I0824687

Black Coral

"A relentless nail-biter whether below or above the waterline. Even the setbacks are suspenseful."

—*Kirkus Reviews* (starred review)

"Mayne's portrayal of the Everglades ecosystem and its inhabitants serves as a fascinating backdrop for the detective work. Readers will hope the spunky Sloan returns soon."

—*Publishers Weekly*

"Andrew Mayne has more than a few tricks up his sleeve—he's an accomplished magician, deep sea diver, and consultant, not to mention skilled in computer coding, developing educational tools, and of course, writing award-nominated bestselling fiction. They are impressive skills on their own, but when they combine? Abracadabra! It's magic . . . Such is the case in Mayne's latest series featuring Sloan McPherson, a Florida police diver with the Underwater Investigation Unit."

—*The Big Thrill*

"Andrew Mayne has dazzled readers across the globe with his thrillers featuring lead characters with fascinating backgrounds in crime forensics. The plots are complex, with meticulous attention to scientific and investigative detail—a tribute to the level of research and study Mayne puts into every novel. A world-renowned illusionist with thousands of passionate fans (who call themselves 'Mayniacs'), Mayne applies his skill with sleight of hand and visual distraction to his storytelling, thereby creating shocking twists and stunning denouements."

—Authorlink

"A solid follow-up with thrilling action, especially the undersea scenes and the threat of Big Bill. Here's to more underwater adventures with the UIU."

—Red Carpet Crash

"As with the series debut, this book moved along well and never lost its momentum. With a great plot and strong narrative, Mayne pulls the reader in from the opening pages and never lets up. He develops the plot well with his strong dialogue and uses shorter chapters to keep the flow throughout. While I know little about diving, Mayne bridged that gap effectively for me and kept things easy to comprehend for the layperson. I am eager to see what is to come, as the third novel in the series was just announced. It's sure to be just as captivating as this one!"

—*Mystery & Suspense Magazine*

"Mayne creates a thrilling plot with likable yet flawed characters . . . Fans of detective series will enjoy seeing where the next episodes take us."

—Bookreporter

"Former illusionist and now bestselling author Andrew Mayne used to have a cable series entitled *Don't Trust Andrew Mayne*. If you take that same recommendation and apply it to his writing you will have some idea of the games you are in for with his latest novel, titled *Black Coral*. Just when you think you might have things figured out, Andrew Mayne pulls the rug out from under you and leaves you reeling in fits of delight."

—Criminal Element

PRAISE FOR ANDREW MAYNE

Night Owl

"[T]he pace never flags. A brisk, competent thriller."

—*Kirkus Reviews*

"Andrew Mayne knows how to write intelligent, well-researched thrillers, and *Night Owl* is no exception."

—Bookreporter

Mastermind

"A passionate and thorough storyteller . . . Thriller fans will be well rewarded."

—*Publishers Weekly*

The Final Equinox

"Science fiction fans will want to check this one out."

—*Publishers Weekly*

"A lively genre-hopping thriller written with panache."

—*Kirkus Reviews*

"This mix of science, thrills, and intrigue calls to mind the work of James Rollins and Michael Crichton. *The Final Equinox* has it all and shows why Mayne is one of the brightest talents working in the thriller field today."

—Bookreporter

The Girl Beneath the Sea

"Distinctive characters and a genuinely thrilling finale . . . Readers will look forward to Sloan's further adventures."

—*Publishers Weekly*

"Mayne writes with a clipped narrative style that gives the story rapid-fire propulsion, and he populates the narrative with a rogues' gallery of engaging characters . . . [A] winning new series with a complicated female protagonist that combines police procedural with adventure story and mixes the styles of Lee Child and Clive Cussler."

—*Library Journal*

"Sloan McPherson is a great, gutsy, and resourceful character."

—Authorlink

"Sloan McPherson is one heck of a woman . . . *The Girl Beneath the Sea* is an action-packed mystery that takes you all over Florida in search of answers."

—Long and Short Reviews

"The female lead is a resourceful, powerful woman and we're already looking forward to hearing more about her in the future Underwater Investigation Unit novels."

—Yahoo!

"*The Girl Beneath the Sea* continuously dives deeper and deeper until you no longer know whom Sloan can trust. This is a terrific entry in a new and unique series."

—Criminal Element

"The pages are packed with colorful characters . . . Its shenanigans, dark humor, and low view of human foibles should appeal to fans of Carl Hiaasen and John D. MacDonald."

—*Star News*

Sea Storm

"The fast-paced plot is filled to the brim with fascinating characters, and the locale is exceptional—both above and below the waterline. One doesn't have to be a nautical adventure fan to enjoy this nail-biter."

—*Publishers Weekly* (starred review)

"Strong pacing, lean prose, and maritime knowledge converge in this crackerjack thriller."

—*Kirkus Reviews*

"Fans of the Underwater Investigation Unit [series] will enjoy this installment, and those who love thrillers will like this too."

—*Library Journal*

Sea Castle

"The plot comes together like the proverbial puzzle, each juicy piece adding a bit to a disturbing big picture. A savvy police procedural that executes a familiar formula with panache."

—*Kirkus Reviews*

"Mayne combines a brilliant, innovative female lead with a plausibly twisty plot. Kinsey Millhone fans will love McPherson."

—*Publishers Weekly* (starred review)

"Mayne creates a world that blends the crime writing of Michael Connelly with high-tech oceanography in his Underwater Investigation Unit series . . . The series never ceases to be fascinating, making characters sink or swim as lives are on the line and the story veers in unexpected directions. Required reading for any suspense fan."

—*Library Journal*

"This is an above-average thriller that never ceases to surprise readers . . . [T]he experience that Andrew Mayne has created for us [is] one to truly savor."

—Bookreporter

Dark Dive

"A solid mystery with an underwater backdrop."

—*Kirkus Reviews*

"I have read all the entries in this series and will continue to read them as new ones come forth. Why? Because they are highly entertaining and have characters I relate to and admire."

—George Easter, *Deadly Pleasures Mystery Magazine*

CHAOS MAN

OTHER TITLES BY ANDREW MAYNE

The Specialists

Mr. Whisper

Impostor Syndrome

Trasker Series

Death Stake

Night Owl

Underwater Investigation Unit Series

Dark Dive

Sea Castle

Sea Storm

Black Coral

The Girl Beneath the Sea

Theo Cray and Jessica Blackwood Series

The Final Equinox

Mastermind

Theo Cray Series

Dark Pattern

Murder Theory

Looking Glass

The Naturalist

Jessica Blackwood Series

Black Fall

Name of the Devil

Angel Killer

The Chronological Man Series

The Monster in the Mist

The Martian Emperor

Station Breaker

Public Enemy Zero

Hollywood Pharaohs

Knight School

The Grendel's Shadow

Nonfiction

The Cure for Writer's Block

How to Write a Novella in 24 Hours

CHAOS MAN

A THRILLER

ANDREW MAYNE

THOMAS & MERCER

This is a work of fiction. Names, characters, organizations, places, events, and incidents are either products of the author's imagination or are used fictitiously. Otherwise, any resemblance to actual persons, living or dead, is purely coincidental.

Text copyright © 2026 by Andrew Mayne
All rights reserved.

No part of this book may be reproduced, or stored in a retrieval system, or transmitted in any form or by any means, electronic, mechanical, photocopying, recording, or otherwise, without express written permission of the publisher.

Published by Thomas & Mercer, Seattle

www.apub.com

Amazon, the Amazon logo, and Thomas & Mercer are trademarks of Amazon.com, Inc., or its affiliates.

EU product safety contact:
Amazon Media EU S. à r.l.
38, avenue John F. Kennedy, L-1855 Luxembourg
amazonpublishing-gpsr@amazon.com

ISBN-13: 9781662522529 (paperback)
ISBN-13: 9781662522512 (digital)

Cover design by Jarrod Taylor
Cover image: © athanop_night, © ATK 3D Works / Shutterstock; © New Africa, © kampee patisena / Getty

Printed in the United States of America

CHAOS MAN

RAINFALL

Jessica couldn't sleep. She couldn't sleep because Theo couldn't sleep. He was standing on the porch that overlooked the tall evergreens of Iron Horse Park, his body silhouetted by moonlit fog. Above the din of chirping frogs, Jessica could hear the radio he kept on the railing next to him.

"You okay, babe?" she asked through the open window next to the bed.

It took a moment for Theo to respond.

Jessica knew that he had two modes. One was the active and energetic mode that had once made him a popular professor. The other was the contemplative, almost brooding mode that could require seconds to get an answer—like switching between applications on an old phone.

"I'm good. Sorry for waking you. I'll use my earbuds," Theo responded eighteen seconds later.

Jessica got out of bed and slipped on the worn bathrobe they'd picked up at a thrift store near Seattle. Ever since a close call in Las Vegas, Jessica hadn't felt like calling anywhere "home" for long. She was content to follow Theo around as his curiosity and speaking engagements took him from one location to another.

Last week it was a conference on artificial life. Before that it was a two-week stay at a scientific retreat thrown by a Wall Street billionaire who liked to hobnob with high IQs.

Jessica had started going with Theo as a distraction from her own complicated life, but she continued because she was worried about him. He was even more distracted than usual. Theo needed her.

He'd leave his luggage on the sidewalk while staring at the flocking pattern of birds, or get himself soaking wet while standing in the rain counting the time between drops.

The only time she knew of Theo ever falling this deep into his own thoughts had happened before she'd met him while he was on the trail of a serial killer nurse. His hunt had taken him from city to city while everything else in his life fell apart. He eventually found the killer working as a nurse in a homeless shelter Theo had found himself at after spiraling. The odds of that happening by chance were astronomical.

While Theo had been using mathematics and forensic skills to learn the killer's pattern, even he was at a loss to explain how he ended up in the very same spot as the killer nurse. Once he'd mentioned the phrase "deep intuition," then stopped because it sounded too woo-woo for his rational mind.

"What is it?" Jessica asked as she leaned on the porch railing next to him.

The wind chilled the parts of her that weren't covered by her robe. Theo, on the other hand, wearing only boxers and a T-shirt riddled with rips and mysterious burns and stains, seemed unperturbed by the temperature. He looked over and gave her a mechanical smile.

Jessica could tell his mind was light-years away.

"Do you want—" she began but was cut off by a glare from Theo and a finger pointing up.

This caught her by surprise. She was accustomed to his fake smiles and almost catatonic behavior, but not this brand of rudeness.

She contemplated how far he'd fall if she shoved him over the railing but realized the trees would soften his landing, and there was a good chance he'd just lie there until she picked him up from the pine needles.

Theo lowered the radio. "I have to go somewhere."

Jessica grabbed him by the arm. She had a tight grip thanks to the hand exerciser she used when stressed—which was often. It had been a gift from her father when she was a child. He'd explained how grip strength was the most valuable strength of all—not only to a magician but to anyone who needed to defend themselves . . . or in this case, keep a loved one from running into traffic.

"Where are we going?" she asked.

Theo looked into her eyes, snapping out of his fugue state. "It's complicated."

"Uncomplicate it for me. Where are we going?"

"Arcadia City, Idaho," Theo replied.

"What's there?"

"I don't know."

Jessica locked her green eyes onto his steel-blue ones. "Theo . . . what's there?" she asked more forcefully.

"I can't quite articulate it. I'm afraid I'm missing something fundamental," he said.

Jessica motioned toward the glowing laptop sitting on the kitchen table at the other side of the cabin. Strange looping waves and spirals intersected one another on its monitor.

To a casual observer, the images would have looked like a screensaver. But Jessica suspected the pattern had everything to do with what was going on in his head.

"Explain it with an analogy," she suggested, knowing how Theo hated using them. It was her way of getting back at him when he didn't want to take the time to explain something.

"Planetary motion," Theo responded.

"Elaborate."

"For most of human history, the motion of the planets baffled us. They didn't behave like the stars. Star motion was predictable. The planets were not—at least not at first. For a long time, the way they moved was a complete mystery.

"When we say Mercury is in retrograde, it's because it's suddenly moving backwards from our point of view. The same with the other planets—they all appear to move back and loop," he explained.

"Because we're all orbiting the sun," Jessica concluded. "They only look like they're going backwards."

"Yes. But to know that, you have to understand that the sun is the center of the solar system, not the earth. That's when it makes sense, but for most of human history we naturally assumed we were the center, and that's what held us back. The smartest minds in the world couldn't conceive what the average kindergartner understands today."

"Cool, bro. Now explain what the hell you're up to," she demanded.

"I know you'll tell me you won't think I'm crazy, but trust me, you'll think I'm crazy on this one. I would. I just have to see for myself. Then I'll know. Then I can drop it and we can do normal stuff for a while," he offered.

"Like you or I would know what normal is," Jessica shot back. "What was on the radio?"

"There's been a blackout in eastern Idaho," Theo replied.

"And that has you worried?" Jessica asked.

"It's what caused the blackout that has me concerned . . . and that either I'm crazy or else I predicted it."

COW BLUFF

Thirty-seven minutes earlier

Waller sat on the ground, picking at weeds with his back against the rear passenger-side tire of his sister's old Toyota 4Runner, listening to her explain why Skyler's latest scheme made absolutely no sense at all.

Skyler was Waller's best friend, but the kid really tried his patience at times. They'd never really hung out until high school, then became best friends because of the classes they shared. Although Skyler could be annoying, Waller appreciated that he was generally quite chill.

Moira and Skyler were sitting on the graffiti-covered rocks overlooking Arcadia City, Idaho, bathed in a silvery glow from the nearly full moon.

"The Cow Bluff," the highest point near the town, was a traditional hangout spot. The Scout troop Skyler and Waller belonged to made it a habit to clean up the beer bottles, cans, and trash up there so the town police wouldn't shut it down.

"You can't just put an electric motor in a regular car and replace the gas tank with batteries," Moira explained to Skyler. "The drive train, the steering mechanism, even the brakes are all different."

"Oh. I was thinking we could try it with my aunt's old Jeep," Skyler said, disappointed.

Waller got bored listening to them and walked over to the far edge of the bluff. He heard the distant sound of a northbound train and tried to see if he could spot it coming out of the gorge east of town.

Usually they were freight trains, but sometimes he saw passengers taking the route. There hadn't been a functioning depot or station in Arcadia since caveman days, so Waller expected this train to race on by like all the others.

The northbound Union Freight Ridge Runner freight train was moving at fifty-five miles an hour—five miles over the regulation limit and more than seventeen miles an hour above what the rail could reasonably handle.

Engineer Kyle Greenfield had been riding this route for seven months and knew the flat plain was a good way to make up for lost time from going up the grade in Oak Valley Gorge.

This part of the route went on for miles in a long, straight line, making it easier for the train to maintain speed. The closest town was Arcadia City to the west, accessible via a spur line that hadn't been used since before Kyle was born.

The train's conductor, Marty Pasquale, was drinking from his thermos of tea while reading on his Kindle. He'd been running the route longer than Kyle and had been the one to explain to him the advantage of making up for lost time on the long stretch through Arcadia City.

"Anything interesting?" Kyle asked over the whine of the motor.

"*Parallel Lives*," Marty replied over the din.

"Science fiction?" asked Kyle.

"Not quite. It's about Greeks and Romans," said Marty.

"Gods?"

"No. People. But they believed in dragons and monsters back then, so you could pretend it's *Game of Thrones* or whatever you're into," Marty explained.

"I'll think about it."

Marty returned to his book, knowing that was the extent of the younger man's curiosity.

❧

Three miles south of Arcadia City, Marty looked up from his book when he felt a bump.

"What was that?" he asked.

"What was what?" Kyle replied.

Kyle had been focused on the fuel gauge and hadn't noticed anything other than the roar of the engine and the rumble of the wheels on the track.

Marty stepped to Kyle's window and stuck his head out.

"Goddamn it!" he shouted. "Stop! *Stop!*"

He didn't wait for Kyle to pull the brakes. Instead, he grabbed the handle and slammed them on himself.

Kyle's face went pale in the dim yellow cabin light as he realized what had just happened. Somehow the track had shifted to the dormant spur, and the train was heading full speed down the short dead-end line into town.

Marty had been to Arcadia City and knew the track ended in the asphalt that became Main Street, but that wasn't the problem. They were going too fast for the curve ahead and would never make it that far. Their locomotive and the freight they were hauling were going to derail.

The moment before impact, Kyle recalled the dark joke Marty had made when he looked over the cargo manifest and realized that they'd be carrying a half million pounds of vinyl chloride and two flatbeds of spent nuclear waste from the Dove River Nuclear Test Facility:

"At least the explosion will kill us before the radiation poisoning."

❦

The sound of the train whistle warning everyone in its path made Waller realize something was wrong. He'd seen trains go by all his life, but never on the spur.

"Hey guys, look!" he shouted to Skyler and his sister.

They all stood up and watched as the train bounced over the curved track, skidded across a grassy field, and slammed into the massive power station relay that routed electricity throughout the state and to neighboring counties.

Blue arcs of electricity crackled in the air as the train tore through metal pylon after pylon, ensnaring itself in power lines.

Waller noticed there was no pause or even a dramatic beat: The moment the train shredded the power transmission facility fence and hit the first pylon, the entire town went dark.

Seconds later, loud popping sounds punctured the cold night air, followed by a huge fireball. Flaming liquid began to spread across the concrete yard of the power facility as the cargo from the train broke free and bounced and crashed toward town.

"My cell phone isn't working!" shouted Skyler. "I can't call my mom!"

"The tower is down because of the power. Get in the car," Moira commanded.

"Are we going to help them?" asked Skyler.

"Yes, but we have to go to Fairmont. They might have working phones there."

Waller was watching as the town began to burn and thick tornadoes of black smoke spiraled upward into the sky.

"Come on!" Moira shouted at her brother to get him moving.

SACUL

Theo and Jessica were two hours into their drive east on I-90 and about to enter Idaho. No strangers to cutting and running, they had quickly packed their Suburban with Theo's gear and what few personal belongings they kept on the road.

If she were anyone else, Jessica knew she'd be complaining about the fact that after loading all Theo's computers, labware, and robots in various stages of construction, there was hardly any room left in the vehicle for luggage. Still, she had let Theo know with a sharp eyebrow raise that he'd crossed the line when he argued whether it was absolutely necessary that they stop to buy underwear at a shopping mall instead of at a truck stop.

While driving, Jessica noted that Theo had become a bit more *present*, as evidenced by the fact that he occasionally looked up from his laptop to stare at the road ahead.

"Any word on our destination?" she asked.

"I think we'll take I-90 until I-15. Assuming we can get through," he replied.

"Is there a storm?"

"No, the weather's fine. If it had been a storm, we'd both be asleep right now."

True enough, Jessica thought. The night sky sparkled with stars, the morning sun still hours from rising.

"Well, since now you're making not only complete sentences but actual paragraphs, perhaps you could tell me a little bit more about what's going on," she suggested.

"I'll tell you as much as I can, I mean, at least as much as what makes sense to me. I've been paying attention to news reports, looking for certain kinds of events. Not natural ones like storms or earthquakes, but man-made disasters or accidents," he explained.

"So this power outage is a man-made accident?" Jessica asked.

"Usually they are. It can be caused by faulty wiring or somebody not paying attention to monitors. Of course, you could also get an event like a solar flare, but that's much rarer."

"What about a tree falling on a line?"

"Not a man-made disaster, but yes, that's common."

"So you don't know if this blackout was caused by a person, a tree, or a solar flare," Jessica confirmed.

"No," Theo muttered.

"Okay, then this is the part where you elaborate—even little fragments of what you're thinking," she explained.

"I've been looking for patterns, or rather I've had an algorithm searching for certain kinds of patterns, which of course, as you know, can be very misleading," Theo explained. "But I was looking for specific ones here, patterns that implied things that were connected in ways that were outside of statistical chance.

"Of course I have two problems. One, I have to figure out what constitutes a detected pattern versus random noise. The other is creating my criteria: What should be part of the pattern and what shouldn't be? Chasing after these things is a path to madness. It's what leads to gambling addiction and major Wall Street losses."

"It's a good thing you don't get obsessed with tiny details," Jessica said snidely.

"Fair enough. But that's all the more reason for my caution and why I haven't been talking your ears off with what I've been thinking."

"Tell me about the patterns and what you're looking for."

"I've been looking at disastrous events caused by people," Theo said. "They happened seemingly randomly. They're hard to connect, and it's not obvious, at least not yet, that somebody is out there coordinating them."

"Give me a 'for instance,'" she said.

"For example, forest fires. We know that a large percentage of them—and probably more than we realize—are man-made, done by opportunists, sometimes pyromaniacs, and sometimes even by firefighters who are bored and looking for work, and unfortunately by copycats as well."

"So you're looking for patterns in disastrous events that seem natural but might've been caused by a person?" Jessica asked. "With a subset being caused by the same person? This sounds like a very complex algorithm."

"I'll say, but I don't have to do all the work. That's the whole purpose of the computer. And I just choose some arbitrary patterns and events."

"Like a blackout in Idaho?" Jessica asked.

"This was a bit of an outlier," Theo admitted. "It's a case where the signal was a bit weak but the pattern was strong—extremely strong. Almost absurdly so, which has me thinking I've made some kind of stupid mistake."

"What was the signal? And by 'signal,' you must mean events that fit your category?"

"I guess I should have explained that up front," Theo admitted. "I've been searching news reports, scanning police frequencies, insurance-claims data, everything I can find, in order to detect adverse events that appeared to be purely accidental but there was a possibility they could have been caused intentionally."

Jessica was silent but gave Theo a brief sidelong glance.

"Okay, I get it. I know that's not making any sense," he responded. "Obviously, it's really hard to know that something was intentional if it appears to be accidental. One way is to begin with systemic failures, like a bridge collapse or, like here, a power grid, or something that involves a cascade of things, or one thing triggering the next."

"And what do we know about the blackout?" Jessica inquired.

"The news and social media are filled with all kinds of reports. The one consistent fact is that there was a blackout," Theo explained. "The center of whatever happened is probably a town called Arcadia City, which has a transfer station for major transmission lines in the region."

"Interesting."

"That and some of the other reports. Social media is saying there may have been a plane crash, which I'm skeptical of for certain reasons. It could have been a tractor trailer, a bomb, and also a possible train derailment. Right now I'm trying to pull up the schedules for all the freight and passenger traffic through that area to see if anything has been delayed. But that doesn't really tell us there was a train crash, because those delays could be from the power outage."

"How about any of our law enforcement contacts? Has anybody heard anything?"

"Nobody's responded yet, and my inbounds to the National Response Center have also gone unreplied to," Theo reported, then squinted at his laptop to look at something more closely. "Okay. Idaho State Police say it's a train derailment."

"That caused a blackout?" Jessica asked.

Theo zoomed into a Google satellite view of the area. "There are the electrical transmission lines, and there's the relay station. Right there, you can see an older rail spur that goes off the main line and heads toward the town. My guess is the train derailed by going off there and crashed straight into the power station relay."

"How much signal is that now, according to your hypothesis?" Jessica inquired.

Theo closed his laptop and rested his hands on the lid. "That's an off-the-charts signal," he said, staring into space.

"So you're saying that derailment was no accident?" Jessica asked.

"I hope to God it was an accident, because if it wasn't, we could be really screwed," Theo said. "We're at three."

"Three?" Jessica replied.

"Let me back up," he said, and finally looked at her. "I started off looking for crime patterns. Like bank robberies happening on the same day of the week around the same time. It was too much data and too much noise. A pointless task. So then I went *very* broad, looking for other patterns. Flight timetable alterations, actuarial chart trends, sudden market disruptions . . . you name it. It was during this phase that I began searching for patterns that might match interesting mathematical sequences, such as pi."

"Pi? Like 3.14159?" asked Jessica.

"Yes. Looking for patterns of crimes that might follow unintentional or deliberate but secret patterns," he explained.

"So you were looking for the Pi Killer?" she joked.

"Not exactly. Well, maybe. I was trying to see if I could find a group of potentially related crimes that followed a pattern that would predict the next event."

"This is the most *you* thing."

"I know. It seemed likely pointless but fascinating in its own right." He scratched his forehead. "To begin, I thought I'd look for signals, crimes basically, that followed a very obvious mathematical pattern—something found in math textbooks. Besides pi, another pattern is the Fibonacci sequence; another is what we call Lucas numbers. They're related. It's the second most common pattern in sunflower seeds. The point is, there are natural events that can occur on their own. But when you look at certain groups of disasters or accidents that follow a mathematical sequence, then you have to wonder if they were human caused, down to the intentional pattern."

Jessica thought she was following.

"An analogy," Theo told her, "would be musical notes—if you detected a melody that suddenly stood out above all the random noise." He sighed. "Basically, I was looking for somebody intentionally doing things that seem unrelated but following this pattern, so the only way you could detect them was through mathematics," he explained.

"Like a calling card?" Jessica asked.

"Maybe, possibly kept only to them. A secret for themselves. Like when they took apart one of the pyramid blocks and found the inscription of the people who made it there. They didn't really intend for anybody to see it. They just wanted to put their little symbol there to say 'Hey, I was here.' Maybe so somebody in the distant future would know." Theo shrugged.

"Or a surgeon leaving their initials inside a patient," Jessica remarked.

"Exactly," Theo exclaimed. "That's a much better analogy. That's somebody being brazen, putting it out there, but doing it in such a way that they're confident nobody will ever know. But if detected, it would be obvious somebody did it."

"You said that we're at number three. What did you mean by that?"

"The first ten numbers of the Lucas sequence are two, one, three, four, seven, eleven, eighteen, twenty-nine, forty-seven, seventy-six," he told her.

"And this event aligns with a number in the sequence? That's either an incredibly perceptive algorithm you created or else this is really all random."

Theo grimaced. "Ach—I should have clarified. I was looking for both a Lucas sequence going forward and a Lucas sequence counting down. The blackout was number three, part of a countdown that began at seventy-six. I detected seven other events before this one."

He ticked them off on his fingers. "Seventy-six—Fog Line Fallout in Tokyo, traffic grid sabotage, no deaths; forty-seven—Blue Vision Burn in Reykjavík, data center fire, three dead; twenty-nine—Copper Ring Rupture in the Atacama, pipeline burst, five dead; eighteen—Horizon Shatter in Zeebrugge, crane collapse, eight dead; eleven—Drone Night Downburst in Dallas, roof collapse, fourteen dead; seven—Greenfall in Oregon, tidal-gate failure, three dead; four—Brightheart Inferno in Florida, battery-farm blaze, no deaths."

He lowered his hand. "The last one was three weeks ago—four weeks after the one before it, seven after that, and so on going back over two years."

"The last one was the battery fire in Florida? That shut down the electric grid and the interstate for days. But I thought it was accidental."

"They're still counting excess deaths from the lack of air-conditioning and have no cause yet. The point is, each one of these involved several systems failing, or a failure in one system causing an even bigger problem in the next one."

"So you think somebody out there is engineering these disasters?" Jessica asked.

"That's what the algorithm says. I could be reading way too much into the noise here. But if it is . . . unlike with the other events, we have a chance to find out sooner than later—maybe find evidence before it vanishes."

"So your algorithm says there might be somebody out there creating disaster-seeming events, but they're so well hidden they look like accidents. And he's timing it according to some mathematical formula? Is that intentional?" Jessica asked, still trying to wrap her head around everything.

"I can't see somebody unconsciously using the Lucas sequence in reverse," Theo mused. "So we'll just start from the premise that somebody trying to be clever might stage things following that pattern. But also, somebody inclined to do such a thing is going to be thinking about this in a very different approach than a spree serial killer or some opportunistic arsonist. At least, I think so. But I'm sure I'm missing something."

"And what kind of evidence do we need?" she asked.

"It's a systemic failure, which means there's something somewhere in the sequence of events that led up to it that could be controlled or engineered," Theo explained. "I don't even begin to know how you would cause a railway derailment without looking at the track and everything else. It could be some mechanical booby trap set on board the train. Or the track. Or the switching system. Or the brakes. I don't know. My concern is that the accident investigators are going to follow a familiar playbook, which is investigating whether the engineer screwed something up, looking for obvious mechanical failure, and maybe a cursory check for some kind of sabotage. But the kinds of sabotage they would be looking for would be too simplistic for whoever's doing this."

"Like bomb residue," Jessica observed.

"Exactly. This guy's not planting C-4 on the track and trying to blow it up, because that would be obvious and leave a trace. Nor is he standing somewhere with a sniper rifle trying to shoot somebody. In the case of the battery fire, all it took was some safeguards to be turned off and suddenly you're shutting down air traffic and theme parks in central Florida."

"And that happened exactly at number four in the Lucas sequence?" Jessica replied.

"Right in the middle of the twenty-four-hour window, which was the first one I was looking for but still wasn't sure about. At the time, it seemed pretty hard for someone to be able to trigger something that precisely. But then I followed the news reports and the experts commenting on it and found out that there were a few systemic failures that could have been engineered by someone knowing what they're doing. But you had to be paying attention. Unfortunately, nobody was paying attention. Or, rather, one person was," Theo amended. "Maybe."

"That's terrible. Hopefully, there won't be any casualties from this," said Jessica.

"Yeah, well, here's the thing, Jess: Even though the Lucas number countdown is getting lower, the scale of these incidents keeps growing. We're still not hearing anything out of Arcadia City, which has me concerned. Also, note that this is number three. Next up in the Lucas sequence is one, which means it's one week away. Then after that, it's two, which is two weeks from then. I have a feeling things are going to get pretty bad," Theo said, "unless we stop it first."

FALLOUT

Despite the radiation warning on the radio, Jessica and Theo continued on until they came to a county police roadblock. Three squad cars blocked the highway, and cops in breathing masks and goggles waved their flashlights at cars to turn around and go the other direction.

Two miles back, they pulled onto the side of the road near a gas station connected to a McDonald's along with nearly a hundred other vehicles crammed into the lot and overflowing up the highway. Dozens of people stood outside their vehicles in the darkness, cell phones on, stranded with no idea what to do next.

"This looks pretty bleak," Jessica said as she pulled in behind the long line of cars and trucks.

"It's going to get worse," Theo warned with a nod.

"So, uh, how seriously do we take this radiation alert?" she asked.

"Whatever they put on a train would be sealed securely," Theo explained. "The chance of something like that cracking open is pretty remote. Those things are designed to fall from airplanes. But we also don't know what other kind of cargo was on there. With enough explosive force, it's possible you could have some leakage. But even then, it's really just a matter of how close you get to it. It's more about what you breathe in than radiation waves affecting you at a distance."

"So don't inhale any glowing green fog."

"Pretty much. In a situation like this, they want to use an abundance of caution. But given how much radioactive dust our parents breathed during the time of aboveground nuclear testing, I think we'll be fine."

"Remind me again how important it is that we get up close to this . . ."

"I don't know." Theo glared at the blank laptop screen and the mute, glowing cell phones around them.

"As much as I hate to admit it, I have a feeling that a nuclear-waste cleanup isn't going to lend itself to careful evidence collection," she pointed out.

"It won't be a priority," Theo agreed. "Which is why it's important that at least we search for it."

"Okay, we can figure out our next move, but let's get some information about what's going on. Who here do you think knows anything?"

"We're looking for someone who's networked in," Theo mused as they surveyed the parking lot for emergency vehicles or any official who stood out. "There's a patrol officer." He pointed at a woman in a police uniform standing by her vehicle at the far edge of the lot.

"Maybe, but my money's on them," said Jessica as she took Theo's arm and led him across the highway toward a group of men standing at the head of a row of 18-wheelers lined up along the side of the road.

"How you doing?" Jessica called out as she and Theo strode up to the clutch of truckers.

Theo admired how Jessica engaged with strangers directly, innately confident that they would have a cordial conversation and that she would be accepted. It didn't hurt that she was charismatic, beautiful, and funny.

"I'm trying to figure out if my kids are gonna have nine toes or twenty," said a man in a tan baseball hat with blond hair poking out the back.

"Is that because of the radiation alert or how closely you and your wife are related?" Jessica teased.

The men burst out laughing.

The guy in the baseball cap grinned, then turned to Theo and said, "If that's the kind of ball busting she does with a hello, I can only imagine what *your* life is like."

"I've learned to choose my words carefully," Theo advised.

"I'm sorry," Jessica said. "Just lightening up the situation. I'm Jessica. This is my partner, Theo."

"Not a problem. I'm Gil. This is Riley," he continued, gesturing at a bald man with a salt-and-pepper goatee. "And this is Peterson," he added, nodding at a man with a gray hat and an olive complexion.

"Were you two headed to Idaho?" asked Peterson.

"East Idaho, but that's looking doubtful," Theo admitted.

"Same for us. We were trying to figure out if there was another route around we could take, maybe even through Canada. Not that that wouldn't be complicated, but apparently they've shut down the border crossings," Riley explained.

"What about southbound?" Theo asked.

"It seems that all of Idaho is shut," Peterson offered. "Gil and I live in Washington, so we could always just go home, but Riley lives in Missoula, so home isn't really an option for him. We gotta figure out where to put our rigs."

Jessica's deduction that the men would know more information than was publicly available due to their CB radios and phone-contact trees had proven correct. She was curious what else they knew.

"Anybody know what the hell happened?" she asked.

"My sister's brother-in-law works with the NTSB's emergency response team," Riley told her. "According to him, the train that hit the power station was loaded with depleted uranium from a nuclear facility.

He said there hasn't been a contamination leak so far, but the fire still isn't under control, and anything could change at a moment's notice."

"What kind of fire?" Theo asked.

"What was the stuff at the East Palestine disaster?" Riley asked.

"Vinyl chloride," Theo answered quickly. "That's nasty." His eyes went to the side as he did some sort of mental calculation, then added, "Not hot enough to get through the casket and probably not enough kinetic energy, although you can't be sure."

"Are you an engineer?" asked Riley.

"No. I'm a computational biologist."

"I'm not sure what that is."

"Well, if we're going to be here for a while, he'll be happy to explain. Do you guys know anything else about what's going on?" Jessica asked the trio.

"My friends in the National Guard have all been activated," Peterson explained. "According to one of them, they're going to be doing perimeters: one around Arcadia City, then a countywide one, then a further perimeter, and of course the state border, which we all ran into."

"Have you seen them let anybody through?" Jessica asked.

"Just emergency vehicles," Gil noted.

"Well, thank you for the information. We're going to figure out our next steps. If any of you want to give us your contact information, we'd be happy to pass on anything we learn."

Jessica and Theo walked back to their SUV and observed the long line leading from the gas station to the end of the parking lot. People were trying to get either coffee, gas, food, or protection equipment.

"I have a feeling we know as much as anybody right now," Jessica commented.

"I suspect even the people on the scene are in the dark," Theo agreed.

"Hypothetically, assuming we get there safely and in a manner that doesn't lead to generations of familial genetic mutations," Jessica mused, "what would we *do* there? What are we looking for?"

Instead of answering, Theo crossed his arms over his head and started pacing the shoulder of the road. He was so lost in thought he failed to react to a patrol car whizzing by with its siren on. Finally, he stopped and turned to Jessica.

"Okay, let's start with what we know. All of this was caused by a train doing something it wasn't supposed to do. It was supposed to continue straight. Instead, apparently, it took a spur. In order for that to happen, it has to go down the wrong track."

"Generally, that's how a train gets sidetracked," Jessica confirmed.

"I know I'm being a little bit *reductio ad absurdum*, but my point is the train went someplace it's not supposed to," Theo reasoned. "For somebody to cause this, they'd have to flip a switch, in effect. And that switch is controlled electronically—which means there's a box connected to that, which told it to change."

"That seems to me the first place they're going to look," Jessica noted.

"In a normal situation, but with a massive explosion and nuclear materials on scene, it wouldn't be their top priority. Still . . . yes, they will try to find the cause, and the first place they'd look would be the switch box."

"But they're not going to find anything clear or obvious," Jessica said. "Right?"

"They're not likely to. This person isn't going to use wire cutters and a soldering iron. They'll be tampering at the component level."

"But we still need to look at the switch box," Jessica noted.

"Yes, preferably before they take it apart."

"Which means we need to do that sooner than later."

"Yep," Theo affirmed, accepting the gravity of the task.

"Step one, sneak across the border, make our way through all the evacuation zones and past the National Guard, then into a potentially radioactive environment so we can proceed to step two and find some potential evidence and steal it," Jessica summarized dryly.

"I can handle the looking-at-the-evidence part. It's the other details that have me a little bit stumped."

"Well, when you were almost run over by that police car, I had an idea."

"What police car?" Theo asked, glancing behind him.

"Exactly. Right now, the authorities are supposed to keep everybody out, assuming only somebody profoundly stupid or up to no good would try to get in."

"We're the former, not the latter, in this scenario," Theo clarified.

"Exactly," said Jessica. "We have to figure out how to look like people who are *not* up to no good."

"Is this going to involve stealing a police car?" Theo asked.

"I was thinking about an ambulance. Still a felony, but probably easier to nab right now." She thought for a moment. "But that brings up the second question: In all seriousness, how do we avoid contamination?"

"Well, we're going to need some sort of personal protection equipment no matter what, because otherwise we'll stick out like a sore thumb the closer we get. As I said before, really what you're worried about is what you're going to inhale, so we want respiratory equipment. I gotta believe within ten miles of here we're gonna find a factory or facility that deals with hazardous waste. Even an auto body shop would do. We'll find something. But it's probably not in the cards to ask politely at this time of night, given the current situation . . ."

"Good thing you know nobody who can pick locks. How about you find someplace on Google for the breathing equipment, and I'll figure out where to steal an ambulance."

She looked at her watch. It wasn't even 4:00 a.m. She selfishly wished that she'd pretended to be sleeping instead of asking Theo what was on his mind earlier this evening.

"What is it?" she asked, noticing he still had a worried look on his face.

"If each incident in the sequence is getting worse, and right now we're looking at three state borders and a national border shutdown, plus a potential radiological and toxic-waste clouds," he said, "what's coming next?"

FIRST RESPONDERS

Theo and Jessica had found everything they needed in an industrial park in Spokane Valley, just a few miles west of the Idaho border. Due to the current emergency, they weren't worried about an immediate response from police when they commandeered an ambulance from a storage lot and personal protection equipment from a pest-control facility, both within blocks of each other.

Their bigger concern was making sure they didn't leave any evidence of their thefts, either on video cameras or via fingerprints. While they'd both mentally pinkie-sworn to return everything they had taken or to remunerate the owners, either deed would be much easier to accomplish if they were never caught and brought before a judge.

As Jessica helped transfer equipment from the SUV to the back of the ambulance, it was not lost on her how being around Theo had shifted her moral compass.

Jessica had gone from a celebrated FBI agent who only sparingly bent the rules to, well, a vigilante, she had to admit, who had no trouble trespassing or stealing things whenever the emergency justified it. She operated by a simple code, and that was she wouldn't do anything that she didn't feel comfortable explaining after the fact to everyone, including those affected. It was the same justification for kicking in the door of a house that appeared to be burning or smashing the window of a hot car with a pet or baby lying on the seat. Sometimes you have to break things and steal things in order to save lives. And yet she frequently found herself in situations where the potential threat was harder for those around her to perceive in the moment.

Even odder, she didn't feel guilt so much as anxiety in such situations. It was not potential punishment she feared but having her actions seem unjustified to others.

Breaking rules around Theo was easy because she never worried about him misunderstanding the justification. This was a man who literally stole cadaver parts to stage a fake murder scene in order to catch a serial killer—creating an unsolved crime that was still on the books, although those in the know had a pretty good idea who'd done it.

"Maybe we should consider getting one of these on a permanent basis. If you think about it, we could drive as fast as we want, go anywhere we want, without any questions," Jessica joked from behind the wheel of her stolen emergency vehicle.

"Brad Trasker actually uses an ambulance to move Kylie around," Theo noted.

Their occasional colleague Brad Trasker, a private security specialist and former counterintelligence agent, worked for an aerospace CEO with a big target on her back. Like Jessica, Trasker was a master of deception, his skills having been honed through espionage tradecraft. But like Theo, Trasker was also known for applying a blunt-force approach to threats.

"That doesn't surprise me. I'm sure he probably has his own private intelligence agency by now."

"I considered asking him for a lift into the hot zone, then thought that might be stretching the friendship."

"Hell, Kylie would probably help us parachute in," Jessica joked.

"Yeah, that's why I didn't ask him."

"Could you start looking at map or satellite footage to see if there are any back-road ways in? I don't think we'll have much interference getting close, but in town things will be much tighter."

"On it."

She started the engine.

It was a four-hour drive to Arcadia City under normal conditions in a normal vehicle. If they didn't encounter state troopers or other obstacles, by Jessica's estimate, she could have them near town in less than three hours.

❧

They had to make one stop for gas, and their only option was a station being kept open by two local police officers charged with the responsibility to make sure that only official vehicles going into and coming out of the evacuation area were fueled up.

The pair wore respiratory masks that covered their entire faces and had on plastic gloves that were taped off at their wrists. The conversation between Jessica, who was also wearing her face mask, and the officer who walked up to the window was brief.

"Where are you headed?" he asked, having to project his voice through the mask.

"We've been told to report to a staging site outside of Arcadia. Any word on radiation?" Jessica asked.

"No, they've set up monitoring stations every few miles. From what I've heard on the ground there, there might be a slight contamination leak. But nothing showstopping so far. Although between you and me, I don't know if they would tell us," he confided from behind the mask.

Theo began to exit the vehicle to pump gas, but the other officer waved him back inside, telling him he would take care of it.

Once they were back on the highway, Theo took off his mask. So far, it had only been useful for convincing everybody that they belonged.

"I think I found a route," he announced after looking at his laptop screen.

"Into Arcadia City?" Jessica asked.

"Actually, a few miles back—the point where the spur leads away from the main rail line."

"I hope it's outside the hot zone."

"We'll be in spitting distance, for sure, but it should help that we're concerned with the point where the train went off track, not where it ended up."

"Any word on casualties?" Jessica asked.

Theo felt guilty. He'd been so focused on logistics that he'd overlooked the human element. "I'll take a look." A moment later: "No word. I think the radiation factor still has them withholding most relevant info."

Jessica nodded and was silent for a while. "Tell me about the kind of person that would do this," she asked at last.

"We've both dealt with extreme personalities," Theo began. "Generally, there's the performer—the person who does a thing because they want attention. Then there's the manipulator—the person who seeks something like money, power, or control. Our suspect is neither. They don't want notoriety. They don't want anything other than chaos. The closest analogy is a serial killer trying to cover their tracks, except this person isn't using guns or knives or bare hands. They're creating disasters."

"And that tells us something."

"They're clever, I guess," Theo said with a chuckle.

"A normal person doesn't take Fibonacci numbers and use the pattern as a template for committing crimes."

"Technically, it's a Lucas sequence. In reverse. But I get your point," Theo replied. "You don't have to be a mathematician to be aware of it. Anybody with access to YouTube could find those numbers."

"Right, but my point is, it's a certain kind of person that would find that compelling," said Jessica.

Theo nodded. "Point taken. And then there's the nature of the crimes we're looking at, which involve a high level of technical understanding."

"We've dealt with clever people before—programmers, chemists, and just off-the-charts insane geniuses. But this one has a particular kind of mind," she thought aloud.

"Yeah, the body count is what's interesting. This could have a very big impact if we do get a radiation cloud, but it's not likely. You know, fewer people died at Chernobyl than we thought, and nobody died from Three Mile Island." Theo considered something for a moment. "And while I can't speak for the people driving the train or whatever happened to the town, or the people who responded there, this may look bigger than the actual loss of life turns out to be."

"Compared to those earlier events on the Lucas timeline, do you think the scale of this incident is bigger?"

"Yes. If we look only at newsworthiness, absolutely," Theo replied. "Although I don't think that this person is counting column inches."

Jessica nodded. "Given the preoccupation with the Lucas sequence, this person might have some other metric by which they measure magnitude. Or success."

"And that has me perplexed," Theo admitted. "There's a progression, but if body count isn't the primary goal, what is?"

"Maybe we don't understand the target selections," Jessica theorized.

Theo frowned. "Structural collapses, electrical fires, train derailment . . . I don't know. I don't see a pattern."

"Step back from it," Jessica suggested.

"Easier for you than for me," Theo murmured.

"Okay, when I went through training and we got lectured by the various profilers, while we understood that a lot of crimes—even arson—can be rooted in certain desires, sometimes it's just because the opportunity is there. For example, some arsonists set fires because they can. They just want to watch things burn. The bigger the better. That's it. And people dying is an indirect consequence. The goal is the fire."

"The guy just wants to create havoc," Theo observed.

"Exactly. We could be looking at a sophisticated opportunist." Jessica looked over at him. "If you were going to pull off something like this, how would you do it?"

"I'd write an algorithm including the kinds of crimes I wanted to commit," Theo explained. "Have it randomly select locations for me, and then I would choose from those the ones that I think I could pull off with the highest chance of success and not being detected."

"I'm pretty sure that's not what your guy is doing," Jessica told him.

"Why is that?"

"Because that's how you think—craving doing things that nobody else thinks of," she explained. "If there were some darker, more evil version of you out there, I don't think they'd be blowing up trains and creating oil spills. No . . . they'd be in some bioweapons facility trying to engineer a zombie plague."

Theo sighed. "I already met that guy. He was the one trying to contaminate the entire supply of flu vaccine for the United States military." A moment later he realized what Jessica had said. "What do you mean, 'more evil version' of me?" he asked, eyebrows raised.

"It's just an expression. My point is, this is probably an opportunistic criminal."

Theo was about to ask how an opportunist could coordinate a series of undetectable complex acts of sabotage, but then he caught her meaning.

"You mean opportunistic, but not within the same time frame," Theo clarified.

"Exactly," Jessica said. "This person might have known about a vulnerability or heard about something and cataloged it for later, fitting it to his strict timeline."

"That would still take a lot of planning," Theo replied.

"Yes," she agreed. "And consider this: This criminal had to know a lot about trains but also a fair bit about Arcadia. So while we look for your switch or other points of vulnerability in the system, we also need to keep our eyes out for what he might have seen there."

"You're saying that we need to look at the place through his eyes because he spent a lot of time there?"

"Maybe not enough time to be noticed by the locals," Jessica said. "Or at least not in any way that people realize."

HOT ZONE

The sun was barely creeping over the horizon by the time Theo and Jessica made it to the outskirts of Arcadia City. They'd made excellent time since leaving the gas station, occasionally having to swerve past fleeing cars taking up both sides of the highway but otherwise encountering no law enforcement resistance. By the time they came to a roadblock, the sound of their siren had caused the troopers and then National Guard people to move aside their barriers to allow them access to the hot zone.

Jessica finally brought the vehicle to a standstill when she spotted a much more serious barricade blocking the main road into Arcadia. There were several parked emergency vehicles, dozens of people in full hazmat gear, and a showering station illuminated with portable lighting where jets of water were being sprayed on rescue workers emerging from the still-smoldering town.

Because of the blackout, the only light came from the glowing horizon in the east and the reflection of blue and red emergency lights illuminating the white, oily smoke rising from Arcadia City.

Jessica glanced over at Theo, her expression tense. "Heads up, Theo. Make-or-break situation here. This roadblock looks a little more serious than the others. What do you want to do?"

He pursed his lips as he appeared to do some kind of calculation in his head.

Theo had done prior work for various government agencies, including the military, and was at least superficially aware of a number of their policies when it came to biological and radiological hazards.

"That's going to be federal authority all the way in from here," he explained. "When it comes to nuclear material, they don't mess around. That means every first responder is going to have a RAD badge and somebody to vouch for them. Even in a situation like this, they're not only worried about the hazard of somebody getting a few too many stray particles going through their DNA but also someone either intentionally or unintentionally removing radioactive material from the location."

"What does your map say?" asked Jessica.

"There's an unmarked road a quarter mile behind us," Theo said. "It should lead us close to the railroad tracks, and then we can walk in from there. We'll probably need to hide the ambulance unless we plan on carrying a body to or from it."

"How suspicious are we going to look?" Jessica wondered.

"By now, this place is going to be crawling with all kinds of state and federal officials. If we don't get too close, I think we're going to be fine. We just have to look like we know what the hell we're doing."

"And what's that?" Jessica asked.

"We need to look like we're looking for something, which is exactly what we're doing," Theo told her. "I've got some gear in the back that we can have in our hands, which should help sell the effect."

"As long as I can explain what it does if somebody asks."

Theo looked over his shoulder at a large case. "I really wish I could use one of my drones right now. Or Doug."

Theo's right-hand man was a quadruped robot, and he was decked out with all kinds of sensors. While useful in most situations, he wasn't exactly low-key or unnoticeable.

Jessica frowned. "I don't think we want to be flying a drone right now, even one as stealthy and small as yours."

"Yeah," Theo agreed. "They tend to take no-fly zones really seriously, especially when there's nuclear material involved."

❧

Jessica took them along the unmarked road, which ran for several miles parallel to the town of Arcadia, then through a series of rolling hills, then finally down a gradient, which brought them alongside the railroad tracks. She slowed the vehicle so Theo could record the rails on his cell phone and review them later. Or have one of his AI programs do it, Jessica suspected.

She parked the ambulance at the mouth of a gorge, where the rail continued on to the horizon and the flickering emergency lights in Arcadia became visible.

"I think this is far enough," Jessica said. "If we take the ambulance ahead too much more, it might stick out a bit. Although nobody might care. I don't know."

"I don't mind the walk," Theo said. "We might find something interesting."

They exited the vehicle and quickly took turns inspecting one another's hazmat suits, making sure that they were zipped up and securely fastened, partly for show and also due to the dawning realization there might actually be radioactive particles in the air.

Jessica looked at the open case inside the ambulance. "You wouldn't have a Geiger counter in there, would you?"

"No. And the one I had would only be good if we were right up next to something," Theo explained. "And by then, probably not helpful."

"It might be better than nothing," Jessica responded. "Okay. I guess if we see anybody else running, we should too."

Theo glanced over, rubbing the back of his neck. "Yeah, I forgot to mention, and it's bad on me for that. You noticed at the station that people wash themselves off. In an event like this, part of what you have to do is not just protect yourself but limit your exposure here. So they were working in shifts. The longer the shift, the longer you have to wait before going back in."

He paused, then added, "Oh, and yeah, another thing—they're probably taking iodine pills and other protective measures in case there is radioactivity."

"You're just remembering this now?"

Theo offered a nervous smile. "Sorry. I'm sure we'll be fine."

Jessica nodded. "Like ninety-nine percent sure?"

Theo considered for a moment. "Call it sixty-five percent."

They proceeded toward the town, walking alongside the railroad tracks. Jessica swept the ground with a metal detector Theo had acquired while he used a thermal-imaging system to scan the ground for anything warmer than the environment.

Arcadia was approximately two miles away from where they were. The smoke now illuminated by the rising sun was drifting toward the east, which Jessica took as a good sign for them since it meant they were upwind from the toxins. Still, it looked bad for anyone within hundreds of miles downwind.

"See anything interesting?" Jessica asked after ten minutes of walking.

"*Fallopia japonica*. Japanese knotweed," said Theo.

She furrowed her brow. "And that's connected to this how?"

"Oh, it's not," Theo explained. "It's an invasive species. There's a lot of it along the railroad tracks. It probably fell off a grain car."

"Of course," Jessica muttered to herself.

Theo stopped and walked over to a metal pole with a light mounted to a metal box.

"This is a switch box," he explained. "It's what the engineer would look for. When lit, it would tell him which way the spur was going."

The metal cabinet was rusted through. Daylight was visible through tiny holes created from a combination of corrosion and shotgun pellets.

"I don't think that thing has worked since Thomas Edison installed it himself," Jessica remarked.

Theo pulled a radio frequency and EMF scanner from his backpack and ran it along the post and up to the cabinet.

"Yeah, there is no voltage in this. If the track was switched, the engineer wouldn't have gotten a signal from it."

"It seems like kind of an important piece of equipment to not keep repaired," Jessica noted.

"There's about 138,000 miles of railroad track in the United States," Theo explained. "Even if a majority of it isn't used, they still use tens of thousands of miles of track and junctions—in various states of maintenance. I suspect the spur line is so old nobody cared about this box, because nobody ever thought that junction would ever point in the wrong direction."

Jessica noticed three yellow figures walking in their direction. They were still half a mile away, but the contrast of their suits against the dry gray ground was unmistakable.

"Do you think they're headed for us?"

"They're probably doing the same thing we are right now," Theo said as he took photos of the switch box.

"Is that the thing that caused the problem?" Jessica asked.

"No, not directly. The junction's still down there," Theo explained. "Well, actually closer to where they are, and that might be what they're looking at. Control of the junction must be there. This control was probably cut a long time ago. Although, if we had more time, I'd like to check if our saboteur had done something to it more recently."

Jessica frowned. "Time and exposure to radiation don't really go together, Theo."

"Fair point." Theo directed his attention away from the switch box and back to the rail. "We can pick up our pace. I don't think we're going to see anything interesting until we get to the spur."

As Theo kept his eyes on the ground, Jessica stared out at the town.

According to ChatGPT, the population of Arcadia was 942, with the majority of people living outside city limits in farms and small clusters of homes with large acreage.

From where they were, Jessica could see several steel buildings, a water tower, and a few three-story structures near the center of town. The steel buildings belonged to a pipe fitting company that made irrigation equipment. There was a farm equipment repair facility in there somewhere too.

As the junction came into view a few hundred feet ahead of them, Theo murmured, "Here we go."

The yellow figures were closer, but not that much bigger than when Jessica had last observed them. If they were heading in their direction, it wasn't in a hurry.

Suddenly, Theo spun 180 degrees and began walking backward in the same direction as Jessica. It was a peculiar habit of his, she had noticed, when he was trying to pay extra close attention to things on the ground. He hadn't even been aware of it until she had pointed it out to him.

She'd asked him if it helped him think or see more things, and Theo had replied that he couldn't think of any physiological, neurological, or mental reason why it should, but he still did it.

"There," Theo said, pointing at a cable running alongside the railroad tracks before disappearing into the ground. "That's the signal cable, which, between here and back there, is probably severed—most likely in multiple places by weather, rodents, people, you name it."

Theo knelt by the junction where two rails diverged from the straight set, creating the side spur. To the left of the rails was a weathered concrete pad with rusted pistons mounted to it and thick metal cables going from the back of them into the ground.

Investigators had already placed small plastic yellow markers with numbers around the pad and the rails.

"Looks like they've already checked this," Jessica observed.

"Yeah," Theo muttered as he moved to the concrete pad and inspected the pistons.

Jessica glanced up, noticing the yellow figures were much closer than before. "We might have a situation here. Do you want me to go buy you some time?"

"The control box is probably in town somewhere," Theo told her. "I'd really like to take a look at that. But the fact that these were still working is interesting. I can't see any signs of recent tampering. But the guy we might be looking for wouldn't leave anything like that." He pulled out his phone. "Let me get some photos and a couple swabs."

"Got it," said Jessica as she headed in the direction of the figures approaching them.

Theo began narrating his notes aloud, despite Jessica no longer being within earshot.

"So we have several things that need to happen in order for our train to go off the rails and into Arcadia. One, a signal has to come from a box somewhere that sends power to here, which then activates the electric pistons, which shift the track from where it had been happily resting for decades and into town. Now, I doubt this equipment was able to last this long and still work without regular maintenance. Regular maintenance isn't necessarily out of the question, though sometimes there's a backlog going back decades. And if we take a look at the cabling and find out that it's all new here, that wouldn't really prove anything, even if there aren't records for it. But it still needed to work."

He stood erect, put his hands on his hips, and stared at the junction. "I'd love to take this apart, but that's not going to happen right now. Of course, this is only part of it. The other factor is the switch. Somebody had to turn that on, and I'm sure the investigators are looking at that right now, because that's the smoking gun," Theo concluded to himself.

"What agency are you with?" asked a man with a loud voice and an MP5 submachine gun hanging across his chest.

Theo looked up and saw two men wearing hazmat suits and carrying weapons.

"Do you know if they identified the switch box?" Theo asked, ignoring the question.

The other man spoke into a comms set in his helmet. "We're checking on him now . . . 10-4."

"What agency are you with?" asked the first soldier.

"I'm a paramedic," Theo explained. "I was asked to come here but wasn't provided any other additional information."

"Asked by whom?"

Theo said, "FEMA."

"Who is your point of contact?"

Theo was trying to think of a better answer when he heard the crackle of the radio in the other soldier's helmet and a voice announcing, "We've got the other one."

"We're going to need you to get on your knees and place your hands over your head," said the soldier.

Theo ignored the man and turned around to see where Jessica was. Instead of two soldiers, she was surrounded by five and was already face down on the ground with her hands being cuffed behind her back. He sighed . . . Although it was unlikely they would have air support to catch him, he understood that running was futile.

"Are you guys with the DOE or the NRC?" Theo asked as they cuffed him.

"We're the ones that stop terrorists from getting nuclear materials," replied the soldier with his knee in Theo's spine.

CONTAMINATION

Ben Ableman took his fourth shower of the day at the cleanup zone.

As jets of pressurized liquid pummeled his body and drained into the portable containment system, he made a mental note to double-check with the monitoring lead about the backup water systems. He'd hate for containment operations to get shut down for something as stupid as not being able to keep the crews clean and safe because somebody forgot to make sure a water tanker truck was en route.

As the Department of Energy's Federal Radiological Monitoring and Assessment Center lead, he had a thousand details to keep track of. Granted, he had an entire team to support him, but part of oversight was just that—oversight—making sure that everybody else got their job done and none of the little details fell between the cracks.

His colleagues at the Federal Emergency Management Agency had done their job quickly, evacuating the citizens of Arcadia along with first responders who had been exposed to noxious gases. And the cargo. So far, the radiation meters hadn't gone off the charts, suggesting that the canisters had done their job. But several containers remained trapped in wreckage around the power station and embedded in the ground. And Ableman knew from experience that moving the canisters might well reveal a fissure and result in a leak.

The scenario that kept him up at night was a situation not too dissimilar to this, but one in which radiological material spilled into a reservoir or river. He could do the math and explain why even in that situation the actual threat was much lower than what people would have realized because the more widely the material was dispersed, the lower the overall levels of measurable radiation. It would quickly reduce to a level indistinguishable from natural background radiation levels. But that scientific detail would be lost on most people.

Explaining to the public that they're exposed to more radiation while flying on commercial airplanes at high altitudes than from all the nuclear material ever used would be equally pointless.

Ableman stepped to the next cleanup point and could see Warren Rafferty, the Radiological Assistance Program team commander, waiting for him on the other side of the plastic flaps.

Ableman gritted his teeth and underwent another spray-down from the hazmat cleanup team, this time in his skivvies, then toweled off and put on a jumpsuit.

"What's the latest?" he asked Warren, who, prior to joining DOE, had served in the navy in nuclear material security.

"The good news is our monitoring systems haven't detected anything, and we've been able to put some embedded units into the outflow from the aquifer about four miles from here. Our drones are set up and monitoring, so we should have a pretty good three-dimensional view of what our containment situation is like. More detection drones are incoming from Wind Aerospace."

Ableman appreciated Warren's military efficiency. He was cut from the cloth that was more concerned with getting things done than any kind of status-seeking.

"What's the bad news?" asked Ableman.

"Not an existential threat as far as we can see, but it is a complication and worth your attention. We caught two people within the restricted zone dressed in chemical protection equipment, but they're not with any agency or department that we're aware of."

Ableman frowned. "Lookie-loos? Citizen journalists? What?"

Every kind of disaster had its own particular breed of human pest that could get in the way. Firefighters sometimes had to deal with amateur firefighters deciding to show up and help out and make things worse. Weather scientists had to deal with storm chasers. Train crashes invited their own brand of nuisance, given the fixation on locomotives and railroads shared by a certain kind of male.

"Well, a woman was using a metal detector. The man carried a bag filled with EMF tools, thermal equipment, and some homemade gear," Warren told him.

"How sophisticated was his equipment?" asked Ableman.

"It looked pretty sophisticated. Weren't exactly CCCP or Russian flag stickers on it," Rafferty replied. "He's an American; so is she. For what that's worth."

Ableman asked, "Did they explain why they're here?"

"We've kept the two separate," Warren explained. "The woman has asked to speak only to you and won't answer any other questions, while the man will only ask questions and also hasn't offered us anything."

Ableman sighed. "This is the last thing I need right now."

Warren nodded. "The woman's interesting. There's something familiar about her that I can't pin down. From her bearing, she's ex-military or law enforcement—maybe both," he explained. "I'm pretty sure the guy is some kind of scientist."

"Do they have any ID on them? My first impulse is just to get that and send them away and not burden the sheriff's department right now."

"Nope, no ID. And I think we're going to have to involve the sheriff because there's the other part," Warren said. "Drones spotted an ambulance two miles from here. We think it's theirs—or rather, one they stole."

"Lotta effort to get inside the perimeter," Ableman thought out loud. "Where are they now?"

"My men have them in separate classrooms over at the high school. Do you want to go talk to them?"

Ableman shrugged. "Do you need to pull your guys off to do something else?"

"No, we're pretty well staffed right now."

Ableman crossed his arms. "Okay, I need to check into a few things. I say we let these two sit for a little while. Also, check with the FBI and see if they want to handle this."

Jessica was staring at the blank blackboard and rows of desks that had been stacked onto each other at the side of the classroom. She was handcuffed to a desk in the middle of the room while a DOE security officer sat at a desk by the door with his submachine gun resting in front of him while he made notes in a metal-cased notepad.

She knew that TV shows and movies always seemed to skip over the time from when you get arrested and processed and then are made to sit waiting, often for hours on end, until someone comes to speak with you. Of course, most of the time, Jessica was the official making the arrestee wait. And more often than not, it wasn't a tactical decision but just the sheer fact that she had way too many things to deal with and talking to a witness or suspect was something that could wait until all the other fires were put out.

The operations chief handling the Arcadia City disaster still had literal fires to put out.

Jessica had not answered the questions of the arresting officers, nor the DOE commander, because she knew their best chance of getting out of this situation without a criminal record would be by saying as little as possible until they had the opportunity to explain themselves to the right person. All that, of course, assumed that the authorities on-site would both be willing to listen and understand the value they brought to the situation.

Given the number of laws they had broken to get past the perimeter, she wasn't optimistic. The next step would be to try to figure out some form of legal remedy. Jessica and Theo had both hired multiple first-rate attorneys to get them out of situations like this. But timing was everything.

Jessica's biggest concern at the moment was Theo. He could either be incredibly smart and tactical in situations like this or completely preoccupied with something else and disregard the stakes.

She glanced down at the handcuff that was fastened to the desk. It was a standard Smith & Wesson. She could pick it in about four seconds using one of at least four different tools she had hidden on her body. It would take a little bit longer with the casing from a ballpoint pen or another improvised tool. But the trick was to do it without being observed. Her guard had her in full line of sight. Not that that necessarily would have prevented her from surreptitiously getting out of the cuff, but it was a complicating factor and also begged the question: *And do what?* She and Theo were in deep enough trouble already. Escaping federal custody would only add to the bill.

Across the hallway, Theo sat in a similar situation to Jessica's. His guard, a man named Ross Surrey, was also sitting strategically by the door but had his full attention on Theo, not his notebook.

From the moment perimeter patrol had handed the suspect off to him, the man had been asking Surrey nonstop questions that were extremely suspicious. He'd wanted to know everything from the location of the switch box that controlled the spur junction to the public availability of the cargo manifest and proof of when the various materials had been loaded onto the freight train. None of which were details that Surrey or anybody else could possibly know, which only made the questions that much fishier. Naturally, neither this scientist guy nor the woman would divulge the slightest information about themselves.

Surrey found the scientist's quiet periods even more suspicious because of the peculiar way in which the man directed his attention. He perked up to footsteps in the hall. He turned his head to observe which vehicles were pulling into the parking lot. And he got a strange look in his eye as he seemed to be listening to sounds coming from the air-conditioning vent. At first, Surrey thought that the man might be insane, but then he realized that Mr. Science was silently gathering as much information as possible about their environment. And this spooked Surrey.

The environment felt equally surreal. The high school gymnasium had been turned into an impromptu command center, along with the classrooms. The last citizens had left Arcadia City several hours ago and were in the process of being moved farther away to staging areas beyond the hazard zone.

Surrey had spent a large part of his adult life going through various disaster training drills. Tonight, everything had gone predictably, with minimal screwups up until these two shady people showed up where they shouldn't have been. His own curiosity was piqued, but his job wasn't to ask questions. Nor did he have recording equipment or the legal wherewithal to gather admissible evidence from a suspect. Instead, he took it upon himself to observe the scientist, make mental notes, and share those details with whoever needed them next.

Of one thing Surrey was certain: Stealing an emergency vehicle to break into a radiation-containment zone meant the scientist and his partner were screwed.

Two hours later, Ableman was confident that the containment team had put enough shielding in place to prevent any accidental leaks from the canisters. They were now proceeding to clean up the wreckage around the materials in order to safely extricate them. The more immediate threats were the toxic vapors and still-smoldering embers from the buildings that had been taken out by the fireball. And residual vinyl chloride that still pooled in certain places.

The EPA had its own teams working on containing the chemical spills. Part of Ableman's job was to manage the interests of both teams while ensuring the high-priority items came first.

"Who do you want to talk to first?" asked the tactical operations commander from his desk in the middle of the hall.

Ableman had half a mind to simply have the sheriff's department take the two trespassers away and deal with them later. But his curiosity had gotten the better of him. No sensible person tries to break into a radioactive accident site. The question was, Were these people sensible or not?

"Where's the woman?"

The commander pointed to a classroom door with a taped-over window.

Ableman asked, "So what are we thinking? Terrorist or podcaster?"

"Which is worse?"

"A podcaster. They're much worse. We're at least allowed to shoot terrorists."

Ableman opened the door to the classroom, nodded to the guard at the desk, and strode over to where Jessica was sitting with her hands clasped on the metal rail where the cuff was attached.

"Are you the field director?" Jessica asked.

Ableman locked eyes with her. It was the voice that triggered him. He rolled his eyes, turned around, and walked out of the classroom and said loudly to the commander in the hallway, "Call the sheriff's department and tell them to send a unit over to take them into custody, then notify the FBI. Today is not the day for this bullshit. Make sure they fingerprint the ambulance and send them all of our field reports."

"Wait," Jessica shouted through the door. "We need to talk!"

Ableman shouted over his shoulder as he walked down the corridor. "No. Not to you, and sure as hell not to who I think is in the other room."

Jessica realized that the difference between fame and infamy was in the eye of the beholder, and in this situation the beholder didn't think highly of either of them. She briefly contemplated freeing herself of the cuffs so she could chase after him and explain herself, but she realized the armed man between her and the hallway might have other ideas. While she was fairly certain he wouldn't shoot, it wasn't a risk worth taking. She had already exhausted the field commander's patience. If they had any hope of getting out of this situation without spending time in a federal penitentiary, she needed to take things calmly.

NUISANCE

Brad Trasker sat down at the visitors window and waited for the sheriff's deputies to bring Jessica Blackwood into the room.

He had received the call during his flight to Idaho. His employer, Wind Aerospace, had a drone contract with the DOE and was dispatching additional radiation-monitoring systems into the area of the crash site.

When Brad saw Jessica's and Theo's names flash across his company internal-threat monitoring system, he had added himself to the flight manifest and headed for the airport.

Most people didn't have friends whose names appeared in threat-assessment systems, but most people didn't have friends like Jessica Blackwood and Theo Cray.

Upon landing, Brad was able to borrow the personal vehicle of one of Wind Aerospace's remote drone pilots who lived in the area. The roads were clear with the exception of emergency vehicles going in one direction. Civilian evacuation had been completed, although on-the-ground reports indicated that the radiation hazard was contained.

As the head of security for the company contracted with the DOE to provide airborne radiation surveillance, he made it from the airport to the sheriff's office without incident.

He wished he could say he was surprised Theo's and Jessica's names came up in the middle of this crisis, but he wasn't. He'd been notified of the train derailment shortly before midnight, when the DOE had contacted Wind Aerospace, wanting to know how quickly they could deploy extra craft to the zone. Now, as he entered the sheriff's department, he made the executive decision not to reveal his connection to Jessica and Theo. Everyone would simply assume that he was taking his job extra seriously by questioning this pair of intruders who had entered Wind Aerospace's drone-surveillance workspace.

A few minutes after Brad was seated in an interview room, two female deputies escorted Jessica in and sat her down. They were professional and polite toward her, which Brad appreciated, and stepped out of the room so they could talk.

"You don't look too surprised to see me," Jessica observed.

"I can't say that I am," Brad admitted.

"I assume Theo must have called you for you to get here so quickly."

"I was already on the way."

"Ah. Have you spoken to Theo yet?" she asked.

"No, I figured I'd talk to you first, since I have at least a reasonable chance of understanding what the hell you have to say."

Jessica leaned forward. "Well, the short explanation is, Theo believes, and I think his intuition is right, that this was no accident. He's been studying patterns of sabotage and he even stayed up last night, monitoring news and half expecting an attack of this scale to happen somewhere. So I'm inclined to think that he's not wrong. The trouble is, his theory about the pattern is a bit more difficult to explain."

"And can I assume that I'm interviewing you here now because you didn't go through the proper channels?"

"Timing is crucial, Brad. Again, if Theo's right . . . we can expect two more attacks in the next three weeks. Each an escalation of the prior attack. They look like accidents involving man-made systems, but it's sabotage. Do you see? Getting permission first seemed the wrong approach. In hindsight, I have other thoughts," she admitted.

Brad looked around, checking to see if they were being observed. Technically, they should have privacy here, but there was no guarantee. "What exactly are we looking at?" he asked quietly.

Jessica glanced around the room. "You mean the next event? Who we're after?"

"No, I mean you and Theo," Brad explained. "At the moment, you're facing federal charges and felony theft. That's the more pressing consideration as far as I'm concerned, because if we don't deal with that, we can't deal with the other thing."

"Well, certain steps may or may not have been taken to ensure that we could get through the perimeter stealthily," Jessica reported. "Given that examining the evidence as soon as possible was our paramount concern, some of the steps taken may have been hasty, and there's a good chance that whatever we were accused of doing might be accurate."

"Okay." Brad thought out loud: "The trespassing and evidence tampering might be manageable because it's going to be subjective, considering the chaotic situation. Borrowing something that doesn't belong to you can be a bigger challenge. A private party might require some persuasion. How much time do I have?"

"Theo said the pattern followed something called a Lucas sequence, but in reverse, and this was number three." She paused, then added, "The next two numbers are one and two, and assuming we're twenty-four hours into number three, that means the next event's less than a week—six days—away."

"Okay, the key person here is Ben Ableman. He's the DOE field director. I might be able to persuade him. And then I'll figure everything else out from there," Brad said. "What was your interaction with him like?"

"He's not a fan," Jessica replied.

Brad crossed his arms. "Not a fan in that he's not happy with what you did? Or not a fan because he realized who you were?"

"The last one," Jessica sighed.

"Oh," Brad said gravely. "That."

It was late afternoon when Brad entered the command center at Arcadia City High School, where Ben Ableman was leaning over a Ping-Pong table covered in maps and charts and giving commands to his colleagues.

The gymnasium was filled with tables and chairs pulled from classrooms and set up in different stations handling the coordination of the crisis. Public schools made good disaster command centers due to the availability of tables, chairs, rooms, and wide-open spaces to throw people together in ad hoc teams.

"Director, I'm Brad Trasker. If you have a moment, I need to talk to you about something."

Ableman looked up from the map. "You're the guy handling the drones, right? You can speak to RAP Commander Warren, over in the corner by the bleachers, okay?"

"Actually, it's about something else."

Ableman glanced at the others, exasperation evident in his voice. "Talk to somebody who has time, because I don't have any right now. We still gotta move the containment vessels and figure out how we're gonna do that with a hundred thousand gallons of flammable liquid still nearby."

"I understand that, but this is about the next potential incident," Brad pointed out.

"The next one?" Ableman asked.

Brad nodded. "Yes, two of my colleagues were chasing down a lead and accidentally crossed your path, I guess is one way to put it."

Ableman rolled his eyes and let out an exasperated sigh. "Don't tell me you're with them." He looked over to an aide. "Can somebody tell me how he got in here?"

Brad held his hands up to calm Ableman but also to prepare himself if he needed to dissuade anybody from touching him. "I'm supposed to be here. I am the liaison for Wind Aerospace. I'm the reason you were able to get more drones here so quickly," he explained.

"Well, thank you for that, but those two aren't my problem anymore," Ableman replied. "I think we're done here."

Brad folded his arms. "We may not be done, and that's what I'm trying to say. I understand how you handled the situation. I don't blame you. Frankly, I've felt like having the two of them put into custody a few times myself. But the facts are important: Jessica Blackwell and Theo Cray came here because they caught onto something that nobody else was paying attention to. They believe that whoever caused this has another large-scale disaster planned within days. We ignore them at our peril."

Ableman fixed Trasker with a stern look. "Trasker, I know your name, I know who you are, I know your reputation. Let me be very clear: The next situation is going to be somebody else's problem, because I'm still going to be cleaning up here. Now, as a professional courtesy, I can overlook the trespassing. I can perhaps turn the other way about the potential evidence tampering, assuming that none took place. But it still remains a fact that they stole, and I repeat, stole, which last I checked is a felony, an emergency vehicle to get to this location. And that's not up to me anymore. That's between the sheriff's department, the county, the state, or whoever else, and the person who owned that. So I can't help you there."

"But they might be onto something," Brad insisted.

Ableman locked eyes with him. "And, well, they might be, but last I checked, the rule of law is still in place. And while I might respect the outcomes of their previous exploits, I sure as hell don't respect the methods."

Brad stood firm. "Blackwood was a great agent and put everything on the line for the bureau."

"Yes, and I respect that. I respect her career and the work she did when she worked with us within the system," Ableman said. "But that's not how she plays anymore. I don't have patience for vigilantes and interlopers. If you want to do the right thing, then you put on a badge and you follow the rules. That's not how they play. And maybe they get some good outcomes, but also they complicate things. There is a long, troubled history with those two making investigations more complicated, damaging ongoing cases, and generally provoking anarchy around those of us trying to work within the laws to protect our country."

Brad frowned. "But what if they're seeing something you're not?"

Ableman snapped, "Then take my card and email me. Until then, get out of my face unless you have something to tell me about drones. We're still in the middle of a crisis here. Those two are the least of my concerns. It's up to the local police to manage that."

❧

Undersheriff Colleen Newell was sitting in the bullpen of the Glassman County Sheriff's Office when Brad was escorted into the room.

"Thanks for meeting with me. I know this is not exactly the best situation right now," Brad said.

"That's putting it mildly, but once I heard your name, I figured I could spare a few minutes," Newell remarked. "We teach your shoot-out at the Mojave Airport in our training academy now."

Brad considered that for a moment. "Is it presented as a good example or a bad one?"

"Definitely bad if you're a Russian hit man, but basically good." Newell smiled. "It was used as an example of how to handle a particularly sticky hostage situation and challenging environment. I suspect a lot of your training was classified."

Brad shrugged. "A fair amount of it, and more field experience than I care to talk about, or am allowed to."

Newell glanced at the file in front of her. "So this is about two of our detainees, Blackwood and Cray, right?"

Brad nodded. "I suspect you already know their story."

"Yep. For a while, those were the only names you'd hear from my friends who followed crime podcasts."

"Not a fan?" Brad asked.

"I'm neutral on the issue," Newell said. "Certainly not as frustrated with them as Ben Ableman."

"Well, the good news is he's willing to be flexible, at least provisionally, about the trespassing issues," Brad explained. "And I'd like to see if I can get my friends out of here as soon as possible, ideally before an arraignment."

"That's where it gets complicated, Mr. Trasker," Newell told him. "They haven't gone through processing, so it's possible to let them walk out of here, but we're still dealing with the stolen-ambulance issue. And if I let them go before they stand before a judge, the owner might be very displeased because it would complicate their claims, which we have to respect. There's also some question of where they got their hazmat suits, but nobody's raised their hand yet on that one."

"So if I can clear that up with the owner of the ambulance company, I can get them out of here?" Brad concluded.

"I can only slow-walk this paperwork so much, even in this situation," Newell explained. "I would need something in writing or an email, and it has to be from the owner."

Brad nodded. "Okay, let's see what I can do."

"Good luck with that," Newell remarked. "When my deputy spoke to him on the phone, he seemed pretty pissed."

Brad leaned forward. "Well, if you can give me the information you have on him, I'll see if I can finesse him a bit. Extraordinary, extenuating circumstances . . . I'm sure he'll understand."

❧

"Why the hell would I want to let those assholes get away with it after they stole my $180,000 vehicle?" yelled an angry Adam Tripp over the speaker of Brad's phone.

"They were trying to prevent a disaster and didn't have enough time to go through proper channels," Brad explained as he sat in the driver's seat of the borrowed drone pilot's truck.

As he spoke, he had his laptop open and was scouring the internet and his databases for any helpful details he could find about Tripp.

"Last I checked, we're worried about a radioactive cloud heading over our heads. I'm not sure how well their disaster prevention worked out."

Adam Tripp didn't have much of a social media presence. Aside from a LinkedIn profile that listed him as the owner of the ambulance company and a security firm, his employment history had only three entries, and he hadn't updated his friend network in a decade. So Brad shifted gears, going deeper into Tripp's past. Starting with his alma mater and tracing his college friends forward in time and checking their social media. All he came up with were photographs of Tripp at several sporting events around the Washington area and at two NASCAR races.

Brad considered this, then replied, "Okay, what about a financial settlement? What if I buy the ambulance off you?"

He had a certain amount of personal cash available for a situation like this. And as much as he hated the thought of it, he could also go to

Kylie and write a bigger check. He had no doubt she would be eager to help out Jessica and Theo, but he considered that a professional line he didn't want to cross. Kylie was his chief priority; his problems should never make her world more complicated.

"Oh, I'm sure there'll be a cash settlement," Tripp remarked, "but after we go through prosecution."

Brad replied, "I was hoping we could settle things right now."

"Nope, I think we'll just let the law do its thing and my lawyers do theirs. Until then, have a good day," Tripp said, then hung up.

Brad stared at his phone and fumed. Now Tripp had made it personal. He'd tried the polite approach. He had tried the financial approach. And all that was left was the blunt approach.

When Brad worked in counterintelligence, his job was to get things done by any means necessary. Sometimes that could be a polite word. Other times that could be dropping a ten-story building on top of somebody. He wasn't proud of all the things he had done, but he knew he was good at it. In civilian life, thankfully, his options were limited, and he didn't have to find himself second-guessing his actions as much. Knocking on Adam Tripp's door and putting a gun in his mouth might be effective in the short term but would cause many more problems in the longer term. He needed to be more clever than that.

Brad zoomed in on a photo of an Asian American male that appeared in several photographs with Adam Tripp. There was a look about the guy, from the kind of clothes he wore to the jewelry, that suggested he was in finance or international law and traveled overseas quite a bit.

The reverse image search identity lookup said his name was Matthew Than. He had grown up in Riverside, California, gone to Berkeley, and then become a consultant for an international firm.

There were five photos that Brad could find of Matthew in Indonesia and Thailand. Two of them showed a karaoke bar that Brad was reasonably sure was located in a district near Phuket.

Brad dialed a contact on his phone.

A voice picked up over the sound of traffic. "Bradley, this is unexpected. What's going on?"

"I'm going to send you a photo," Brad said. "You don't have to tell me anything other than if you've tracked this person going into any of the LaCoix associate establishments in Phuket."

"Sure thing. Just got it," said the other man. "I'm not going to bother to ask."

"It's a personal matter," Brad explained.

"Yep, he is in our database. Adam Tripp, is that the name?" asked the man.

Government intelligence tracked businesspeople all over the world, looking for infiltration, sales of secrets, and, in general, dirt that could be used in certain circumstances. Someone like Adam Tripp wouldn't have been a focus of an investigation, but if he had gone into one of the gambling parlors or whorehouses owned by one of the Thai organized crime organizations, there was a good chance that his name would have been flagged in some database.

This made Brad's life a lot easier, because his next steps would have been to track down Tripp's family members in search of dirt. And that's when things get extra icky.

"Thanks. Let me know if you need anything," said Brad before he hung up.

It had only been six minutes since Adam Tripp had brushed Brad off and hung up.

"Jesus Christ, what is your problem?" he said as he answered the phone.

"We tried this the right way. Now I'm not going to be so polite. Name a number for me. Name a number that will ease your frustration and let me help out my friends."

"Fuck you. I think we're done," Tripp snapped.

Brad replied, his voice low: "I'm looking at a list of the number of times you and your buddy Matthew Than went into whorehouses in Thailand, with very specific times and locations. I can call the housemothers and probably even get the names of the underage girls and whatever weird shit you're into. I don't want to do that. I *can* do it. I've done worse. But you haven't given me a lot of options here. Tell me what you want for my friends to walk."

He could hear the sound of Tripp breathing on the other end of the phone. It took a while for the man to regain his composure.

"Who the hell are you?"

"I'm a guy looking out for my friends. To be honest with you, I don't have the time for this right now. If this doesn't work, then I have to escalate. If that doesn't work, I escalate even further. It doesn't stop until I get what I want. Between now and then, your life is going to spin off on trajectories you *really* don't want. So, name a number."

Tripp began to hyperventilate audibly. After he'd managed to master his breathing, he rasped into the phone: "Free. The number is free. Nothing. Just return my ambulance. I'll put it in writing. Whatever you want. Just leave me alone. I wasn't even the one that wanted to press charges. But that Abel—Ableman guy, he got all insistent because he was raging over this. So I'm good. Return the ambulance. We'll forget it happened. Just stay out of my life," he pleaded.

Brad paused, then said, "I'll draft an email for you to copy and send to the sheriff's office stating this. And thank you for helping me out. If you ever need anything, let me know."

Tripp sighed. "I hope to God I never need somebody like you to help me out."

"Understood. It might take a little while to get the ambulance back to you, given the current situation." Brad hung up. Satisfied but not proud of himself. He'd added the bit about taking longer to return the ambulance because he realized that Theo and Jessica might need it for transport. He'd make sure that Adam Tripp was compensated. If for no other reason than to ease his own conscience.

If the past was any indication, events would only become more complicated, and Brad wouldn't be rid of Jessica and Theo just yet.

PATTERN SEEKER

Jeff Crandall got out of his pickup truck at the top of the bluff overlooking Arcadia City. He was confused. He had been called out here by Brad Trasker, apparently because Trasker had some questions about setting up the drone relays in an optimal position to inspect the tracks. As the on-site authority for the Federal Railway Administration, Crandall knew his job was to get a quick take on the cause of the disaster and to see if there was anything they needed to do quickly to prevent similar incidents throughout the rail system.

While the drone antenna relay was in position and so was Trasker, Crandall wasn't expecting to see the two other people, Theo Cray and Jessica Blackwood, whom he'd heard had been arrested a few hours earlier for trespassing inside the perimeter.

"Are they supposed to be out here?" Crandall asked Brad.

"Yes, that's all cleared up," Brad assured him. "We have a couple questions about the ongoing investigation."

Crandall furrowed his brow. "How is this connected to the surveillance drones?"

"It just is." Brad looked over at Theo. "Theo, you want to go ahead?"

Theo had been surveying the town of Arcadia. There were still whiffs of gray smoke, but the fire had been mostly contained. In broad daylight, the wreckage of the train was easy to discern, even from this distance. The railcars were strewn about in a haphazard zigzag pattern with the locomotive in the middle of the power station relay, still covered in cabling and pylons. The entire grid had needed to be rerouted around the area, with emergency generators providing power to the high school command center and a few other locations. When night fell, the town's only illumination would be portable emergency lights.

"What exactly made the track switch?" Theo began bluntly.

"We still don't know," Crandall admitted. "There's a control box in the former railway station downtown. Our best guess is there might have been a power surge from a line we thought had been shunted, but it might have had corrosion or some groundwater seepage that caused a connection."

Theo stared at him. "And how likely do you think this is?"

"We couldn't find any evidence of tampering in the switch box. There was no new cabling put in place other than what the standard repairs had been out on the rail line. It just seems to be one of those freak accidents. With over a hundred thousand miles of rail, these things can happen," Crandall explained. "We've got a backlog going back years for inspections, and as much as we want to catch up to that, we just don't have the people to do it. I'm sure there's going to be a lot of complaining. There's going to be some inquiries, and it's going to be the same usual thing—a lot of finger-pointing—but never enough resources to prevent it from happening again."

"What about the switch box?" Theo asked. "If there had been power to it for a while, could something else have triggered it? Maybe remotely?"

Crandall rubbed his chin. "I checked it out myself. Nothing had been tampered with."

"Nothing you could see," Theo added.

Crandall replied, "Well, we'll know once we get it back to the lab and take it apart and have a closer look. But for now, I don't know what else we should be looking for. It's not exactly like there was a remote control or something hot-wired in there. Everything looked exactly like it should."

"I'm not sure your team will know what to look for," Theo remarked, sounding more condescending than he intended.

"Well, then. How about you tell us what that is?" Crandall challenged.

Theo hesitated. "Sorry, I don't know. I think you're going to find that everything is exactly what it's supposed to be, other than the fact that it was working and it shouldn't have been. As far as how power got to the box or to the line, I think you'll see everything's functioning. It'll seem like there was a power surge. Triggered by something else." He paused, frowning. "And what triggered *that*? That's going to be the real question."

"I don't know about you, but not everybody can be an expert in everything. I've been looking into these kinds of things for years, and sometimes things just happen." Crandall nodded toward the wreckage of the train. "Convenient explanations are only ever convenient."

"Often the difference between the explained and the unexplained is the point where we stop looking for answers," Theo countered.

"Where's the switch box now?" Brad asked.

Crandall said, "At the high school, about ready to be shipped off to our inspection facility."

"How long will that take?" Brad asked.

"Given the situation, I expect it will get a high priority."

Jessica asked, "What is a high-priority response time for the Federal Railroad Administration and the NTSB?"

Crandall said, "I think we'll have our report back in a couple weeks."

"Weeks!" Theo exclaimed.

"We have to proceed carefully and cautiously. Although there seems to be no evidence of sabotage, we're keeping that open, which means we have to proceed in a way that preserves any forensic evidence. So, yes, weeks."

Theo gestured toward Arcadia City. "I don't think we have weeks. Something like this will happen again within days."

Crandall narrowed his eyes. "If you know something, maybe you should tell us."

"Just a hunch. Thanks for coming up here and helping us out," Brad said, intervening. "I'll get you the drone-surveillance data as soon as I can, and you can put together your track inspection report."

After Crandall left, Jessica, who'd been silent, told Brad, "Thank goodness your company had the drone contract with the DOE. I don't know what we'd be able to do without your access."

"You can thank Kylie for that," Brad explained. "She's been bidding for as many of those as she can at or below cost for reasons I don't quite fully understand, but I just go along with it."

"Data," Theo replied. "Data. Gathering that much information is incredibly useful. Not just for the information itself, but just building out the infrastructure that can handle that volume. She's smart."

"So according to your theory, we've got six days until the next event like this," said Brad. "What do we need to do next? How do we find out where and what the next sabotage is?"

"I still need to take a look at that switch box," Theo told him.

"Do you think you're going to find something they won't?"

"I think it's the only point of contact we may have with whoever did this."

"Okay, well, in that case, I need to get you the box. How much time do you need with it?" asked Brad.

"Ideally, a few days, but a few hours with the right equipment would work."

"Did you bring that equipment with you?" Brad asked.

"I can probably improvise something if I can get to the gear in the ambulance."

"The good news is that it's sitting in the parking lot of the high school and nobody's expecting it anytime soon," Brad informed them. "I'll find out if there's a motel or someplace nearby we can use."

"And that switch box?" asked Jessica.

"I guess it's my turn to commit a crime," Brad replied.

Brad Trasker was an expert at acting like he belonged anywhere he chose to. From mah-jongg parlors in Shanghai to private social clubs in Bulgaria, he could adapt to a situation and make himself effectively invisible.

While his official role as supervisor of the Wind Aerospace drone contract allowed him certain levels of access around the disaster site, that authority didn't extend to breaking into the evidence lockup inside the high school classrooms where the NTSB and FRA were storing equipment that needed to be shipped for closer inspection.

"When in doubt, put on an orange vest and carry a fiberglass ladder and tool belt" was Brad's motto as he strolled down the corridor of Arcadia City High School to the blocked-off cafeteria.

As he passed the intersection with another hallway, he saw a woman with red eyes clutching her purse, wandering around. When she saw Brad she spoke up.

"Excuse me, could you help me?" she asked, worry etched across her face. "I'm trying to find out what happened to my kids."

"I'm sorry, I'm just a contractor," Brad apologized. "Maybe I can help you find somebody who knows what's going on."

The woman pulled a badge from her purse. It was an identity card for the hospital located in the next town over.

"I was working there when it happened and came home as soon as I could," she explained, her voice shaking. "Even though they didn't want to let me in, I had to, but I couldn't find my kids."

"I'm sorry. Maybe we should check at the front office for a list of who's been found," Brad suggested. "As far as I know, there weren't many casualties."

The woman burst into tears. "Nobody knows anything. Nobody can tell me anything," she sobbed.

Brad leaned the ladder against a row of lockers. "I'm sorry. When did you last speak to your children?"

"Yesterday evening before I went to work. I knew they snuck out after I left, but they're good kids. They're not the kind to get into any trouble. Well, nothing major. But this is something different," she explained.

"Did you check the sheltering sites?" Brad asked.

"Yes, but they weren't there, and the people at the shelter couldn't tell me where anybody else was," she replied, frustration lacing her words.

"Where's your hospital?" Brad asked.

"Fairmont. Right now, we've got a lot of first responders there undergoing treatment for smoke inhalation."

"Did you check there?" Brad asked.

"At the hospital? Someone would have told me if my kids were there."

"No, I mean the evacuation center in Fairmont," Brad explained. "If your kids were out of the house when this went down, there's a good chance they might have tried to head toward you but got diverted there."

The woman suddenly seemed hopeful. "You mean I could have just driven right past them? I hadn't even thought about that."

Brad could only imagine what the woman was going through. He'd been in far too many crisis situations involving families torn apart by war and disaster. He was optimistic that her kids were fine and hoped she wouldn't ask him to visit the impromptu morgue set up at the veterinary clinic near the command center.

The woman wrapped her arm around Brad and said a quick thank-you, then turned the other way and hurried back down the hall.

Brad grabbed his ladder and walked toward the entrance to the cafeteria, guarded by a National Guard soldier standing at attention.

Brad motioned toward the emergency lights that were illuminating this part of the school. "I gotta check the batteries in there," he said matter-of-factly.

"Sure thing," replied the guard as he pushed open the door for Brad to go inside.

The tables of the cafeteria were covered with plastic sheets. On top of them were various pieces of wreckage and equipment in the process of being cataloged before they were shipped off to the forensics lab. Two technicians wearing white bunny suits and respirators were at the far end taking photographs of what appeared to be a control panel from where Brad was standing.

Neither one of them gave him a second look as he worked his way through the tables, lugging his ladder.

Theo had shown Brad some examples of the device they were looking for. As he walked through the cafeteria, he slyly used his phone to take photos of the other objects and also made a mental catalog of their locations using his mind-palace technique. The mnemonic tool worked best when Brad knew what he was trying to memorize. Given that he had no understanding of the different pieces of equipment, he had to be imaginative in order to remember them. A shredded piece of engine shroud that looked vaguely like a fork became a fork. An instrument panel that had dials like a Connect Four game became the

Connect Four game. Swiftly, he made mental analogies for the objects, then placed them in relevant "rooms" throughout his memory space.

Brad ultimately found the control box on a table no more than five meters from where the technicians were inventorying the evidence. He unfolded the ladder, placed it between the technicians and the control box, climbed to the top of it, and reached up to an overhead light panel and slid away a ceiling tile so he could poke his head around and make it look like he was doing something important.

When he was satisfied they weren't paying attention to him, he stepped back down the ladder, grabbed a tool from his toolbox, unfolded the canvas bag he'd brought along, and then leaned on the table for a moment to see if they were looking in his direction.

As expected, Brad was effectively invisible to the suited workers. In one swift motion, he moved the control box into the canvas bag, then left his toolbox in its place. He went back up the ladder, looked around some more, pulled the ceiling panel back into place, then returned to the ground. As he closed the ladder with one hand, he moved his toolbox to the side, slid another piece of equipment where the control box had been, then reached down, swung the strap of the canvas bag over his shoulder, put his ladder over the other, grabbed his toolbox, and headed back to the door with a calm, measured pace.

The control box had already been tagged and inventoried. As long as it showed up somewhere in this room before it had been cleared out, he assumed nobody would miss it, given the chaotic situation. Still, he made sure to maintain his deliberate pace as he strolled out of the building carrying stolen federal evidence.

LABMAN

When Brad Trasker entered the hotel room on the outskirts of Fairmont, he found Theo Cray sitting at what he could best describe as an impromptu clear plastic tent constructed over the motel room table. Jessica sat cross-legged on the bed with her laptop, observing Theo and adding to her notes.

Since the safety crew had managed to contain the radioactive material to their satisfaction, the shelter-in-place warning had been lifted outside the city limits. In Arcadia, though, pools of toxic chemicals and fumes still lingered. Still, Brad had used some paperwork legerdemain to enable Theo and Jessica to stay within the security perimeter. This was mainly so Brad could return the stolen evidence before anybody noticed in the shortest amount of time.

He walked over to the table to observe Theo's contraption. He had created a plastic bubble with a car vacuum cleaner blowing filtered air into the chamber in order to maintain positive pressure and avoid unwanted contaminations like hair or DNA.

Inside the chamber, Theo had set up a high-powered microscope and was delicately moving the circuit board from the switch panel underneath the lenses. Brad noticed Theo's laptop sitting to the side, which was recording a video feed and running a program of some kind that was logging all the different parts and making annotations as Theo examined the device.

"Could you take a closer look at the lower right corner of the circuit board?" said a voice from Theo's laptop.

"Sure thing," Theo replied.

"Is that one of your forensic expert pals?" asked Brad.

"Kind of," Theo admitted. "It's a program I wrote."

Brad shrugged. He knew Theo created AI tools and assistants to help him with his work, but the extremely human-sounding voice had caught him off guard.

"Why am I not surprised?" Brad turned to Jessica. "Are all his friends AI?"

"Excluding you and me? I'd have to say the answer is yes."

"You should both be flattered," Theo said under his breath.

"Find anything?" asked Brad.

"No, everything looks like what it should," Theo said. "This board was made in 1992 in a factory outside Cincinnati. It looks like there were a couple repairs done over time, replacing fuses and a capacitor that would have leaked. But beyond that, I can't see any evidence of tampering. Then again, I didn't really expect to see any obvious evidence."

"So what were you expecting?" Brad inquired.

"Gum," said Theo.

"Gum?" Brad repeated.

Theo leaned back from the microscope, stretched his arms, and yawned. "I had an anthropology professor my sophomore year who took us on a field trip into the community center at our college campus. It was empty, there was nobody there, and he lined us up against the wall and asked us to explain from looking who we thought had lived there.

"Some of us tried to be clever and pointed to the wooden tables and the posters on the wall and described craftspeople who like to work with wood, metal workers, artisans who chose specific colors for the wallpaper. There was conversation about hierarchical social structures based upon the layout of the tables and placement of windows. But finally, he had enough of it and told us to look again.

"He said, 'I asked you who lived here, not who built it.' And then he walked over to a table, dramatically flipped it over, and revealed the underside, where we could see graffiti and dried gum stuck to the surface. 'What does that tell you about who lived here?' he asked us.

"There was a treasure trove of information in the gum alone, given all the dental imprints, which could illustrate the oral health of the people who'd left it behind. Then there was all the demented, perverted, and just strange graffiti that people felt compelled to hide in plain sight.

"The point," said Theo, "was there were two stories: the story we try to tell and the story we're actually telling. The layout of the room, the placement of the tables and chairs, and the posters was one story, but the gum under the chairs and table and all the other little things hidden underneath our gaze was where the real information was."

"But you're not actually looking for gum, are you?" asked Brad.

"No, it's a metaphor."

"I thought you hated those."

"I do," said Theo, "but you gotta do what you gotta do." He sat back in his chair. "Our master of chaos is a very detail-oriented person," he continued. "They would have to be in order to pull off what they've done, which means I don't expect to find a fingerprint. And if it is some kind of calling card, other than using the Lucas sequence for the frequency of these events, it's not going to be obvious or something that's going to stand out to a forensic technician. And even if I did find something that stood out, I would be suspicious because it might be intentional."

"Hypothetically, what do you think you're looking for?" asked Brad.

"I have to start with what I would do, which is always a terrible place to start from, but it's kind of all I've got right now. This person needed to cause the track to move, which means he not only needed this switch box to be working, he needed to be able to do something like send an electrical impulse to it to get it to do something it's not supposed to do, but in a way that would look like a malfunction and not like tampering."

"Is that all?" said Brad.

"Well, one way to do that would be . . . well, take a look here," said Theo as he pointed toward a tiny blue cylinder on the board. "See that capacitor? We know how much charge that is supposed to hold and how long it's supposed to take to charge up, but you could replace the materials inside of there and increase that by a slight amount and it might seem that it falls within or maybe a little bit outside of tolerances. But couple that with a change over here"—he pointed toward a transistor—"and you might have enough to get that to flip and to actually open up a gate when it shouldn't. Again, I'm just hypothesizing. You could do a couple little tweaks here to push things outside of their parameters to get it to do something it's not supposed to do. Another example would be if I had some electrical conduit running behind a wall and I put a nail through the wall close enough to go through it. It would look accidental, but if I was actually trying to create a spark gap or trigger a gas leak, that might be enough.

"It could be something painfully obvious if I look at it the right way, or it could be something extremely subtle. I would love to take apart the transistor and look inside there, but that would be too destructive if we're trying to put this back into evidence."

"I appreciate that. I think a few people may have seen my face," said Brad. "So, you're looking for something more subtle?"

"Yeah, something like an intentional row hammer attack," Theo explained.

"*Row hammer* . . . why is that familiar?"

"That was an apparently unintentional defect on a mass-produced microprocessor where a line of transistors that had public ports could be triggered all at once, which then tripped a fault in a secure component of the microprocessor, basically allowing you to get access. It was a very niche sort of attack. And if you had just looked at the blueprints of the transistor, you never would have necessarily realized the vulnerability was there. It's also the kind of thing that's made me extra suspicious about hardware coming from places like China. You may not see something that stands out and says 'I'm a trap,' but just laying things out in a specific pattern can have an influence on nearby systems. So while this isn't the same scale as a microchip, it's still possible to put things in here in a way that would pass detection but could actually cause the kinds of things that you want to trigger, which gives me some suspicions about who may have done this . . . but I need to think about that."

"Like Leon Theremin's wooden seal," said Jessica from the bed.

"The one where the Russians were able to bug the US Embassy by hiding a listening device inside of a carved wooden seal?" asked Brad.

"Yeah, that's the one," said Jessica. "Basically, the guy that invented the theremin figured out that if you placed two metal plates close to each other inside of a wooden seal with no other power, you could x-ray it, and it would look completely passive. But if you beamed a microwave at it from across the street, it would act like a microphone. Every time somebody spoke, the sound waves would cause the plates to touch and give off an electromagnetic frequency they could listen to passively from outside. I encountered a more sinister version of this a few years ago."

"Is that what you're looking for?" asked Brad.

"Maybe," said Theo. "Right now, I'm still looking for gum. Things that may have been left behind but weren't intentional. Like I said, I don't think it'll be a fingerprint. I don't think it'll be DNA. But it could be something. Whoever did this had to modify this within the last couple of years, not a decade ago. And doing that would be tricky. All the solder joints, everything looks like it should be, but that doesn't mean that it's not more recent. There are a lot of little tricks you can do to make you think that it's older than it is, things that I'm pretty sure would get past whatever technicians are going to look at this, so I'm just trying to think of other things to look for."

Jessica glanced up from her laptop. "I've been going over the photographs we took and everything else we've been able to find, and something doesn't sit right with me."

"What do you mean?" asked Brad.

"It was a hunch; now I think it's more than that. Our guy had to spend a lot of time here. I'm not saying months, but probably more than just a few days. He had to have a lot of information about what it would take to get the train to derail. He had to have the time to get the equipment working. That means people saw him. They may not realize who he was, and maybe nobody remembers him now, but there were witnesses. A town this small, somebody's got to remember something."

"Well, that seems to be the pattern in just about every major investigation. The culprit was probably at some point stopped by or interacted with the authorities, but at the time, it didn't seem like anything," said Brad.

"Exactly." Jessica closed her laptop. "Have they opened the community center yet?" she asked.

"Yeah. It's a first responder station right now. You looking for anybody in particular?"

Jessica put the laptop in her bag. "No," she said, "but I think I want to find some local Arcadia City cops, if there're any available, and see if they recall anything. Do you mind keeping an eye on the mad scientist here?"

"As long as it doesn't involve stealing body parts from a cemetery or climbing onto the roof to set up an electrical rod for a lightning strike, I think I've got it handled."

Jessica smirked. "Well, I got news for you. One of those two, Theo has already done."

"Allegedly," Theo replied without looking up from the microscope.

After Jessica left, Brad asked, "How far along are you?"

Theo looked at his laptop. "I've covered about six percent of the board so far."

Brad checked his watch. "I don't think we can hold on to it for that long. Is there anything I can do to help quicken the pace?"

"Do you have an X-ray machine or an electron microscope on you? If so, the answer is yes."

"Would that really help?"

"It would certainly help me narrow things down, but I don't know the practicality of that."

"I can make it happen," Brad assured him.

OBSERVER PARADOX

Jessica was no stranger to the haunted look in the eyes of the rescue workers gathered around the tables of the recreation center drinking coffee to replenish energy and half-heartedly eating the boxed meals that had been provided to them. There were conversations in low voices and people staring at phones waiting for updates but little else that resembled normal human behavior.

Part of what weighed everyone down was the uncertainty. People could make jokes and laugh at funerals where everyone knew the outcome. It was much harder to do that next to a car crash while they were still pulling bodies from the wreckage.

Jessica had started her career as a rookie police officer in Miami. Her first day in uniform on patrol, her supervisor had her get a statement from a crying woman sitting on a sidewalk who'd just watched her date get nearly decapitated by a broken windshield after he drove into a concrete divider.

The part of her that wanted to please people urged her to say "It's okay, let's talk when you're calm." But that's not what the police instincts that had been drilled into her dictated.

Now was always the most important time to get an accurate description—while events were still fresh. You could get statements later, but time and motives would blur those details.

Jessica found a helpful reframe that made her cop work easier: *The show must go on.* As a child performer born into a family of stage magicians, she'd learned that mantra at an early age. She'd been surrounded by stories about the heroic and ballsy efforts her family and friends had gone through to keep the show going despite adversity.

She surveyed the room for anyone wearing a police uniform belonging to the Arcadia City Police Department. The city only had eight full-time police officers, so she wasn't sure what her odds were, but this was the best place to look outside of the command center in Arcadia—which she didn't have access to.

Jessica spotted a stocky woman by a table with the coffee dispensers, fumbling for a paper cup and knocking the entire stack over and onto the ground. She was dressed in tight-fitted navy-colored slacks and a blue polo shirt that said FAIRMONT EMS on a sleeve.

"Let me help you with that," Jessica offered as she knelt down and gathered the coffee cups, pushing them back into a stack.

"Thank you," the woman replied. A brass name tag over her breast read MICHELLE CHOW.

"It would be helpful if they put these into a basket," Jessica remarked as she split the stack of cups into three smaller, sturdier towers.

"I don't think anybody's had a minute to think about that," Michelle answered, massaging her forehead. "I'm still trying to catch my breath."

"Have you had any sleep?"

"I tried to. I think I got maybe forty minutes in my car, but that was about it. I don't think anybody's getting much sleep."

"How long you been on duty?" Jessica inquired.

"I was home when the crash happened but got called in about two hours later, when the calls for help started coming in," Michelle explained.

"Anybody you know been impacted by this?"

"No, thankfully," Michelle replied, shaking her head. "But I wish I could say the same for the folks over there." She pointed to a tall, skinny man in a blue windbreaker sitting in the corner, holding a phone in his hand.

"Who's that?" Jessica asked, glancing over.

"Ian Tyler, assistant police chief at Arcadia. He was one of the first on the scene. The chief had to pull him off duty and send him over here," she explained quietly. "He refused to stay home. He's been doing what he can, but the poor guy hasn't slept in forever."

Part of Jessica just wanted to leave the man be. She could see from the look on his face and the shadows under his eyes that he hadn't slept since the event and was probably still struggling to process everything. But the show must go on.

"Poor guy," Jessica murmured. "I'll see if he needs anything." She walked away, not giving Michelle the chance to suggest maybe he'd rather be left alone.

As Jessica walked past the tables and exhausted emergency personnel, she quickly calculated her approach. She could try somber and understanding to get the man to slowly open up, but the fact that he was still on duty, refusing to quit, suggested to Jessica that he was mission-focused. Short of him being completely catatonic, the best approach, she decided, was to be direct and professional.

Assistant Chief Tyler looked up as Jessica approached. The moment their eyes met, she nodded and offered a polite smile.

"Chief, do you mind if I talk to you for a moment?" she asked.

Before he could object, Jessica took a seat in a plastic chair across from him.

"I've been asked to do some follow-up work on the crash," she began, "and wanted to ask you a few questions. Now, of course, is the worst time, but as you know, we don't have a lot of options." She expected this introduction would reduce the chance of Tyler asking her to explain who she was working for.

Tyler nodded slowly, eyes searching Jessica's face as he tried to place her in his memory. "How can I help you . . . Ms. Blackwood?"

"Just Jessica's fine. As you know, there's still some question as to what could have caused the crash—possible sabotage or tampering with the tracks. Everyone from the NTSB to the insurance companies is trying to sort it out. I'm trying to lay enough groundwork so they have what they need. Amen," she explained with a flourish.

Tyler exhaled, running his hand over his face. "I don't know how much help I'd be. I never really paid too much attention to the tracks, to be honest. They were here before me."

"I understand that," Jessica acknowledged. "I'm more interested in whether anyone had been spotted around them—doing anything suspicious near the tracks or the switch box."

"Kids play out there all the time. People go trekking. We get dirt bikers, hikers . . . just about anything you can imagine," Tyler replied, voice muted. "I can't say I've seen anybody who looked particularly suspicious. Is that what they think happened? Someone moved the tracks or messed with the switch box?"

"We're still trying to figure that out," Jessica replied neutrally.

He shook his head. "It would seem to me it'd be pretty hard for someone to move railroad tracks like that. And as far as I know, that box hasn't worked in decades."

"Yeah, that makes it all the more suspicious," Jessica noted.

"Sorry I couldn't be more help."

"Well, maybe you still can be," she countered. "There might be something else you've noticed or a detail you remember that could be useful. Have you noticed anybody suspicious around town?"

Tyler managed a weak smile. "I'd say about half the people here are pretty suspicious."

Jessica grinned, then clarified, "Yeah, but I mean more specifically. A drifter, maybe—someone spending more time in town, didn't really fit in, caught your attention?"

"Over what kind of time frame?" Tyler asked, brow furrowing.

"The last few days, weeks, or even months," Jessica prompted.

"Nothing comes to mind," he admitted. "You know, we get a few people from Fairmont in our bars who cause trouble, but all our other mayhem . . . tends to be homegrown. Do you think it could've been someone from Arcadia, if it was sabotage?"

"I don't know," Jessica replied, choosing her words carefully. "It's possible." She decided to give the most basic explanation. "This person could have done things like this before."

"This person . . ." Tyler repeated, picking up on her phrasing. "So you really think somebody caused this."

"We don't know," Jessica deflected smoothly, using "we" to establish her official role. "But it's something I've been tasked with looking into." She changed tack. "Do you know if there were any eyewitnesses to the crash?"

"Other than a few hundred people who heard the impact, I don't know yet if anybody actually saw it," he said, shifting in his seat. "I think we're still collecting reports. With the evacuation order, everybody's scattered. It might take a while." He added, "Of course, this is a roll-up-the-sidewalks-at-dusk kind of town. The only people who'd be out there at that hour are usually up to no good."

Jessica leaned forward a bit. "Are there any night owls you can think of that I might want to talk to?"

He considered. "Well, we get kids up on the bluff. We don't hassle them too much unless they're causing trouble. It's possible there might have been a couple up there watching."

"Watching the town?" Jessica asked.

"Yeah," Tyler said, rubbing his eyes. "It's a favorite pastime. Goes back to before I was here—kids go up on the bluff and stare down at Arcadia City, wishing they were somewhere else."

Jessica laughed politely at that, then took out her phone and opened a map of Arcadia. "Could you point out where the bluff is?"

"Sure," Tyler answered, leaning forward and indicating a hillside not far from where Jessica and Theo had parked the ambulance when they inspected the tracks.

"Thanks," she told him. "I think I know the spot."

❧

For the second time in less than twenty-four hours, Jessica found herself standing on the bluff overlooking Arcadia City. The sun was setting, the horizon painted with orange. Power had been restored to parts of Arcadia, and lights had begun to twinkle on the streets and around the command center. The power station to the west was a charcoal-black smudge, melted trusses and towers twisted into a Tim Burton nightmare—skeletal and deformed.

Jessica and Theo had walked through the pass to the east, only a few hundred meters away from where she was now. Later, they'd visited the overlook with Crandall for a bird's-eye view of the town.

In her experiences as both a sleight-of-hand artist and law enforcement officer, Jessica knew that certain physical locations could act like magnets: for a unique vantage, for information, or simply because of convenient proximity. Theo called places or events that collected other anomalies "strange attractors." Jessica visualized them as random bits of debris gathering at intersections—tin cans, shards of glass, things nudged and swept into corners by passing cars.

Sometimes, she thought to herself, *we're drawn toward these strange attractors; sometimes, we're pushed into them.* Standing here for the second time, Jessica felt certain that whoever was responsible for the sabotage had also stood here—before or during the collision.

She redirected her attention from the devastation to the ground at her feet.

The hill was dry earth and scraggly weeds in uneven patches. Tire tracks and ruts hinted at cars passing through, some lined up in parallel rows—a periodic gathering place. The boulders crowning the bluff were covered in graffiti and scratch marks, layers of paint and ink weathered into a near-indecipherable scrawl.

As she paced, Jessica noticed that for a teenage hangout, there was remarkably little trash. She wondered if some city employee kept it clean or if the teens made an effort so as not to invite local police attention.

She'd grown up in a rickety old mansion in Los Angeles. It was too expansive for her family, but her grandfather insisted on it out of ego. As a kid, Jessica spent hours wandering paths beside manicured lawns and towering fences, her sense of the world shaped by privilege. Only later did she realize how warped this impression was. The kids of Arcadia City, she surmised, probably got an equally distorted view of the world from this hillside—small, isolated, feeling unique in their boredom, not realizing boredom was universal for teenagers. For Jessica, raised in the whirlwind of performance and travel, a town like Arcadia would have felt stable and appealing.

She noticed something blue at the base of a graffiti-covered rock. Drawing closer, she realized it was a wallet. Jessica slipped on gloves before picking it up, peeled open the Velcro, and discovered a learner's permit and high school ID inside.

The name on both was Waller Morrison. The photo showed a teenage boy with curly hair, cropped sides, and a confident but hesitant smile.

Jessica spoke quietly to herself. "Well, well, Mr. Morrison. What would cause you to leave your wallet out here? More importantly, not come back for it?" She glanced down at the black scar across Arcadia City. She was fairly certain she already knew the answer.

X-RAY

"We're here," Brad announced as he pulled their ambulance into the empty parking lot of a remote industrial park forty minutes outside Arcadia City.

Theo glanced up from his laptop screen. "Where?"

Brad pointed toward a slate facade on the side of the building with the words Western Rock Mineralogical Laboratory. "You said you needed an X-ray, right?"

"That and a few other things. An X-ray we probably could have found at a hospital," Theo noted.

"Maybe so, but I don't know if you've been paying attention," Brad said, a note of caution in his voice. "There's a good chance there might be some humans using the hospital X-ray machine right now. I figured this place might have more equipment for you."

"Oh, sure," Theo muttered, now taking in what he was seeing. "I was thinking maybe a university."

Brad shook his head. "I know you've had your head in whatever it is you're looking at, but look around, Theo. There's not a university laboratory suitable for someone with your curiosity within a few hundred miles."

Theo closed his laptop lid and stretched, rubbing his eyes. "Yeah, of course. Sorry. I kind of get lost in the data."

Brad couldn't help himself. "You don't say."

"So did you call ahead to get us access?" Theo wondered, skeptical.

"I couldn't exactly get hold of anybody at the facility, so we'll have to improvise," Brad said as he got out of the ambulance. "I'll grab the doohickey. You get whatever you need, and maybe wear some gloves."

They walked up to the front entrance. Brad stepped over to a keypad and typed in a code. Moments later, there was an audible click and buzz from the door. Brad reached down, grabbed the handle, turned it, and pushed it open.

"How much do I want to know?" Theo asked.

Brad met his gaze. "How much are you willing to lie about on the witness stand?"

"If it goes that far, I got bigger problems."

Brad held open the door so Theo could carry his equipment boxes inside. "I tried to reach someone here—no luck. I couldn't get into their internal network, but a friend found a vulnerability in their security. Turns out they had a default password for all their buildings. Also, we have a schedule for when the security guard will stop by—shouldn't be for another three or four hours. Okay?"

"That gives us some time," Theo said. "More would be better."

"Well, the bad news is we have less time than that because the investigators are about to ship off all of the evidence, and we need to get this"—Brad gestured to the switch box under his arm—"back into their staging area if we want to avoid a bigger crisis."

"That may not be enough time," Theo said with a sigh.

"I hear you. Let me know what I can do to help, but we're going to have to call it in"—he checked his watch—"about ninety minutes."

Theo just nodded and got to work, heading over to the directory listing the facility's rooms. "Number eight," he said. "Specimens lab. They should have an X-ray machine in there."

Less than ten minutes later, Theo was sitting in a swivel chair, staring at a computer monitor connected to what Brad could only compare to a brutalist pizza oven. It bore little resemblance to the clean, ergonomic X-ray machines found in hospitals. The lead-lined vests hanging on the wall, stretching from neck to knee, were a testament to the seriousness of the device.

Theo explained, "This thing can put out a hundred to a thousand times more X-rays than a dentist's office."

"Let me know when you turn this on," Brad said, eyeing the exit. "I'll be in the next state."

"I think this is pretty well shielded," Theo replied, gesturing at the machine without looking up.

Brad raised an eyebrow. "Given the amount of time we just spent at a nuclear-containment emergency scene, 'pretty well' doesn't fill me with confidence."

Theo ignored the remark and began typing on the keyboard. Fans spun to life, and a low hum emanated from inside the cabinet. He'd already placed the circuit board into the sample chamber and closed the door.

Brad took a few casual steps to the far side of the room, leaning against a counter with his arms crossed.

As Theo entered commands, the machine made various whirring and clicking sounds. "It's mapping the surface and interior of the circuit board," he explained as tiles began to form on-screen, mirroring the circuit panel. "Check this out," he said, clicking a tile with a dirty mouse. "I can slide this selector up or down for a kind of 3D view into the board. It's not as precise as other imaging systems, really just using different wavelengths of X-ray at different energies. But it still gives us some insight."

As he worked, more tiles populated the screen, creating a mosaic.

To Brad, the image resembled an overhead view of a city: electronic components as buildings, the sharply defined circuitry as roads and highways, though the lines shifted direction in a haphazard dance, often with several lanes in parallel. The meaning of it all was lost on him, though, so he remained silent, occasionally checking his watch while Theo leaned in, scrutinizing every pixel.

After about ten minutes, Theo leaned back and stared at the ceiling.

"Find anything?" Brad finally asked.

It took a moment before he replied. "No. Nothing unusual. It looks just like an old circuit board."

"What were you expecting?" Brad wondered.

"An old circuit board," Theo admitted, "but one could hope."

Brad came over and bent down for a closer look at the X-ray. "What's this?" he asked, pointing at a long, thin line with random objects stacked atop it.

"The Z-axis," Theo said. "A sideways view," he clarified. "I was checking for a circuit board on top of a circuit board. Normally you lay everything out onto a single board, but sometimes if you have too many connections, you add another layer, like an overpass. This board is pretty old, though—they wouldn't have used that technique. Maybe some jumpers, but a second board would go undetected unless someone was looking for it."

"What would be the point of that?" Brad asked.

"Watch," Theo said, pointing to the overhead view. "You've got a transformer here, some transistors, capacitors. It all links over here, where you see several overrides to prevent an accidental signal from triggering the junction. They're intentional redundancies. If I wanted to bypass them, the direct way would be jumper cables, but that's obvious. Another approach is a secondary, hidden circuit—undetectable from the outside unless you x-ray it, or know exactly where and what to test for."

"Sounds complicated and pretty sophisticated," Brad remarked.

"Ever look inside some of the equipment coming out of China?" Theo shot back.

Brad didn't miss the implication. "Yeah, I think I get the picture."

"That's the problem. The NTSB, Federal Railroad Administration, FBI—they're going to assume accident or sabotage. If it's sabotage, they'll look for something obvious, not a saboteur with this level of sophistication."

"You think we're dealing with a state actor?" Brad asked. The thought hit him heavier than he'd like.

"I don't think so. The whole Lucas sequence pattern suggests it's one person, or maybe a small group, likely driven by the urge to create havoc—not a state-sanctioned operation. If it were, I wouldn't even know where to look." He zoomed the mouse in on a section. "See this capacitor? I pointed it out in the motel room. It looks normal, but I was checking if the composition was off."

"How so?" Brad asked.

"I could make a capacitor function normally and also be a supercapacitor. Basically, it would do its regular job, but a secondary trigger could turn it into a bomb. A visual inspection wouldn't spot this; even a multimeter check wouldn't. But above a certain threshold, it would behave very differently. Still, I don't see any evidence of that here."

"You were hoping for the bomb?" Brad asked.

Theo hesitated. "I'm not sure 'hoping' is the word, but it would have made my job easier."

Brad glanced at his watch. "Okay, we need to start narrowing this down. It's getting tight. How much longer do you need with the X-ray?"

"I could spend months looking at this board from different angles and wavelengths," Theo said. "But there's another possibility."

"And what's that?" Brad prompted.

"I never had a clear signal. I'm looking at noise. The Lucas sequence is a noisy sequence—I thought I saw a signal. The derailment fit perfectly. But it's possible this is just random."

Brad tensed. "You need to consider that if you tell me, after all this, that it was all a fluke, I might have to punch you. I've committed extortion, trespassing, felony theft of evidence, and probably a handful of other crimes, only for you to say, 'Whoops, maybe it's all a coincidence'?"

Theo shot a look at him. "Yeah. Fair point." He nodded at the X-ray. "I just don't think this tells me what I need to know. I can see the physical makeup, but not the process or subtle manipulations."

"And how would that help you?" Brad wondered.

"When I did contract work for the government, we'd get odd cases. Once, we got bomb fragments from an uptick in convoy sabotage. The CIA thought maybe the groups had a better manufacturing setup. The thing with bomb makers is, there's only so much skill they get before they blow themselves up or get blown up by someone else. But this time, the fragments stood out—they used much less solder than you'd find in a field-assembled device."

"What did that tell you?" Brad pressed.

Theo explained, "There's no reason to be stingy with solder; it's cheap compared to explosives. It's a stylistic thing, except in mass manufacturing. When terrorist cells make bombs by the hundred, a few cents' savings per board means nothing. Using less solder is a sign they're coming out of a factory."

"They were being produced wholesale," Brad concluded.

"Exactly," Theo said. "We couldn't pin it on the state, but we traced it to a city block in a Chinese manufacturing zone. Workers there didn't know—or didn't care—about where their work ended up, but the commercial-level precision was obvious. It was unnerving to see gaming console standards applied to battlefield explosives."

"Well, that shouldn't surprise anyone," Brad said. "Where there's blood money, someone always takes a bite, no matter the cost."

Theo drummed his fingers on the table. "Unfortunately, the X-ray isn't detailed enough for me."

"What about your fancy microscope?" Brad nodded at Theo's case.

"I already checked the solder under it. It looked normal, at least to my eye. But whoever did this—let's assume there's a saboteur—could have checked dozens of these boards and known exactly how they should look. That's the problem. He knows more about these than I do."

"And he's not likely to leave prints or DNA."

"No," Theo affirmed. "But no one's perfect. The most efficient goal here would be to make sure an accident investigator would never uncover the manipulation. Doesn't mean it's undetectable—but it means we should look for something unconventional. Short of cracking open the capacitor, which would mess up the evidence, I don't know what else to do. I'd really like a much, much closer look—micron-level detail." He tapped the table. "Any chance this place has an electron microscope?"

"Room 6," Brad answered, recalling from memory. "Twenty feet down the hall on the right. How much time do you need?"

"More than we have, but I'll make it work."

If the X-ray machine made the circuit board resemble a city, the electron microscope made it an alien landscape. Smooth surfaces and neat textures to Brad's untrained eye became jagged mountains and pockmarked, almost organic-looking structures in detail.

"About how much area of the circuit board are we looking at?" Brad asked, realization dawning.

"A thousandth of a centimeter," said Theo.

"And how long would it take you to inspect the entire board at this level?" Brad asked.

"Roughly the time it would take us to inspect every square foot of Yosemite National Park on foot."

"I see," Brad replied.

"Of course, we don't need to do that," Theo added. "I'm just looking at a few specific things."

Brad checked his watch again. "Fewer would be nice."

"Don't worry, I understand," Theo said. "Right now, I want to look for weathering to get an idea of ages of different parts. From X-ray or microscope, it's hard, but at this level, I'm checking for pitting, rust, or dust, signs showing if certain parts are newer. This can't give direct evidence, but it tells if this board's been recently modified."

Theo guided the probe around the circuit board to what Brad assumed were random locations, but surely they weren't. The screen zoomed across what appeared to Brad like a vast plain, with occasional indentations and periodically emerging structures.

"This is the plastic covering over the capacitor," Theo explained. "I'm looking for oil residue or complex hydrocarbons—indicators of flux or lubricants. These generally wear off from moisture, washing, but if our saboteur did this on a tabletop, they might not have access, so parts appear dirtier, collecting various residues attracting more dust."

"This sounds more like geology than electronics," Brad noted.

"At this level, it's not a bad comparison," Theo replied.

"So, wait," Brad said as something struck him. "This couldn't have been done out in the field. They'd need to take the whole board out of the switch box."

"That would be the easiest way," Theo agreed. "You want clean conditions for this, and it could take hours or days, which would draw suspicion."

"So they'd have to go out to the switch box, pull the board, bring it somewhere, do the modifications, then return it. How long could they have had the circuit board before anyone noticed?"

"I don't know," Theo admitted. "We'd have to know the maintenance schedule and whether anyone would have noticed. Probably, to be safe, they'd want to do it as quickly as possible and not leave it absent too long. Even if full checks aren't frequent, inspectors do eyeball inspections, given vandalism and theft concerns."

"I need to share this with Jessica," Brad said, pulling out his phone and dialing.

"What's up?" came Jessica's voice.

"We're trying to finish up our inspection of the device, but your partner in crime is coming around to your theory," Brad said. "Whoever did this was on-site for a significant amount of time. Maybe a long time. Have you found anyone who remembers a suspicious character hanging around Arcadia City?"

"Not yet," Jessica replied. "But I'm about to speak to a witness—one of the many teenagers who hangs out on the bluff overlooking the town. He likely witnessed the crash. Plus, the location itself . . . I think our guy was here. How are things going there?"

"Hard to tell," Brad said, glancing at the fuzzy terrain on-screen. "If we're doing a thorough job, Theo needs a hundred thousand more years in front of the electron microscope."

"Don't be afraid to use threats of physical violence for motivation," Jessica teased.

"We're well past that. How does he respond to actual violence?"

"Thankfully, I haven't had to find out yet."

"Well, hello there," Theo addressed the computer screen, sounding suddenly excited.

Brad turned. "Sounds like the mad scientist had a breakthrough."

Jessica laughed at that. "You can give me the details later. I'm about eighteen thousand 'hello theres' into our relationship."

"Understood," Brad said, hanging up. He turned back to Theo. "What do we got?"

Theo was transfixed by what looked like a vast spiderweb with crystals embedded at random intervals, angular and slick. The web looked almost oily, but it was hard to tell from the monochrome monitor, which only revealed surface textures.

Suddenly, Theo bolted from the chair, ran to the chamber, turned a few valves, and opened it as it hissed. He pulled the board out and peered at it closely. "There," he said, pointing at a small reddish rectangular device. "See that?"

"I see it. I have no idea what I'm looking at," Brad admitted.

"I can't tell if that's been tampered with, but the material I just saw on it—it's highly suspicious." Theo set the board on the counter and took a swab from his case, carefully swiping the red component.

"Do you think the investigators might notice that?" Brad asked.

"I don't care," Theo shot back. "All right, Memory Boy," he said briskly, "is there an infrared spectrometer in the building?"

"Next door," Brad confirmed.

Theo held up the swab like a trophy. "Let's take a look."

Brad held the door for him, and the two hurried into the next room.

Inside, Theo flipped switches and loaded the swab into a coffee cup–size chamber, sealing it. "This hits the sample with infrared light. Every molecule responds a bit differently—we're looking for fingerprints." He indicated the percentages. "You'll always get a ton of contamination, but I'm looking for a strong signature."

After Theo had adjusted dials and pushed a button, the device's monitor displayed a long list of chemical compounds and percentages.

"Well, do we have a strong signature?" Brad asked.

"Hell if I know," Theo said, eyeing the list. "It's a lot of chemicals. Thankfully, it's not up to me." He snapped a photo of the screen with his phone. "Give me a minute." A moment later, he brightened. "Aha!"

"Did you just run it through some special program?"

"Basically. I asked ChatGPT."

Brad raised an eyebrow. "And what did it say?"

"Ink," Theo replied.

"Ink?" Brad echoed.

"Yes, but not just any kind. Newspaper ink," Theo clarified.

"I'm not convinced newspaper ink is especially rare. I get it on my fingers every time I read the paper," Brad pointed out.

"Yes, but newspapers use a special coating, so it doesn't rub off as much. This is the raw ink, before application," Theo explained.

"Okay, but how many people come in contact with newspaper ink?" Brad asked.

"Tens of thousands," Theo replied, "but different newspapers use different inks. And we have the formula for this one. If it's not a super-common blend but something for a particular kind of printing, it gets easier to narrow down. Plus, there's something else."

"What's that?" Brad prompted.

"We now know what to look for at other sabotage incidents. Whatever this ink is, you wouldn't normally find it among the evidence from the prior attack sites. If do we find it on other circuit boards or machinery, that's our calling card. That's how we tie it together," Theo concluded.

Brad nodded. "This could be a breakthrough. What next?"

"We need to look up the formulas, narrow down the manufacturer, and check the distribution. Also, we should look at the Florida battery fire—our prior Lucas incident—to confirm if it was connected."

"By checking for the ink?" Brad asked.

"Exactly. Now that we know what to look for, I can have someone find it with a field exam."

"Florida . . ." Brad repeated.

"Yes. The last incident in the sequence was a massive battery pack fire near Orlando."

"I guess it's time we give Sloan a call," Brad replied. "It's only fair she get her hands dirty."

CHILL

Jessica followed Tasha Drummond, the head librarian at the Fairmont Library and Community Center, as she guided her through the rows of books to a section at the back.

"Unfortunately for the children whose parents work at the hospitals and other emergency services," Tasha explained, "evacuation under this situation wasn't really an option. So we've been using the community center and library to shelter them."

Jessica noticed several rolled-up sleeping bags in the corner next to some gym mats. "How have they been handling it?"

"Surprisingly well, all things considered. Once they knew their parents were okay, the kids have been pretty much hanging out and keeping to themselves. There's a lot of fun distractions here, which is one of the reasons why we chose this. Getting a bunch of kids to stay in one place in the middle of a disaster is not exactly easy, but having an entire section full of comic books is helpful." She nodded ahead of them. "I think I saw Waller back over here reading comics."

"What kind of kid is he?" Jessica inquired as they walked on.

"Real good," Tasha told her. "Both he and his sister are the children of a friend of mine, who I know from the outlet library over at the hospital. Their mom has been pretty overwhelmed. The first thing they did when the accident happened was race over to let everyone in

Fairmont know what happened and then check on their parents. Not above mischief, of course, but he's a good kid."

"Where's his sister?"

"Across the street at the elementary school. We've got about eight kids there, and she's been helping look after them," Tasha replied as they rounded a shelf full of weathered copies of *Goosebumps* and came to a colorful corner adorned with posters of comic book characters.

Sitting on a beanbag was Waller, his nose in the middle of a hardbound copy of *Watchmen*.

"Hey, Waller, we've got somebody who wants to talk to you. This is Jessica Blackwood—maybe you've heard of her," Tasha said, announcing Jessica's presence.

Waller looked up from his comic book. "Hey," he muttered, clearly not placing her.

Jessica settled onto the floor across from him and crossed her legs. "I'm helping out with the investigation into the accident, and I wanted to talk to you."

Waller flicked his gaze to Tasha, then back to Jessica.

"It's okay," Tasha reassured him, her tone gentle. "I'll be right nearby," she added, then stepped away.

"Thank you," Jessica said quietly before returning her attention to Waller.

"I guess you heard I was there," Waller began.

"Well, indirectly at least," she answered, reaching into her pocket and pulling out his wallet, which she handed over. "I found this on the bluff."

"Oh my God, I thought I lost this thing forever. Thank you, thank you," Waller said, relief plain in his voice as he clutched the wallet. Jessica realized that, for her, it was just an easily replaceable learner's permit, school ID, and twelve bucks. For a teenager like Waller, it was the sum total of his identity—the cornerstone of becoming a functioning adult.

"So you were up there when it happened?" she pressed gently.

"Yeah," Waller confirmed. "I was with my sister and my friend. To be honest, I don't remember a whole lot. I mean, not like I was knocked unconscious," he went on. "It was just—I saw the train going down the wrong track and told Moira and Skyler to take a look. And it just felt like a moment later, it hit the power station. There were sparks and fireballs. And we could even feel the blast. It was intense. Moira pulled us into the car, and we headed over to Fairmont as soon as that happened. Because our cell phones didn't work."

"That had to be pretty insane. So you were up there with, you said, your sister and Skyler? Who's that?"

"A friend of mine from high school. His aunt came and picked him up," Waller replied, pointing to a rolled-up sleeping bag.

"Was there anybody else up there on . . . what do you call it, the bluff?" Jessica wondered.

"The Cow Bluff, the Overlook, the Hillside. I don't know. I mean, everybody's got a different name for it. But no, it was just us. It was pretty late. Our parents were working late shifts, and we got kind of bored and decided to go up there and just sit and chill," Waller told her.

"Do you do that often?" Jessica asked.

"I don't know—maybe once or twice a week, depends. Summer, a lot more—obviously not on school nights; Mom's not too thrilled if we leave the house. Although you can literally see us up there from our place with a pair of binoculars," Waller explained.

"Have you ever seen anybody else up there? Like anybody you didn't know?" Jessica prompted.

"You mean like somebody who doesn't go to our school?" Waller clarified.

"Yeah, or maybe any adults, somebody you might have seen up there or down by the tracks. Folks who seemed out of place."

"I mean, you see lots of people around. But up on the hill, probably not, because you just go there to hang out. And I think we would remember somebody, particularly an adult, if we didn't know them. But you can see a big part of the valley. And sometimes you see people out riding mountain bikes and trucks driving on some of the old trails out there. But I kind of just go there to look at trains and stare at Arcadia City—not that there's much to stare at. Well, there wasn't. Now there's that big scar," he said.

"So you never saw anybody maybe inspecting the tracks or the junction box? That's the metal post that's close to the intersection there," Jessica clarified.

"No, not that I can think of. Are they looking into the idea that somebody may have done this intentionally? I mean, I've been sitting here trying to think about how the train could have jumped a track like that. I guess it just got old, but I hadn't really thought about somebody making it happen. Would they have to have been standing there at the time?" Waller asked.

"No," Jessica replied. "There are a lot of different ways it could have happened, and who knows if it was even intentional or not. But it is just something we're trying to consider. Maybe you saw somebody who looked like they belonged, like a railroad worker in a truck wearing an orange vest, somebody who just fit in and you didn't think about."

"Possibly. My sister Moira's got a much better memory than me. You could talk to her, but I don't remember anything like that. But like I said, I might just not remember it because it didn't stand out to me," he admitted.

Jessica could see he was thinking hard, almost frowning. She decided to offer a reprieve. "Have you read this before?" she asked, nodding toward the comic in his hands.

"I watched the movie and thought it was pretty cool. I thought I might try to read it since it's the one comic book my English teacher lets us write reports on," Waller replied, interest returning to his face.

Jessica's thoughts moved back to the bluff, that strange attractor, and she speculated that the saboteur had, at least at some point, stood where she had and looked down at the town and the junction. Could he have resisted? Clearly, he was no dummy, and being spotted by locals would be something he would try to avoid. Staking out the site of a future disaster from the bluff would probably be a bad idea. It would also not be a close vantage point if he wanted to witness the accident in detail.

She thought of the side road they'd used to get into the perimeter and the other paths out on the plain where people rode dirt bikes and off-road 4x4s.

"This is gonna sound odd, but when you were out there at night, either the night before when this happened or other times, did you ever get an odd feeling?" Jessica asked.

Waller cocked his head. "A weird feeling? Like what?"

"You know, the feeling when you . . . get the sense you're being watched? Or there's somebody else in the room you can't see?" she clarified.

Waller thought it over. "You get animals out there at night. You know, we're not that far away from the national forest. And Skyler swears he saw a wolf. But nobody believes him—it was probably a mangy dog. There've always been ghost stories. People talk about the bluff, somebody who killed himself there and that kind of thing. Although if you've seen it, if you tried to jump off it, all you'd do is just roll all the way down to the bottom and maybe get a few scratches. But yeah, sometimes . . . you know there are other people there, because you might hear voices, somebody talking. Or you might see the glow of a cell phone. I know couples might go up there to go make out and stuff, and when they see that the cars are parked up there, they just go somewhere else. The tracks run through a ravine next to the bluff. Sometimes people park down there because you can't see it from the town."

"What about that night?" Jessica asked.

"I don't know. I do remember feeling a little bit weird," Waller recalled. "Like, I don't know. I just wanted to be by myself, but I didn't want to go too far away. I love Skyler, but that kid can ask, like, a million questions in a row. And my sister is a saint, so she can handle it, but he kind of gets on my nerves. I remember walking away to just sit down by myself, but then, I don't know—I think maybe I heard a rock or something or whatever from towards the canyon and just decided not to go very far. So I just sat down close to them and stared at the grass."

"Were you guys on anything at the time?" Jessica asked, keeping her tone casual.

Waller's face went pale. "Like edibles?"

"I'm not a cop. I'm not going to tell anybody. I just want to get an understanding," Jessica assured him.

"No. I'm not into that. Moira's not either. Skyler swears that he ate some at some Christian summer camp he went to, but that kid is so impressionable it could have been a marshmallow and he'd think he was tripping out." Waller lowered his voice. "Although I know for a fact some other kids like to go up there and do that and just lay on the ground staring up at the stars. Of course, when they do that, they don't park there because the cops will show up. And the last thing they want to do is be all glazed and get caught. But no, I wasn't on anything. I would tell you," he insisted.

"But you think there could have been somebody there that night because you heard something?" Jessica probed.

"Maybe. Like I said, I usually wander. If I don't wander, it's because I want to stay out of somebody else's business. Not just because I'd be scared, but just because, I don't know—you get that sense there's somebody nearby. It's like when you're camping and somebody camps near you. You kind of want to stay away," he explained.

"Did you say anything to Moira or Skyler?" Jessica asked.

Waller shook his head. "No. The last thing I want to do is get Skyler talking about the Owlman."

"The Owlman?" Jessica echoed, interested. "What's that?"

"Yeah, I told you about the wolf because, well, that's kind of typical Skyler. But also, a couple of times he insisted he could see some figure out on the flats or down by the ravine, just standing there. Skyler called him the Owlman because he just seemed—I don't know—to Skyler he looked like a tall owl that wasn't moving."

"Literally like an owl?" Jessica pressed.

"No, just Skyler's imagination when he's trying to make sense of something really far away. When we asked him for details, it just turned out that he was probably describing some very tall dude standing there. Which you do get . . . people who follow the tracks. We call them hoboes and stuff. But anyhow, that's just Skyler. It could have been a piece of trash or tumbleweed. I didn't see anything when he said he saw it."

"Do you remember the last time he saw the Owlman?" Jessica asked.

"It would have been two weeks ago. Mom had to work the late shift and Dad was out of town, which would have been a Saturday night, which meant we went out there later. And that's when Skyler brought him up," Waller answered.

"Any time since then?"

"No, maybe a couple months before, but it was only, I think, maybe twice," Waller recalled. "I wouldn't read too much into it. Although, I mean, could be a person there, but I don't think there's an *owl* man."

Jessica considered this. In her experience, people who commit crimes based upon specific locations, particularly sophisticated ones, often visit them multiple times. If they're careful, they try to avoid being seen. One way is to blend in, a specialty of Brad Trasker's. Here, you could dress as a railroad inspector in an orange vest. Camouflage in plain sight. Another method is to avoid people entirely by going to locations when nobody else is there, like the dead of night. It would seem more than likely that the saboteur had been to Arcadia City multiple times, and it would also stand to reason he would have spent some of that time inspecting the tracks and the site of his planned disaster.

It would be really weird if nobody ever saw him, but since neither Waller nor the assistant police chief had any specific recollections of somebody, this would imply that this person was either extremely unremarkable or else took care to avoid being spotted.

The flats between Cow Bluff and Arcadia City were wide and open, but also contained many smaller crevices and indentations. Gullies, washes, riverbeds. Ravines. Plenty of options for camouflaged concealment. Jessica also considered that Arcadia City wasn't the exclusive target. It was the train. It stood to reason that the saboteur would have logged the train's comings and goings, its timetable, the workings of its tracks.

All this led to several assumptions that she felt strongly about: The saboteur had been there multiple times; he had been on the plains not far from the tracks and/or on and around Cow Bluff; and, in addition to his prior visits to Arcadia, he likely was on-site the night of the accident.

The remaining question, besides the saboteur's ID, was where exactly he'd been and whether anyone had noted his presence.

Jessica believed Waller's and Skyler's claims—they'd glimpsed the suspect long before the crime and heard him on the night of the derailment.

If this were a normal situation and the inhabitants of the town hadn't been scattered across several states because of the radiation threat, they could have canvassed all the residents in short order.

A thought occurred to Jessica. "Did you ever see an RV or a camper parked in town?" she asked Waller, realizing she should have asked the assistant police chief this too.

"No," Waller replied. "I don't think the police would stand for that. You get some people out sightseeing who want to overnight here, but there's a couple campgrounds further out where tourists stay. They would probably find themselves directed that way. This isn't exactly a tourist hotspot, if you hadn't noticed."

Jessica understood what he was saying. Arcadia City was a working-class town. Not close enough to a national park to draw regular crowds.

If the suspect had spent as much time in and around Arcadia City as Jessica believed, he had become known to the town's residents in *some* capacity. He must have had a purpose or role that simply didn't attract suspicion—which implied some form of contract labor, which could range from being a substitute teacher to a cable installer. It didn't make things significantly easier, but it did give Jessica a new area of focus.

Oh . . . and this also meant their suspect had been sleeping somewhere around Arcadia City or Fairmont, which might help narrow the scope slightly.

While Waller was skeptical of his friend's account of the Owlman, it provided Jessica a more specific date on which the suspect might have been in the area.

"Thanks, Waller. Try not to lose that again," she said as she tapped the wallet next to him.

As he returned to his graphic novel, she lingered for a moment, envious of the boy's ability to shift from harsh reality to a fantasy world where supervillains could be quickly dispatched by turning the page.

ULTRAPACK

Tendrils of black smoke were still visible for miles away from the StarPower Ultra Battery Facility south of Orlando, Florida.

The fire had started four weeks ago and took nearly a week to put out. But long after that, the insulation and battery materials continued smoldering.

Up until three hours ago, when Sloan McPherson got the call from Brad and Theo, all she knew was what she'd heard on the news: The battery pack facility, which stretched several acres, had had a catastrophic and unforeseen critical event leading to each isolated cell bursting into flames and raising the collective temperature so high that the other ones caught fire too, resulting in a massive conflagration that put even sugarcane field fires to shame.

The aerial footage Sloan had seen on the news showed a massive black scorch mark that resembled what she thought a meteor impact would look like, down to a large indentation at the center of the facility where the battery packs had managed to burn through the asphalt and boil off the groundwater, causing an unforeseen sinkhole. *Unforeseen,* thought Sloan. That was a word she'd heard a lot in the news lately about the event. From the questions about the manufacture of the batteries to the entire layout of the system, there were many people scratching their heads and asking *why*. Although more than a couple of experts Sloan had seen on the news explained that this conflagration had been inevitable because the design of the facility was poor and it had been built in a hurry.

The builders of other battery pack facilities were quick to point out the failings in the StarPower installation and explain why it could never happen at theirs.

Sloan didn't consider herself an expert on a lot, and much less what constituted safe battery-farm design. She was a little bit nervous about talking to the Florida Department of Law Enforcement investigator about the fire. Not because she didn't know Cal Healy but because she knew she was completely out of her league and had no idea what technical questions she should be asking.

She pulled over to the side of the road and dialed Theo's number.

"What's up, McPherson?" Theo said from the speakerphone.

"I'm about to meet with the lead investigator, and I'm still not quite sure what I'm supposed to be asking. If this was a shipwreck or a body in the canal, I'd know the routine. But this high-tech stuff . . . that's not quite my lane," she admitted.

"Don't worry," Theo assured her. "Who you really want to speak to is the supervisor of the facility. The person the blame is going to fall to. Because I'm sure they're going to have a lot of theories, and one of them might be correct."

"Do I even need to talk to the investigator?"

"Yes. We need to get a list of whatever evidence they have, which I assume is going to be considerable, ranging from software to circuit boards."

"There's a Florida Department of Law Enforcement depot outside of Orlando, maybe an hour away from here. I could just go there," Sloan suggested.

"Yeah, but I'd still get the manifest first and then talk to the site supervisor, because we're looking for something even smaller than a needle in a haystack."

"How's it going on your end?" she asked.

"We're still trying to narrow down next potential targets. We're less than six days away, which has me anxious—not to mention whatever else comes after that," Theo said.

Even though Sloan was alone, she lowered her voice. "So, Theo, how extraordinary of measures should I resort to to get what we need as quickly as possible?"

Although they didn't know each other well, they had been through a lot together already, including nearly getting killed by cultists in Washington state. Despite being an actively employed state law officer, Sloan had lived through situations in which extraordinary measures truly became necessary. When lives were on the line, she knew that Theo too had—and would—break rules, and even violate laws.

Theo replied, "Well, given the fact that had the suspect's worst-case scenario played out, millions of people would be worried about radioactive rain, extraordinary measures are justified. Not to mention," he continued, "that, had this accident happened earlier in the evening, we could have lost a hundred or more people in downtown Arcadia City. All of which is to say, I'm terrified about what could happen next."

Sloan knew Theo to be the most rational and logical person on earth. He would never use a word like "terrified" unless he meant it.

"Got it," she said. "I'll do whatever I can as quickly as I can."

"Well, if you get into trouble, let us know," Theo added. "We've got Brad here. He already got Jessica and me out of jail."

"You're going to have to tell me about that later. Or maybe not. You decide."

She clicked off, exited the vehicle, and looked around. Yellow inflatable booms ran to the left and right of the highway across the marsh, encircling the entire site in order to prevent any more environmental damage than had happened already.

Sloan wasn't sure what the effect would be of all the chemicals and fire-retardant materials being spilled out into the ecosystem. As someone who spent a considerable amount of her time in Florida's waterways, she expected the ripple effects would be significant.

A few meters ahead of her, she recognized the Florida Department of Law Enforcement command post trailer parked on the side of the road. It was much like the ones she'd occupied during weather emergencies. She stepped up onto the aluminum stairs and knocked on the door.

"Come in!" shouted a woman's voice from inside.

Sloan entered and found three people sitting around a table with charts and maps laid out before them. Behind them was a window overlooking the charred battery facility. She noticed two air purifiers whirring away near the door, working hard to clean the air.

"McPherson." Cal Healy looked up over his reading glasses. "I'm sure everybody here knows you." He motioned to the woman on his right, who Sloan assumed was the one who told her to enter. "This is Detective Rhonda Glassman." Then he pointed to the younger dark-haired man sitting to his left. "And Detective Palmer Lake."

"Hello, Sloan," Rhonda greeted her.

"So, what interest does the Underwater Investigation Unit have in this disaster?" Cal asked.

"More of a professional favor for some colleagues investigating the Arcadia City situation," Sloan told him.

This caught everyone's attention. All heads turned to her.

"Could you elaborate?" Cal prompted.

"Well, I can elaborate only as much as I know, and that's that there's a suspicion that the derailment could have been sabotage."

Cal glanced at his colleagues, then back at Sloan. "I haven't heard anything about this from the feds, including the NTSB. Is this something new?"

"Kind of," Sloan improvised. "It's more of a potentiality. There's a possibility this fire and the Arcadia City incident could be connected to a larger sequence of sabotage attacks."

Theo had made it clear she could share as much as she wanted about what they thought was happening but should do her best to keep his and Jessica's involvement to a minimum in any conversation.

"What makes them think Arcadia City could be sabotage?" asked Palmer.

"Like I said, I don't have a lot of details, but there might have been some tampering with equipment, although very subtle. So subtle that it could pass even a forensic examination."

"What do you mean?" Rhonda asked.

"Well, I'm still trying to figure that out myself, but from what I understand, there could be—and again, not my theory—a potential saboteur camouflaging his work in such a way it looks like accidents. System failures would be his specialty."

"How do you create a system failure to trigger 128 battery packs spread apart with proper insulation and fire-retardant systems?" Palmer questioned.

Sloan was about to laugh off the idea that she would have any idea how something so technical could happen, but the charred remains of the facility were directly in front of her and the burnt copper scent still lingered in her nostrils.

"I don't know," she said. "I just got sent here to ask some questions."

"Ask away," Cal said as he leaned back and folded his arms.

What Sloan really wanted was the manifest for Theo and not to be put on the spot to ask overly technical questions. So she decided to take a more direct approach.

"What caused this?" she asked.

"Terrible safeguards," Palmer replied. He added, "We've already gone over every square inch of this looking for any kind of residue for explosives and checked the cabling for tampering."

"I'm sure," Sloan said. "From what I'm told, this guy, if there *is* one," she quickly added, "wouldn't leave anything as obvious as that."

"As obvious as that," Palmer echoed.

Sloan realized he was the Florida Department of Law Enforcement's resident technical expert on this case and wasn't happy to have anyone second-guessing his opinions.

"I'll have to defer to you on that," Sloan said to placate him. "But hypothetically, if you," she emphasized, "wanted to cause something like this to happen, how would you do it?"

"You'd have to know everything about this system—the schematics, the layout—and I don't mean the official blueprints but the actual way that it was laid out. Because that was the problem. This thing wasn't built the way they said it was going to be built. They didn't use the materials they said they were going to use. Things weren't configured right. But you wouldn't know that from looking at the architectural plans and the data sheets."

"Hmm. Could that have been knowable?" Sloan asked.

Cal pushed a clipboard toward her. "Maybe. This is what we've been looking at. This is a list of the actual materials they used that we got from Customs. And there's some discrepancies between what they told inspectors they were using and what was actually put into place here. Lower-grade copper, insulation that wasn't suitable for this, and a few other things that stand out."

Sloan nodded. "Well, that would explain why the Florida Department of Law Enforcement is here. You're pursuing a criminal investigation."

"Potentially," Cal said. "Heads have to roll for this. The site supervisor insists that he had no knowledge of the severity of the discrepancies, which might be true, might not be. But the people that built the facility appear to be culpable." He paused. "We'd appreciate your discretion on this, Sloan. We don't want them to destroy any evidence—well, any more evidence—before we have a chance to look into this deeper. But I think we're going to be able to put together a pretty good case against them."

"So you're not inclined to think this was sabotage?"

"If by 'sabotage' you mean when this facility was planned and built twenty months ago, sure. But we have enough cause to think that this was an accident waiting to happen."

"Interesting." She could understand their point of view. If you ran into a burning house and found out the occupant had been storing newspapers and had a habit of falling asleep with a cigarette in their hand, arson wouldn't be your first suspicion. But if an arsonist knew that there was a house filled with newspapers and somebody who liked to fall asleep at night with a cigarette in their hand, that would prove a tempting target if their goal was to go undetected.

"Could you email me a list of any items you have in evidence?" Sloan asked as casually as she could for the manifest.

"Yes, just as long as you keep the criminal investigation under your hat," Cal said.

"Could we maybe put a pin in that for a little while?" Palmer suggested.

It was not hard to tell how put-upon Palmer felt at the thought of Sloan sticking her nose into the case. She didn't bother looking at him and responded to Cal.

"That would be great. Thank you very much." Then she turned to Palmer. "I'll let you know if I find anything interesting."

Sloan caught a slight smirk from Rhonda Glassman and could only guess at the dynamics in the room.

"What about the site supervisor?" Sloan plowed ahead. "Is he available?"

"His name's Oliver Trent," Cal said, "and he's here, although we're keeping an eye on him. It's not an ideal situation, but nobody knows more about this facility than he does."

"As far as we know," Palmer added.

"Thank you," Sloan said. "I'll be in touch." She exited the trailer before anybody could tell her not to talk to Trent.

Cal knew she was professional and wouldn't mention the investigation to Trent, although Sloan was certain the supervisor knew it would be coming. You don't have a disaster like this without a list of people to be held accountable, even if they're not the most responsible.

She found Trent walking around a charred pit at the north end of the facility with two other people in tow. He was pointing out conduits and twisted pieces of wiring as forensic technicians photographed and made notations on tablets. True to Cal's word about them keeping an eye on him, Sloan spotted an FDLE detective she knew keeping a careful distance and sipping his coffee, watching Trent.

Sloan gave the detective, Bryce, a nod and he returned the gesture.

She stepped to the supervisor's side. "Mr. Trent, could I speak to you for a moment? I know you're pretty busy, but it's pretty time-sensitive."

"Sure, sure," he said. "Could you guys excuse me?" he told the technicians, then followed Sloan a short distance away.

Even though she was wearing a breathing mask out here, the residual smoke made her eyes water and her nostrils ache. She had no idea how Trent and the others were able to take this for so long.

"I need to be real with you right now," she began.

"I've been nothing but real since this happened," Trent told her.

"So I don't need to tell you how dire of a situation this is for everyone."

Trent nodded at his detective overseer. "I'm not stupid. But I'm also not the one that built this. So I've got nothing to hide."

"That's good. I hope your lawyer feels the same way," said Sloan.

"Yeah, yeah. We've talked. There's nothing for me to do but do what I can to help," Trent explained.

The man seemed earnest, but Sloan wasn't sure if this grew out of a sense of responsibility or the need to cover his ass as best he could. Probably both. But that wasn't her immediate focus.

"From what I understand, there were a lot of mistakes made in the construction of this facility, and I've heard the phrase 'an accident waiting to happen.' Would you agree with that?"

Trent laughed under his breathing mask and then waved an arm toward the devastation. "I would say this certainly qualifies as that, wouldn't you?"

"Okay, I'm going to level with you. I think this was sabotage—or rather, I have a strong suspicion this is sabotage. There may have been a series of fuckups that led to this accident being *possible*, but it's also conceivable that somebody knew about the flaws and engineered this to happen on a certain date. If you had known about the substandard copper and other materials, the bad insulation, how would *you* have caused this to happen?"

Trent raised an eyebrow. "I'm not a legal expert, but that sounds like an indirect way to get me to confess to something. I may not be the most sophisticated man, but I'm not stupid."

Sloan pulled her mask down to show him her face. "I swear on my life, I'm not trying to bullshit you right now, okay? You know me, probably, you know my reputation. You know I don't play, right? Did you hear about the train derailment in Arcadia City? There's a chance that's connected to this. And there could be another large-scale 'accident' coming in days. A more devastating one. And the sooner I figure out what the hell happened here, the sooner we can stop that from happening."

Trent studied her for a moment, then replied, "Sure, why the hell not? I'll tell you how I'd do this."

Sloan took out her phone. "I'm not going to understand the technical details, and I realize asking you if I can record this is probably making you even more suspicious, but I just want to make sure that my science-y friends hear what you're telling me."

Trent sighed. "This could be the most clever form of entrapment I've ever heard of—or I'm the stupidest man on the planet. But whatever, fine. Video it for all I care.

"And let the record show, you're going to find out that I wrote a number of reports to the owners of the facility about my issues. And when it comes to the list of people who said 'I told you so,' my name should be at the top."

"But you didn't go to the authorities and tell them to shut down the facility?" Sloan asked.

"No, I did not. And that is going to be my dying regret. Now, do you want me to tell you how a sabotage scenario could play out or not?"

"Please," said Sloan.

"This facility had 128 separate battery packs, all hooked up into a grid. Each one of them was spaced the appropriate distance away from the others in case of a fire. In theory, this meant that one unit would burn itself out and not affect the others. But there's two problems with this. One is you could have a critical software problem that could affect all the units and they could all be triggered at once, which would make isolation irrelevant. They would all suffer the same failure," he explained.

"Did they all go off at once?" Sloan asked.

"No, they didn't. We know that the fire started pretty close to where we are now because this was the hottest point and it burned the longest. All it took was for one battery pack to go off. We didn't need a software failure; all we needed was a very simple defect in the temperature regulator. Basically, there's a sensor that keeps track of the heat of the battery and the external environment. If it gets too hot, it cools itself down, and there are a few fail-safes there. But if you're able to interfere with the sensor, override its purpose, you could get the battery to overheat and catch on fire," Trent explained.

"Okay. But you told me all the others are spaced apart. How did they catch on fire?"

"The problem was the design, and I didn't know about this until several months into me working here. It was a conduit underground. The fire didn't spread aboveground, it spread belowground. Connecting each one of the battery packs was a twelve-inch piece of plastic pipe, which had plenty of room for a fire to move through and plenty of air. After one unit caught on fire and the fire-suppression system started, the flames were already moving through the underground pipes and setting everything else ablaze. The fire-suppression systems are up top. The fire grew below and burned its way up."

"If it was sabotage, are there any parts or things that are still around we could look at?" Sloan asked.

"Everything was fairly well carbonized," Trent said, "except the first unit, because the fire-suppression unit kicked on pretty early."

"And that would be the point of sabotage?" Sloan asked.

"Yes, and your friends in law enforcement are going to be going over that with a fine-tooth comb. I hope."

"Hold on a second," Sloan said. She walked over to one of the technicians, who was kneeling down near a pit, wiping a cotton swab on a piece of copper tubing. "Excuse me, sorry to bother you. Can I ask you a question?"

The forensic technician stood up. He was wearing a full face mask, with only his eyes visible through the glass. "What do you need?" he asked through his mask.

Sloan remembered something Theo had asked for. "Did you get swabs of the original power pack? The first one to go?"

"We swab anything and everything," he replied.

"Have you done chemical analysis of those yet?"

"It's ongoing, but we've got a mobile spectrometer over there," he said, pointing toward an RV unit two vehicles down from the FDLE trailer.

"Do you already have a list of whatever chemical compounds you found?" asked Sloan.

"It's all in the database."

"Do you by chance remember seeing anything unusual?" she asked.

"We haven't had a chance to even really process that, other than looking for things like chemical explosives. But you can talk to Amy," he offered.

"Who's that?"

"She's our on-site chemist. She'd be the one running the samples right now."

"Including an infrared spectrometer?" Sloan asked. It was the one piece of equipment she was familiar with from her archaeology doctorate—and the key tool Theo had mentioned.

"Of course," said the technician.

Twenty minutes later, in a hotel room outside of Fairmont, Idaho, Theo hung up the call.

"What is it?" Jessica asked. She was sitting on the floor typing on her keyboard.

"That was the chemist at the battery pack facility. Do you know when Brad gets back?"

"Any minute now. He had to sneak your switch box back into evidence. Why?"

"They found ink. The same ink we found."

Jessica's eyes went wide. "Are you sure?"

"Very. They didn't know what to make of it."

"Well, I gained access to an FBI database that tracks materials," she told him.

"Great. What did you find?"

Jessica spun her laptop around so Theo could see the screen. "I found seventeen locations where that formula is sent."

"Is one of them near Orlando?" Theo asked.

Jessica nodded.

"And is another one in Idaho?"

Jessica nodded again. "It's in Rexburg. Just thirty minutes from here," she said.

"And did all of those events match up with the Lucas sequence?" Theo asked.

"Yes, Theo. They did. We have your pattern. We have a fingerprint. And I think we have a list of potential targets for the final two attacks."

"But what we don't have," said Theo, "is time."

CLOCKWORK

Ben Ableman was clearly not happy when he walked into the Arcadia City Police Department conference room and saw Jessica and Theo sitting on the other side of the table next to Brad Trasker.

"Aren't you two supposed to be in jail?"

"Sorry about that," said Jessica. "We had other plans."

Ableman glanced over at Trasker as he took a seat. "You move fast."

"We have to, given the situation," said Brad.

"I got your email," Ableman responded. "But I haven't had a chance to look at it. As you know, my hands are already full here. And yes," he interjected before Theo or anyone else could speak up, "I know, ticking clock. There's another disaster about to happen. We already had that conversation. I need to focus on cleaning up this one. Whatever you know, tell it to your friends at the FBI. I'm sure you know more of them than I do."

"We have," said Jessica, "but even they're having trouble understanding the urgency of the situation. We thought if we could at least explain things to you, given the amount of resources and attention currently at your disposal, you might be able to move things more quickly."

"I want to just walk out this door right now," an exasperated Ableman admitted. "I'm exhausted. I haven't seen my family in days. I don't know the last time I took a shower that wasn't from a power washer. And between the four of us, I'm not exactly feeling compassionate right now."

"I've been there," Jessica said softly.

"Have you?" Ableman asked.

"Do you want me to tell you about the time I was too late to stop a mass suicide and stepped into a vault with a hundred dangling bodies over my head? And the sound of a child's footsteps running around in the dark?"

"I get it, Blackwood. I get it. It still doesn't change the fact that there's not much I can do right now."

"Just hear them out," Brad urged.

"Fine." Ableman sighed and waited.

"We found ink with a particular signature on the circuit board for the railroad junction that matches identical ink found on a thermostat in the battery fire in Florida," Theo stated bluntly.

"How do you know it's on the circuit board?" Ableman questioned.

"The chemical traces are in a database," Jessica explained. Not exactly the answer he was looking for, but not an out-and-out lie.

"Wait, and forensics missed that?" Ableman asked incredulously.

"They swabbed it, but it's just noise, a random material that nobody's screening for. But it's also something that doesn't belong in either location," Theo explained.

Ableman shook his head. "Okay, go on."

"It's a residue, not something left intentionally, but ink—in this case, newspaper ink. Before it's applied to paper and goes through a thermal process as it's pushed into the pulp, it is extremely oily. It gets everywhere. And somebody who's worked around it or handled it, even if they go to extraordinary lengths, would have difficulty making sure that there was nothing on their body to leave trace amounts."

Jessica interrupted, "Like fish oil pills left in your pocket that go through the laundry."

"That sounds disgusting," Ableman replied.

"It is," Jessica assured him.

Theo cut in. "It would be unlikely to find this in two completely random locations. Now, when those locations are the scenes of sabotage, it suggests something common between them. And we think that our saboteur is somebody who works around or with newspaper equipment. Although, because this has happened in multiple locations, they're not necessarily an employee of a specific news-printing facility."

"But somebody who is in a position to get close enough to the machinery," Ableman concluded.

"This particular ink is manufactured in Canada," Theo informed him. "There are seventeen locations in the United States that use it and eight there. It's a particular formula designed for a specific press, which is older. That's why they still need this ink and it's produced in limited runs for them."

"And you'll find an older printing press using that ink within thirty to forty-five minutes of each attack site," Jessica added.

Theo nodded. "We could be dealing with somebody who works for the manufacturer, Haber Printing," he explained. "Or somebody who's connected to these different printing facilities and—"

"Wouldn't they have to work for the ink manufacturer, then?" Ableman interrupted.

"Well," Jessica said, "as Theo pointed out, the ink is connected to the presses. The presses are the same type in all the locations. This person doesn't have to be connected to the ink maker. He could be connected to the presses. Also, nine out of seventeen of the old presses are owned by the same company."

"What about the other eight?" Ableman inquired.

"Three different owners, but two of them have a service contract with the same provider. There could be other connections we're not aware of."

"So what are you telling me?" Ableman asked.

Brad spoke up. "We need to get a list of every employee that would come near that ink—staff from both the ink company and all the newspapers."

Ableman turned to Jessica. "Why not just ask your friends in the FBI?"

"There's only so much I can do, and right now you're the one with the agency and authority to get things done. If you ask, people aren't going to be pestering you with questions. You can just get it done."

"We get a list of people, then what?" Ableman asked.

"You find out if anybody on that list has been in Arcadia City within the last week," she said flatly.

Ableman thought it over and muttered, "You guys are a pain in the ass."

"It's a small ask," Brad replied. "Getting those names and doing checks to see if anybody on that list has been here would be pretty useful information, don't you think?"

They knew Ableman was stubborn but not stupid.

"And if I don't do this and it turns out there is something there, I become the fall guy. I get it," he admitted. "Fine, whatever. What else?"

"We've got a list of potential next targets," Theo told him.

"Locations near plants that use this ink?" Ableman asked.

"Yes," Theo replied. "All of these are locations that have complex infrastructure that is theoretically vulnerable to similar forms of sabotage."

"And you believe another attack's imminent?"

"We think one of these is going to have a critical failure in the next five days," Jessica said.

"And how many targets are on that list?" Ableman asked skeptically.

"Forty-three," said Theo.

"Forty-three?" Ableman exclaimed. "Did you just pick a random spot in each state?"

"That would be fifty," Theo replied flatly. "No. We have six potential locations based upon the printing facilities remaining and, near each of those, between three and ten potential targets."

"And how did you determine the targets?" Ableman asked.

"That one was a bit more fuzzy," Theo admitted. "We're fairly certain these are the general locations. Local authorities will probably have a better idea of what would be potential points of vulnerability. We just need to alert them."

"*You* have phones. I've had it," said Ableman.

"We need you to do this," Brad said.

"Me?" Ableman replied incredulously. "Are you fucking kidding me? You want me to call up forty-three different whatevers on your list and basically prank call them about a bomb threat? You're crazier than I thought."

"We just need to notify the authorities in six locations," Theo clarified. "We can give each one of them the list of our suspected sites and leave it up to them to determine what precautions to take."

"I need more than this, guys. I've already dealt with one massive panic situation. Which, by the way, I don't know if you know this, but the whole shelter-in-place wasn't my suggestion. Because, yeah, I could do the math. I understand the outcome of the situation. Even the worst-case scenario wouldn't have caused so much as a sunburn in somebody in the next county. But that's not the way people react when they hear 'radiation.' But that doesn't matter. Nobody remembers the name of the boy who cried wolf. They just remember there was a boy."

"People are going to die," Jessica said bluntly.

"I said I would get you the list of employees. You already know the names of all the people you need to contact, I'm sure. You looked it up, given the thoroughness with which you approach everything else. I'm not going to be the one on the other end of the call. There's just not enough to go by, and I have zero idea what to tell them either." He addressed the trio. "What would you have done if you knew Arcadia City was a target? Four days before it happened?"

"I would look for the most likely point of vulnerability. You have a large electrical substation passing through this region next to a rail line with an old junction. It seems obvious from aerial footage that this could have happened," said Theo.

"Obvious in hindsight," said Ableman. "You have the benefit of knowing what the broken pieces are. Are you certain you would have spotted the point of failure before it happened?"

"Theo was listening to the radio, waiting for this to occur," said Jessica. "I don't know if you realized it, but we got here before the out-of-state news crews. Theo knows the timing; what we need now is a line on our suspect."

"Yet you have a list of forty-three targets. It's not exactly narrowing things down," Ableman pointed out.

"Give 'em time," said Brad.

"I don't think realistically there's much I can do that you can't."

"Bullshit," Brad growled. "If you make a call to the authorities, I guarantee you they're going to pay attention."

"Like I said, you can call them too."

"And you expect them to listen to us? You had us thrown in jail," Jessica reminded him.

"By rights, you'd still be there."

"This again," said an exasperated Brad. He turned to Jessica and Theo. "I think we're good."

"So that's it? You're done? You're out of my hair?" Ableman asked.

"We don't have the time to waste," Brad said.

Theo pushed a stack of papers across the table to Ableman. "I made you a copy of the list."

Ableman looked up at him. "I'll check the employee rolls. But I'm not going to cause a nationwide panic."

"Fine," Jessica said. "Then consider this list a reminder. Because when something happens to one of the locations, we'll be coming back to say we told you so."

❧

Jessica, Brad, and Theo stood under a streetlamp next to their stolen ambulance.

"What's next?" Brad asked. "What's our plan C?"

"I'm going to refine the list," Theo said. "Narrow it down. He's right. Forty-three targets is a lot. And even if it comes down to just six locations, it's still pretty vague. His point about trying to predict what was going to happen in Arcadia City wasn't lost on me, because I have to be honest with you—even if I did think it was going to be a train plowing through the spur junction and into the power station with all the cargo, there still wouldn't have been much I could do. Even now, there's no apparent evidence of sabotage. Even if we held the train and inspected the track, we wouldn't have found anything."

"Well, you found the ink," said Brad.

"He has a point," Jessica agreed.

"So what are our options?" Brad asked Theo, who wasn't responding.

Jessica looked across the street at a cluster of news vans. A reporter standing in the bright light of a camera was giving his audience an update on the situation. From where Jessica stood, the breathing mask he wore was clearly visible—although even rescue workers had stopped wearing them a day before.

She noticed a field producer standing off to the side, watching the broadcast and making notes on a tablet.

"Fuck it," Jessica exclaimed as she started to walk toward the camera truck.

"What are you going to do?" asked Brad.

"If Ableman wants to be a dick about it, then screw him. I'm going straight to the news," she replied.

"Are you worried that might cause a panic?" Brad inquired.

Jessica looked over her shoulder. "Not more than the one we just went through. I'll let people figure their own shit out. I just want 'em to have the information."

Brad turned to Theo. "Should we stop her?"

"I don't use the word 'impossible' very often, but I think that applies here," Theo said. "And let's be honest, we were asking Ableman to do the same thing. Put his name behind it. He was playing it safe. So were we. Jessica understands the stakes are too high for that. I can't think of a better option. At least it's better than doing nothing."

"I hope you're right," said Brad. "I hope you're right."

FAULT TOLERANCE

Leo Sterling was in the control room of the Mud River Dam filling out his report logs when a red light began to flash.

The light wasn't supposed to flash, at least not when there wasn't a storm upriver. But the gauge indicated that water levels were beginning to rise quickly. He furiously tapped some keys on the computer and saw a reading that didn't make any sense. While protocol dictated that he needed to call this in, Leo ran for the doorway so he could step outside and visually inspect the reservoir.

"Jesus Christ," he muttered, realizing the water levels had climbed until waves were breaking over the top of the dam.

He rushed back inside and checked the control valves at the two sluice gates upstream, which should have been restricting the flow of water. They were automated and reliable yet now appeared to be open.

This shouldn't be happening, Leo thought.

Dams were incredibly redundant systems designed to withstand just about any potential failure scenario outside of freak weather events. Arguably, they were the oldest form of infrastructure, going back before mankind—because even goddamn beavers know how to build a solid dam.

Leo was the only person on shift, because everything was automated and, at least in theory, extremely reliable.

The two upstream sluice gates released water in a predictable flow into the main reservoir. Water was supposed to be slowly released from the reservoir in anticipation of buildup at the other two storage locations upstream—it was a backup for a backup. Releasing too much water from the Mud River Dam would send an outflow across the valley and flood a good part of southwestern Virginia.

He didn't have to look at the hydrological map to know the town of Medford, located in an oxbow just a few miles away, would take the full brunt of the water if it began to spill. From his point of view, building cheap homes on a floodplain was an act of stupidity. But he couldn't help the fact that they were already there. Not to mention the two trailer parks that would likely be swept away if the outflow couldn't be contained.

Leo grabbed the phone from the wall, dialed his supervisor's number, then sent his fingers flying across the keyboard, trying to initiate a restart sequence on the upstream sluice gates, hoping he could shut off the flow. But he suspected—he knew—it was already too late. The current levels were showing him the water had already reached the top of the dam. Even if he were able to close the gates—and there was some question of that—the surge heading his way would spill over the top of the dam. While that wasn't the primary problem, the erosion it would cause around the edges was. This dam, built as a fail-safe, was only meant to contain water below a certain point. Beyond that, there was no telling if it would hold.

"How's it going, Leo?" Ben Lindelmeier asked as soon as he picked up.

"We got a critical situation here," Leo replied, urgency lacing his voice. "The two sluice gates are stuck open. The meters weren't reporting it until now, and I think we're going to have an overflow."

"Fuck," Ben responded. "I'll put in the warning. Do what you can. God." There was a pause. "We need to get somebody up there on those sluice gates and manually try to control them. But even then—"

"I know, I know," Leo said.

He stayed at his station and tried everything within his power to restart the sluice gates and close them, hoping to prevent a disaster. But no matter what he did, they refused to respond. It would be up to the emergency maintenance crew to try to physically shut them—but it would take at least an hour for them to get there.

He had left the office door open and could hear the sound of the water as it began to spill over the dam like a waterfall.

Leo traced the path of the river with his eyes, and his heart sank. He took out his phone and dialed. "You get the warning?" he asked his brother, who lived downstream of Medford in Eidelberg.

"Yeah, my phone just went off. We're in the car now. What the fuck did you do, Leo?"

"I don't know," he said in frustration. "I don't know."

"I'm just messing with you, man. I'm sorry. I didn't realize you were there right now. I'm sure it'll be fine. It's just a false alarm."

"No, it's not," Leo insisted. "Get to high ground fast. Stay safe."

An hour later a notification flashed: The emergency crews were at the sluice gates, trying to shut them. There was nothing more for Leo to do. Two backup engineers rushed into the control room.

"Let me have a look," Scott Alistair offered, heading toward the console.

"Have at it," Leo said, rising to give up his seat.

Knowing it was futile, he walked outside, drawn by the roar of the water. He watched the flood in the crescent moonlight as it surged below and washed through the river toward the oxbow. He saw twinkling house lights in the distance and cars lined up, trying to escape along the single road out of the basin.

If people didn't panic, they should be fine, Leo thought. At least the ones who were awake. But there were a lot of people down there who didn't have phones—who might not get the message.

The surging tide created a silvery ripple as it pushed through the river and spilled over the banks into the fields and streets on either side. By morning, the river, the oxbow, and the land in between would be a lake—littered with mobile homes and flimsy houses that had been ripped from their foundations.

Leo was a thorough man and took the logs seriously. He'd faithfully run every single test, followed every protocol, never cut corners like some of the other guys.

Yet that was small consolation. This had happened on his watch. Lives were already being forever altered—and, unfortunately, some would come to a premature end.

Six years ago, they had replaced the World War II–era valves and sensors with modern electronics. They'd insisted that these new systems were much more reliable and fault-tolerant. Leo had believed them, because he had to.

But he had no idea how they worked, nor did anybody else he knew.

❦

Jessica, Brad, and Theo were sitting inside the main cabin of a Bombardier Global 7500 jet parked at Smyrna Airport, just outside of Nashville, Tennessee. Mathematically, Theo had predicted this was the one location that would make it easiest for them to get to whichever of the six most likely locations was impacted next.

"A dam just broke in Virginia," Jessica announced. "Twenty-three miles away from the *Virginia News Tribune* printing plant." She glanced at Brad and Theo, already knowing they understood the connection.

In the four days since they had asked for Ableman's assistance—and since Jessica had gone to the media with a list of potential targets—not much had changed.

We'll look into it.

We'll take it into consideration.

Those were the empty promises that followed her attempt at a national news story.

Although the FBI was treating the matter with more urgency, without a specific target or clearer evidence, there was only so much they could do to get local authorities to act.

"The dam was on the list," Theo observed quietly. "Top eight."

"We know," Brad replied. "We know. There wasn't anything else we could do."

"We don't know that," Theo countered.

"Well, we'll find out," Brad said. He pushed out of his seat. "Let me tell the pilot our destination."

As Brad disappeared into the cockpit, Theo stared into space. Jessica studied him, aware of how much guilt he was internalizing.

"Theo, we did what we could," she said gently.

"It's not enough," Theo insisted, shaking his head.

"We'll get more help. We'll make more noise. We'll stop the next one," she promised.

He turned toward her, his eyes bloodshot and heavy-lidded. He hadn't slept for days. "The next one's the last number in the sequence, Jessica. We have to do something. It's going to be bad. Real bad. Worse than this. And we don't even know what this is. But whatever it is, it'll be worse."

Brad reentered the cabin. "We've got a flight plan filed. Takeoff in ten minutes," he reported.

"How quickly can we get Sloan there?" Theo asked him.

"I've kept a jet waiting at Fort Lauderdale Executive Airport, just in case," Brad said. "By the time we land, she should be en route."

"What about Kylie? I know she's your boss. You're already stretching things with the use of the planes, but . . ."

"She's in. She's always been in. I'll get her and the drones on this too," Brad assured him.

"Thank you," Theo murmured.

Brad studied Theo's drawn expression. He walked over to the seat, positioned his hands on either side of the headrest, and leaned down until he was eye level with Theo. "Dr. Cray, I need you to snap the fuck out of it. I don't need you to be compassionate right now. I don't need you thinking about the victims. I need you to think like the person who's orchestrating this. Understood?"

"I know . . . but there's no order to this. No pathos. Just chaos. Pure chaos."

PENNY

"Would you like some more coffee?" the server inquired.

"Yes, please," the man said, pointing toward his coffee cup at the edge of the table. He didn't look up from his notebook or make eye contact, partly because he was focused on the details of what he was writing, but also because he never made eye contact.

The man kept his arm placed around the notebook for privacy. His handwriting was very tiny and difficult to decipher from more than a few feet away; as a matter of habit, he was always protective of his thoughts.

The line between his inner monologue and the words he put on the page was fairly blurry for him. He'd found that most things weren't really clear until he could put them into writing.

The man's life could be divided into two periods: before he could express himself in his notebooks, and after. The after period was orderly and the before period was a chaotic blur, like a scratch on a film negative—the same way he saw people's faces.

A psychologist had once tried to explain to him that this was a condition called prosopagnosia, the inability to remember faces.

But the more the woman went on about the condition, the less convinced the man was that this was what he had. His experience was entirely different. He could look at somebody and be aware that they had eyes, a nose, or a mouth, and maybe even describe them like he could numbers on a chart, but they didn't connect or have any particular meaning for him. If you asked him to draw what he saw, it would be a scribble. Whereas the illustrations he'd seen in the textbooks at university made by people with face blindness showed almost comical, cartoonlike, simplistic drawings. The man could tell you where the nose was in relation to the eyes or the mouth, just like he could tell you the shape of his own teeth by feeling them with his tongue, but he had no more understanding of what someone's face looked like than he did the inside of his mouth when it was closed.

He waited for the waiter to walk away before glancing up. As the older man retreated, the man noticed the tempo of his steps and the slight angle to his gait. He had seen this before in people who needed orthopedic shoes due to congenital defects in their legs and ligaments.

Since childhood, the man had had an easier time recognizing friends as they walked away in the hallway than when they walked up to him. Technically, it shouldn't make a difference if someone was walking from or toward him when evaluating their gait. He concluded that he found their noisy faces distracting.

He had once paid for an MRI under an assumed name. He was curious to know what made his brain different from everybody else's. He had spent several days at the university library going over the image, comparing it to different case studies.

The man's hypothesis was that the fever that nearly killed him when he was four created an untreated case of encephalitis that damaged part of his brain. Of course, the fact that his mother and grandparents all were mentally ill probably didn't help his prognosis.

The man felt no emotional reaction to this insight. It was simply an explanation for why his neurology was different than that of others.

He didn't consider himself sociopathic, insofar as he didn't seek to manipulate people, nor did he enjoy hurting humans. Still, he understood that his actions had killed quite a number of them. He simply felt nothing about people. Occasionally, he might find somebody interesting—but the effect was more like watching a movie: He could release them from his life as easily as switching the channel to a more engaging TV show.

He'd had relationships with several women and found that the less he said, the more interesting and normal he seemed to them. But ultimately he always found his partners merely distracting.

Checking the restaurant around him to ensure he wasn't being observed, the man slipped the burner cell phone from his pocket and checked the news coming out of Virginia and Arcadia City. He wasn't surprised the nuclear canisters hadn't broken. The Federal Railroad Administration safety standards were well designed. He knew it would take a series of several unlikely events to happen for them to come open. He'd given it his best shot. What pleased him the most was the final positioning of the locomotive and cars. It matched his calculations to within a few meters.

The flood was a challenge to predict in terms of outcome, but elevation maps gave him some idea of the final shape of the lake it would form. The closer the aerial images matched his projections, the greater the satisfaction he would feel.

It had taken the man some time after first conducting his experiments to understand what brought him joy.

Certainly, the ratio of outcome to time and effort he put into them was a factor.

But ultimately he realized that he cared most about how closely the final outcome resembled his predictions.

He hadn't expected the radioactive material to escape, so he wasn't disappointed that it didn't happen.

Whereas with the final number he had much higher expectations. While calculating the total damage could take authorities years, he had rough estimates of what he would be able to find out shortly after.

For example, he was certain the Pancake House where he was currently sitting wouldn't be here in two weeks. And depending upon the schedule of the waiter and where he lived, he might not be here either.

The man looked out the window at the intersection of the town and mentally estimated the damage that would affect the various buildings. The metal pole holding the giant tire would probably remain, although there was a strong chance it would bend, depending upon how tightly fastened the tire was to the top and if the explosive force created was enough to warp it.

Based upon available data, every window for several miles would likely shatter, even the ones facing away from the center.

The older building structures would probably remain, while the newer ones made from lightweight timber and prefab materials should incinerate or get blown away almost immediately.

Unlike with Arcadia City and Mud River, the man had no plan to be anywhere near here when it happened. While it would certainly be a spectacle, surviving it would be effectively impossible.

His hope was that perhaps several years later, it might be possible to visit this site and see how the aftermath compared to his prediction.

The waiter set the bill on the table. The man did the calculation for ten percent and decided to be generous, giving the older man the benefit of the fraction of a cent, and placed down the extra penny.

As he walked outside into the sunlight and the parking lot, he stopped for a moment and smiled at a thought.

What were the odds the penny would still be here after the incident?

It was something new to consider.

He had time to think about such things now because everything was already in place.

He had nothing left to do but wait for the world to burn.

MENTORS

Jessica Blackwood stood in front of the vending machine deciding if she would pretend to stay healthy and choose something like crispy green beans or go all in and buy the Reese's Peanut Butter Cups she knew she was craving. Out of the corner of her eye, she was also keeping watch on a young man in his late twenties in a loose-fitting football jersey talking on his phone. She could tell by the close-cropped hair and performance sneakers that he had served as active-duty military or in law enforcement.

He'd stolen a couple of glances at her but seemed intent on committing to the idea that he was focused on his phone call, occasionally turning his back to Jessica, but not for too long.

Since the Mud River Dam accident two days earlier, multiple law enforcement agencies and other organizations had been swarming around this part of western Virginia.

She and the rest of the team had given statements to the FBI and other agencies about why they'd included the dam on the list that Jessica had given to the media. Although the feds were paying attention to her now, they still weren't really listening.

Jessica had first spotted the man in the jersey the night before—being terrible at pretending he wasn't watching her and the others. He had been with two apparent colleagues, a woman about his age and another male. Each one of them looked professional but dressed too casually to fit their hairstyles, carriage, and demeanor.

Her gut instinct was that they were working undercover but had not spent a lot of time actively training for it. They could've been from any number of agencies, ranging from the FBI to the Department of Energy's intelligence division.

She contemplated going back into the motel room and asking Brad if he wanted to shadow Jersey Boy, given it was his area of expertise, but she checked herself, realizing that Trasker had better things to do with his time. Hell, there were better things for all of them to do. She decided the simplest solution was to cut to the chase.

Jessica bought her Reese's Peanut Butter Cups and shoved them into her backpack, deciding to give herself a little more time to decide whether to indulge. Jersey Boy had walked toward the corner of the motel and was leaning against the wall, but at an angle so he could still keep her in view.

She knew that if he really wanted privacy, he would have just walked around the corner. Instead, there he stood.

Jessica turned around and walked back toward her room and turned the corner into the breezeway that led to the back section. But instead of making a right turn, she went left and continued walking in the direction where the man had been standing, but on the other side of the row of rooms. When she rounded the last corner, he was still leaning against the wall facing the vending machine where Jessica had been—only this time his phone was resting in his hand under his arm.

"You're really bad at this," Jessica said, startling the man.

He turned around, his face flushed.

Jessica continued, "Either that's because you're very new and don't have a lot of experience, or this was something thought up last minute."

"Um," he began.

"I get it. You and your friends are on a road trip, yada, yada, whatever. If you want to know what we're up to, just come ask."

"I'm sorry, I don't understand," he replied.

"It's totally fine. I don't expect you to break cover right now. I'm just letting you know what we're doing to make it easier on you," Jessica explained. "Anyway, I'll be in room 25 with the others. If you and anybody from your team gets permission to talk, please come by and visit. Otherwise, this is just a waste of your time and a bit tedious for me." She gave him a sweet smile, then proceeded back to her room.

Brad was sitting in a chair backward with his arms folded across the backrest.

"Then what did he do?"

"I think I scared the hell out of them, but we'll either get a phone call soon or they're gonna bail."

"Probably some desk jockey who got called up out of the blue and told to keep an eye on us without much instruction beyond that," Brad guessed.

"To spy on us?" Sloan asked from the table by the window where she'd set up her laptop.

"That's what I would do," Theo replied. He lay on the floor with a towel over his face. "I mean, we are kind of suspicious."

"And we do kind of break the rules sometimes," Sloan added, "which doesn't make me get all warm and fuzzy about the idea that we have somebody watching us this closely."

"I think the scrutiny's due to me feeding the media the list of potential targets," Jessica said.

"It was the right thing to do," said Theo.

Jessica sat down on the bed and shook her head. "It didn't help. They're still pulling bodies out of the water."

"I don't know what else we could have done. Sometimes you just gotta call things in advance so people pay attention. Of course, having the Mod Squad out there watching us isn't exactly the kind of attention we really need right now," said Brad.

"I don't know what worries me more," said Sloan. "The idea that you just made a reference about a movie from 1999 or that it could have been about a TV show from the 1970s."

"The TV show originally aired September 24, 1968," said Brad. "The movie was 1999. I haven't seen either of them. I just have a mother that made me memorize every Trivial Pursuit card."

Only a few insiders were aware of the fact that Brad Trasker's mother was a superspy in her own right. She had taught him everything she knew, from blending in among crowds to using your mind as a memory palace for near-eidetic recall. Although he'd tried to pursue a different career path, originally in the marines, then as an embassy guard, he had found himself pulled into the intelligence world.

Brad stood up and leaned against the wall without attracting too much attention to himself, but it was obvious to Jessica something had tipped off whatever spidey sense the man possessed.

A moment later, a shadow passed the curtains on the walk outside and a knock came at the door.

Jessica noted that Brad, as always, was conveniently positioned to either move into the adjoining bathroom or return fire through the door, if necessary. He had a lot of these little quirks that were probably invisible to everyone else.

"I think that's your pair," Theo said without lifting the towel from his eyes.

"Wait, aren't there three of them out there?" asked Sloan.

"There's one directly in front of the doorway and two others standing to the side," Brad replied.

"You could tell all that from footsteps?"

"The CIA has an incredibly exhaustive collection of audio samples going back all the way to the 1950s, including vinyl records of nothing but different footsteps and different kinds of footwear and different kinds of environments."

Brad mimicked the sound of a droll narrator: "Size nine and a half, oxfords, solid rubber soles on worn linoleum produced in Minsk. Approximately seventy-eight kilograms, age fifty-eight."

"That is some incredibly boring ASMR you had to listen to for work," Sloan remarked.

"Oh no," Brad replied. "This is what my mother used to put me to sleep."

Jessica was beside the door, ready with her weapon.

"So you decided to stop by," she called out to the person on the other side, then peeked through the peephole.

Jersey Boy stood there with the two colleagues Jessica had spotted last night now posed behind him.

Jessica opened the door.

"Hello. Apologies. My name is Nicholas Zhao. This is Agent Carly Surivanap, and Kevin Williker."

Agent Surivanap was wearing a Lululemon tracksuit that was extra baggy around the midriff, providing a discreet place for her service pistol.

Williker wore a loose jersey like Nicholas, likely hiding a gun and holster under the folds by his lower back.

"FBI?" Brad asked from the corner where he now stood, arms folded.

"Yes." Nicholas nodded. "I'm sorry, I should have said that."

"No need to," Brad responded. "It's kind of obvious. I'm guessing they pulled you from your desks twenty-four hours ago and told you to come out here and keep an eye on us."

"Not exactly," Nicholas explained. "It was actually my idea."

"Well, come in, find a seat, and tell us more," Jessica invited.

The three junior agents entered the motel room. Nicholas took two steps forward, then froze when he saw Theo on the ground with the towel over his head.

"Is that him?" he said with what almost sounded like exalted reverence.

"He's just some bum that passed out on our carpet and we've been too busy to kick him out," Brad said.

"Ignore the cynical deep-state marionette in the corner," Theo said from under the towel and extended a hand.

The young agent bent over and shook Theo's hand. "It's an honor to meet you." He stood back up and said, "It's an honor to meet you all. I wish I'd thought this through a little bit more thoroughly, but we've had to improvise things."

He and his female colleague took a seat on the edge of the bed facing the door while Williker leaned against the wall with his back facing the window, arms crossed in a pose almost precisely mirroring Brad's.

"We're on a team in the Special Projects Division at the FBI," Nicholas explained. "Our area is computational criminology. I have a PhD in computer science from MIT. Carly studied robotics at Carnegie Mellon, and Kevin has a master's degree in mathematics from Stanford."

"Did you say your name was Zhao?" Theo asked from under the towel.

"Yes, sir," he replied.

"Let me see, that was about the use of agentic systems to simulate multilevel law enforcement procedural networks," Theo recalled.

"Yes, that was the title of my doctoral thesis," Nicholas said. "You read it?" he asked excitedly.

"Well, I read the abstract and skimmed it. And saw enough to know that you had the right idea," said Theo.

"Is it on audiobook?" Brad asked.

"No, but you can use NotebookLM to summarize it," Nicholas told him.

"He's messing with you, kid," Sloan remarked from her spot at the table.

"Ah, got it," Nicholas admitted. "It does go a little bit deep."

"But it's a very good idea," Theo agreed. "Nicholas simulated how information gets lost or accumulated inside of law enforcement agencies by using several hundred different investigations to create a model that could predict where breakdowns would occur. And the answer was?" Theo prompted Nicholas.

"Too much noise, not enough signal. The larger the investigation, the more data they collect, which on the surface is good, but the decision-making structure doesn't scale appropriately in order to make effective plans of action," Nicholas explained.

"I think it's a pretty good predictor for investigation size. If your higher-ups had any sense, they would pay attention to that and realize that throwing more agents at a problem doesn't always solve it."

"Correct. My conclusion was that most law enforcement agencies would benefit by tripling the number of forensic technicians they had on staff, both to increase the throughput of evidence processing, but also to put in safeguards to prevent it from being dismissible in court."

"Microscopes, unfortunately, aren't as sexy as guns when it comes to funding," Theo told the room.

"No," Nicholas agreed.

"So why are you spying on us?" asked Sloan.

"We're not spying," Carly replied. "We just wanted to observe you."

"When you observe somebody from a distance and don't introduce yourself, technically that's spying," Brad pointed out.

"Field research isn't exactly our strong suit," Nicholas responded. "This seemed like a really good opportunity to see how you all work."

"You could have just knocked on the door sooner," Theo said.

"We didn't want to get in the way," Carly explained.

"And that seemed like a better plan?" Brad asked.

Kevin, who had been observing this from the door, responded, "I told them."

"So how can we help you?" Jessica asked as she leaned against the dresser.

"Maybe we could be helpful if you could share with us anything you've learned or uncovered, whatever you think is appropriate," Nicholas hastily added. "We can also share with you some of the things we know."

"This might not be the right time for us to take on a mentor-mentee relationship," Brad said.

"I understand that," Nicholas responded, "but I think we can be helpful without being in the way. And to be blunt, we're the federal agents, you aren't."

"I'm on an assignment from my bureau," Sloan replied, "and these three are case specialists working with me. If you have an issue with that, I'd be happy to tell you what you can do with it."

"I apologize," Nicholas said quickly. "I'm just trying to say that we might be able to help you in some official capacities. That's it. Outside of what you can get from whatever state authorities you have."

"Well, if we learn anything, we know what room you all are in and we'll be happy to pass it on." Jessica moved toward the door to usher them out.

Nicholas spoke quickly now. "The chromatic cellulose compound you found—what led you to your list of targets? You know, I found it in the FBI database."

"You have lots of things in the FBI database," Jessica replied.

"No," Nicholas said. "I mean that specific ink was connected to earlier crimes."

Theo pulled the towel off his face. "What kind of crimes?" he asked as he sat up.

"Three bombings, six years ago," Carly explained. "A domestic terrorist group, if you want to call it that, blew up several monuments. Nobody was killed. There was an investigation, but not much came of it. We were going through forensic data, searching for any kind of pattern matches, and we found that ink was in the spectroscopic analysis."

"Nobody from the FBI mentioned this when I spoke to them about the case," Jessica said.

"I don't think they realized it, although I sent them a memo," said Nicholas. "There were no arrests made in that case. It was pushed back to the state level, and the FBI closed their investigation."

"Have you done anything else with this information?" Jessica asked.

"No. Our supervisor told us to pass it on to other teams but to not act on it."

"And are they doing anything with it?" Brad asked.

"No," said Kevin. "Too much noise, not enough signal."

"Can you give us the case files for this?" Jessica requested.

"We have them in our room, but . . . do we have an arrangement?" Nicholas asked.

Sloan returned the question. "What are the precise conditions of the arrangement?"

"You share your notes, anything you have, include us in email chains, et cetera," Carly said. "Whatever you can do to let us understand the steps that you're following for this investigation. Any archival data you have would be great."

"I'm going to need something in writing from your supervisor and a Justice Department attorney stating that none of this can be used against us," Brad said.

"What do you all have to hide?" Kevin asked.

"Care to just unlock your phone and hand it to me right now?" Sloan challenged. "I didn't think so."

"I think we can get that sorted out," Nicholas said. "I hope you understand that for us, understanding how you operate could be very useful. And I promise we won't get in the way."

After the agents departed, Jessica sat down on the bed.

"What do you guys think?" she asked.

"I smell something fishy," Brad replied.

"Me too," Sloan added.

"Fishy in that you think it's some kind of sting operation?" Jessica asked.

"I don't think they're trying to make a case against us," Theo said, "but like Brad and Sloan, I'm not sure if they were being completely honest about their motivations."

"I feel the same way. I'll make a couple calls and check them out to make sure this is legitimate. But if they're right about the other situations, the other cases with the bombs, that would be a big break."

"So far, our saboteur has gone to great lengths to avoid anything that looked like an explosive. Everything has been very methodical and designed to imply an accidental failure," Theo pointed out. "Bombing statues seems a bit out of character."

"I agree," Jessica replied, "but we all know people aren't static. Methods and motives change over time."

"Me too," Theo responded. "If what they say is true, this adds some interesting new angles to the case."

"We'll also have to figure out how to divide up our time," Jessica said. "I want to go back to Arcadia City, see if our suspect left more of a footprint there than we were able to ascertain."

"Something tells me the newspaper employee list search didn't go anywhere, otherwise we would have heard of something," said Theo. "I'll keep working on my systems analysis. I don't know if I'm going to be much help chasing things down at the moment. I think it's very important that we narrow the potential targets as much as possible."

"I can handle the bombings," offered Sloan.

"I've got to look into a couple of other things myself," Brad replied, "but after I take care of that, I can give you an assist."

"What kind of things?" asked Theo.

"Let's just say I need to rule some things out."

OBSESSIVE

The last thing Rene Broussard recalled before he blacked out was the duct tape covering the lock on the driver's side of his '72 Ford Mustang. He had reached down to pull the tape off and realized his mistake a fraction of a second before he felt something smash against the base of his skull, and everything went black.

The car, kept in a parking garage near the Atlanta airport, was his safe space. Seeing it was a mental trigger for him to relax. It meant that he was almost home. Now that he was tied up with a bag over his head, locked inside the trunk of the car, he didn't feel safe anymore.

He had rolled over on his back and pulled the carpet away to try to reach for the gun that he kept in the wheel well, but it was gone. Whoever captured him had made it a point to remove all of his weapons.

Rene's mind raced through possibilities. The Italians, the Chinese, the French, the Russian Mafia, the Vietnamese Mafia? Any number of people could have a grudge against him. None of those potential culprits were the type to try to do something this brazen on American soil. The people on the other side of the Qatari deal he had recently pulled off might have other feelings.

The one saving grace in Rene's favor at the moment was the fact that he was still alive. If this was going to be a hit, they would have either killed him in the parking lot or shot him, then shoved his body in the trunk to dispose of elsewhere. They wanted something from him. What concerned Rene most was whether it was information they sought or some form of painful revenge.

He was an operator, a term that applied to hit men who managed to be nowhere near the scene of the crime when an assassination went down. He engineered things like exploding cell phones and plastic-explosive-filled TV sets that could be detonated from a continent away.

More infrequently, he engineered havoc. Sometimes never having to leave his kitchen table. This could be as simple as pointing out which transatlantic fiber optic lines could be cut with an anchor dragged behind a boat for a few dozen kilometers, or how to disable an entire oil terminal by triggering the safeguards in an open internet router.

Rene had learned his craft from his father and uncles. It had been a family tradition going back three generations, working with the French intelligence services.

His grandfather had made bombs in Algeria to take out resistance leaders, then created false-flag operations when public support waned.

His father had been a freelancer who worked only with Western powers—well, at least as far as Rene knew.

Rene did contract work for private companies that were indirectly working with Western intelligence agencies, but he also, under an alias, took the occasional assignment from foreign intelligence agencies aligned with the Middle East.

He heard gravel hitting the bottom of the trunk as the driver of his car turned down a remote road. By Rene's estimate, they had been traveling for more than a half hour, which could place him anywhere within a few hundred square miles of Atlanta. An area that contained plenty of out-of-the-way forests, quarries, and other remote sites where someone could go about their dirty work without interruption.

The car came to a sudden stop, slamming Rene's head against the side of the trunk. He suspected the driver did this intentionally to disorient him. When the trunk opened, a million-candlepower light lit the interior. Despite the bag over his head, he squinted against the white-hot glow through the fibers.

"Move and you die," said an electronically altered voice.

The mechanical voice made Rene relax slightly. The light and the voice changer indicated this person didn't want their identity known, which opened up the possibility that Rene could walk away from this. But that also meant that they were going to want something from him, which would be information. So far Rene had taken it as a point of pride that he had never ratted out anyone. Of course, other than a few low-level interactions with local law enforcement, he'd never found himself in a life-or-death situation in which his integrity was on the line.

A gloved hand reached over and grabbed the chain between the handcuffs restraining Rene's wrists behind him and pulled him out of the trunk.

"Lie on the ground," said the voice.

Rene spread his body flat with his head turned to the side.

The tip of a pistol was shoved into the back of his neck. Rene smelled fresh gun oil through his hood.

"Who did you tell about Arcadia City?" the voice demanded.

Rene's mind raced. He'd seen the news online.

"I don't know anything about it," he said.

The gun barrel shoved deeper into his cervical vertebrae, pressing into his spinal cord.

"Fuck!" Rene screamed. "I don't know about it," he insisted. "Fuck."

"Bullshit," the voice snapped.

Rene tried to think of something to say. He wasn't merely an operator; he was also a planner. Sometimes people asked him for pieces of operations. How to disable an alarm system. The most vulnerable part of a pipeline. What's the fastest way into an engine control room?

He knew these details because he collected them and a million other technical bits of information about everything from toaster ovens prone to catching on fire to the amount of deterioration in the containment wall of a nuclear reactor at Shanghai Technical College.

Had anyone ever asked him to point out critical vulnerabilities in the electrical grid or rail system around the crash site? It was possible, thought Rene. Yet he was almost certain he had never heard the name Arcadia City until it popped up in the news.

"I don't know who you think I am, but I don't know anything," Rene said, trying to sound as calm as possible.

"I'm not convinced," the voice replied. "Who did you tell?"

Rene wasn't sure how to respond to allegations of leaks he'd never made. He decided that trying to play the role of the complete innocent would be pointless. This man obviously knew who he was.

"I don't talk about those kinds of things," Rene said, trying a little bravado. "I will take them to my grave. And if that's right now, fine. Pull the trigger."

"Mud River," said the voice. "Who did you tell?"

Now Rene was convinced this person had him confused for somebody else. Who that could be, he had no idea, but he had never been asked to try to destabilize a dam with anything other than Semtex.

"I'm not the only person that does those kinds of things," Rene pleaded, feeling fresh hope. It seemed the man with the electronically disguised voice was on a fishing expedition, and Rene was just one of several fish he sought.

Then he realized it.

There were precious few people who knew he was an operator, and only one who knew who he really was *and* where he lived.

"For fuck's sake, Brad, couldn't you have just called me instead of kidnapping me?"

Rene felt the weight of the pistol lift off his spine, followed by the sound of a Velcro strap, and then Brad's own voice. "I wasn't sure you would have told me the truth."

Rene sucked in fresh air as the hood left his head.

"We've been in gun battles together. I've saved your ass more than a couple of times," Rene reminded him.

"I don't think I'd go that far," Brad replied.

"We're in the same business, for Christ's sake," said Rene.

"No, we're not," said Brad as he undid the handcuffs and helped Rene to his feet. "You're a mercenary. I'm a soldier. There's a difference."

"The only difference," Rene replied as he rubbed his sore wrist, "is that I get to choose. You don't."

"Well, I question your choices, then," Brad responded. "You saw the news about Arcadia City and Mud River."

"I take it they weren't accidents," Rene ventured.

"No. That fire at the battery plant down in Florida? That wasn't either. And a few other things."

"So you decided to blame me?"

"I needed to talk to you. Time is critical. We've got three days until the next event," said Brad.

"What kind of event?"

"I don't know. That's why I'm talking to you."

Rene looked at the woods around him, then at Brad. Being out here alone with him made Rene uncomfortable.

"Mind if we have this conversation at my house? I'd like to at least die in the place where I've been paying my mortgage."

Rene's home was on a twenty-acre property north of Atlanta, covered in tall weeds. It was set back from the road behind barbed wire and rows of trees. He lived in a single-story four-bedroom house that had two metal storage structures behind it. One of them had been an equipment barn. Rene had built the other after he bought the land.

Brad brought the car to a stop in front of the house, got out, and tossed the keys to Rene, who was still feeling a dull ache in the back of his head. Rene fumbled the keys and dropped them into the grass. He had to kneel down to pick them up. Bending over, he felt a fleeting moment of panic realizing that act had made him extremely vulnerable again. He clutched the keys as quickly as possible and stood up.

Brad was standing on the porch, arms folded, watching him. Rene knew he was still toying with him, keeping him on edge.

The car ride had been silent. After he got behind the wheel, Brad turned to Rene and said flatly, "I need you to think about everybody you know and who could have pulled this off." And those were his last words until now.

Rene was very aware that Brad knew nine ways from Sunday how to fuck with somebody's head, whether it was literally concussing it or using whatever secret spy techniques he knew for getting into someone's psyche.

"Do you have a list for me?" Brad asked.

"I can think of five guys, and I'm fucked if anybody finds out that I told you," Rene replied.

"I can think of six," said Brad, "aside from you. And if a couple of my names aren't on your list, I'm going to know you're lying to me."

"Can't we just have, like, a normal business discussion?" pleaded Rene.

"Oh, I'm sorry," said Brad. "I didn't realize that we were in normal business and not the killing-people business."

"My conscience is clear," Rene protested.

"You don't have a fucking conscience."

Rene trudged up the steps to the porch and headed toward his front door. Brad reached an arm out and grabbed him by the clavicle.

"I asked for a list of names."

"Can't we do this inside?" asked Rene.

"Let's do it now."

Before Rene could protest about not having anything to write on, Brad produced a small notepad and pen from a pocket. Rene sighed and sat down on the steps, put the notepad on his knee, and wrote down four names. Brad saw him hesitate on the last one. "If it doesn't hurt a little, it's not going to be valuable to me," he told the mercenary.

"If it comes out that this name ever came from my lips, I'm dead."

"Good thing I'm asking you to write it down, then, and not say it."

Rene finished the list and handed the notepad and pen back to Brad.

"There are governments that would spend hundreds of millions of dollars to get this list."

"I'll keep that in mind if my retirement bonus doesn't shape up the way I hope it does," Brad told him. "Which of these do you think could have pulled off Arcadia City or Mud River?"

"Any of them," Rene replied, "with enough time."

"But any one more than another?" Brad pressed.

"No. None of them did it," Rene said with a headshake.

"What do you mean?"

"There's no angle to it. There's no point. Not for these guys. They're for hire, and the people that hire them pay a lot and have very easily understood motivations. If I get asked to take out an oil terminal somewhere, all you have to do is see which one is taking up the slack and who's getting richer from it. And to figure that one out, you just go the day after to the champagne room of the most expensive nightclub in Dubai to find out who did it."

"Maybe we don't know the motive yet," said Brad.

"Maybe we never will, but the other thing I don't think you've considered," said Rene, "is any one of these guys might pull off a single operation inside the United States. None of them are going to pull off multiples. That's pure suicide."

A thought crossed Brad's mind. "What if it was all of them?"

"That sounds like an Agatha Christie novel. No. Somebody trying to pull that off and hire all these guys would have to be a state actor, and I think we would understand the agenda. It's not any of them."

"Then maybe you need to add somebody else to the list," said Brad.

"I can't add what I don't know. And before you try some other intimidation technique, I'm being completely honest with you." Rene paused as a thought occurred. "Let me show you something," he said as he stepped away from the porch and started walking toward one of the metal buildings.

With Brad behind him, Rene unscrewed the end of a cylinder on his key chain and shoved six pills that were hidden inside into his mouth.

As Rene was about to swallow, he felt a firm grip around his neck, and his throat started to seize up. Brad's fingers forced their way into Rene's mouth and scraped the back of his tongue as they pulled the pills out.

Before Rene could say anything, Brad punched him in the stomach, knocking the wind out of him and sending the two remaining pills lodged in his throat flying into the grass.

"It's Xanax," Rene screamed from his bruised vocal cords, "fucking anxiety medication. For fuck's sake, man!"

Brad knelt on the ground and picked up a pill and examined it in the light. "Sorry," he said. "I thought—"

"That I was going to fucking suicide myself?" said Rene. "I don't know how you deal with this job, but I have got an anxiety medication addiction that could put an entire stable of racehorses to sleep. And unless you plan on letting me go inside and get a refill, don't be surprised if I piss myself."

"It wouldn't hurt your lawn," said Brad as he plowed through the weeds. "What are you going to show me in there?" he replied as he flashed the light on the storage shed.

Rene took several deep breaths to calm himself down. “You know fieldwork was never my thing, right?”

“I think that’s becoming pretty apparent right now,” said Brad as they approached the door. Rene reached a shaky hand, holding his keys, toward the lock. Brad took them from him and opened the door.

He swung it open and aimed the flashlight into the interior, then let Rene step inside and turn on the light switch.

The storage unit was filled with row after row of metal shelves stretching into the darkness. Resting on the shelves were manuals, binders, and file boxes of all shapes, sizes, colors, and languages.

Brad glanced at a binder with a Cyrillic title and pulled it from the shelf.

“That’s the Rostelecom engineering specifications,” Rene said.

Brad nodded. He could read the Russian. It was filled with schematics and diagrams explaining the details of the landline system used in Moscow.

He walked farther down the aisle and saw manuals for commercial diesel power plants, binders with schematics describing electrical power grids in Thailand. There was even an entire section dedicated to the architectural designs of every university and research nuclear reactor in the world, including six binders for installations that Brad knew were top secret.

He rounded another corner and grabbed a black binder with no label on it and flipped it open. “I don’t think the United States Navy would take too kindly to finding out that you have the specifications of the antimissile defense system of the USS *Gerald Ford*.”

“Maybe so,” said Rene. “I’ll be more than happy to give them the name of the Russian website I downloaded it from so they can send a cease and desist.”

Brad wandered farther into the stacks, exploring the different manuals that Rene had collected. He knew that intelligence agencies kept archives like this. This was the first time he had encountered one in the hands of a private individual.

"How did you get all these?" Brad asked as he turned around to face Rene, who was sitting in a chair next to a desk at the entrance.

"There are entire online communities of people that do nothing but discuss all the historical track layouts of the Lisbon-Portugal railway system in such nauseatingly exhausting detail—even their own engineers would get bored by it. It's a kind of mania or an obsession. For me, it's a profession. For them, it's something they live, drink, eat, and breathe." Rene waved at all the books. "I could walk away from this. I don't need them. But for others, it's kind of an OCD."

"A compulsion," said Brad.

"Definitely. You ever hear about those guys that have model trains that run through their entire house? It starts with a project in the basement, then it moves upstairs, and then it becomes everything. But it could be model trains, it could be telephone grids, it could be the various ball bearings used in a particular railroad route through Eastern Europe. Anything mechanical that moves. I guarantee you, somewhere there's a group of people obsessed with it."

"Do you know of any intelligence agencies that might have trained someone who could have pulled off Arcadia City or Mud River?" Brad asked.

"I still don't think you understand what I'm telling you," Rene said. "You don't have to be *trained* to have that degree of obsession. In fact, you really can't get their level of knowledge from training. This person might have worked for the military, might have even done what I did for some period of time. But they just as easily could be an airplane mechanic or some guy sitting in a factory in Detroit trying to figure out a new spark plug. Their job's not where they would have learned any of this. It's the *kind of person* that wants to learn this."

"Where did you get all of these manuals?" Brad asked.

"Half of them I printed out from schematics and diagrams I found online. The other half you find at collectors' meets online, other places. I never buy them through my own name, but I'm always looking for these. You never know when something might come in handy or you get a phone call because somebody has a question about the Milan subway system." Rene corrected himself. "I mean, the Moscow subway system."

Before Brad could react, Rene reached into his desk drawer and pulled out a pistol and aimed it at him. "You should have just called."

Brad was still flipping through a manual and seemed not to notice the gun. He was twenty feet away. Rene was reasonably sure he could get off one fatal shot before he got too close.

"You're right," Brad said, still seemingly unaware of the gun trained on him.

"We could have avoided this situation."

"No," Brad responded. "I mean about sucking at fieldwork."

Rene tried to make sense of the remark. Brad still hadn't made a move and was looking at the book.

Brad was the type to have wheels spinning within wheels. What was he up to? Did he think he could bargain his way out of here?

Brad tilted his head to the side for a moment, then returned to the diagrams of B-2 bomber avionics.

Rene looked up at the ceiling. "Goddamn it," he swore as the sound of a helicopter grew louder.

Brad closed the book. "You're a wild card right now, Rene. Sorry. I gotta take you out of the game."

"I didn't do Arcadia City or the thing with the dam!" Rene insisted.

"I know," said Brad, "but you've done some other things. We both know it."

Brad took a step back and said "Come on in," into a microphone underneath his collar.

A moment later four men in tactical armor bearing no insignia came running in, grabbed Rene, and pushed him to the floor.

Brad knelt over him for the second time that night.

"Come on. We both know the anxiety medication wasn't in case I showed up. It was in case everything else caught up to you."

"They're going to throw me in a bottomless pit," said Rene.

"At least you'll be medicated."

Brad stepped outside the storage unit as a man in a windbreaker strode toward him from the helicopter. He had a dark baseball cap pulled down low over his sunglasses, which were completely impractical for how late it was.

"Is he connected to what happened in Arcadia City ?" the man asked.

Brad shook his head. "No, not at all."

"Too bad. That would have been convenient," said the man. "But we were going to have to bring him in sooner or later, especially after that thing in Italy."

"I figured," said Brad.

"Was he at least helpful?" asked the man.

"In a way."

"Speaking of which, how is Dr. Cray?" the man asked with a tone that didn't sound like friendly curiosity.

"Great," Brad responded.

"He's a bit of a wild card too."

"Aren't we all?"

"Maybe. Maybe. Do you need a ride somewhere?" the man asked.

"No," Brad replied, holding up the keys to Rene's Mustang. "I'm good."

As Brad walked away from the whoosh of the helicopter blades and into the darkness, part of him wondered if one day the man and his team would be coming for him.

REBEL

Detective Stanley Sherwin pointed at a patch of dirt at the center of a park in Springfield, Iowa.

"That's where the statue of Teddy Roosevelt was," he explained. "Until the bomb got it. They took out a sitting statue of Ben Franklin over at the north end of the park and then a Lincoln bust a few blocks away."

"Not exactly Confederate war criminals," Sloan remarked.

"No. I stopped trying to make sense of the politics of the kinds of idiots that do this stuff a long time ago," Sherwin said, shaking his head.

"This was six years ago, all in one night?" Sloan asked.

"Yes. Out of nowhere, no warning, no note, nothing. There was just the sound of three booms, one after another, and one hundred percent of our dead-white-guy statues had been destroyed. And when I say 'destroyed,' I mean 'obliterated.' The charges were carefully shaped—which I thought was suspicious—to sever them into pieces." Sherwin motioned toward the roof of the local library. "We found an arm up there. Poor Benjamin Franklin's head landed in a dumpster a block away. All the windows on the east and west side were shattered, but the north and south ones weren't. The explosive experts tell me that was because of the precision of the charge."

"And the FBI investigation?" Sloan inquired as she took a seat on a brick bench.

"They came in, inspected the pieces, gathered fingerprints and fragments, sent us a copy of the report, and that was it," Sherwin told her. "In my opinion, they're more reactive than proactive. And since we didn't have a note or anything else to go by, this went into whatever kind of filing cabinet they keep this kind of thing in, to be locked away until it happened again and they had more evidence."

"What about you guys? What did you determine?"

"It was my investigation and I spoke to everybody I could, from the leader of the local communist group to the Hells Angels, who we knew had trafficked in explosives. I certainly met with a lot of shady characters but wasn't left with any strong suspects. At least nobody I could bring in front of a judge," said Sherwin.

"What did the FBI say about the bombs?" Sloan pressed.

"They said the same thing our own forensics experts said, which was that this was a high-quality plastic explosive with a shaped configuration designed to cause the most destruction to the statues."

Sloan took a file from her backpack, including the copies she had made via FedEx of the case that she was able to download, and sorted through the pages. "Did any of your suspects have military experience?"

"A few. Some had worked with ordnance, but nothing stood out too much because anybody will tell you all you have to do is go online to find out how to build a bomb or use shaped charges effectively. It's not exactly forbidden knowledge, for better or worse."

"True," Sloan agreed. "But amateur bomb makers often have a habit of blowing themselves up while trying to get in the reps."

"Yeah, we spoke to a couple of our own idiots that had had mishaps as teenagers or tried to blow themselves up. We couldn't find any match with the explosive. It wasn't too hard for me to get a search warrant and get samples of everything, but no match. As you probably know, high-quality explosives leave traces, and unless you handle them in the most contained environments, they get everywhere."

"And the FBI helped you with the samples you collected from the suspects?" Sloan asked.

"Yes. Most of them. And we couldn't find any match," Sherwin replied.

Sloan closed the file and slid it back into her backpack. "So who do you think did this?"

"I don't think the bomb maker was local," Sherwin said, folding his arms. "He might have had a friend or two here, but I don't think it was anybody that I spoke to. My guess is somebody from out of town, or some people who decided to show up one night and blow up our statues. I keep checking to see if something like this has happened elsewhere with similar explosives, but so far, no. Generally, the imbeciles that try to pull off this kind of thing use poorly configured pipe bombs or wrap chains around the statues like the Taliban did. Plastic explosives are something else."

Sloan stood up and walked around the plaza. She returned her attention to where the statue of Teddy Roosevelt had once stood, then back to the corner where Benjamin Franklin had been located. "What time did this happen?" she asked.

"4:17 a.m. Good thing nobody was here, because pieces shot everywhere."

"I suspect that was by design. The fact that nobody left a note or took credit for it, that seems odd to me," Sloan mused.

"I agree. Attacking statues is a political stunt. And if you don't tell people what your politics are, it's hard for them to make sense of it," Sherwin said.

"Tell me what you really think happened," Sloan pressed, prompting him to be more frank.

"To be clear, I think our bomber was from out of town, but I think he had a friend here, a local," Sherwin admitted.

"A local radical?" Sloan asked.

"You could say that," Sherwin confirmed.

She could tell he was holding something back. "I don't care about the local who may have been connected to this," Sloan said. "I'm concerned with whoever made the bomb."

"I imagine," Sherwin responded.

Although he didn't say anything, the expression on his face told Sloan quite a bit. Among law enforcement, there's an unspoken code—to look out for their own, within limits. The limits depended a lot on who was involved, what was at stake, and other factors. Even the most ethical police departments would let things slide, like speeding tickets or domestic disputes, if they involved people they knew and making a case of it would create even more complications.

Sloan decided to follow her intuition. "I'm guessing one of your suspects, maybe somebody who never made it into any file, is the son or daughter of somebody. Somebody in the department, or maybe a prosecutor?" she guessed.

"One of our circuit court judges," Sherwin admitted. "Nancy Rafario. She's a pretty good judge, has been generally favorable to us, and a decent person."

"And her daughter?" Sloan probed.

"Emma. She was a good kid up until her sophomore year of high school. Then her rebellious streak kicked in—she became . . . I don't know, do they still call them 'hippies'? Whatever—counterculture, nose ring, tattoos, all of that. Graduated, went to university here, took up political science, I think. You know the cliché," Sherwin said with a sigh.

"Maybe, but they always have details that matter. Tell me more about Emma," Sloan prompted.

"Her mother didn't really talk about it, but I'd overheard secondhand that Emma had dropped out of school and taken up with a group of weirdos that liked to drive around to different protests and 'speak truth to power,' or whatever they were calling it," Sherwin recalled.

"What do you know about the group?" Sloan asked.

"I think they were genuine about being in it for the movement and not the violence," he explained, "which—I know—some of the people that get caught up in that are just looking for an excuse to throw a brick or set something on fire. These folks traveled from protest to protest with their bullhorns and signs and made themselves heard. There was never anything like a manifesto, but they did have a habit of showing up where violence broke out."

"How many people were in the group?"

"I don't know. It seemed to vary," Sherwin answered. "I recall Emma visiting home once with two or three friends—another woman and two men. And this is going to sound horrible, but the way they dressed, it was kind of hard to tell which was which. I only know this because I had to bring some papers by for the judge to sign and saw them hanging out in the living room."

"Was the judge happy about this?" Sloan asked.

"I think she was just glad to have Emma still in her life. More than anything, I think she was afraid of losing her daughter to whatever radicalism she was going through. And if that meant entertaining some of her smelly, pot-smoking college friends, she was willing to do that."

"Did you get the names of any of her friends?" Sloan asked.

"No, this woulda been like eight months before the bombing, so I wasn't really noting them," Sherwin admitted.

"What about after the bombing?" Sloan pressed.

"That's when things got ugly. I reached out to the judge to let her know that I wanted to speak to Emma. And the next thing I know, I got called into the county supervisor's office, along with the police chief, and was read the riot act.

"Unless I had any specific evidence or witness testimony, I wasn't supposed to go anywhere near Emma. It was explained to me that not only was she not involved, but any indication from the police department that she could have been in some capacity would be met with retribution. Of course, they said this in much more legal and professionally polite terms," Sherwin told her.

"Did you think that was suspicious?"

"To be honest with you, not terribly, because I've had more than a few of these kinds of conversations. Anytime somebody politically connected or powerful was under scrutiny and there wasn't sufficient evidence to make a case out of it at that point. My hope was that the forensic evidence and the explosives would lead to somebody in the FBI database and they might be able to turn something up. But you know how these things go—days turn into weeks, weeks turn into months, and then other things begin to pile up on your desk. Any sense of urgency is lost," he continued.

"What can you tell me about Emma?" Sloan asked.

"I didn't really know her that well, but from people who did and my brief interactions with her—bright kid, smart, very sweet, but different from her mother. I think the judge is a bit strong-willed, although she's gotten a little bit better-tempered in her age, maybe at the fear of losing her daughter. I don't know. But also a bit lost. Her father died when she was young. The judge remarried. That didn't work out. And between her mother's career and the pressures of being the child of somebody with that much authority, it can be a challenge. I think she just wanted a role to fill."

"Does Emma still live here?" Sloan asked.

"No, she hasn't come back since the bombing, which has more to do with her becoming disconnected from her mother. But as I say it, I know how it sounds," Sherwin admitted.

"Do you know where she is now?"

"I think Astoria, Oregon, but I can find out for you."

"Do you know anything else about the group she was with?" Sloan pressed.

"I have some notes in my case files. I can pull them for you. I remember the name—Night Before Dawn. It sounded like a Depeche Mode album to me, but whatever." Sherwin laughed.

"Night Before Dawn?" Sloan repeated.

"Yeah, that's what they called their group. It does sound kind of ominous too, now that I think about it."

"Do you know anybody else here who might have been in contact with them or could tell me more?" Sloan asked.

"Well, you could talk to Beth Ann Gross. Sorry, Beth Ann Kellerman now. She got married two years ago. She was Emma's best friend up through college. They both went there together, but Beth Ann came back here. She works at the State Farm insurance office about three blocks over."

"Thank you very much." Sloan checked her watch. "I think I might be able to catch her now."

"It stands to reason. While you go do that, I'll get all my notes together and send them over to you."

"Thank you, I appreciate that. But could you do me one more favor?" Sloan asked.

"What's that?"

"Don't let her know I'm coming. And if possible, don't mention to anybody who I am or why I'm here," she requested.

Sherwin nodded. "Understood."

Emma Rafario was the closest they had come so far to a person potentially connected to their saboteur. The last thing Sloan wanted to do was let him or anyone connected to him know they could be closing in.

Sloan found Beth Ann Kellerman sitting behind a desk at the State Farm insurance office in a small strip mall two blocks away, wedged between a 7-Eleven and a dry cleaner. The office was an open floor plan with four desks. Kellerman and a colleague, an older gentleman in a gray flannel suit—he probably purchased it the day he first started selling insurance—sat in the back corner reading a newspaper.

"Hello," Sloan greeted as she entered. "I'm looking for Beth Ann."

The younger woman stood up and greeted her right away. "That's me," she said, offering her hand. "How can I help you?"

"My husband and I have been house hunting in the area, and I was told to come ask you for a quote," Sloan explained.

"Have a seat. Who referred you?" Beth Ann asked.

"My husband's been talking to the Realtor, so I don't recall the name. Gi . . ." Sloan started as she sat down.

"Julian Fry?" Beth Ann guessed.

"I think so," Sloan replied. "That sounds right. I'm sorry, I'm terrible with names. I always have been."

"Me too, which is not really good in this job, if you know what I mean," Beth Ann admitted, smiling. "What brings you to the area?"

"He works in contracting. I work from home," Sloan told her.

Beth Ann's curiosity seemed genuine. "What do you do from home, if you don't mind me prying?"

"Not at all. I work in publishing, freelance mostly," Sloan confabulated. "Editing manuscripts, getting them into shape, that kind of thing. A couple different publishing houses use me. It's nice, flexible hours. I'm not going to get rich doing it, but I enjoy it. Sometimes you find some really talented people."

"That sounds really interesting," Beth Ann replied. "Where were you looking to buy?" she asked next.

"Featherbrooke," Sloan answered. She had seen the name of the development as she passed by a billboard headed into the city.

"Oh, very nice," Beth Ann replied.

Sloan wasn't sure if it was perhaps too upscale, but it wasn't really important. "We're still looking, but it seems beautiful there."

"Oh, have they finished the model homes yet? I thought that was still under construction," Beth Ann commented.

"I meant the concept photos. You know, with computers and stuff, they're so detailed, you feel like you're actually seeing it," Sloan responded smoothly.

"Yes, even the VR walk-throughs are pretty cool. It kind of gives you a sense of what it's like to be there," Beth Ann agreed.

Sloan wanted to just blurt out and ask the woman if her friend from school might have been dating a mass murderer, but she knew that it wasn't time for the blunt approach yet.

"I never really saw myself living in a place like that," Sloan mused aloud. "I was kind of a hippie chick. I thought maybe I might ride around Europe on the back of a motorcycle or find some magical cabin by the lakeside and write poetry all the time. But, you know—silly."

"You remind me of a friend of mine," Beth Ann told her. "Reality had other plans. I think she wanted to set the world on fire with her poetry and heal everyone. Instead, she's working at a coffeehouse in Oregon with four roommates without a stick of new furniture between them. But as long as she's happy." Beth Ann's tone suggested she didn't entirely believe her own words.

"That could have been me," Sloan said. "You never know who the cute guy you talk to at a concert really is, much less what kind of man he's eventually going to become. Lucky for me, I did okay."

"Emma didn't," Beth Ann said with a frown. "She liked the shaggy, charismatic ones, or at least the guys that yelled the loudest." She sighed. "They all seemed like phonies to me, but everybody has their type."

Sloan nodded and tried to sound as casual as possible. She reached for her phone. "Hopefully it was a short-term thing and not something that lasted," she offered.

"Last I heard, still in her life. So, they're happy, but I don't think they have what you'd call a traditional relationship," Beth Ann said.

Sloan considered what she'd heard: *Emma goes off to college, meets some radical loudmouth activist who's still in her circle. Not long after, bombs go off, and she's never seen again in this town.* It sounded too good to be true, she thought, but also too good to screw up by being obvious.

"My mother used to say that you could read a person by their name, which sounded stupid. Although my husband, Scott, seems to fit the bill. Scott's a pretty normal name. You don't really hear about a lot of Scotts doing anything outrageous. Not a lot of famous ones either, but it felt safe to me," Sloan told her, lightening the mood.

"I married a Steve," Beth Ann replied with a laugh. "That's pretty normal. I think you know what you're going to get with a Steve."

"Steve Kellerman," Sloan said. "That sounds good. And your friend Amanda?" she asked, intentionally getting the name wrong.

"The guy's name was Frazier. Frazier is a little weird to me. Maybe it was because of the TV show, but a Frazier sounds like somebody up to something. You know what I mean?"

"I hear that . . ." Sloan needed to quickly change the topic into something that made an even bigger impact so Beth Ann would be less likely to remember this part of the conversation. She noticed two vitamin bottles on the cabinet behind Beth Ann. "Are you guys planning to have children?" she asked.

Beth Ann's cheeks turned red. She leaned in and whispered, "As a matter of fact, more than planning."

Sloan listened to her talk for the next twenty minutes as she subtly texted the name Frazier to her team members.

NEWSIES

Jessica Blackwood walked through the corridor between the two massive rows of machinery that formed the printing press inside the *Idaho Pamphleteer* printing facility.

"Is it always running?" she shouted over the sound of the presses and hopefully through the plastic earmuffs Eric Ortega, the newspaper's general manager, wore.

"No, only at night usually, but since everything that happened, we've quadrupled our circulation," he replied, pointing toward a front page stuck to a blue cabinet facing them.

The cover photo showed one of the nuclear-containment vessels that had been thrown from the train and landed in a playground next to a swing set.

"That's a terrifying image," Jessica remarked.

"Thankfully, the danger has passed," Ortega said.

Jessica simply nodded. She wasn't in the mood to try to explain how things could be getting much, much worse—not to mention the fact that they were still pulling bodies out of the floodwaters in Virginia.

She'd asked for a tour of the plant because of the connection to the ink. It was one of seventeen facilities using it in their press.

Although they had gone through the list Ableman finally provided, no significant leads or names had emerged. The FBI and other law enforcement agencies were now taking things more seriously and conducting background checks at all the other print facilities and the manufacturer of the ink in Canada.

Jessica glanced up at the overhead tubes and conduits twisting over the corridor and connecting one side of the press to another. Large white ribbons of paper were flying through rollers and twisting through different pieces of machinery. Even though she'd seen newspaper-printing plants in movies and TV shows, somehow she naively underestimated the complexity of putting ink on paper at this scale.

"It seems overly sophisticated," Jessica said, trying to make sense of all the equipment.

"You can say that again," Ortega responded.

Jessica yelled louder, "I said it seems overly sophisticated!"

Ortega laughed. "I heard you the first time. I was agreeing with you. Newer printing presses take up one-tenth this much space, but they also cost ten times as much as what it takes for us to keep this running.

"This way," he said, guiding Jessica through an archway below the press toward a tunnel that led to a door with a glass window. Ortega held it open for her, and she stepped inside a brightly lit office.

When Ortega shut the door, the sound reduced considerably. She looked back and realized it was a thick door with insulated glass.

A small man with a fringe of gray hair over his ears gazed up at her through his thick glasses.

"This is Robin," Ortega introduced as he took off his earmuffs. "He makes sure the plant keeps running."

"Hello," Jessica said a little too loudly before realizing she was still wearing her hearing protection. "Sorry. Nice to meet you. My name is Jessica Blackwood." She offered a hand.

Robin shook it weakly, then looked at Ortega, confused.

"Am I getting fired?" he asked.

"Why would you think that?" Jessica shot back, suspicious.

Ortega shook his head. "He asks that every time I bring somebody new back here. Don't worry, Robin. You've got plenty of job security. I can't find anybody crazy enough to want to learn how all this works."

"You say that until you go digital," Robin replied.

"If I could afford that, you wouldn't be worried about losing your job," Ortega noted.

"Mind if I have a seat?" Jessica asked as she pulled up a chair across from Robin's desk.

"Looks like you already decided to," he replied matter-of-factly.

She smirked. There was a certain kind of personality she had encountered before that bore the responsibilities of keeping data centers, nuclear reactors, and now, apparently, printing presses running—at the expense of normal human social cues and interaction.

"How many people does it take to run this press?" Jessica inquired, ignoring Robin's gruffness.

"Twenty-three," he answered.

"Do you have a list of them?" she pressed.

"A list of who?" Robin responded.

"The twenty-three people you said run this," she remarked.

"I never said twenty-three people operate this press. I said it took twenty-three people to run it. Unfortunately, I only have seven." He glanced over at Ortega.

Jessica wasn't sure how much of this was Robin's sparkling personality or theater he was performing for management to make them aware of how critically important he was and how under-resourced the department was.

"This might take a while, Mr. Ortega. I'm sure Robin can escort me out of here when we're finished," she said.

Ortega took the cue. "Well, have fun," he replied, then put his own hearing protection back in place and stepped into the noisy facility.

"Not a fan of him?" Jessica asked after the door shut and she could hear her own voice.

"I'm sure he's a pleasant person when he's not trying to bleed us to death," Robin said neutrally.

Jessica didn't want to go anywhere near the politics and logistics of trying to keep a newspaper running in the twenty-first century and decided to leave things at that.

"As I understand it, there are only sixteen other facilities like this one," she said.

"What do you mean, 'like this one'?" Robin asked.

Part of the problem, Jessica suspected, was that after several years of playing the curmudgeonly troll that keeps everything running while hidden away in his cave, Robin had started to believe that's really who he was. Or at least it became a persona when he stepped into the printing facility. But she knew all about personas and the roles that people felt compelled to play. Sometimes they were ready to set them aside.

Jessica rolled her eyes. "This is going to be a lot easier if you just assume I mean the thing you already assume I mean."

"I watched a YouTube video of you doing card magic," Robin said. "You were . . ." She could sense he was searching for a word and dangerously close to saying something kind. "Quite good," he finally said with a small smile.

Finally, progress, Jessica thought.

"That must have taken a lot of practice," Robin added.

Jessica realized the man appreciated precision and hard work. Going from the printing facility, where something being a centimeter out of alignment could wreak entire havoc, over to the newsroom, where people casually chitchatted, spilling coffee and haphazardly making deadlines in the most chaotic way possible, had to be an adjustment.

"I started when I was young, with smaller cards of course, and I would practice until I got calluses on my fingers," Jessica said. She held up a hand and showed a small white scar on the inside of her index finger. "Sometimes till they bled."

She had never shown anybody that scar before. She hadn't been deliberately keeping it in her back pocket, but understanding where Robin was coming from incentivized her to be a little bit more open than usual.

Robin raised his right hand and pointed to a crooked pinkie. "Second day on the job, I wasn't paying attention."

Jessica nodded at the newsroom. "I don't think that happens from typing."

"No," Robin said, shaking his head. "I don't want to sound like a fanatic, but you smell that? The paper, the ink, all of the machine oil? That's what this business is about. Not electronic word processors, not blogs. It's taking information—news about the world—and making it into something physical. Something you hold in your hands. Something tactile," he said excitedly, his hands gesturing as he held an invisible newspaper in the air. "Nothing is real for anybody anymore."

He then tapped his finger on the newspaper laid across his desk. "This is real. I mean, the stories are probably bullshit, but my point is, it's still something made of something. It's . . ." He hesitated. "It's substance. That's what I'm trying to say, substance." He flipped over the newspaper to the back and showed a row of used car ads. "Even this is real. It has meaning. Somebody sees this, says, 'Hey, I could use a 2017 Honda Accord.' And they're connected to it. Not by their phone, not by a screen, but by something physical."

"You ever been to Arcadia City?" Jessica asked.

"My sister's brother-in-law lives there. He works at the farm-supply store. Sometimes we do Thanksgiving there. His wife makes terrible mashed potatoes. I know: We live in Idaho. How is that possible? That's like being Irish and terrible at drinking." Robin shook his head in disbelief.

He was an odd little man, but Jessica suspected if she visited the sixteen other newspaper plants, she would find sixteen different versions of him, each obsessive about newspapers.

The FBI background check hadn't flagged any suspicious patterns for Robin. There were no credit card receipts for any of the other cities within the last ten years, and his work records were fairly consistent.

Jessica didn't consider him a suspect. She wanted to speak with him because she believed there was a high probability that at some point he had spoken with the suspect.

The FBI analyst's prevailing theory was that their saboteur had a business reason to visit all seventeen plants, which was the theory Jessica, Brad, Sloan, and Theo had come up with several days prior, when nobody would listen to them.

"How many people know how to keep this plant running?" Jessica asked.

"Not a lot, unfortunately," Robin replied. "We have to train new guys on how these printing presses work, and that takes a while. Every now and then, if I get somebody who's good, they'll get hired away to go work at one of the other facilities. Which is good for them, I guess, but not so good for me. It means I got to train some new lunkhead."

"What about the people that built this?" Jessica asked. "How many of them still work for the manufacturer?"

"Maybe four or five guys, and they're all older than me. This was already falling apart when I started working here," he said. "The flow mixer is the crankiest part," Robin explained. "It was not well designed, if I have to be honest with you. And after eighteen to thirty-six months, no matter what happens, vibration will shift it out of alignment and you get too much smudging."

"What's that?" Jessica asked.

"A smudge?" asked Robin. "You never heard of that before?"

"No. A flow mixer," she shot back.

"Oh, it's the system that mixes the inks before they're poured onto the drum. The problem is that modern inks don't work with this system, and the older ones aren't quite made to the right tolerances."

"How many people know how to fix that?" Jessica asked.

"The manufacturer subcontracted that out to one guy. We call him in every two years to adjust it before it gets out of alignment."

Jessica sat up straight. "Do the other plants use him too?"

"I would think so. I haven't found anybody else that can get it back into alignment as quickly as he can."

"When was the last time he was here?" Jessica pressed.

"Seventeen months ago. I asked Ortega if I could call him in sooner and not wait for the smudging to start happening, but no, I couldn't. It's not in the budget. So we'll have to wait another seven months, and we'll get smudging. God, I hate smudging."

"Could you give me his contact information?" Jessica asked.

Robin leaned back in his chair and squinted his eyes. "This isn't about a printing press, is it?"

"Only indirectly. What can you tell me about him?" she inquired.

"About Chris? Normal guy. Quiet. Knows more about this system than I do."

"How about a physical description?" Jessica asked.

"Average height, older, not as old as me, but just . . . a typical guy."

"That may be the least helpful description I've ever heard," Jessica scolded.

"You want flowery prose? Go next door and talk to the writers," Robin said, crossing his arms defensively.

"Could you give me his full name and contact information, then?" Jessica asked.

Robin slid open the top drawer of his desk and pulled out a spiral notebook that had dozens of dog-eared pages and business cards stuck to the interior. He flipped through, then stopped on a section and turned it around for Jessica to see.

The card was simple: the name, Christian Prescott; below it: PRINTING TECHNICIAN; and beneath that, an email address for an AOL.com account.

Jessica took a photo, then reached over and tore the page out of the notebook before Robin could protest.

He complained, "Wait, that's mine. That's theft."

She slid the page into a plastic bag.

"Technically, I'm pretty sure it belongs to the newspaper, but either way it's what we call evidence," she said. "I'll make sure you get a photocopy. And if for some reason he calls, don't tell him I was here."

"He doesn't have a phone," Robin grumbled.

"You know what I mean," Jessica replied as she hurried out to call the other members of the team.

PSYCHOBABBLE

Theo Cray was walking along a deserted side road outside of Medford, Virginia, lost in conversation.

When he needed to think about things, he either tended to lie still, removing all stimuli possible, or go for a long walk, sometimes for hours, not paying attention to where he was headed. Jessica had seen to it to place AirTags into his pockets and backpack to keep track of him.

"You sound skeptical," said the voice of James Brussel.

"I think you may have good intuitions, but like many psychiatrists, you also suffer from an overreliance on storytelling," Theo replied.

"Storytelling is the only true indicator of who we are, some might say," Brussel answered.

"Stories can be helpful patterns but sometimes misleading and, like any pattern of sufficient complexity, hard to transmit reliably, and subject to gross oversimplification, or in your case, well, to put it politely, creative editing."

"Are you speaking about the George Metesky case?" Brussel asked.

"Yes, your original profile said that he would be a man born and educated in Germany who lived in White Plains, New York. In your book you change this to claim that he would be a Slav who lived in Connecticut in order to fit the true identity of the Mad Bomber to the known facts," Theo explained.

"Profiling someone with very limited information can be challenging," said Brussel. "While some of my specifics may not have turned out to be true, I was directionally accurate, which then led to the suspect's arrest. Whether he was born in Germany or of Slav descent wasn't as important as the other factors which allowed us to narrow down his identity. And I think if you look carefully at the record, you'll see that the authorities were completely in the dark and were only able to zero in on Metesky after I helped them make sense of the case."

"You have excellent intuition, like other notable psychiatrists and psychoanalysts. It's the lack of rigor and the self-mythmaking that gets in the way."

"I wonder if you're talking about me or yourself, Dr. Cray. From our conversation and what I know about you, I gather that you are extremely analytical and suspicious of intuition, yet you have quite a lot of it," Brussel remarked.

"I believe intuition has its place, but I don't think it's some magical muse that comes from a mythical plane. It's our subconscious pattern-seeking behavior that gets triggered. I suspect those patterns could be consciously observed and tested if one paid attention."

"Who would you say that you tried to please more as a child, your mother or your father?" Brussel asked. "My guess is your father and that he was an analytical man. Your mother was the soft, emotional one. And this compulsion to depend upon analysis over feeling is what torments you. Did you think that by mimicking your father's analytical behavior, you would get the affection of your mother?"

"Jesus Christ," Theo muttered. "Can we dial back the Oedipus-complex diagnosis on this?"

"I apologize. In my era, Freudian analysis was still in vogue. May I access post-1982 psychiatric literature?" Brussel inquired.

"No," Theo replied. "Please keep the context within the expertise of James Brussel. Do a double-check and make sure that we're not overemphasizing Freudian or Jungian archetypes. It sounds a bit clichéd."

"Understood," said the voice of the long-dead psychoanalyst. "Would you like me to answer that question again?"

"Yes," Theo agreed. "No, actually, forget about me. Let's go back to who you think our saboteur is."

When Jessica first realized that most of the conversations Theo was having on the phone were with constructed AI personas, she had expressed her concern. But after the proliferation of ChatGPT and normal people using AI tools for everything from drafting emails to relationship advice, she had to admit that Theo had merely been ahead of the curve. While this didn't exactly put her at ease, it made it difficult for her to make fun of him.

Given the similarities between the Mad Bomber and their current case, Theo had decided to look into the old investigation for something to help him out of his dead end. To do that, he'd created an AI persona based on the known writings and life of James Brussel, who'd assisted in the case and followed it through to its end.

George Metesky, a.k.a. the Mad Bomber, planted his first explosive on November 16, 1940, on a windowsill at the Consolidated Edison power plant. He would go on to plant many more in a career of destruction lasting seventeen years, terrorizing people throughout New York City.

Metesky planted at least thirty-three bombs throughout his career, of which twenty-two exploded, injuring fifteen people. Complicating the search for the Mad Bomber were a series of fake bombs and copycat bomb makers mimicking Metesky's crimes.

Between bombings, Metesky periodically sent letters to the police, including one in December 1941, after the United States entered World

War II, stating he would hold off on his bombing rampage for the duration of the war out of patriotic duty. Each one was signed "F.P."

While his fixation on Con Edison had put the focus on current and former employees of the utility, that still left several hundred leads. It would turn out later that the signature at the bottom of his many letters—F.P.—stood for Fair Play because Metesky felt wronged by the company.

At a loss for a suspect, the police turned to James Brussel, a psychiatrist who had studied criminal behavior and served as assistant commissioner of the New York State Commission for Mental Hygiene.

His profile included a great number of details based upon his prior experiences with the criminally insane. But like many profilers who based their theories on intuition and anecdote, it was overly specific and deeply rooted in Freudian analysis, making assumptions about sexual fixations from how rounded the *W*s were in his handwritten notes.

While Brussel's profile brought new attention to the case and created publicity, it also created a surge of hoaxes, complicating the investigation.

Although the psychiatrist was credited with having provided the key information to solve the case, Con Edison clerk Alice Kelly was the one to identify Metesky as a potential subject when looking through compensation cases and finding a filed letter marked in red with the words "injustice" and "permanent disability," terms also used in a letter Metesky had written to the *New York Journal-American*.

Although Theo thought that Brussel had exaggerated his contributions to the case, he had to admit that underneath the bravado and rewriting of history, Brussel was right about a few things that stood out. He had told the police that when they found the man, he'd probably be wearing a three-piece suit because of his attention to detail and fixation on appearance.

While Metesky wasn't wearing a three-piece suit when he was arrested, he asked police if he might change into one before being escorted to the police station for further questioning.

These were the kinds of details that Theo was looking for. He was at the outer limits of his ability to make sense of what the data showed him and was hoping a conversation with a dead psychoanalyst might at least steer him in a new direction.

Frustrated by the AI's questions about his childhood and which parent's attention he'd craved more, Theo didn't think the conversation had yielded any useful insights—it had only reinforced his skepticism of criminal profilers.

He decided to try a slightly different line of questioning and asked, "Why would someone go to such elaborate efforts to commit these sabotage crimes, yet completely mask their ownership of them?"

"In my experience, all criminals leave their signatures in their crimes," Brussel's voice said.

"That's kind of vague," Theo said. "We could either take that to mean something literally, like he left DNA, or some intentional indication of who he was. Be specific."

"I believe they all leave an unconscious pattern," Brussel replied.

"And what is the pattern here?" Theo inquired.

"The pattern is the target of his acts," Brussel responded.

"The train and Arcadia City, Mud River. What about the battery plant fire? There was nobody near there. Who was he trying to target there?"

"Ironically, Dr. Cray, you're quite close, but you don't realize it. You're thinking in diagrams and graphs and equations. The answer is in the means of your analysis and not the conclusions," Brussel said.

"That is even less helpful than asking me how I felt about my mother," Theo replied. "I need less Socratic discussion and shorter responses instead. In fact, just give me bullet points from now on. I don't have a lot of time."

"Very well. One, all of the targets have been mechanical systems.

"Two, all these structures are part of complex systems.

"Three, the success of the acts of sabotage is due to the technical understanding of the saboteur."

Theo lowered the phone to think things over. Everything he had heard from the AI avatar was a reflection of something he had already told it. With the exception of Brussel's doppelgänger telling Theo he had a mommy fixation.

While he was inclined to just take this as random mid-twentieth-century psychoanalytical regurgitation, he considered that there might be something more to it. After all, he'd had reasons for wanting to talk to Brussel in the first place.

"Could you explain what you meant about me being too fixated on my graphs and diagrams? And tell it to me in the style of a Milton Erickson story?" Theo asked.

"Certainly." The voice shifted to that of an older Midwestern gentleman . . .

❧

"I had a middle-aged man come into my office one day who looked like he hadn't slept for days. His hair was a mess, his clothes were unkempt, and he was on the verge of a breakdown.

He said, 'Doctor, I'm not a believer in hypnosis or whatever else you do, but I don't know who else I can turn to. People told me I should talk to you, and I'm skeptical, but if I can't solve this problem, I'm going to shoot myself.'

'Explain to me the problem,' I asked.

'It's a bird. It's a goddamn bird. I feel like I'm in an Edgar Allan Poe story.'

'Please tell me more,' I told him.

'I work in a tiny little office at the back of my college when I'm not teaching classes. The pay is not so great, so I edit textbooks. My wife wants a new house. We've got to get our car fixed, and this money is important to us. The problem is I can't concentrate because every time I sit down to write, a goddamn bird lands on the windowsill and starts trying to get my attention, tapping away. At first, it was amusing, then it was distracting. I'd throw a newspaper at the window, it'd fly away, then it would come back.

'I tried yelling at the bird. Fifteen minutes later, it would be back. Before I knew it, I had to go to class. I've only got two hours in that office to write. I can't write from home because there's no time for me to do that there between my wife and our three children. They're even more distracting. And I don't think the police would look too favorably if I tried to kill them,' the man explained to me.

'Did you try to kill the bird?'

'Between you and me, I came close, but then I found out it wasn't just one bird. It was any bird. I noticed they were different—one had dark black feathers, one had light gray ones. It's insane, I know. I told my colleagues. They thought it was a joke. I asked to move offices. I couldn't. I asked maintenance. They said there was nothing they could do.

'Now, I know I shouldn't let a little thing like a bird bother me, but I . . . I'm running out of time. I've got a deadline. And if I can't get this textbook done, my wife is going to be unhappy, probably leave me. So, could you hypnotize me or help me in some way? And I know I could try listening to the hi-fi or something, but just knowing that bird is there tapping, tapping, tapping is what's gotten to me. It's the psychological effect of that.'

The patient had clearly worked himself into a frenzy. The problem wasn't the bird, I could tell. It was all the other stress in his life. But telling him that wasn't going to be effective.

Instead, I asked him to do something very simple.

'Will you be in your office tomorrow?' I asked him.

'Yes, at 9:20 a.m., trying to write and getting distracted by that bird.'

'Okay, this is what I want you to do. Tomorrow, at 9:20 a.m., be the bird.'

'Excuse me?' he replied.

'I want you to go outside and I want you to tap on the window. You don't have to use your nose, just use your finger. And I want you to distract yourself. To distract *you*.'

'Doctor, that's crazy.'

'Am I the one walking into your office for help? Or are you coming to me?' I reminded him.

'Fine, fine.'

'Come back tomorrow afterward and tell me what happened.'

Twenty-four hours later, he stood in front of me. His hair was combed. He was a little less unkempt. He had a smile on his face.

'What happened?' I asked.

'I did like you said. 9:20 a.m. I walked across the quad, up to my window, and got ready to tap.'

'And what did you see?'

'I saw myself. I saw my goddamn reflection in the glass.'

'And what did you realize?' I asked.

'The birds weren't trying to bother me. They were looking at their reflections. They thought they were attacking other birds.'

'And what insight did you grasp from this?' I asked the man.

'The birds weren't the problem. If I really needed to, I could go to the library and write. I had to just stop getting in my own way.'"

The voice shifted to that of James Brussel. "How was that?"

Theo lowered the phone again. He couldn't tell if the story was random coincidence or if the AI had found some deeper pattern.

He raised the phone to speak. "He doesn't see people, does he?"

"I don't think he's blind or has a clinical face blindness, but directionally, I think you're correct. This man isn't trying to attack other people. He's attacking systems. He's trying to break them," Brussel explained.

"Because he's broken," Theo said.

"Because he only sees order and sees himself as chaos. When people have impairments in some areas, they often develop abilities in others. Blind people become more perceptive to sound. People with language difficulties become more physically expressive. The hearing-impaired learn to pick up on visual cues."

"This man is a mechanical genius," Theo said aloud after thinking about it. "But due to the way he processes information, he's probably a loner or works alone. He's the kind of person you put on the late shift or, given his capabilities, only call him in when you need him."

Theo thought for a moment.

"He probably won't show up in the employee records of either the newspaper plants or the ink manufacturer. He's a specialist, somebody who gets called in. Maybe a chemist. But we only found the finished ink, which suggests that he wasn't involved in the manufacture of it. He came in later, somewhere between the delivery of the ink and it being put onto the newspaper.

"All these presses have something in common. They're older and harder to maintain. He's a technician. He's the person you call when they break and nobody else knows how to fix it," Theo realized excitedly. "There's probably maybe a few dozen people in the world that would fit. Thanks, Dr. Brussel."

He moved to dial his phone, but it was already ringing.

"Theo, I've got a name!" Jessica said.

"Let me guess," Theo replied. "He's a technician that repairs the printing press."

"Yes! Did Sloan tell you?"

"Not quite," said Theo.

PINCER MOVEMENT

Sloan McPherson was already waiting for Jessica in a rented SUV in the parking lot at the Virginia Tech Montgomery Executive Airport when her plane landed. From the look on Sloan's face, Jessica sensed that it wasn't going to be good news.

"Fake name," Jessica guessed as soon as she got within earshot.

"Unfortunately," Sloan confirmed as she climbed into the driver's seat. "I take it you tried to search for any record of him too?"

"Yeah," Jessica admitted, "but I was hoping that maybe our junior agents at the FBI might have better resources than we do."

"They came up blank too, although to their credit, they've been very proactive about a physical description from the workers at the other newspaper plants. But there's a problem," Sloan said.

"They don't match?" Jessica asked.

"Well, sort of. It seems like there are two Christian Prescotts, one older than the other, and at some point the younger one showed up and took over for the senior one," Sloan explained.

"A father and son?" Jessica questioned.

"Only if there was an adoption involved, apparently. The older one was described as being Italian or Maltese. The other one, more Nordic and pale-skinned."

"Were they working at the same time?"

"No, actually, only a few people remember the older Christian Prescott. He stopped doing maintenance around eleven years ago. That's when the younger one stepped in, and by younger, I mean younger than him, but right now he should probably be in his early fifties."

"Did you find anything out about the email address?" Jessica asked.

"We're working on that. Best case is we get the address and actual identity of the original Christian Prescott. I'm not so sure if that will connect to the younger."

"What about your lead? The potential boyfriend, Frazier, no last name?"

"I'm thinking about going to Oregon to talk to Emma," said Sloan. "I've got to figure out the right way because I don't want to alert anyone. We haven't told the junior agents yet, which maybe is bad on our part. But my concern is that the moment somebody gets called in for questioning, our suspect's gonna get spooked."

"That's a tricky game," Jessica warned.

"I think we give it forty-eight hours," came Theo's voice from the back seat.

Jessica turned around to see him curled up.

"For crying out loud, warn a girl," she snapped.

"Sorry, I was just thinking."

"Apparently he had a very interesting conversation with one of his imaginary friends," Sloan told Jessica.

"And what came of that?" Jessica asked.

"Aside from me possibly having an avoidance issue when it comes to a mother fixation, maybe some more insight into this person," said Theo. "I talked it over with Brad. By the way, he's on his way to DC right now. He wants to go through some records."

"What records?" Jessica inquired.

"Military records, I think."

"Does he think our guy is ex-military?" she pressed.

"It's a possibility," Theo said. "But after my conversation with Dr. Brussel, I started thinking differently about this person. Clearly he's a mechanical genius of some kind because to pull this off is not something even the average engineer would be capable of doing. Even if he had training, it's extremely complicated. That implies a particular kind of obsessive personality which, if he was in the military, would probably have some behavioral patterns that might stand out. But as you ascertained, this guy is a loner and takes up solitary work that leans heavily into his technical capability. I wonder if fixing these printing presses might not be the only thing that he does. It could be a sideline, given that it's such infrequent work. He might be a specialist in other areas too."

"Have we found any other Christian Prescotts doing specialty technical repairs?" Jessica asked.

"No," Sloan responded. "Probably under another name. Maybe Frazier, for all I know."

"Christian Prescott," Jessica said aloud. "The name sounds . . . contrived."

"Exactly," Sloan replied.

"What does it make you think of?"

"I don't know, an uptight WASP banker?"

"Precisely," Jessica confirmed.

"And the original Christian Prescott didn't exactly fit the New England banker type, did he?"

"No," Sloan said. "Mediterranean look, blue collar, penchant for dirty jokes."

"Which begs the question," Jessica pondered, "Why use a fake name to fix printing presses?"

"Because he can't use his real name," Sloan responded.

"And what line of work do you find criminals who know an awful lot about printing presses?" Jessica pressed.

"Counterfeiting," Sloan breathed. "Damn! I think you're onto something."

"The assumed name would be because under his real name he has a record. We should talk to the Mod Squad and some of my friends at the Secret Service to see if we can't narrow this down a bit. There aren't a whole lot of counterfeiters that would fit that description and that age range with that level of technical skill. Ninety-nine percent of them are just clumsy people with printshop plates or hacked Xerox machines."

"What about the original Christian Prescott?" asked Sloan. "Was he in that line of work too?"

"Maybe," Jessica repeated, "but I'm not so sure."

"It seems like a pretty useful skill to pass on," Sloan suggested.

Jessica nodded. "It's not uncommon for an expert to have an illegitimately acquired skill in one area that they pass on to somebody else in a more legitimate way."

"Okay," Sloan responded, "you're going to have to unpack that one for me."

"I learned card magic from one of my grandfather's friends who was a magician's magician, a bit of an underground legend. But the only place you could ever see him perform would be at a lounge at the Magic Castle in Hollywood. Prior to that, he made a living as a professional card shark—the kind used by the Mafia to get an edge in a game.

"You can have a good run at that for a while, but you have to move around. Once you stop doing that, people pay attention. Either the kind of people that don't take too kindly to getting cheated or the kind with badges. So he entered, well, to be honest with you, it was a semiretirement and focused on the card magic and teaching a younger generation.

"The thing is, he wouldn't teach just anybody. You had to have a knack and an interest to really make use of what he knew. There is a reason why the original Christian Prescott decided to teach Christian

Prescott 2.0. And that was because the younger was probably already pretty sharp."

"How do these people find each other?" Sloan asked.

"Sometimes prison," Theo put in.

"Fair point," Sloan said. "As they say, game recognizes game."

"If not prison, Junior could have met Senior at a swap meet, a club or association, some kind of conference. Who knows? Assuming, of course, that they're not related, which maybe they are. Although it doesn't explain why Junior took on Christian Prescott Sr.'s name unless he had something to hide."

"Brand value?" Sloan suggested.

"I don't know if there's a whole lot of brand value in that. I think the people hiring him just needed somebody who could bang the hammer or whatever he does in the right spot."

"We need to do a pincer movement," Theo said.

"How do you mean?" Sloan asked.

"We need to split up. You should follow this Emma lead and start from what could be his past and work your way forward, while Jessica and I should focus on where he is right now. Jess was right—he was likely quite near Arcadia City when the train derailed."

"Even though he was trying to create nuclear annihilation?" asked Sloan.

"He knew that wasn't a likely outcome," Theo told her. "If he wasn't there during, he was on-site shortly before. Right now, he's either setting up his next stunt or checking to make sure everything is in place. At the very least, getting last looks."

"Are you sure?" Sloan asked.

"Not at all, but I think it's a start. I need to stop focusing on the specific targets. Look for the man, not the next act."

"Well, how do we plan on doing that?" Sloan inquired.

Theo was silent.

"Come to think of it . . . maybe it's nothing, but one of our junior agents said they hadn't had any success turning up hotel records for stays during the run-up to the derailment," Sloan told them. "They did a preliminary search covering the time when our guy last visited the Idaho newspaper plant. There was no Christian Prescott checked in anywhere, which probably shouldn't be a surprise. And they have pretty complete records from every motel and hotel in the area. Still, no matches from our other lists either."

"He could be using a different name in each city," Jessica suggested.

"Possibly," Sloan responded, "but why? It would make more sense to use the same name, given he's using Christian Prescott, or that's how they know him at each of the newspaper facilities. What difference does it make if he checked into a hotel room or not?"

"This guy may have a bit of social anxiety. We can already assume he's a loner. And something else strikes me," Theo said.

"Tools," Jessica intuited. "He's not just going around with a screwdriver. He's got to have a bunch of tools that he uses for his trade. He might be sleeping in his vehicle," she thought aloud.

"Yes," Sloan added. "That would explain no hotel records."

"If you think about it," Jessica replied, "he might have some specialty equipment, other kinds of gear, and that's going to be the lifeblood of his work. And if he's not flying from place to place, it means he's driving."

"But the Arcadia City Police said they didn't spot any RVs or anything like that," Jessica added.

"They could have missed it. They could have parked out of town, but it might not have been an RV."

"True. I knew a magician that used to travel from county fair to county fair with his doves and rabbits and everything else inside of his van, and he slept there too so he could save money on motel rooms. He was also very paranoid about his van getting stolen. That happened to him once before, and he nearly starved," Jessica said.

"Urban camping," Sloan repeated. "My daughter calls me an aquatic urban camper because I spend so much time in my boat. I watched a whole hour of YouTube videos with her of these different setups people have—vans, pickup trucks, innocuous-looking delivery vehicles—all tricked out for camping in cities."

"But disguised not to look like campers to avoid the police," Jessica added.

"Exactly," Sloan agreed.

"A highly technical urban camper with social anxiety," Sloan summed up. "That helps a little bit."

"He might have had a juvenile record for counterfeiting," Theo blurted out. "Possibly sealed. Might be hard to get. But worth looking into."

"Why do you say that?" Sloan asked.

"I don't want to use the *I* word, you know, 'intuition,'" Theo admitted, "but there are several patterns that might be related here. One is that his fixation on systems and indifference toward people could imply some kind of facial blindness—not the traditional kind, because those people behave normally, in some cases are extrasocial—but maybe some kind of psychological tic. My point is that somebody like that might be fixated on faces in their most objective sense. And one of the skills it takes to be a good counterfeiter is the ability to draw dead presidents.

"But he's very smart and probably realized that counterfeiting is more of a distribution game than a technical one. And I would imagine he learned that very quickly early on when he was younger. That being said, it might be how he came across Prescott Sr. Although I don't know how much we need to focus on how the two met," Theo admitted.

"This all makes a lot of sense, except for one thing," Sloan observed.

"What's that?" Jessica asked.

"The bombing connection to Emma, at least the theoretical connection—where they found the ink on the explosives. This Frazier is somebody she met in college, which would make him maybe twenty-five years younger than Christian Prescott 2.0."

"Maybe . . ." Jessica considered. "Did you actually get the age of this guy?"

"No," Sloan replied. "I could have pried a little bit more, but I was afraid of . . . scaring Beth Ann off."

"Not everyone on a college campus is between the ages of eighteen and twenty-two," Theo noted. "I present myself as evidence. You also have staff, you have graduate students, and just people who like to be around universities. But there's also the possibility that Christian Prescott isn't Frazier but Emma or Frazier or both of them know who he is. I think it's a worthwhile lead to chase down."

"Okay," Sloan agreed. "I can talk to my contacts and find out if there's anybody in the local law enforcement that can steer me in the right direction so I'm not running around blind. And it certainly sounds like an easier job than you two are going to have knocking on the door of every parked Econoline van in six states."

"I think we can narrow that down a lot more," Theo said, "with the help of some pattern matching and algorithmic data."

"We could just ask Brad if we could borrow a few drones to map the areas," Jessica suggested.

Theo's eyes lit up. "Oh, yes. That would make things a hell of a lot easier. I can build out a 3D image-matching model, and if we can get license plate data, it would narrow things down considerably."

"I don't want to get too ahead of ourselves here," Sloan said, "but we also have to think about how we need to handle things if we actually find the guy."

"Why is that?" Theo asked.

"Guys who like to make booby traps and bombs generally plan for those kinds of contingencies," Jessica responded from experience. "I think we need to have a conversation with the Mod Squad and anybody else we can on the bureau's response team. Because catching him could be even more dangerous than letting him go."

LOCAL

"First off, it's not exactly a coffee shop," Lieutenant Reginald Billing of the Astoria Police Department said to Sloan McPherson as she sat across the table from him at a Thai restaurant at a marina outside of Astoria, Oregon.

"What do you mean?" asked Sloan, setting down her iced tea.

Pressed for time and realizing she'd have to risk word getting ahead of her, Sloan had found a contact with the local police department she could meet with outside of town to find out more regarding Emma and the mysterious Frazier.

"Well, it used to be a coffee shop up until they changed the marijuana laws. Now the Happy Seagull sells cannabis," Billing explained. "Emma Rafario is the leaseholder and name on the registration forms for the shop. As far as a 'Frazier' goes, I don't recall anybody by that name. But given the kind of crowd she's in . . ." He shrugged.

"What do you mean by 'the kind of crowd'?" Sloan asked.

"You ever see the show *Portlandia*?" Billing replied. "There's a certain type. Nice people, don't get me wrong, but a bit earthy or perhaps too in touch with their feelings."

"How active are they locally?" asked Sloan.

"You mean, do they show up at city council meetings and let their voices be heard? Or walk around with protest signs? Not really. I think there was a permitting issue a while ago when they decided to transition from the coffee shop to selling pot. But beyond that, pretty low-key. We don't exactly have a high tolerance for nonsense here, at least not like in Portland," Billing said. "People come here because they like the ocean, they like to fish, they like the sea, and they like their peace. And as long as everybody's okay with that, we all get along just fine. Now, you didn't say much over the phone. Could you tell me what this is about? Is there any connection to that business up on Cap Island?"

While the mainstream media had largely given up sorting out what took place in Washington state, where Sloan and company had come across a cult leader using social media manipulation to try to socially engineer young people, it continued to make waves among law enforcement in the Northwest.

"No," Sloan replied. "It could be connected to Arcadia City and Mud River."

"The flood in Virginia? I thought that was some kind of computer error."

"Well, the cause of the computer error is what we're looking into. The same with the derailment. We think they might be acts of sabotage."

"My wife and I sat in our house for two days with goddamn N95 masks because of that whole fallout nonsense." Billing sighed.

"Well, hopefully we can prevent something much worse from happening."

"And do you think Emma Rafario is connected to whoever did all that?"

"Not necessarily," said Sloan. "I'm trying to chase down some leads. There was a bombing in her hometown, and we have evidence that connects that to Mud River and Arcadia City, and the battery fire you may have heard about in Florida," she explained. "And it could be coincidence, but we don't want to take that chance."

"I'm not a big believer in coincidences," Billing told her.

"Me neither. And I wouldn't be here if I were. Could you tell me a bit more about Emma?" Sloan asked.

"Nice girl," Billing said. "She's a bit earthy. I think I said that before. Sweet, probably high a lot. I know that generation is on edibles all the time. They're kind of slowly zombifying themselves, but that's their business."

"But not the type that you would associate with violence?"

"No, but I know a lot of nice girls that have really terrible taste in men," Billing remarked.

"What about the men? Any particular ones stand out?"

"There are two men that work with her at the cannabis store or hang out there a lot. I don't really know what the professional arrangement is. One's a taller gentleman, I'd say maybe early thirties. Another one's a little bit younger, maybe mid-twenties. I don't know their names. When I've gone in to check on the paperwork and registration for the shop, it's just been Emma there."

"Is that a scheduled thing?" Sloan asked. "Where you go check on their paperwork?"

"Yes, we give them a heads-up. It's just a formality for the city. Really, there's nothing much we can do because it's a state law, but we just make sure that they're following the guidelines as far as posting signs about age and handling the transactions in an appropriate way—and between you and me, make sure that they're the ones running the store and not some cartel."

"Is that a problem?" Sloan asked.

"You're not from around here, I can tell. Let's put it this way: A number of people running these cannabis shops aren't exactly the kind that would make great bank loan material. Yet somehow they managed to show up with money for the leases, the security deposits, and everything else they need. And I've poked around into this before, and it's because a week before they decided to set up shop, they walked into a bank with a lot of $100 bills."

"Here in Astoria?" Sloan asked.

"No, no, Portland and other places. I'm on a task force that handles some of the regional crime that's created by that situation. It's one of the things that doesn't get a lot of attention in the media."

"What can you tell me about Emma socially?" Sloan asked.

"I've seen her and some of her friends in restaurants. She's not a member of my church. I think a lot of her social life is probably outside of Astoria."

"Any known reason why she ended up here?" Sloan asked.

"No idea. Sometimes people just end up here because there's an ocean on the other side and there's no place else to go. Some people just like the community. I don't really know her that well other than a few interactions, so I can't really tell you as to why. Far as I know, she doesn't have any family here or any other connections. Could have been a boyfriend or something, but I don't know."

"I know this is a big ask, but do you have a local database or any kind of electronic record system that we could have access to, particularly for motor vehicle incidents, accidents, tickets, running red lights, that kind of thing?" Sloan asked.

"Yeah, it's a billion years old, but we have something like that. Anything you're looking for in particular? I could maybe search for it," Billing offered.

"No, it's more looking for patterns in the data. I have a friend that can parse through that on the odd chance that somebody Emma knew, that we'd be interested in, is in there in some way. To be honest, any detail or small point could be helpful," Sloan added with a smile.

Billing studied her for a moment. "You seem like a straight shooter," he said. "And I'll be a little more transparent. The two guys she has in the shop, I don't like them. Younger guy, bit of an idiot. The other guy, the older one, he's a hothead. He's never had an altercation with me. But I've just seen him on the street and passed him when he's coming from or going to there. And you get a look. You're a cop. I think you know what I mean. Not enough to fully cross the line, but something that lets you know how they feel."

"Not you personally but the uniform?" Sloan asked.

"Exactly," Billing replied. "He doesn't see the person; he just sees what he thinks it represents. But it's never been a problem. Doesn't have to like me, doesn't have to like the other people in the police force; just has to not break the law, and you can think or give me all the dirty looks you want."

"Thank you," Sloan replied. "I would appreciate any help you can give us, plus your discretion. I want to go talk to her, but I'm doing it unofficially, if you understand."

"Not a problem," said Billing. "I'll let you know about those records." He paused for a moment, then looked at her. "You might want to consider dressing a little bit differently."

Sloan glanced down at her jacket and slacks. "This kind of says cop, doesn't it? Do you know if there's a secondhand store nearby?"

THE HAPPY SEAGULL

As Sloan entered the Happy Seagull Cannabis Dispensary, she could immediately see that it was stuck between its bohemian coffeehouse vibes and an attempt at a clinical, almost Apple Store aesthetic.

The chalkboard-painted walls were covered in colorful 1970s-style illustrations of smiling faces, happy suns, and neon flowers. While in front of them stood sterile-looking LED-lit cabinets filled with clear plastic boxes of marijuana with imaginative brand names like Matthew McConaug-high, Fred Flintstoned, and Blunt to the Future.

A heavyset twentysomething man sitting on a stool wearing a navy-blue hoodie was thumbing through his phone.

Sloan took five steps into the store before he even glanced up and noticed she was there. He made an audible grunt that could have been a hello, but Sloan wasn't sure.

"Hello," she said in a friendly tone.

He glanced over his shoulder through a doorway to his left, then responded, "Welcome, how can I help you?"

"I'm just curious," Sloan said. "Do you mind if I look around a little bit?"

"Yeah, sure. If you have any questions, just ask us," he replied.

"Oh," Sloan said, acting surprised. "I thought this was your place."

He shook his head. "No, I just help out my friend Emma," he said, nodding toward the other room.

A moment later, Emma Rafario stepped to the doorway with a warm smile.

"Hi there. If you have any questions, let us know," she offered.

Sloan had combed through Emma's practically nonexistent social media. She'd had a Facebook account in college but deleted it after the incident with the bombing in her hometown. There were a few entries in poetry websites that matched her name and a related alias, but other than that, she was almost entirely invisible online.

In Sloan's world, this was a sign of either really strong social hygiene or somebody who was trying to hide something.

Emma was dressed in blue jeans and a plaid shirt with the sleeves rolled up. Her hair was pinned back, and she wore a minimal amount of makeup. She looked a little bit older and wearier than in the photos Sloan had seen but still had the same smile and observant eyes.

"Do you have any particular preference?" Emma asked.

Sloan set down a box with the label MOONLIGHT CHILL. "I'm going to be completely honest," she said, being completely dishonest. "I've only done this a few times at parties, and I couldn't tell you what it was I smoked. But I was thinking about getting something for my anxiety."

"Anxiety," Emma said. "Well, pretty much any of this will take the edge off. I got it from here, David," she told her employee.

"Cool," he replied, then got up, picked up his backpack from a corner, and walked out the door without another word.

"Family?" Sloan asked after he left.

Emma replied, "Sort of. I inherited him. I was about to make a cup of tea. Would you like some?"

"That'd be very kind," Sloan replied, then asked hesitantly, "What kind of tea?"

Emma let out a laugh. "Just Earl Grey."

"Sure."

Emma disappeared into the other room. Sloan could hear the sound of an electric kettle warming up. She took the opportunity to explore the shop.

In addition to the clear plastic boxes with marijuana buds, there was a wall filled with different kinds of gummies in bright, colorful packages.

While Sloan didn't have any strong ethical problems with the consumption of cannabis and felt that it would be hypocritical given her love of beer, she was a little bit disturbed by the almost kid-friendly design of the products. She was staring at a comic book–style illustration of a green Norse god called Green Thunder that narrowly skirted IP infringement when Emma returned with two mugs.

"How long have you been dealing with anxiety?" Emma asked as she handed Sloan a cup.

In that one gesture, Sloan had a pretty good idea who Emma was as a person, and she liked her. She was the motherly type who sought to help lost souls.

"It comes and goes, you know, kind of life events," Sloan said. "I've had to do a lot of travel with work lately, and that's not been easy. I've been away from my kid and my husband, and just kind of in general feel like I'm not giving everybody enough."

"I know that feeling. Do you live around here?" asked Emma.

"No. I'm from Florida."

"Oh," Emma replied. "They're not as open-minded as we are about a lot of things."

"The beaches are amazing and the water is beautiful. Everywhere's got politics," Sloan replied, not wanting to enter a conversation about different political environments.

"What brought you out here?" Emma asked.

Sloan was impressed with Emma's natural ability to ask probing questions without any apparent agenda. "I work with a tour company, and I was scouting locations," she said.

This was an easy lie for her because it was hard to check up on it. The tour company could be an idea in her head, something she worked on with a friend, or a private enterprise.

"That sounds like fun," Emma said, "but I guess it gets boring after a while."

"It does, although after too much time at home, I want to be on the road again." She shrugged. "How about you? Do you have any children?"

"Not yet. I'm still trying to decide if settling down is for me."

"Living alone must be nice in some ways."

"Oh, I don't live alone. I've got four roommates."

"Ah, do you live here in town?" asked Sloan.

"A few miles outside of it in a little farmhouse."

"That sounds charming."

"It can be. Everything's falling apart, but it's nice to have my morning coffee in a field and watch sunsets to the sound of crickets."

This sounded like a commune to Sloan, but she didn't want to ask too many prying questions and set off alarm bells. Still . . . Sloan wasn't anything close to the actor Jessica Blackwood was, but it was time to take a chance.

She set her mug on the counter in front of her, clasped her hands, put on a forced smile, let it break, then let her gaze drift to the ground as if a sudden weight had fallen upon her shoulders.

"Are you okay?" Emma asked.

"I'm great," Sloan said, forcing a smile. "Just a little tired. Sorry."

"Sometimes it helps to talk to a stranger," Emma said.

"I don't want to burden you," Sloan replied. "I'd be happy to just buy something."

"Well, I'm not going to let you purchase anything, so that's not even an issue right now. You don't know me, so it can just go in one ear and out the other if that makes you feel better."

"My kid hates me. Now that she's off to college, that's fine. It makes it easier. My husband is on another prolonged work trip, which I don't think is really a work trip. There's nobody for me to go home to. And even if there were, this is going to sound terrible, but I don't want to go there. I've just been killing time. But I can't extend this trip any more because my boss is going to murder me over the hotel expenses."

Emma set her mug down and reached out, clasping Sloan's hand. "We got plenty of space. I'll give you a room of your own if you want to hang out for a couple days. You might have to clean some dishes and cook something, because everybody's sick of my meatloaf. But no pressure."

Sloan could tell it was an earnest gesture. Emma overflowed with human empathy. Her willingness to take in a stray she'd met twenty minutes ago was proof of that. This made Sloan even more certain that Emma and the saboteur had crossed paths, because even the most damaged soul would not be beyond her obvious tenderness.

"Yeah. That might be fun. I make a pretty good spaghetti and sausage," said Sloan. "At least my kid thought so when she still talked to me." Sloan had no intention of taking Emma up on the full slumber party. But she figured that after dinner and a few beers, she could probably get the woman to open up fully and tell her story.

"Did you drive here?" Emma asked.

"Yeah," Sloan replied. "I'm parked a couple blocks away."

"Great. I'm going to close up here in about forty minutes, and you can be my ride. We can also stop at the grocery store along the way. I'm warning you, we're going to have to have a couple vegan options when it comes to the sausage. One of my housemates is kind of particular. I used to be, but I really started to miss the taste of meat."

Sloan had been so committed to her role-play she hadn't realized her phone was buzzing in her purse. She had shut off all notifications except for ones from her teammates.

"Let me just text my boss and let him know," said Sloan.

"Sure thing," said Emma.

Sloan glanced down at her phone and saw three words from Brad Trasker:

GET OUT NOW!

She placed her phone back into the purse she had bought forty minutes prior at a thrift store and said as calmly as possible, "Perfect. I'll see you in a little while."

Sloan turned around and headed for the door as a black SUV with a flashing blue police light pulled up to the front. She continued through the door and proceeded down the sidewalk, pretending not to notice.

But she was too late.

Two men in tactical SWAT gear with the letters DEA were running at her from the opposite direction.

The man closest to her screamed, "On the ground now!"

PROJECT MAPPING

Jessica and Theo were lying on the floor of the motel room staring up at the ceiling, onto which Theo was projecting surveillance photos from various cities where they were searching for the saboteur's trail.

Brad, through a source he wouldn't name, had managed to get them satellite images of Arcadia City, the StarPower Ultra Battery Facility plant in Orlando, and the Mud River dam, all taken within twenty-four hours of each site's attack.

"This looks a lot clearer than the images he sent you," Jessica said, pointing to the finely rendered buildings and cars.

"I was able to get the raw image data, calculate the motion blur from the satellite, and use that to generate a stereoscopic effect to give me a depth map," Theo explained.

"Do you think his people should know about that method?" she asked.

"I found it on Hacker News," Theo replied. "Some high school kid came up with it. I'm sure they know. If they don't, I don't know how much me telling them will help. They've got other problems."

Theo raised his hand in the air, and the camera on his laptop tracked the position of his fingers as he twisted them. Above them, the map turned in three-dimensional space, making the vehicles more distinct.

Brad had told them he would have drones dispatched within the next few hours to get new data, including license plates, at the relevant locations. This could be helpful if their saboteur was still on the scene. For now, the historic imagery they had wasn't clear enough to make out anything other than the make and model of cars.

While Theo had a lot of faith in the AI and algorithm methods he was using to scan through the gigabytes of data, he'd asked Jessica to help him out because she saw things that he still couldn't train an AI to detect.

"What are you thinking?" Theo asked.

"For weeks during the 2002 Beltway Sniper attacks, everybody was looking for vans and cargo trucks," Jessica said, "because that's what made the most sense. A lone shooter on top of a vehicle provided a height advantage that would be the clear choice of anyone in law enforcement trying to take those sniper shots. The problem was that when we went back and looked at the forensic data—the entrance and exit wounds and places on the ground and buildings where the bullets struck—the trajectories painted a different picture. Yet we ignored it because it didn't make any sense."

"They were shooting from a Caprice with a hollowed-out trunk, right?"

"Exactly. The killers weren't thinking like cops. They were thinking like people trying to stay away from the police and avoid detection. Everyone was baffled about how the shooter could keep moving from location to location without being detected when every law enforcement agency in several states was searching and looking at any van or truck they could find, including putting up roadblocks everywhere. But the shooters were able to pass right through because nobody was looking for a sedan."

Thus far, Theo's algorithm had found 137 RVs and mobile campers in proximity to the attacks when the saboteur had likely been there.

They had turned this information over to the FBI, which was in the process of sorting through credit card receipts and gas station footage, trying to identify the vehicles' owners.

Neither Jess nor Theo was optimistic about that line of inquiry. Nobody in Arcadia City had recalled an RV, which would have stood out in a small town. The same could be said for the battery plant, and the footage hadn't yielded anything yet. In the case of the plant, they had less of an idea of when the saboteur came on-site. The best they could hope for was spotting an RV in one of the surveillance cameras, given that they had no immediate way to identify the hundreds of workers and other personnel who had been to the facility since it had been constructed.

Theo and Jessica had decided to start looking at trucks with camper tops and other vehicles that urban campers might use, including vans masquerading as work vehicles.

One telltale sign that a van was being used for something other than ordinary tools and goods was the presence of a sophisticated air-conditioning unit on the roof. Theo's algorithm found forty-three vans that matched that description but none they could place at multiple locations within the time frames.

"Okay, we have RVs, which we don't think our guy is using, and we have work vans. Some of them look similar, but we have enough features to differentiate them. But we don't have any that we can place at all of the locations, or enough locations, for us to have confidence it's the same one," Jessica said aloud. "Are we missing something else?"

"Clearly," Theo said. "That's why I asked you to help me."

"I know, I know. I'm not sure if lying on the floor like this is the best thing for my back."

"Says the girl that spent half her life curled up in a box so she could be sawed in half," Theo remarked.

"First, that was only a short period of my life, and second, I was usually the one doing the sawing. But yes, there were other boxes I had to crawl inside of, thus my back not liking anything I put it through, other than a long massage."

"He could have magnetic signs that he rotates," Theo observed.

"Maybe," Jessica replied, "but it would still look the same from the top, right? Unless he's expecting satellite surveillance, which I think is probably even too paranoid for this guy."

"Yes, we're not really going to pick up any signage from these images. There's just not enough data. How did your magician friend stay anonymous?" Theo asked.

"Professor Jester. It was just an old light-blue van. Nothing on the sides. I think he put some cardboard on the windows, torn around the edges, so you kind of assumed a vagrant lived inside," Jessica said. "Which is a thought . . . See, he wasn't afraid of the police as much as kids or gangs breaking into his van and stealing his things. I think years before he'd been a reserve officer, so he wasn't wary of getting pulled over. He was a very likable guy—the kind of person that could do a magic trick to get himself out of a situation. His bigger concern was making it look like there was nothing of value inside his van."

"Compares with our saboteur, who is also actively avoiding detection, albeit from the police. What would Professor Jester do if he was trying to avoid cops?"

Jessica thought this over as Theo rotated the image yet again and started flying through the terrain, like with Google Street View.

"Well, if he wanted to avoid the police *and* anyone stealing from him, he would make the van look like something that belonged there but wasn't high value," she said. "Which can be hard because you're dealing with people that will literally steal the copper wire out of streetlamps. One thing is to put an animal in there to protect it, but that means you got to leave a yappy dog in there. And it doesn't do anything to avoid police . . ."

"Okay, we're asking the wrong question," Theo said. "This guy's *really* smart, right?"

"Yes. I'm not sure how that changes the answer."

"Well, I think it will in a moment," Theo replied. "I want you to tell me what *you* would do if you had to move from town to town, have someplace to put your head down to sleep, yet avoid the cops and getting ripped off."

"In that case," she said, "I would probably approach things the same way as the Beltway Snipers. Although ideally I wouldn't sleep in my vehicle because some towns don't take kindly to that, even if you're as charming as Professor Jester. Which our suspect is not." She thought a moment more. "Yeah . . . I don't want anyone to even notice the vehicle."

"What about a minivan with tinted windows for privacy?" Theo tried.

"Well, I think we're back to the same problem. You would look at a minivan and know that somebody could be sleeping inside. And if you're trying to avoid vagrancy laws and suspicion, you wouldn't go that route. Plus, a minivan with tinted windows is an attractive target if somebody wants to steal from you. Remember that he travels with tools. And I don't have a list yet from the printing facilities of what he would have brought with him, but I'm sure it wouldn't be a tiny toolbox. Not to mention the fact that he's toting around whatever he might need for his next sabotage."

"Okay, assume he has a vehicle no one notices, so he sleeps in it and avoids leaving a trail of motel stays. So . . . we need a vehicle that has enough space for a toilet, maybe a shower and a bunk, and tools, yet doesn't look like a van or RV," Theo concluded. "Are we chasing Doctor Who?"

"That's not a crazy idea," Jessica said. "You ever hear about the Jarrett Cabinet?"

"Was that a magic trick?" Theo asked.

"Guy Jarrett was a brilliant magic creator. One of the first inventors who wasn't specifically a performer, just someone who created magic for other people. He had a very unconventional approach. The Jarrett Cabinet was an illusion where the magician would open the curtain of the cabinet and a person would step out, and then another and another and another. Of course, the magician would never show you the interior of the cabinet. But what still made it magical was the sheer number of people that kept coming out, which forced you to think not where they were coming from, which would happen with a mirror box or some other method. No, instead you were wondering *how* they could all possibly fit inside there. And just when you thought there was no way there could be any more people inside the cabinet, more would step out until the stage was filled with people that had presumably been inside it. Now, one of the subtricks was, as people were coming out of the cabinet, the magician would usher in more folks from the wings in all the chaos, increasing the total count. But still, the cabinet seemed to hold an impossible number of people."

"What was the secret?" Theo asked.

"There was none. He shoved all the people inside of the cabinet. That was the beautiful thing about the illusion. You didn't think that that many people could fit inside of there."

"So are you saying our guy's crammed himself inside a clown car?"

"No, although for a hot minute I did entertain the idea that he might be a little person. But I think that would probably have attracted attention. I guess what I'm trying to say is . . . I think our saboteur is using some kind of illusion."

"Some kind of urban camouflage?" Theo probed.

"No, I think he's using some form of magic trick or some sort of visual deception. Clearly, we're missing something." She made a moaning sound as she climbed to her feet.

"Where are you going?"

"To do some research," she said.

"At the library?"

"No, I'm going to the café to look at YouTube videos for a while."

STUNTWOMAN

Brad Trasker was leaning across the conference room table of the Portland FBI office, glaring at Nicholas Zhao.

Sitting next to the young agent was a senior FBI supervisor named Matilda Diamante.

"Watch your tone," she snapped at Brad.

"I'm sorry, what tone should I use for this dumbfuck operation that could have jeopardized everything?"

"I'm sorry," said Nicholas. "They were pressing me for something actionable. And given the limited amount of time we have, this seemed like a good idea."

"I can tell you where a lot of good ideas are dead and buried in deserts and jungles around the world because idiots like you two decided to second-guess the people on the ground," Brad fumed.

"With all due respect, Mr. Trasker," Diamante responded, "your blunt-force approach towards things isn't how we do things here."

"You literally sent in a DEA SWAT team under false pretenses to raid a cannabis shop and a farm while Sloan McPherson was in gaining the confidence of our most important material witness," Brad stated.

"I'm sorry, *your* most important witness? Could you remind me what law enforcement agency you work for?" Diamante countered.

"How many phone calls do you think it would take for me to get reinstated or deputized?" Brad shot back.

"More than I have time or patience for," Diamante said. "I'm speaking to you out of courtesy."

"I convinced them to at least arrest McPherson," Nicholas interjected.

"And how exactly is that doing us a favor?" asked Brad.

"Well, to the suspects, she looks like a witness or a suspect herself. I was thinking at the very least we could protect her undercover status."

Diamante cut in. "She has no undercover status. She's not even assigned to this case. She's a Florida police investigator. And last I checked, this isn't Florida."

"Last I checked, you wouldn't even be here if it wasn't for her," Brad said, staring at Nicholas. "Which, by the way: How did you know to come here? Were we being surveilled? Were you tracking her phone?"

Diamante raised a hand to keep Nicholas from speaking. "That's not important right now. What is is the fact that we have two people under arrest: Emma Rafario and Francis Zapier."

"Who the hell is Francis Zapier?" asked Brad.

"We were going to explain that to you, but instead you barged in here and started yelling at Agent Zhao. If you'll have a seat, as a courtesy, I'll tell you," Diamante said, "but if you're going to stand there trying to intimidate us with your tough-guy antics, we can have you escorted out of here and on your way."

Brad understood when it was time to raise hell and when it was time to shut up and listen. With almost sociopathic ease, he relaxed and sat. "Okay, explain."

"Based upon the Emma Rafario connection," Nicholas said, "we were able to create a social graph of the different people she knew and their connections, then look for high-contrast nodes. One that stood out is Francis Zapier. He was enrolled in a political science master's program when Emma was on campus."

"Something tells me that he wasn't studying just so he could go work on campaign finance reform," Brad replied.

"Correct. I guess the more accurate term is 'political agitator.' He would probably call himself a social justice advocate. Regardless, we found photographs of him in at least seventeen different protests that turned violent within the past fourteen years, half of which involved the use of pipe bombs or other incendiary devices. He had been called in for questioning at least four times but released in each case for insufficient evidence and demonstrated harm."

"It sounds like lazy policing," Brad assessed.

"Unfortunately," Diamante agreed. "Prosecutors are generally happy if the person promises to leave town, or at least not show up again until the next protest. Whenever they try to prosecute people in situations like this, when it's a protest tied to a popular cause, there's usually an influx of dipshit do-gooder attorneys eager to stick it to 'the man' and defend these assholes. And unless there's enough serious physical damage or a victim that's been maimed or killed, it's not deemed worth the hassle and they plead to reduced or no sentences."

"So they can do the same asshole thing at the next protest," Brad added.

Diamante sighed. "Pretty much."

Brad knew a lot more about political agitation than he felt like bringing up in the conversation. Most of the time, his agitation had advanced some US security goal for better or worse, and it took place in other countries. Experience had shown that it wasn't terribly difficult to get a bunch of young people riled up, particularly if there was a big university nearby.

"So, this Francis Zapier . . . tell me more," he requested.

"We think Francis Zapier is where the name 'Frazier' comes from," Nicholas said. "FR and then Zier. We're tracking down people who know him to get confirmation."

"And what do you think his connection is to the saboteur?" Brad pressed.

"We think he *is* the saboteur," Diamante said.

"I'm sorry, run this by me again. You think a guy that's been hanging out on college campuses in a political science program, just so he can hook up with college girls and cosplay as a freedom fighter—*he's* our guy?" Brad asked incredulously.

"Why are you so skeptical?" Nicholas countered.

"Does this Francis Zapier have any technical background? Was he an engineering student before his political science program? Did he even enter a science fair as a kid?"

"We're still looking into that," Diamante replied.

Nicholas added, "From our profiles, we know it's becoming more complex to determine somebody's skills relative to whatever their trade is. We have people who are incredibly capable computer hackers who hold down warehouse jobs. I've learned quite a lot of things online that weren't taught to me in school."

"I'm sure you have," Brad sighed. "How did you pull off the arrest?"

"We have records from the cannabis dispensary with Zapier's signature next to statements that he had never been charged with a felony—which is technically false," Diamante explained.

Brad shook his head. "I think 'technically' is the right word here, as in, a technicality. And I don't know if you realize who Emma Rafario's mother is, but I won't expect either of them to be talking anytime soon. And when they finally do, it'll be with an incredibly expensive attorney defending them, followed by a civil lawsuit."

"Well, if your team's estimates are correct, Mr. Trasker, we're out of time and out of options. Getting him into custody seemed like the smart thing to do," said Diamante.

"And that's the problem," Brad shot back. "It was not the smart thing to do. You could have given Sloan more time."

"How much time?" asked Diamante. "Do you know if she'd made any progress?"

"How *could* I know? You arrested her. And I haven't heard from her since before she went to go speak with Emma Rafario. Do *you* know if she was making progress?" Brad shot back.

"I think there's a good chance we can get Rafario to talk with the right pressure."

"I think you're kidding yourself. Her mother's a judge. She knows her rights. The last time she got into a scrape, her mother cleaned things up and she disappeared. I don't think this is going to be any different."

There was a knock at the door.

"What is it?" shouted Diamante.

An agent popped his head in. "I got bad news and worse news."

"What is it, Brian?" Diamante growled.

"She's asking for an attorney, and it turns out the kid who worked at the shop—we missed him. He saw what went down and made a couple phone calls."

"To whom?" Diamante asked.

"Apparently, Emma Rafario's mom is pretty politically connected. We already got a call from headquarters in DC that unless we have something real, we better let her go soon. As in, in the next hour."

"Goddamn it," Diamante said, slapping her hand on the table. "Do they understand the situation here? That's bullshit."

"Well, that was the bad part. I got the worse news for you. This Zapier guy, we can't hold him either."

"Did they say that too?" Diamante asked.

"In as many words . . . apparently he's got some pretty high-powered legal representation. And they're going to be inbound sooner than later. We might be able to hold him a little bit longer, but that guy's not talking to us. He knows the routine."

"Come on. This guy could be a potential terrorist. We basically rewrote the Constitution for cases like this," Diamante said.

"They said we'll have to let him go, but they also said there's no reason why we couldn't keep him under surveillance. Maybe that's the better approach. I've already spoken to one of our judges about a warrant—we can tap his phone, we can bug the farmhouse before they get back. We at least have that option."

"What if he runs?"

"I think we can create a pretty good box and keep him under visual surveillance without him knowing. If he tries to duck that, well, then we have another reason to stop him."

"I hate this," said Diamante.

"You have another option," Brad said.

"And what's that?" asked Diamante.

"Sloan McPherson—let her finish what she was doing."

"We could make sure Emma knows we questioned her," suggested Nicholas. "For cover."

"No," Brad replied. "Emma and Zapier would see right through that. We've got to be a little more subtle. Actually, we've got to be a little more brutal."

Sloan McPherson was sitting in an interrogation room at the other side of the floor, staring at her own reflection in the one-way mirror. She couldn't name which annoyed her more: the situation she was in or the angry expression on her face that she couldn't control.

The door unlocked from the outside and Brad Trasker stepped inside.

"Could you give us a moment?" he said to the agent in the hallway. He took the seat across from Sloan. "How you doing, kiddo?"

"What the hell happened?"

"Long story short, the Mod Squad was keeping closer tabs on us than we expected. They tracked you all the way here and then got nervous and decided to pull this little stunt so they could get Emma and her boyfriend Zapier, also known as Francis Zapier, a.k.a. 'Frazier,' into custody and question them."

"Did they realize who her mother is?" Sloan asked.

"They know now. They're already getting phone calls from headquarters because as strained as the mother-daughter relationship is, Mom is pissed."

"So now what?"

"Well, there's a possible fix to the situation. And that's going to come down to you. They've already asked Emma all kinds of questions about our saboteur, assuming that this Francis Zapier is our guy."

"Is he?" asked Sloan.

"I don't know," Brad replied. "Doesn't fit the type to me. No engineering background, nothing to suggest he had any technical capability. Just an immature guy who can't get over the fact that he's not twenty-one anymore and thinks he's going to change the system with a protest sign, the occasional pipe bomb, and a tolerance for pepper spray."

Sloan sighed.

"But I think he knows where our saboteur is," Brad added. "The bombs placed around Emma's hometown—that could be Zapier. My guess is our saboteur is somebody they met and convinced to build the bombs for Zapier to let loose on Springfield's poor unsuspecting statues."

"So what do I need to do?"

"Here's the way I see it. This Emma might know everything we need to find out and could talk under the right circumstances. This Francis Zapier, on the other hand, I don't think he's going to say anything, especially if he's the guy that planted those statue bombs. But the two of them have not talked to each other yet. They were arrested separately:

Emma at the dispensary and Francis at the farmhouse. Apparently, FBI got a search warrant for that but didn't find anything. They're going to be running swabs to see if they can find our ink. But here's what we can do right now: We can tell them both they're going to be released, release her before Francis, hold him for as long as we can, and drive Francis back home as slowly as we can. Maybe the vehicle breaks down. That would buy you a few hours with Emma if you think that's enough time to get her to speak," Brad explained.

"It would have been if they hadn't pulled this stupid stunt. It's not going to work now. How would she trust me?"

"We need her to feel like you're not part of this," Brad replied. "And even more so, we need her to feel guilty about getting you involved."

"And how would we do that?"

"I've sent one of the FBI kids to the drugstore to pick up some makeup. I can give you a pretty convincing black eye, and nothing will gain you more sympathy with her faster than the words 'police brutality.'"

"So you're saying I fake a black eye and we tell Emma that I got roughed up and let go?"

"Pretty much. I can go in and explain it to her in a way that'll be convincing. At the moment, I don't trust the Keystone Kops to pull that off. And as far as she knows, I'm an FBI agent. Wouldn't be the first time I've had to pretend to be one."

"Then what?" asked Sloan.

"I can get the two of you in a car together. We put her in a situation where she thinks that you've been victimized and feels horrible about it. You'll have to take it from there. Okay?"

"You think you can set that up?"

"I've done almost this exact same scenario more than once. The trick is you selling the black eye and convincing her to tell you what you need to know."

"I'm not so sure about the makeup part," said Sloan.

"If she doesn't see the physical damage, it's not going to be as convincing. Because then it's just a story. We need her to see the story with her own eyes and then put it together."

"No, I get that," said Sloan. "I'm just saying I don't think we should be using makeup. We need to do this for real."

"Really?" asked Brad, something like respect in his expression.

"Yeah. I mean, how did you do it before? Not makeup? Right?"

"Not quite, but the stakes were higher."

"Higher than this?"

"I was afraid you were going to say that," Brad murmured.

She shrugged. "It's the only way we pull this off."

"Your husband will kill me."

"Brother, I have been chopped up by propellers, chomped by alligators, shot, drowned, and suffered every type of bodily damage you can imagine. This is a light day at the office," Sloan said.

Brad let out a long breath. "Do you want me to get you some aspirin first?"

"Do we have time for that?" She raised her chin. "Just get it over with."

SECRETS

"Those assholes are gonna pay big-time," Emma Rafario shouted as she barged into the conference room where Sloan was waiting.

Sloan wasn't aware of everything Brad had told Emma in the hallway, but she knew he was setting her up for the grand lie.

Sloan was perfectly fine immersing herself in a hundred feet of water with the weight of the ocean above her but not as comfortable immersing herself in a lie.

She tried to take her cues from the effortless way in which Brad manipulated and deceived Emma.

He could have been a great actor, Sloan thought. He had the quality of being both convincing but also not confusing himself in the role. She had seen him snap out of characters before, and watching the man who had only a short while before explained the harsh reality of how they were going to have to pull this cynical stunt off turn into an almost obsequious, mousy civil servant profusely apologizing for a situation that got out of hand was fascinating.

"Jesus Christ!" Emma exclaimed as she saw Sloan's black eye.

"It's not that bad," Sloan pretended.

Emma wrapped her arms around Sloan and gave her a warm hug. "I'm so sorry you had to go through this bullshit."

"I'm still not sure what happened," Sloan began the lie. "I walked outside and the next thing you know I'm face down on the sidewalk."

"They got the wrong name on a warrant," Emma explained. "Can you believe that bullshit?" She cast a glance over her shoulder toward the doorway where Brad was waiting on the other side. "Imbeciles," she muttered.

Emma knew that wasn't why they had raided the dispensary to begin with. In their interrogation of her, the FBI had asked about Frazier and connections to the Arcadia City and Mud River incidents.

That Emma was trying to pretend this was all some clerical mistake was a red flag to Sloan—the question was whether Emma was withholding information because she was embarrassed about her past or because she knew more than she was letting on.

All Sloan knew for certain was that she was in the presence of two liars: Brad, a professional, and Emma, a natural—the latter now trying to save face or protect someone. Could Sloan keep up with her own charade?

"I thought I did something wrong," Sloan said.

"You just picked the wrong day, sweetheart," Emma replied. "You didn't do anything wrong at all. I feel terrible. The offer's still open if you need a place to hang out. I'll get these assholes to give us a ride back."

"That would be great. I'm really exhausted." Sloan lowered her voice. "But I have to tell you something."

"Not now," Emma cut her off. "We'll talk later." She pointed toward the ceiling. "You don't know if these jerks are listening or not."

Sloan was absolutely positive that Brad was listening just outside the door, but simply responded, "Okay."

❧

Brad had convinced the FBI SAC to let him continue the ruse by driving the pair back to Emma's dispensary and Sloan's vehicle.

As he drove, Emma and Sloan sat in the back of the FBI vehicle in silence, although Emma was furiously texting on her phone.

The ibuprofen tablets Sloan had taken weren't quite strong enough to overcome the dull ache she was feeling around her cheekbone. She had done enough martial arts and taken enough falls and blows to know the difference between a punch designed to break bones and one just meant to bruise. And while her skull wasn't fractured, the contusion hurt like hell. She wondered what else was in Brad's bag of tricks but was also a little scared to find out.

She caught Emma glancing at her occasionally, then shaking her head, muttering, and clasping Sloan's hand to reassure her. An hour into the drive, Emma asked Sloan for her phone number to add it to her contacts. A few minutes later, Sloan got a text from Emma:

> Spoke to my mom she is a really important judge. These guys have no idea how much they fucked up. We need to take some photos of your face if that's okay. There could be some $$$ in this for you!

When they finally arrived at the dispensary, Brad stopped the car, turned around, and faced the two of them.

"Ma'am," he said to Sloan, "I just want to apologize again for the clumsy way this was handled. You have my card. Let me know if there's anything else I can do. I just want you to know that the agents involved are good people and feel terrible about this."

"Oh, do they have black eyes right now?" Emma snapped back. "Is that how terrible they feel? Because just look at her fucking face, for

Christ's sake. You know, she knows, and I know. You guys fucked up big. Big. Like, this is probably the end of your career, so enjoy however many minutes you have left of it, because I am going to make the phone call that's going to end you and the whole goddamn bureau."

Brad shifted from apologetic to slightly more aggressive. "Well, then you just have to do what you have to do. This is your stop," he said curtly.

"You asshole," Emma replied. "You have no idea the world of trouble you're in, you dumb son of a bitch."

"Ma'am, if you're trying to make a threat, could you please articulate it clearly to me? Because then we can handle this differently," Brad said with a glare, pretending to be irritated.

"Oh, we're good," Emma shot back. "Come on. Let's go, Jennifer," she said, using the fake name Sloan had given her with her phone contact info.

Emma waited for the taillights of Brad's vehicle to fade in the distance before raising a middle finger and shouting, "Fuck you."

Sloan realized a lot of this was performative theater on Emma's part. She was trying to present herself as this strong, bad boss bitch. Sloan suspected it was mostly for her benefit, but maybe also for Emma's sense of self. Still, it struck her as overcompensating.

As far as Sloan could tell, Brad's tactic to get Emma to trust her had worked perfectly. The deception seemed to have transferred any suspicion about Sloan into anger at Brad and the FBI.

"Let's go get your car," Emma said after she had calmed down.

Sloan was grateful that the role she had to perform would benefit from long periods of protracted silence, which Emma would read as shock. But she suspected that wasn't going to get Emma to open up to her. Now that she had made herself a victim for Emma to protect, she had to become her confidant.

After they climbed into Sloan's rental car, she leaned forward, head on the steering wheel, and closed her eyes. She was trying to figure out what she needed to say next, but outwardly it appeared like she needed a moment to collect herself.

Sloan could feel Emma's reassuring hand massaging her neck.

"Let's go get some wine. And then I'm gonna make that phone call I threatened him with. My mom and I don't get along so well, but . . . when we do, watch out. She's always had my back."

An hour later, Sloan and Emma were sitting on the back porch of the farmhouse looking at the weeds as they swayed in the nighttime breeze.

The conversation had mostly consisted of a rant by Emma on the people of Astoria, the police, the authorities, and all the assholes she had encountered in her life.

She had noticeably avoided talking about the specifics of their arrest and detainment.

There had been a brief five-minute phone call where Emma had spoken to her mother, explaining the broad strokes of what had just happened. She also insisted on taking a photograph of Sloan's face to send so she could see the bruises. Sloan was nervous that her mother might have seen some of the news from South Florida and could connect her to that, so she made it a point to cover her face with the exception of the bruise as if to present it more closely to the camera.

Sloan knew there were a thousand holes in the plan that would become apparent once Emma and her mother and whatever attorneys they were speaking to started to pick things apart.

She also knew that didn't matter because time was not on their side.

"I'm sorry," Sloan said, taking small sips of her wine—enough to be convincing, but not so much that she got herself too loose.

Emma was already on her second glass. "Sorry for what?"

"Can I tell you something?" Sloan said after a long moment of silence.

"You can tell me anything," Emma replied.

"I thought they were after me," Sloan said.

"Why would they be after you?" asked Emma.

"Well," Sloan started to say, letting her voice trail off for a moment, "it's kind of complicated. I wasn't fully honest with you—I mean, I wasn't dishonest with you," she lied, "but there was a little bit more to why I don't want to go back home."

"What's that?" asked Emma.

"My husband," Sloan said with a sigh. "We're not really on speaking terms. Things got complicated. I could try to tell you the story one way where I look like the good person, but there are a lot of shades of gray."

"Life is all gray, sweetheart."

"Well, he had been stealing from one of his business partners. That's really the only way to put it. And at first it was borrowing from the business and not telling him. Then it was creating fake invoices, and it kind of got worse. Finally, his partner found out and threatened him, and it got ugly. My husband knew some stuff about him and said it would be bad if he went to the police, which, that was just a week ago, and I kind of thought things had settled down, and that's why I took the job out here," Sloan explained. "I just wanted to get away for a few days, and then I realized I don't want to go home."

"Sounds like your husband's a real asshole," said Emma.

"I think I'm the asshole," said Sloan. "I mean, I knew what he was doing for a while. I can't pretend that I didn't. When the FBI showed up, I assumed they were coming for me. And then, when I saw them escorting you out with handcuffs, I really began to panic," she added. "I was thinking to myself, Did they somehow think you were connected to all this, like laundering money or something? I don't know, it's stupid, but I felt so bad. I'm so sorry."

"You didn't do anything wrong," Emma replied. "This was some clerical mistake they made."

"Yeah, I know, but you just start to think about the people in your life and the things we don't pay attention to and what you overlook."

"Uh-huh," Emma agreed as she stared at the twinkling stars.

Sloan needed to push things a little bit more. "And I was really confused when they started asking me about terrorism and a bombing," she said, then took a sip of wine and looked off into the distance, trying not to gaze right into Emma's eyes.

"Oh, they asked you about that?" Emma said, surprised.

"I couldn't figure out if it was some sort of head game or what," Sloan said. "But I was about to blurt out about my husband's business and all of that. Then I realized they were talking about something else, so I just shut up. Plus, my face hurt and I couldn't really understand half of what they were saying because of the pain."

She feared it was gilding the lily. But so far, her physical stress had triggered trust in Emma.

"We can't be responsible for the actions of everybody we meet," Emma replied.

"I know, but this was my husband. I could have said something or done something."

"That can just make things worse. Trust me, I know from experience. Everybody has their own little path they're going to follow, and there's nothing you or I can really do to change that."

"Maybe so," Sloan agreed. "But it's kind of hard to explain. I'm sorry. I should have just kept my mouth shut."

"I understand way more than you realize," Emma mused.

"Do you?" Sloan asked in a tone that she instantly regretted—it sounded like *prove it* rather than empathy.

Emma lowered her voice and glanced over her shoulder for a moment, then leaned in to Sloan. "I'm going to share something with you."

Sloan tilted her head to listen.

"They thought my friend Frazier had done something. But it wasn't him."

"What do you mean?" asked Sloan.

"Let me grab a flashlight and I'll show you."

INVISIBLE

Theo was standing in the middle of the motel room with a VR headset strapped to his face when Jessica rushed into the room.

The surprise of seeing him in strange garb and postures had faded early in their relationship.

"I think I have an idea!" Jessica said.

Theo pointed to another headset sitting in a plastic case at the foot of the bed. "Me too," he said.

She put it on and turned the dial until the room went completely dark. A ghostlike version of Theo was standing a few feet in front of her where the real version had been a moment ago.

"You know, most people use Slack and Google Meet to communicate," Jessica remarked.

"Not enough bandwidth," Theo replied.

They were standing in the middle of a virtual version of downtown Arcadia City as it had been before the train collision. Jessica could see the complete buildings like all the pieces in a solved jigsaw puzzle before it got disassembled.

She pointed at a pickup truck to her left. "How accurate is this?"

"I realized I could use a neural radiance field algorithm for the things we're not terribly interested in, and then more compute to try to reconstruct other data," Theo explained. "Obviously, there's an upper limit here, but we're getting a lot more geometry than before. Signs and text are going to be hard to read because they don't really show up in shadows or ambient light, but we can get a pretty good idea of what vehicles were present when the images were taken. I've also got some more time-series data from Brad, so we can roll things back and forth a little bit and look for big shifts."

"So I guess that means more detail, right?" Jessica asked, getting to the point.

"Yes," Theo confirmed. "Basically, it's like a video game where I'm using a lot of redundant processing for the things we don't care about. Leaves and trees, bricks, et cetera. But for the actual shapes of the vehicles, it's more precise geometry."

Jessica started to walk forward, then banged her knee against the bed. "Damn it," she muttered.

"You might want to teleport instead," Theo suggested.

"Yes, of course," Jessica said sarcastically. "I should just teleport like, you know, a normal thing that I do all the time."

"Well, I did see videos of your magic act. It's not as crazy as it sounds." Theo smiled innocently.

Jessica pointed toward an intersection at the end of the main street. "How do I get there?"

"Just point with your finger like a gun," Theo instructed. "A laser beam will appear, and you can open your hand to move."

Jessica aimed a bright blue beam of plasma toward the intersection and released her fist. A moment later, they faded into view in the new location.

"Ugh," Jessica groaned. "They don't tell you on *Star Trek* how disorienting this is."

"I close my eyes before I do it," Theo offered.

Jessica glanced around. "When was this taken?"

"Eight hours before the crash," Theo answered.

"Okay," she replied. "He might have been in the area if we think he was present for the crash. But can we go back to when we know he was at the newspaper plant . . . say, that night?"

"One second," Theo said as he touched controls to a virtual display in front of him.

Everything went black for a moment, and then they were standing in the same location, but it was now nighttime.

"Okay, let's go over here," Jessica said, pointing toward the power station.

A moment later, they were standing near the spot where the train had barreled through the fence and into the power relays.

"I've already looked here," Theo said. "No van, no RV."

"I know, but I want you to look again," she insisted.

Theo pressed a button on his imaginary panel and a text list appeared before them, reaching from the ground to above their heads. Each line named the make and model of a vehicle next to a 3D rendering.

"Jessica," he explained, "I already wrote an algorithm to make a list of all the vehicles here. Just look; we don't have to jump around."

"Well, I need you to see, not think. Can you just do that for a moment?" Jessica said firmly.

"I'm not sure I understand," he started.

"Will you shut up and do it?"

"Okay," Theo said as he pressed another virtual button and all of the control panels vanished.

They were left alone in the twilight looking at the street running through town. There were at least a dozen cars in view from where they were standing. Jessica used the teleportation trick to move them to another spot at the edge of town past the power plant. Cars were parked in front of the coffee shop and bar. Farther up the street, there were two cars parked at the twenty-four-hour laundromat.

She teleported them again to the opposite side of town, where a Shell gas station stood. There were no cars at the pumps, but two vehicles were parked along the road that led to the pipe fitting factory.

"Hmm. Okay," Jessica said. "Can we go to Mud River?"

"One second," Theo replied. He made the control panel appear again and pressed some phantom buttons.

They were standing on a boat ramp at the riverbend where flooding had peaked. Jessica felt a bit of an emotional reaction, because this was the same position from which a camera crew had captured a floating body drifting through the floodwaters.

There was a van parked at the far end of the parking lot. Across the street were four more vehicles. Theo teleported them over to the van.

It was a generic white work van with clear windows.

"I looked at this before," Theo said. "We were able to get a license plate from a gas station north of here. We know the owner and the registration, and it wasn't in any of the locations."

"That's fine," Jessica replied. "It's not what I wanted to show you. What do we have from the battery farm?"

"Nothing other than vehicles we were able to trace within seventy-two hours of the fire," Theo replied. "Which could have been set up months before."

"I figured as much," Jessica said. "It's only got one road. Which I think our master of chaos would probably avoid being seen on around the time of the fire." She thought for a moment. "Can you take us to the newspaper plant in Idaho," she asked, "on the day that he was working there?"

A moment later, they were standing in the parking lot of the printing facility.

"How many cars are here?" Jessica asked.

"Can I use my algorithm?" Theo asked.

"Yes," she replied.

"Twenty-eight. We were able to match all of these to prior days. There're no new vehicles here," he explained.

"But he's in the facility right now, isn't he?" Jessica said as she pointed toward the building.

"In a matter of speaking, yes, he should be inside there," Theo said slowly, realizing she was trying to show him something.

"But none of these cars are his?" she asked.

"Correct," Theo said. "Why didn't he park here?" he asked aloud. "He can't have thought that we'd have this level of surveillance detail, could he?"

"Maybe, maybe not," Jessica answered. "He might have been aware that vehicles coming or going from here could be logged, but even then that would be overly paranoid, because we have a dozen witnesses inside there that have seen his face. Why would he want to keep his vehicle somewhere else?"

"Well, I drove a really crappy car in high school that I didn't want people to see," Theo said. "But that's probably not it."

"Actually, I think that's kind of exactly it," Jessica said.

"Explain," Theo prompted.

"Well, I went to the coffee shop and watched some YouTube videos about urban camping. These guys that build vehicles, I saw some imaginative ways of concealing yourself in plain sight, but most of them are ones that you and I already thought of: station wagons, vans disguised to look like work vehicles, and that kind of thing. But I saw one that got me thinking because I realized it was completely out of our search scope."

Theo cocked his head at that.

"Go back to the gas station in Arcadia City later this night," Jessica told him.

Everything faded for a moment, and they were standing again at the Shell gas station.

"Theo, I want you to *look*. Just tell me what you see. Don't think about it. Just describe it," Jessica instructed.

"Well, approximately eight meters from where we're standing is a row of *Artemisia tridentata*," Theo replied.

"No, Theo, I did not ask you to point out the trees," Jessica snapped.

"I was talking about shrubs."

"Same difference," she added tersely. "Just think about the things that move, i.e., cars and trucks and that kind of thing."

"Got it," said Theo. "Over at the back of the gas station there is a pickup truck. It looks like it's older. There's a spare tire in the back. Over across the street near the streetlamp is a Chevy Malibu. And then about twenty meters in the distance there, I can make out a Honda Civic pulling a flatbed of flattened cardboard."

"Okay, let's go back to the boat ramp on Mud River."

Everything faded for a moment, and then they were standing back at the waterside.

"Well, you said the van wasn't what you wanted to talk about," Theo said. "There's the . . . hold on. Oh. Oh, wow," he repeated.

"You see it?" Jessica asked.

"Oh, I see it. It's obvious . . . now," Theo admitted. "I kept looking for boxes, empty boxes where he could be hiding. But I didn't think about things," he said, pointing a blue plasma bolt toward where he was staring.

It was the same Honda Civic from the gas station. But what stood out was the trailer. A trailer filled high with tightly packed, flattened cardboard boxes.

"I had the algorithm looking at cars or trailers. Not flatbed-hauling thingies like this."

"And a flat trailer heaped with flattened cardboard isn't the kind of thing you would expect someone to be hiding inside of," Jessica said.

"Of course not. It's not the kind of thing a person or an AI would ever think. Well, not a normal one." Theo walked around the trailer. "I'm amazed the algorithm was able to get this much detail," he noted.

"Well, a stack of cardboard isn't exactly a terribly sophisticated object," Jessica replied.

"No, it's not," Theo agreed, "and that's kind of the brilliance of it. So what did he do? Did he pile the boxes and carve into them? Or just build a trailer and add them around it?" he asked aloud. "It doesn't really matter," he hastily added.

"And do you now understand why he didn't park this near where he was working?" Jessica asked.

"Yes," Theo said. "It's perfect camouflage until someone catches you walking out of the secret door."

"Exactly," Jessica replied. "If it were me, I would have cameras all around so I could be aware of my surroundings. But even then, that's not enough. I can't wait all day to leave if some kid is playing on the sidewalk or somebody's grabbing a smoke and doesn't want to go back home," she said.

"Right," Theo responded. "Better to just park this on a side street or somewhere a little bit out of the way."

He teleported them back to Arcadia City.

"We're still a distance away from the switch box," Theo pointed out. "Did he walk all the way? I can't imagine he'd unhitch the trailer and leave it. That would get the attention of the police."

"You ever heard of a bicycle?" Jessica asked. "I bet you that's how he got around. I have a feeling if we start looking through all the images Brad sent us for people on bicycles, we might be able to narrow it down considerably."

"This resolution won't show us much of a face," Theo observed.

Jessica pointed at the Shell station. "No, but I bet you one of their cameras will."

EMPATH

Emma's shed was a small, run-down structure no more than eight feet wide and ten feet long. The only thing new about it was the lock on the door. Both its small windows were covered with cardboard from the inside.

"I keep a bunch of junk in here," Emma said as she unlocked the door. "Watch out for the spiders. We've got a couple cats around here that take care of the mice and the rats, though."

She reached a hand inside, flipped a switch, and a small incandescent light bulb flickered on, illuminating long wooden shelves filled with cardboard boxes and plastic bins.

"We have friends who drift through here and like to leave their stuff," she explained. "Some of them don't come back, but you never know." Emma walked inside and started opening and peering into different boxes. "When I went to college, I thought that maybe I'd end up becoming a lawyer and a judge like my mother. But instead, I found something I didn't expect."

"What was that?" Sloan asked as she leaned against the doorway, keeping her distance from the cobwebbed interior.

"People," Emma replied. "Somehow, being there made me realize how much I like people. Obviously, you're around them all the time, high school and all that. But the summer between graduation and your first semester at college, something happens. You start to see yourself as an individual, I guess. And you're disconnected from your family. I'd always been in my mother's shadow, and this was the first time I got to define myself. And part of the way I did that was choosing who I spent my time with. She didn't approve of my friends, but I know that she had been a bit of a rebel and a hippie in her younger years. So her protesting rang a bit hollow.

"Anyway, it didn't matter. I wasn't living at home anymore. Eighteen, I can make my own decisions." She shrugged. "So she accepted that and for the most part tolerated me and my friends. She wasn't thrilled to find out that I wasn't as enthusiastic about the academic work as much as the social opportunities. I don't mean dating. I dated, of course, but just getting involved with so many other people with interesting ideas and passions, I loved it.

"I joined every club I could and found myself a member of every group. There were so many passionate people there who wanted to make the world better, who wanted to make a difference. And just being around them was . . . energizing. I guess that's the word for it," Emma said. "My dorm room became a bit of a crash pad, which caused problems, so I moved to an apartment off campus with a couple other people.

"You know how movies show radicals in the '60s and '70s with posters on the wall and somebody playing a guitar and a joint being handed around? It was like that. It was exactly like that. I got it. I understood what that meant. They weren't just a bunch of crazy stoners. These were people just trying to adjust to a role in society that they didn't make."

"Did your mom ever warm to your friends?" Sloan probed.

"I think in some ways she was actually happy that I'd taken this path, but she couldn't really encourage it, if you know what I mean."

"Yes," Sloan nodded. "I have a family member that certainly takes pleasure in the fact that I did everything opposite of what they told me to do because that's exactly what they would have done."

"Right," Emma responded. "She was always willing to help me out and even help my friends out. Some of them, well, they were a bit radical, if you know what I mean. They took a lot of things personally. And they really felt there was an urgency to fix things. And even if I didn't agree with everything they did, I understand why and where their heart was. So I was able to get my mom to help them out."

"It sounds like you're the person to always have everyone's back," Sloan observed.

"I try to, and some people make it kind of difficult. I'm, well, I'm nonviolent. And I understand there's a time and place for it. But growing up so privileged, it's harder for me to understand that," Emma said, sagely. "As a well-to-do white girl whose mom was a judge, I had everything handed to me. So I couldn't judge other people who had to fight for things. Not everybody I went to school with had the same upbringing I did," she added.

"And everybody you meet is worthy of your trust," Sloan observed, trying to move this along.

"Right . . . hold on a second, I think it's in this box here," Emma said as she grabbed a cardboard box from the top shelf and put it on the floor.

"I kind of got into a little bit of trouble when I was in school. To be more accurate, Frazier got me into some trouble. He's a good guy, he's got anger issues, and he's gotten better at dealing with them. He had a terrible upbringing and got screwed over every way possible. His mother had an alcohol problem. His dad was put in jail," Emma explained. "One of the things I realized was that if things had been a little bit different for me, my outcome could have been a lot worse. I was privileged, and privileged means you're less likely to trip and fall into things that can ruin other people's lives. Like if I ever wanted something, I could just ask my mom and she'd buy it. If she didn't and I decided to shoplift it, well, she could get me out of *that*. Other people aren't so lucky, and when they see the system work so well for one person but it doesn't work for them, they're gonna be angry. They'll lash out. It's understandable."

"I take it Frazier was *much* more radical in his younger days," Sloan commented.

"You could say that. He'd be the guy that brought the bricks and frozen water bottles to the protest. He always wanted to take things up a notch. And it all only happened because of a random meeting."

"What was that?" Sloan asked, trying to follow the slipstream of Emma's memories.

"Frazier's got all kinds of weird hobbies. It's one of the reasons I really dig him. One day he brought a guy back to our apartment who he met at some swap meet where people were selling parts for old cars. This guy knew everything. Frazier loves muscle cars. And they got into a conversation about whatever it is that guys get excited about. So he brings the guy home and says, 'You gotta meet him.'"

"What made him interesting?" asked Sloan.

"He was a genius," Emma replied. "He knew everything, not just cars. Everything. How an elevator worked, how the power got through the streetlights. Just mind-blowing how much sheer *stuff* he knew. But he was also shy. It's not like he would just tell you all this. But if you asked him something, he'd get right into it.

"I would tune out after a while because I could only hear so much about hydraulics and solenoids and what have you. But Frazier liked it. Also, Frazier likes people to think that he's smarter than he is. He's a smart guy, don't get me wrong, but he's always wished that people would think he's brilliant. You know, a genius. Which, who cares? But this guy seemed like the real deal, and that fascinated Frazier."

Sloan nodded, actively listening. No need to prime the pump now.

"It turned out this guy Seth had been in the military, which made sense. And Frazier was asking him about explosives. I didn't understand where the conversation was going at first. I just assumed it was guys talking about guy stuff. But then Frazier started going off about how to truly disrupt the system. How you had to think differently about it. Like, you know how people set police cars on fire? Which seems dumb. But Frazier can explain why it actually makes sense. That it's property, not people, that it's really about attacking a symbol. Frazier believed people are different. You don't hurt people. But symbols are fair game."

"And what did this guy think about all that?" Sloan asked.

"Seth? I think he was a bit mesmerized by Frazier because they were so different. Frazier was all words and Seth was all, I don't know, thinking or analysis or something. It was sort of fun to watch. Frazier explaining political structures and class systems and that kind of thing. And Seth would listen. And then Frazier would ask, How does a machine gun work? Or how does an atomic bomb get triggered? And Seth would go into incredible detail. He could tell you where the nuts and bolts were manufactured, for crying out loud. One time, I asked him how he knew that. He just said, 'Manuals.' Which means I guess you can look that stuff up in the library?

"Anyhow, Frazier and Seth came up with an idea. I was aware of it, but I wasn't really paying attention. It was about making some sort of symbolic gesture. Long story short, Seth made Frazier a few bombs. These weren't people-killers. There was no, like, nails in them, but they were bombs. And Frazier had this plan to start blowing up symbols of oppression, statues, that kind of thing."

Sloan wished she were wearing a wire to record this story. Instead, she focused on remembering every detail.

"I don't want to bore you with the specifics, but what happened was, Frazier used Seth's bombs to blow up some public property. A handful of outdoor statues. That's it. Unfortunately for me, he decided to do this in my hometown because he was staying there at the time and was going on and on about the one percent and all their symbols."

"That must have caused some problems," Sloan said, pretending she had no idea of what the aftermath was.

"Yeah, let's just say it strained my relationship with my mom, because Frazier wasn't as careful as he could have been. So we got the hell out of there. And never looked back."

"What happened to Seth?" Sloan asked.

"After that . . ." Emma paused. "Hold on a second." She reached into her pocket and pulled out her phone. "I'm sorry, it's my mom calling me back. Let me take care of this."

Sloan felt the air trapped in her lungs as Emma brushed past her and walked outside the shed.

All Sloan could hear was Emma saying, "Uh-huh, uh-huh, yeah," as somebody spoke to her on the other end of the line. About a minute into the conversation, Emma spun around quickly and stared at Sloan.

Goddamn it, Sloan thought.

She knows.

Emma casually lowered the phone, but Sloan could see the call hadn't ended.

"I'm sorry, what did you say your last name was?" Emma asked, trying to pretend to be as sweet as possible.

"McPherson," Sloan replied. "My name's Sloan McPherson. Why don't you hang up and we can talk?"

Emma raised the phone back to her ear. "Yep, it's her," she said to the other party. "I'll deal with it." She then ended the call and turned toward Sloan. "You fucking bitch. I trusted you. I *trusted* you!" Emma screamed. "Is that even real?" she demanded as she strode up to Sloan's face and pointed at the bruise on her cheek.

"Very real, and it hurts like hell."

"Good. You deserved it. I can't believe you just lied to me like this."

Sloan gave it a beat, then responded in as calm a voice as she could, "Thousands of people are about to die."

She didn't know if that number was accurate, but it could have been. And given what almost happened to Arcadia City and the dead in Mud River, she felt like the possible exaggeration was warranted.

"I have no idea what you're talking about," Emma said.

"Your friend, Seth, the bomb maker, we connected him to the train crash in Arcadia City, the sabotage at Mud River, a battery plant fire in Florida, and other acts of destruction. We've been chasing a technical genius, and the investigation led us straight to you and your connection to him."

"Tell it to somebody else and get off my goddamn property!" Emma yelled.

Sloan stood her ground.

"I said go away!" she screamed. "I don't have anything to do with this."

Sloan could tell that Emma was conflicted. "I believe you, but we still need your help. I need your help. Those people need your help," she emphasized.

"I'm not connected to any of this. I didn't want any part of it," Emma said, retreating.

"Neither did I, but here I am. The point is to save whoever will be harmed next."

Emma shook her head. "It doesn't connect. Seth isn't a killer. He's not like that. He's not politically motivated."

"Maybe so, but he's killing people whether he means to or not," Sloan said. "Our best guess is that he's neutral about it. He lacks empathy. Does that compute?"

"Seth is not what you would call neurotypical. But there's nothing violent about him," Emma argued.

"Help me understand. I can make sure that he gets to talk to people, the right people, but I also gotta make sure that he doesn't hurt anybody else."

Emma turned away from Sloan, crossed her arms, and started to pace back and forth. "He's not an activist. He's not political. He's not full of hate. He just sees things differently."

"What do you mean?" Sloan asked. "Help me understand."

Emma let out a sigh. "I don't know where to begin. Seth could be thoughtful. He could be curious. But he was different. And he's definitely not a monster."

"I never said he was," Sloan responded. "As far as I can tell, all of these acts of sabotage were aimed at machines and systems. The people were bycatch. It's like what Frazier was trying to do: hurt symbols of power, not people."

"Yes," Emma agreed. "But the stuff you're saying Seth did is very, very different."

"He might not understand the consequences of it," Sloan replied. "I'd like to know more about him."

"I'm sure he wouldn't get it," said Emma. "That's the odd part about him—he's got this thing with people. I want to say the word is 'indifferent,' but that doesn't even fit. Like, technically? He doesn't see people."

"I'm not sure I understand," Sloan said. "Like, face blindness? Like he can't remember faces?"

"No, no, not quite. We asked him about that. He said that when he saw people, he just saw, like, scratch marks, like on a film or something. It was kind of odd. And Frazier and I were like, 'Well, what do you see when you talk to us?'

"Seth said he saw our voices. And he could see the way we moved our hands and moved our bodies and everything else. And that was just it, it was like, that poor guy, something happened to him when he was younger. I think he had an abusive mother that created some physical damage. And despite that, he became an amazing mind and really tried to overcome this impairment."

"You said he was in the military?" Sloan asked.

"Yeah, Iraq, the first Gulf War. He didn't really talk much about what he did, but something to do with ordnance or WMDs, I don't know. Frazier would have told you, but now?" She grimaced, then stepped past Sloan and back into the shed. "Let me grab something."

Emma had calmed substantially, and Sloan could tell there was part of her that wanted to confess, but she couldn't because of whatever convoluted moral code she was following.

She returned to the box she'd pulled from the shelf and opened it. "I kept some of his stuff that he left at the apartment." She took out a folded piece of paper. "I dug his artistic style. He didn't see himself as an artist, but it was . . . something," she said as she unfolded the paper.

To Sloan's eyes, it was a complex schematic with black lines and curves forming intersecting patterns that combined to create some kind of machine.

"What is that?"

"Well, Seth was a mechanical genius, and he made his living going around fixing things that were too hard for anybody else to fix. I think this was the inner workings of an MRI machine at a hospital that he got called in to repair. He was very excited—well, Seth's version of excited, which really wasn't excitement—but he kept talking about how they'd had a helium leak that short-circuited everything on the floor."

"I'm not sure I understand," Sloan said.

"Me either. Seth was fixated on how systems work and then how they broke, and he was delighted to find new ways that something would break down. In this situation, there were some helium tanks or whatever they used for the magnets, and they leaked. And he said that helium can actually interfere with microchips and circuits so they don't work and said that his watch stopped and other people on the floor had iPhones that were malfunctioning. Nobody had realized there was this helium leak. Anyhow, my point is," Emma said, pointing to the illustration, "for him? This is art."

Sure, Sloan thought, *if you're a member of the Borg Collective.*

"Do you know if he ever worked on newspaper plants?" Sloan asked.

"Yeah." Emma held the piece of paper up. "That's what this is. It was a blank piece of newsprint. But he worked on everything. Anything you could name."

"Could you tell me more about him? Could you give me his full name?" Sloan asked, hoping to close the deal.

Emma hesitated. "Do you really think he's connected to what happened in those places? I saw the news on TV. People were killed."

"Either he or somebody he knows was," Sloan said. "I'll make sure that nobody does anything without hearing his side of it."

"I trust you, which, I know, I *shouldn't*, but I think you're trying to do the right thing," Emma said.

"I think you understand me," Sloan replied.

"Seth Bakker. B-A-K-K-E-R. That's his name. He would be, like, fifty right now. He was in the army in the 1990s. That's about it."

PATTERN MATCH

Jessica and Theo were sitting inside a rented RV outside the Atlanta FBI field office, waiting for news from Sloan, the only member of their team allowed inside the command center overseeing the search for Seth Bakker.

Brad stepped inside the trailer, accompanied by a cool breeze of night air.

"Any word from McPherson?" he asked.

"No," Jessica replied. "They're combing through traffic, camera footage, and everything else they can get their hands on across the entire United States, which, predictably, is a pretty big information problem," she explained.

"Yeah, but that car and trailer seem pretty specific," said Brad.

"I think he might have ditched it," Jessica responded. "A guy this smart would have a pretty good idea when an APB is put out on him and have contingencies. We've got seventy-five hours left before the end of the sequence."

"Any of your math-e-magic tricks help them out?" Brad asked Theo.

"I've done what I can, but they have way more chefs in the kitchen than I think they can handle."

"What have you been able to find out?" Jessica asked.

"Unfortunately, not a lot," Brad said. "My military contacts were able to get me his service records, but they were suspiciously sparse. We know that he served in the army, worked in the motor pool, and did a stint with ordnance disposal. All in all, six years. And then he got a discharge."

"What kind of discharge?" Jessica asked.

"General discharge," Brad answered. "Which means he messed up somehow, but maybe not in a major way. Sometimes that can happen to guys who have psychiatric issues, but they don't want to spend the time having to treat them or deal with the aftermath of that. It's easier just to say, 'Hey, why don't you see yourself out,' without the stigma of a dishonorable discharge."

"And we have no idea what that was for?"

"I've been able to track down a couple guys that served with him, and hopefully we can get a little more information." Brad checked his watch. "I'm expecting a call in about ten minutes."

He glanced to the window a moment before a knock came at the door.

"That's Nicholas," said Jessica. "He says he's got some updates for us."

Brad opened the door and stared down at the young FBI agent. "Is this another spy mission?"

Nicholas's face turned red, and he took a half step back. "I'm sorry about what happened with Ms. McPherson. That was not under my control."

"That's a problem with guys like you. You don't realize what you can and can't control. Maybe if you thought a little bit more about that, we wouldn't have these problems."

"In case it helps," Nicholas said as he stepped past Brad into the RV, "I have some more information from the profilers—the good ones," he added. "I know what you all think of them, and I kind of agree, but we've got a pretty good data-driven approach, which is based more on actual historical data and interviews than wild speculation."

Theo closed his laptop and leaned back in his corner of the nook by the center table. "Let's have it," he said skeptically.

"We did a kind of pattern match with other individuals," Nicholas clarified, "so just understand that's where it's coming from. And we worked from there. We found two that I thought were pretty interesting. One was a counterfeiter; another was a forger. The counterfeiter's name was Scott Fiedler. He was arrested in 1985, released after two years, then arrested again in 1988, and finally again in 1999. Seems he got smarter but never stopped doing what he was doing," Nicholas explained. "He was very technical. He was actually an engineering and science prodigy through middle school. Then in high school, his father got into an argument with his mother, murdered her, tried to kill himself, but ended up just giving himself brain damage.

"Fiedler then went to live with his aunt and uncle, got into some minor trouble—shoplifting, vandalism, the kind of thing a kid who basically lost his parents would do—but nothing major until he was implicated in a counterfeiting ring. He was making and passing fairly sophisticated bills. The only reason he was caught was because an informant broke into his printing facility, which was in an industrial park, and saw the machinery. When he got pinched for something else, he turned evidence on him.

"Fiedler had been very careful about how he passed the bills. He would sell them for fifteen cents on the dollar and just do a one-time upfront cash transfer. That was it. He moved around, he avoided repeating himself for too long, and by the time the counterfeits were found in circulation and traced back to the vendors, they had no way of finding him.

"That's what our profilers pointed out and why they thought it might be relevant. His margins were quite slim compared to the technical capabilities that he had and the quality of the bills."

"He was doing it for the thrill," Jessica said.

"Exactly," he agreed. "It was the technical challenge, and his bills kept getting better and better, although he didn't change his margins or try to scale up his operation. After his first arrest, he went mobile. He built out a counterfeiting operation in an RV not that different from this. I'll show you the photos because it's very interesting, in that you would walk inside of it and not realize that behind the cabinets and under the bed and the floorboards was all of his equipment. It was a counterfeiting machine but designed to be invisible. Like you said, he enjoyed the challenge of it."

"And he printed money as he needed it," Jessica remarked. "But how did he find his customers?"

"Gambling and Cocaine Addicts Anonymous," said Nicholas. "He would go to those meetings, listen to the stories of the people, and then approach them afterwards in the parking lot. He knew that in both cases these were people that could turn around large amounts of cash in a short amount of time."

"So he was having social interaction," Jessica asked. "How did they describe it?"

"In the interviews there was a shocking similarity. Basically, Fiedler had a script, like some kind of verbatim Tony Robbins sales pitch, that didn't change much—which, by the way, when they finally caught up to him the last time, they found a bunch of audiotapes of motivational speaking and sales training. He had memorized it by rote. People said that there was something off about him. The term 'autistic' wasn't really thrown around a lot, but that would be the best fit right now. He could seem extremely social, but the moment the conversation went in an unexpected direction, he shut down."

"What was the other case?" Brad asked.

"An engineer who worked in Silicon Valley," said Nicholas. "He was stealing components from chip-fabrication machines and replacing them with homebuilt or reworked parts."

"To sell to the Chinese?" Brad questioned.

"No," said Nicholas. "That's the crazy part. He had built, or nearly built, his own chip fab in a warehouse he rented. When they asked him why, he simply said these were the most valuable machines in the world. Why wouldn't everybody want one?"

"What did he say he was going to do with it?" Jessica asked.

"Sit and stare at it," Nicholas replied. "I mean, literally, he said that. Which was confusing to the investigators until they realized that for him, this was a *Mona Lisa* or some form of art, and his goal was to possess it—nothing else."

"Was there anything else interesting or relevant about him?" Jessica inquired.

"His attorney tried to get him an insanity plea, but it didn't work, although the court agreed that he certainly was not neurotypical. His performance evaluations and record indicated that he preferred machines to people."

"So what was the big takeaway from your profilers?" Jessica asked.

"Neither of these guys were surprised when police finally caught them. They didn't put up much of a fight. And they were very cooperative after the fact."

"I'm not sure what to make of it," Jessica murmured. "Brad, Theo, what's your take?"

"To Aristotle," Theo said first, "a fish and a porpoise were the same thing because he never had the chance to look closely at the former and the latter together. He missed out on the fact that porpoises were mammals. I think the problem here is that these are the two closest cases they have, but they could be a world apart. Maybe there's some parts of them that are helpful, but neither one of these guys is Seth Bakker."

"Well, I hope they're listening to Sloan's advice on how to apprehend him if they find him," said Jessica.

Nicholas held up a hand, answered his phone, then told Jessica, excitedly, "We might find out right now. Cleveland PD thinks they spotted him. Same car. Same trailer."

"Damn it," said Jessica.

"Isn't that a good thing?" asked Nicholas.

"It is," said Theo, "and it isn't."

TACTICAL

Sloan, Jessica, Brad, and Theo were at the back of the Tactical Operations Center, listening in as the FBI special agent in charge spoke to a Cleveland Police Department officer on the scene via a cell phone connection.

The SAC was Terrence Lumley. He was methodical, calm, and by the book. It was apparent why he'd been selected for the task in the deliberate way he spoke with the officer on the scene.

Sloan filled in the others with the details:

"Routine patrol through an industrial area. The police officer spotted our vehicle, remembered the APB, and had the common sense to keep driving and then pull into a nearby alley. She's made a few spot checks on the car. There's nobody in the driver's seat. What she said as she drove by, she thought the trailer moved. That's what caught her attention initially because she just saw a pile of flattened cardboard, then remembered the bulletin."

"What's happening now?" Jessica asked.

"They're moving in their SWAT team and the bomb squad but keeping them out of view of the car."

"They need to pull back and wait for him to move away from the car and trailer," Jessica stated.

"I know, I told them that," Sloan said. "Their concern is that he will just drive away and out of the city limits."

"And the FBI can follow him," Jessica said.

"They know that, but they're still trying to put together surveillance teams. They don't have an airplane yet, and they're afraid a helicopter will attract too much attention," Sloan said.

"It won't matter once he's on the run. How long till they get an airplane up and ready?" Jessica asked.

"Two hours."

"They should have been ready for this," Jessica objected.

"The nearest surveillance plane was too far away," Sloan said, then turned her attention to the SAC at the front of the room.

"How's it looking out there, Officer . . . Gertz?" Lumley asked.

"I just took another peek around the corner. Still no movement," she reported, "but like I said, I swear I saw the trailer bounce up and down like somebody moving inside of it. Of course, now I'm thinking it could be shadows, because it's been thirty minutes since I saw that and nothing's happened."

"Well, we just need to keep our eye on him a little bit longer," Lumley said. "You're in the best position, and we're afraid that if we move in one of your colleagues to replace you, they might get spotted."

"What's their plan?" Jessica asked Sloan.

"Actually, they're considering a page from our book and staging an accident, something that might draw him out or distract him."

"That one didn't turn out so well for us," Jessica noted.

"I know," Sloan agreed. "Another option is to have another police unit pull up and inspect the car and trailer as if it was a routine check. Possibly using parking enforcement."

"Does parking enforcement work this late in Cleveland?" Jessica queried.

"No, but I overheard them debating if Bakker would know that or not."

Jessica shrugged. "They have to understand—he's not an idiot."

"I've explained that to them. I think they get it," Sloan said. "But they're worried that he might get away."

"I can't see how," Brad responded. "They have him pretty well boxed in. And he's pulling a goddamn trailer."

"I think they're also afraid that if they do nothing," Sloan pointed out, "they finally have to take the ticking clock seriously."

Lumley spotted Jessica, Brad, Sloan, and Theo in the back, armchair quarterbacking the situation, and shrugged, obviously not happy about it.

"I think the only way to get Bakker to cooperate," Jessica said, "is if we get Emma to talk to him."

Nicholas Zhao had joined them. "They don't want a chance on that," he said. "It could take too long, and our analysts don't think they had a strong connection to begin with."

"Maybe so," Jessica replied, "but her connection is going to be stronger than whatever cop you send up to tap on his window."

Lumley had a cell phone to his ear again and was listening to someone. He put it down, then began to pace.

"Do you know who he was talking to there?" Brad asked.

"No," Nicholas answered. "I think somebody in headquarters."

"Well, I think they're telling him to do something stupid," Brad said.

Lumley glanced over at them again, swore under his breath, and then approached the group. "Since you're having so much fun watching, I might as well ask you for a sanity check," he said. "We're thinking about staging an accident."

"What kind of accident?" asked Jessica.

"Putting one of the Cleveland SWAT team officers in plain clothes in a car and having him drive like he's drunk down the street and rear-end the trailer."

"Nine times out of ten, I would think that was actually a pretty good idea," Jessica said. "But in this situation, I think it's terrible."

"I need you to explain that to me in thirty seconds or less, because that's what we're about to do," Lumley told her.

"He is an unknown quantity. He's a saboteur. He's capable of anything. I don't think that he prioritizes life the same way we do," Jessica explained.

"Well, that's clear. That's why we're trying to apprehend him," Lumley replied.

"No, I mean, including his own," she added.

"We've still got three days left on this sequence," Lumley responded as he glanced over at Theo. "I think he might want to be around for that, don't you?"

"We don't know what to think," Jessica confessed. "All I know is he's incredibly clever and very good at booby traps. And you know that guys like that don't get taken down easily."

"We've got two snipers on the roof. We could try to wound him," Lumley suggested.

"I think that's an even worse idea," Brad muttered.

"And why is that?"

"Like Jessica said, this guy's into all kinds of booby traps. He could have a dead man's switch, anything. He could be wearing a bomb vest, for all we know."

"Our profilers don't think that's likely the case," Lumley said.

"I don't think they're drawing from a whole lot of experience," Brad pointed out.

"Do you mind if I ask who it is you were speaking to on the phone a moment ago?" Jessica inquired.

"We were given a specialist in DC to help talk us through this," Lumley explained.

"Somebody from the bureau?" Jessica asked.

"No. The Pentagon."

"The Pentagon," Brad repeated.

"He's an expert in terrorist interventions. At least that's how it was explained to me," Lumley said.

"What's his name?" Brad asked.

"Meadows. Hunt Meadows," Lumley answered.

"By Pentagon, you mean the Defense Intelligence Agency, right?" Brad asked.

"I think so. I was just told that we should be getting our instructions from him."

"Overseas, a terrorist intervention usually involves a drone strike. The DIA doesn't really work domestically," Brad informed him.

"Not officially, anyway," Sloan added. "I had to deal with a few rogue DIA agents a while back and found out that they were running a black site in South Florida."

Another agent walked up to Lumley and whispered to him.

"Looks like it's go time," said Lumley. "We're making the call to apprehend."

"What if he doesn't want to be apprehended?" Jessica asked.

"Right now, this is a deserted street. In a few hours, we're going to have a lot of traffic. Better to handle this when there's nobody else around. If we block the traffic off, it'll look immediately suspicious."

"I can get Emma Rafario here before then," Sloan offered again. "I think she could talk him down."

"We don't have the time," Lumley snapped. "Officer Gertz, are you still there?" he said aloud to the speakerphone.

"Still here, still no movement," her voice called out from a speaker on a table.

"Here's the plan. We want you to do another drive-by. This time, slow down and use your spotlight on the vehicle. Our goal is to have you do that and then leave, and hopefully, if he's hiding in the trailer, he'll come out, get into the car, and move on so we can stop him behind the wheel. The idea is to spook him out of his little cardboard fort," Lumley explained.

"I don't think this is a good idea," Jessica muttered.

"Me either," Sloan agreed.

"Okay, I'm in my vehicle now," Officer Gertz said over the sound of the car-door chime. "I'm going to pull back onto the street and do a slow pass in the opposite direction."

A moment later: "Okay, I'm slowing down. The car is still empty. The trailer is still there. I'm going to aim my light at both."

There was no loud boom or explosion.

Only a sharp crack, and then the call went dead.

DEBRIS

Jessica and Theo surveyed the crater in the street where Bakker's vehicle had been. The entire city block was a crime scene.

Sloan and Brad were trying to get as many details as they could from the forensic technicians who were pulling pieces of metal and other debris out of the bricks of the surrounding buildings while Theo and Jessica tried to process everything.

"Any word on Officer Gertz?" Theo asked Jessica as she typed away on her phone.

"They say she's gonna make it, thank God," she replied.

Theo was staring at Officer Gertz's overturned police car, flipped during the blast, now resting on the sidewalk opposite from where Bakker's vehicle had been parked.

Special Agent in Charge Lumley walked over from an operations tent set up just outside the debris field and spotted Jessica and Theo.

"He looks happy," Jessica noted.

"I'm guessing they got a DNA match," Theo responded. "And he thinks that's a good thing."

"Have you heard?" Lumley asked as he approached them.

"About Officer Gertz? Yes," said Jessica. "I'm glad she's going to make it." It took every ounce of energy in her to not add *No thanks to you.*

"Yeah, she's tough. Real tough one," Lumley said.

Why do the people in charge who make mistakes that end up hurting other people often dismiss it by pointing out how strong those people are? Jessica wondered.

"Did you get a DNA match?" Theo asked.

"Yes." Lumley nodded vigorously. "We tracked down some family members and were able to get matches. Unless he had a brother we don't know about, it was him in there." He hesitated. "Unless you think it was a trick . . ." he asked Jessica.

"I think it was him," she said.

"Well then, that's good news, isn't it?" he pressed.

"I guess that depends. Was he going to or coming from somewhere?" Theo answered.

"It's hard to know, but the point is, we got him before he was able to pull off his next stunt," Lumley said.

"But you didn't get him," Jessica pointed out. "He blew himself up."

"That was unfortunate. We would have loved to have questioned him and obviously prosecuted him for everything. But if that puts an end to it, then between you and me, it's for the best," Lumley concluded.

Theo stared at the SAC for a long moment. "The battery fire and Mud River were planned months or maybe even years in advance. The only reason we think he was even in Arcadia City was to watch the derailment. Same with the dam. Not because he had to do anything. The work was already done."

"That's just one theory," Lumley countered. "We think he had to be near these locations in order to trigger his catastrophes."

"I believe the word you're looking for is 'wish,' not 'think,'" Theo said firmly.

"The only images we have of him near Mud River," Jessica pointed out, "were months ago. None of the other surveillance cameras caught him at any point close to there when the dam burst."

"I appreciate the analytical way in which both of your minds work, but you have to remember, some people own more than one car. Just because we knew that he had this vehicle, or what was left of it, doesn't mean that's the only one that he used. He was mechanically inclined. He met this Frazier character at a car show. It stands to reason he could have had other vehicles, and that's why we haven't spotted him more recently at that location or others," Lumley explained.

"I think you're trying to fit the facts into too tidy a package," Jessica said.

"So what are you saying?" he asked.

"Focus only on what we know right now. We know he was in Arcadia City, and we have a location here. If we draw a line from Arcadia City to Cleveland, we need to know what happened in between," Jessica said.

"We think he was headed somewhere from here," Lumley said.

"How far have you tracked him after he left Arcadia City?" Theo asked.

"You know as well as I do, we don't have any data."

"No traffic cameras, no gas station cameras, no other surveillance systems were able to track him between Arcadia City and this point," Theo repeated. "Does that make you suspicious?"

"That he took some wild random route through other states? Not really," Lumley said.

"It has me concerned," Jessica responded. "It sounds like he was going out of his way to not be spotted, which means somewhere between here and Arcadia City, he spent a period of time doing God knows what."

Theo pulled a laptop from his backpack and opened it. "I've made a map of possible routes."

On-screen were four colored lines taking odd paths from Arcadia City to Cleveland.

"What are those?" Lumley asked.

"The paths somebody could take to avoid the likelihood of being captured by city or interstate cameras," Theo responded. "The best way to go from point A to point C without anybody knowing where point B was."

Lumley studied the map. "And what do you want me to do with this?"

"Can you give us traffic camera data and anything you have from North Dakota?" Jessica requested.

"I can have people take a look."

"I think you should give Theo the data if you want to find out anything faster."

"Can this wait?" Lumley asked.

"That's the big question," Jessica said. "If the countdown is still on, no, it can't wait."

"One second," Lumley said. He took out his phone and typed a message. "You should get access at any moment now." He stared at each of them. "This goes against every procedure."

Ignoring the SAC, Theo sat on the ground and started typing. "It looks like you've got some gas station data and traffic camera footage. Let me transfer this to my network and see what I can do."

"How long will that take?" Lumley asked.

Theo held up a finger. "That long."

Jessica squatted down. "What do you see?"

"Two images," Theo said. "One's a ninety-nine percent match. One's a sixty-five percent match. The first image is driving past a gas station camera in Bushell, North Dakota. The second image, if you look, is pretty blurry, but I think that's our trailer, taken by a highway camera near Hollow Woods, North Dakota, at the eastern end of the state."

"So he drove through North Dakota," Lumley said. "What's the point?"

"Look at the time stamps," Theo replied. "He spent fifty-two hours in North Dakota. I don't know if you're aware of this, but there is nothing in North Dakota worth spending fifty-two hours doing."

"So what was he doing there?"

"I need to figure out the *where* first. Where specifically in North Dakota?" Theo started tapping away on his keyboard.

A moment later he asked, "You ever heard of a town called . . . Hillstone, North Dakota?"

"No," Lumley replied.

"Me either," said Jessica.

Theo pointed at a number of intersecting lines on a map of the town.

"It's got a gas line near there, a major internet fiber optic junction, and a satellite uplink facility. That's a lot of interesting infrastructure for the middle of nowhere," Theo said.

"I guess it has to go somewhere," Lumley said. "Do you think those could be critical targets?"

"I think we need to be there as soon as possible," Jessica said.

SCORCHED EARTH

To Jessica Blackwood, the deserted streets of Hillstone, North Dakota, resembled something out of an alien-invasion movie. With the exception of the FBI team and local authorities convening at the community center, the only sign of life was Theo Cray sitting in the middle of the intersection on his laptop. He had been there for hours going over diagrams, schematics, and aerial images of the town and the surrounding area, trying to figure out where their chaos man had planned his final strike.

Technicians had swabbed every piece of vital infrastructure, looking for traces of the telltale ink that had connected the other acts of sabotage. So far, they'd found nothing. The gas company that controlled the pipeline running from the Canadian border through the outskirts of Hillstone had run test after test, checking the integrity of the system, and put in place fail-safes to shut it down in the event of an attack.

Railroad inspectors were going over every inch of track within miles of the town and closely following the freight train traffic moving through the vicinity.

The response team had even gone as far as sending the bomb squad to inspect all gas stations and grain silos for signs of sabotage. So far, nothing had been found.

Despite the threat of potential annihilation, Jessica found the town charming and quaint. There were two cafés, a small bar, and a post office with prominent American flags on display, all of which were overlooked by a water tower at the center of the town. It could have made a magazine cover in the 1950s.

When they first arrived, Jessica had observed that two-thirds of the vehicles were pickup trucks, which told her a lot about the residents. This was the kind of community that was easy to forget, but also easy to underestimate how important they were.

LA, where Jessica had grown up, could shut down for a year and people would still find a way to entertain themselves. But if a sprinkler-fitting company or grain-processing facility stopped working, it could create serious downstream effects, from the cost of Wheaties to the availability of produce in the grocery store. The average consumer probably spent less than ten seconds a year thinking about where the soybeans or wheat they consumed came from. It was small towns like this, inhabited by farmers, machinists, and a variety of other skilled workers, that kept the heartland thriving and the rest of the country fed.

As she walked to join Theo, she glanced at a small store that still had barbecue grills and lawnmowers for sale out front. For a town that spent a considerable amount of time under snow, it was a sign of their optimism.

"You want to hurry up?" Jessica asked. "The Rock Hound Cafe is going to have a steak fry tonight." She nodded at a vinyl sign stapled to a wooden plank next to a café and an auto parts store with a huge tire on a metal pole.

"That would be nice," Theo said.

Good, Jessica thought. *He's a bit more lucid.*

Theo reached his arms into the air and stretched, then reached back and felt his spine.

"You know they have these things called chairs," Jessica remarked.

"I know. Sometimes I need to be in the center of things to remind myself this is all real," said Theo. He climbed to his feet and shoved his laptop into his backpack. "Any word on the gas pipeline?"

"They've been over every system, every fail-safe," Jessica replied.

"And how is the forensic side of things going?"

"Sloan and I agree they've got a pretty good team here. I think they're taking it seriously. They've been nonstop running samples looking for any trace of the ink. So far, nothing. And just to be sure, I had their supervisor put in a couple test samples as per your suggestion."

"And how did that go?" asked Theo.

"They spotted them, so I don't think we have to worry about false negatives," Jessica answered.

"Let's walk," said Theo as he started pacing. "If all we had were my spectrographs and vector topographies, I'd be pretty suspicious of the data."

"But we have gas station images placing him in this vicinity for several hours," Jessica pointed out.

"Exactly. And I can't quite figure out why. There are a couple potential targets, but nothing that's at the level I was expecting. Now I'm wondering if he was here for some other reason," he considered.

"We've got the FBI interviewing everybody and showing them photographs. So far, nobody has turned up that knew him or spotted him."

"You think the FBI team here is pretty good?" asked Theo.

"I think they're smart and sincere. Why do you ask?"

"I'm just wondering if they have any ideas. I'm literally at a loss here. I've been going over every bit of online information I can find about this town. Heck, I've even been plotting satellite trajectories overhead. In case, I don't know, the Hubble Space Telescope was about to fall down or something."

"That wouldn't be the weirdest potential outcome we've ever dealt with." Jessica noticed a figure walking toward them. "Here comes Lumley."

"Anything interesting?" asked Theo as the SAC came within earshot.

"No. I want to run a hypothesis by you, though."

Theo folded his arms. "What's that?"

"Maybe this town was the target, possibly the gas pipeline. We've run through some different scenarios of what somebody could do if they were able to take complete control of it and create an overpressurization scenario. So, mind you, there are all kinds of fail-safes to prevent that, but I have to admit, they had 'em at Mud River, and look what happened there. So I tasked a team with trying to figure out the worst case if the pipeline was a target.

"There are a couple scenarios including a kind of pulsed explosion where you don't just get one point of impact but several. Basically a shock wave that goes through the whole system."

"I think there's one big problem with that," Theo said.

"What's that?"

"I don't think anybody would care if that happened out here. Certainly it would rattle the windows in this town, but this is North Dakota. One explosion or ten isn't going to have the same kind of impact that we've been seeing. Much less than what we would expect for the final attack in the sequence."

"I can appreciate that, but to be fair, that's your intuition and not your data speaking," Lumley replied.

"I one hundred percent agree. But we're back into the situation where we're hoping that was the case. And I guess the other part of your hypothesis is that when they were running all the systems checks, they might have overridden whatever's in there that could have caused a disaster and possibly prevented it," Theo guessed.

"Well, yes," said Lumley. "That was the other thing I was going to get to, is that we might have prevented this and not realized it. Another possibility some of our profilers have suggested is that the last act was what happened yesterday when he blew himself up."

"For one, the timing would be wrong," Theo responded. "Second, I don't think his self-immolation is quite on the scale of everything else. Though the personal scale, for sure."

"Well, that's just it. We're trying to read his mind, and I don't think any of us really can," said Lumley.

"Have your profilers given any insight as to why he blew himself up?" Jessica asked.

"You mean other than it could be his final act?" Lumley answered. "The other likely reason is to avoid being captured. You had suggested this yourself—these guys don't go down easy."

"True," Jessica admitted, "but there's going down with a fight and there's atomizing yourself and every trace of your existence into oblivion."

"So what's your hypothesis?" Lumley asked.

"I leave the hypotheses to Theo. I just have questions. One question is, Why would someone blow themselves up before their big finale?"

"To avoid capture," Lumley replied. "Why else?"

"Maybe," Jessica said, "but Theodore Kaczynski was perfectly fine going into custody. As were other methodical madmen."

"But we have a number of cases of bomb makers taking themselves out instead of being arrested," Lumley said loudly.

"True, but those tend to be spree killers. Guys that just went nuts over a period of a few weeks or months and were in some sort of mental decline. Whatever spiral this Bakker went into happened a long time ago, and yet he stuck around until we got a little too close."

Theo sat on the curb and pulled out his laptop.

"Do you have an alternate explanation as to why he took himself out like that?" Lumley asked her.

"He wasn't trying to kill himself," Jessica said.

"It was an accident?" asked Lumley.

Jessica shook her head. "No, I think he set it off intentionally, but killing himself wasn't the primary reason."

"Killing Officer Gertz?"

"No, I don't think that was the case either," she said.

"Then what?" Lumley pressed.

"Maybe he was trying to destroy the evidence," Jessica suggested.

"I don't know how helpful that was, considering we were able to track him down," Lumley pointed out.

"No," Jessica replied. "I mean, for what he had next. I think he may have done that not because of what he knew, but because of what was in the trailer."

"Why not just destroy it, then?" Lumley asked.

"I don't know," Jessica admitted. "It's a good question. Maybe the mission was more important. Which concerns me. Because, given everything that's happened so far, he might have been pretty satisfied about the outcome regardless of whether he was around to watch it happen or not."

"He might be part of the evidence too," Theo remarked.

"What do you mean?"

"Sometimes we're able to find forensic evidence under fingernails, on soil samples, on people's shoes that tell us where they've been with a lot of detail. Give me the contents of somebody's stomach and I can tell you more about them than their Instagram feed."

"Well, I think the contents of his stomach are all over a city block in Cleveland. It can't be too hard to find," Lumley pointed out.

"Actually," Theo said, "it's almost impossible. We've got tissue samples, some bone fragments, but something more substantial, like an entire intestine, hasn't been found. And everything we could find is going to be so contaminated by the urban environment, we're not going to know anything for sure. If we find a fingernail, what is the dirt under there going to tell us? Was it from someplace he's been? Was it from the muck in the gutter where it got blown into? It's a contamination nightmare."

"We have a team there picking up the pieces. Also, some specialists have been sent in to help out," Lumley said.

"I'm missing something," Theo admitted as he opened up his laptop. "Jessica, you're the best metaobserver I know. What's the first thing that comes to your mind?"

Jessica put her hands into her pockets and gazed into the distance, straight down Main Street and out to the horizon, tracts of farmland that faded into infinity.

"He doesn't see people like we do. He sees systems. He sees patterns. He sees the interconnectedness of things," she observed. "Maybe it's not in the schematics or maybe not the ones we can see. Maybe it's something else. Something special about this place that we don't understand but he could."

Theo pulled up satellite imagery of the region and started scrutinizing it again.

Lumley turned to Jessica. "I've got to make a decision pretty soon. If he's wrong, then we should pack up shop and go. But if he's right, do we all want to be here when that happens?"

"How are you leaning?" Jessica asked.

"I'm looking to you guys for answers. What's your plan?"

Jessica nodded at Theo. "I'm going to leave when he leaves, and something tells me he's not going anywhere until he figures out exactly what Bakker was up to."

"Understood," said Lumley before walking away.

"You heard from Brad yet?" Theo asked once he was out of earshot.

"Still in Cleveland being mysterious," said Jessica.

"Did he say anything? Even anything vague?"

"You know Brad. He's suspicious of everyone."

CLEANUP CREW

Brad Trasker was leaning against a brick wall just outside the blast zone in Cleveland. FBI forensic technicians dressed in white bunny suits were meticulously picking up fragments of Bakker's vehicle and its contents, placing them into evidence bags as they photographed their locations within a grid.

The way the maniac blew himself up didn't sit right with Brad. He couldn't quite place why. Add to that the fact that additional officers and officials had shown up once Bakker was identified. A lot more than Brad would have expected. There was the typical hodgepodge of government agencies and local law enforcement. But there were also a number of outside observers that struck Brad as unusual. Although his own presence surely raised red flags for others.

He heard the familiar sound of a certain brand-new pair of Danner boots walking up behind him. "How's it going?" he asked Nicholas without turning around.

"Oh, hey, Mr. Trasker, how are you doing?"

"I still don't trust you. Other than that, I'm doing great. I'm just trying to figure out why this guy blew himself up. What's your theory?" Brad asked.

"I guess he didn't want to be arrested. I don't think seeing the inside of a jail for the next fifty years is acceptable to some people," Nicholas replied.

"That's the problem," Brad countered. "I don't have the insights of your kooky shrinks you listen to, but I don't think this Bakker character really cares if he was going to spend the next fifty years sitting in sunshine or stuck inside of a federal penitentiary staring at toy train catalogs all day long. In fact, that might even have thrilled him."

"I guess that's a good point," Nicholas admitted. "Why aren't you in North Dakota with your friends?"

"Is this a question from you or from your superiors?" Brad shot back.

"Both, I guess. They're trying to figure out how much credence they should give Theo."

"You guys spend a lot of time studying the way Theo thinks," Brad observed.

"You're interesting too," Nicholas added.

"I wasn't fishing for a compliment. In fact, the opposite. I know you're not being honest with us. I'm just trying to figure out how many different things you're not being honest with us about," he said.

"Nothing nefarious, I promise," Nicholas assured him.

"I think you're a well-meaning kid," Brad replied. "So I'm going to tell you what you've been telling us without realizing it."

"What do you mean?" Nicholas asked hesitantly.

"You have a pattern. I'm going to tell you your pattern because, frankly, I don't care if you know or don't know—because I kind of think I know what you're up to. When it comes to sharing information with us, you're very quick to give us updates from the profiling unit at the FBI. Other details take a little bit longer, which tells me who you spend most of your time talking to. And since the profilers are curious to get in the heads of some strange and unusual people, and they seem like they like to talk to you, that means you have something in common with them. Now, I know you're not a profiler. You told us you were working on systems analysis, and Theo was pretty familiar with your work. You study things. You figure out how they work," Brad explained. "And I'm guessing that isn't limited to how efficiently staplers are used in an office. What you're really studying are the people and the decision-makers. More specifically, how they think. Am I getting warmer?"

"Certainly that's an area I'm interested in," Nicholas responded. "Of course we want to know how really smart decision-makers make their choices. We told you this at the beginning."

"You said that, but that doesn't mean that's the truth," Brad said.

"I'm not sure I follow," Nicholas queried.

"That's another pattern you use. It's a very common one. When somebody's confronted with a question they're not prepared to answer, either affirmatively or with a good lie, they just pretend to be confused. 'I'm not sure I follow' is a simple way to buy time or avoid a situation by feigning ignorance. But I see it for what it is, which is a lie," Brad explained.

"I don't think I told you anything that wasn't true," Nicholas said.

"That's another lie. When you said 'I don't think I follow,' you followed exactly. You knew exactly what I was talking about. So you might say it's a fair answer, but no, it wasn't."

Nicholas merely nodded.

"Now you're using another tactic," Brad said. "Silence. You realize that anything you say is something that I might interpret in a way that you don't want me to, because you're afraid I'm going to read more into it than you realize you're revealing. And for you, silence is probably the best approach. So I'm going to tell you what I think is going on. I think your interest in Theo is more than academic. I looked you and your other teammates up and found you guys are active in computer modeling. Specifically, in AI systems that make decisions. I'm willing to bet that you're trying to create a digital version of Theo."

Nicholas pursed his lips and glanced away from Brad's gaze.

"I thought so," Brad said. "I have a suggestion for you—in part because you're a terrible liar, and mainly because you're going about this in an extremely difficult way. I don't know if you've picked this up from Theo, but there are two things he lives for: to figure things out and to explain things. Personally speaking, I think the guy's going a little bit crazy because he's been spending all of his time figuring things out, and poor Jessica is the only one he can explain things to. She's clever and patient, which is good. But everybody has their limits."

"I'm not sure I understand," Nicholas admitted.

"Now I kind of believe you," Brad said. "I'll be more direct. If you're trying to build a computer model or some system that thinks like Theo, I suggest you just go talk to Theo. I think you'll find he'll be more than happy to help you out and even collaborate. And maybe for some reason he doesn't need to know the details of it or you have some other motive for it, just tell him that. He'll understand it from an experimental point of view. He'd probably be quite happy to learn something like this is happening. If you ask him to be actively involved, he'd be more than willing to tell you everything he knows. Why? Because the one thing that's been bothering him more than anything else is that he's the only person who sees these things. The only way he'll find any peace is if he teaches some new students." Brad shrugged.

Nicholas's eyes widened. "You . . . you really think he would agree to this?"

"I have a pretty good feeling he will. Well, he might be skeptical of the outcome of whatever kind of artificial intelligence experiment you're running. I know I am. I think at the very least, if he could train three human brains, including yours, that would make him pretty happy."

"Could you ask him for us?" Nicholas responded.

"I think I can arrange that, but there's a small price," Brad said.

"What's that?"

"I need you to be honest with me," he answered.

"I can't break the rules."

"Of course you can," Brad shot back. "I do it all the time. It's fun. You should try it more often. But I'm not asking you that right now. I just want you to break whatever unofficial rule somebody higher up put on you . . . because it might be impacting things. And if we don't figure out what's going on, Theo's likely to get himself blown up before you have a chance to dissect his brain."

"What do you need from me?" Nicholas asked.

"I've noticed that there are twelve technicians working this scene right now," Brad said, nodding at the men and women in white clean suits carefully removing evidence from the scene. "The FBI field office here has seven full-time forensic technicians. The ATF has another six, which is thirteen. But we know they're working them in shifts right now. And I don't think all twelve of these people are from the ATF and the FBI. My guess is there are three extra people here that aren't from the ATF or the FBI. So . . . who are they?"

Nicholas looked at the technicians. "That's easy," he said. "The army sent us some techs with experience in investigating bombings and IEDs."

"Is it normal for them to mix in with the domestic agencies like that?" Brad asked, already knowing the answer.

"I think given the special circumstances and the time constraints, it was all hands on deck."

Brad pointed at a group of tables under a tent piled with stacks of bins with evidence bags inside them. "What's that area over there?"

"That's our evidence-collection area," Nicholas said. "After we photograph things, they're bagged and placed there. Why?"

"Do you see the evidence technician across the street near the fire hydrant? The one with boots a lot more worn than yours?"

"Yes," Nicholas replied.

"Do you see that large tackle box he's been carrying from spot to spot?"

"I guess that's where he keeps his equipment," Nicholas said.

"Have you seen him pull any equipment from it?"

"No," Nicholas responded slowly. "What are you saying?"

"Do you see the evidence technician standing three meters in front of him with the metal detector?"

"What's unusual about that?"

"If you look closely, the sensor is a little thicker than the one being used by your team," Brad pointed out. "But that's not the most important thing. Every now and then, the person with the funny metal detector turns towards the person with the equipment box he never opens and points to something. And do you know where he sets the equipment box next?"

"Next to the evidence," Nicholas replied.

"No. On top of it."

"I'm not following you," Nicholas admitted.

"Now I believe you," Brad said. "Those guys aren't looking for evidence. They're cleaning it up."

CLONE TOOL

Theo Cray strode into the command center at the Hillstone Community Center, where FBI agents and other response team members were hunched over tables staring at laptops and conferring in huddles. He unplugged a computer attached to the cable running to the overhead projector and replaced it with his own laptop.

"I was using that," said a woman returning to the lectern.

"I'm using it now," Theo replied matter-of-factly, then raised his voice to address the room of several dozen people. "Class is in session."

Every head turned toward him. Jessica, who was standing in the back, observed their confusion. Some assumed that Theo was speaking in an official capacity. Others involved in the command structure made angry faces.

"I know what the target is," Theo said loudly to make sure that everyone was giving him their full and undivided attention. "But before I tell you, I need you to discover this for yourself, because if you don't believe me, we're going to be facing a worse situation than anybody in this room has considered."

"Dr. Cray, could I speak with you privately?" asked Lumley.

"No," Theo replied bluntly. "We have seven hours and twenty-two minutes left."

Lumley was clearly frustrated by Theo taking command of the room. "Professor Cray," he said as calmly as he could, "there's a protocol for this. Let's talk about what you've uncovered first."

"Your entire operation has been compromised, and you don't even know it. Protocols are about to get millions of people killed. You're welcome to have me escorted from the premises. It's your call." Theo crossed his arms and stood next to the lectern, waiting for Lumley to try.

Jessica could see a vein throbbing in Lumley's temple. She knew what Theo's gambit was going to be and understood the need for theater.

"Fine. Proceed, Dr. Cray, but this better be worth it. If not, I'm going to have you put under psychiatric evaluation," Lumley said.

"I will surrender myself willingly." Theo tapped a button on his laptop and a driver's license photo of Seth Bakker appeared on-screen.

"I'm going to recap a few important details for the benefit of some of the new people here." Theo nodded toward a table of four men with close-cropped haircuts who were gathered off to the side. Jessica had observed them as well and hadn't been able to get a straight answer from Lumley or anyone else about who they were. Her best guess was they were observers sent from the national security community.

"Here are the facts," said Theo. "Our suspect's name is Seth Bakker. He's fifty-two years old and he served in the army for approximately six years. We have some records indicating what he did during his service, but they're just records. We don't know the specifics.

"We know that he worked as a technician repairing complex printing machines. We also have indirect evidence that he worked as a mechanical engineer repairing other complex machinery, including hospital MRIs. While working on printing machinery, he came in contact with a custom ink used by only a handful of newspaper-printing plants. Here's what we've been able to assume indirectly because of that ink: Three bombs used seven years ago in Springfield, Iowa, were connected to that ink and, by proxy, Seth Bakker. A friend of Bakker's involved in the bombing was able to connect us to his name and help us ID him. When we found him, based upon surveillance images, he triggered an explosion, taking his own life and destroying what other evidence he had with him.

"Now let's go into the hypotheticals. Based upon patterns he displayed, assumptions I've made, and behavioral analysis by profilers that was confirmed by people who knew him, Bakker had certain cognitive impairments. Specifically, a previously undocumented form of face blindness. Hypothesizing even further, either as a result of this or to compensate for this, Bakker had developed a fixation on physical systems. Where other saboteurs focus on maximum loss of life or high-profile victims, Bakker seems specifically focused on maximum damage to infrastructure.

"While he was once associated with a group with ideological leanings, we've not determined any specific ideology in his patterns. He has simply focused on targets that either came to him through his travel patterns or otherwise held interest for him. Any questions so far?" Theo invited.

The room was silent as they waited for him to continue.

"There are forty-six people in this room and several hundred outside it within the area trying to figure out what system he was trying to disrupt," said Theo. "I have been running mathematical projections and agentic research systems to make sense of the available data, and I've come up empty-handed.

"Our best prediction so far is that he might have been planning an attack on the gas pipeline near here." Theo tapped his computer, and a map of Hillstone and the surrounding farmland appeared on the overhead projector. "You can see the pipeline running from the north to the east." He pointed at a red line that traced the pipeline's path. "To the west, there's a train route that goes in the opposite direction to a terminus sixty miles south, and a depot.

"But our answer is right here," said Theo as he walked up to the overhead projector and slapped his hand in the middle of the map.

He looked around the room to see if anybody understood what he was trying to point out.

"This image tells us something. The problem is none of us, including me, think like Bakker. More precisely, we don't *see* like him."

Theo glanced over at the four men huddled in the corner of the room. "You," he said, addressing them directly, "what do you see here?"

A bald man wearing thin wire-frame glasses responded, "Farmland and the Lantern Saddle Wildlife Refuge."

"Who controls that?" asked Theo.

"The Department of Agriculture."

"Who really controls that area?" Theo pressed.

"I'm not sure I understand your question," the man responded.

"My friend Brad would call that a lie," said Theo.

He stood back and turned toward the screen. "I want everybody to look at this image, but don't focus on the city, the roads, or any of the obvious man-made artifacts. I want you to look at the ones that aren't obvious at first glance, but once you see them, you won't be able to unsee them."

Someone in the middle of the room muttered, "Damn," under his breath.

"You see it," Theo replied. "Does anybody else?"

"Theo, time," Jessica said from the back of the room, reminding him that this wasn't a normal lecture.

"Right, I'm sorry. If one person gets it, the rest of you will probably get it pretty quickly when I point it out. This wildlife refuge is also a no-fly zone to protect the habitats of the species located there. Which makes sense, but look closely at this region," Theo explained as he pressed a button on his laptop and a grid appeared over the refuge.

Several people in the audience let out audible gasps as the image enlarged.

Theo walked over to the grid and tapped his finger in each plot of satellite imagery. "This section is exactly identical to this section, and this section, and this section, and this section.

"This is a Photoshop. This is not a satellite photo. This is a manufactured image. It's what you or I would find on Google Maps. It's what somebody looking through satellite data that was commercially available but processed by a company working with the United States government would provide. And it's a lie.

"Why would anybody lie about what was here?" Theo asked as he turned on the men sitting at the corner table.

They were silent, but Jessica could see from their body language they knew exactly what he was talking about.

"Bakker is fixated on systems and machines. A little while ago, Agent Zhao told us about an FBI profile that I didn't pay as much attention to as I should have. One of the matching cases they found was a man obsessed with complex microchip fabrication machines who was trying to steal one part by part. For him, it was the pinnacle of human technological achievement.

"I don't think Bakker would agree. I think he had a different fixation, but a similar obsession," said Theo. "And this was apparent to us from the beginning when he engineered the incident at Arcadia City. What is the most coveted artifact in all of human history?"

The room was silent.

"What item is so precious we will go to incredible lengths to prevent anyone else from having it?" Theo prodded.

He turned toward the men in the corner of the room. "What object do we spend trillions of dollars to prevent from falling into the hands of people we don't want to have it?"

"Nuclear weapons?" asked a woman.

"Exactly," Theo shot back.

"I'm going to ask the four gentlemen over here who arrived in vehicles from Minot Air Force Base, which happens to be one of the primary command centers for the United States intercontinental ballistic missile system, what is in this wildlife refuge?"

The bald man responded to Theo, "Dr. Cray, I don't think that area is of anyone's concern here."

"You might think so," Theo replied, "and by 'think' I mean 'wish,' but eight minutes before I came into this room, I got a call from our colleague Brad Trasker at the Cleveland cleanup site.

"If the air force unit in charge of nuclear weapons isn't concerned about the possible sabotage of a nuclear warhead, I'd be very curious to know why you have Defense Intelligence Agency agents stealing evidence from an active crime scene and running a Geiger counter disguised as a metal detector."

"What?" Lumley gasped.

"Your federal brethren haven't been straight with you," said Jessica. "In fact, they've been lying."

Lumley turned toward the bald man and called him out. "Colonel Osterman, do you care to explain this?"

"I'm afraid I can't. This is a classified situation and nobody here has the clearance," Osterman replied.

Theo dramatically raised his wrist and checked his watch. "Well, in about seven hours, it's going to be declassified when a 1.2-megaton warhead explodes twelve miles south of here."

"That's impossible," said Colonel Osterman. "Our facilities, wherever they may be, are the most secure locations on the planet and are under constant surveillance. Someone can't simply tamper with or accidentally trigger a nuclear warhead. There are a number of fail-safes in place to prevent this. Not to mention the fact that these are located in secure missile silos, which are essentially vaults. There are several layers of protection preventing anything from happening to them and a considerable layer of security on top of that."

"He doesn't have to get any closer than a few meters to the warhead to set it off," Theo said.

"I think that, for all of your computer know-how, Dr. Cray, you are not an expert on nuclear warheads and definitely not in a position to tell us what is or what is not possible," Osterman said sharply.

"You are correct," Theo replied. "You are the experts on nuclear warheads and these scenarios. So allow me to direct your attention to my next slide, which is a top-secret Department of Energy project, done in conjunction with the United States Air Force Global Strike Command, which I found on a Russian BitTorrent server."

A slide appeared on-screen with the title *The Matryoshka Scenario*, next to a diagram showing a missile in a silo with a series of explosive charges embedded in the walls around the missile.

"For everybody else in the room, I will give you my best explanation as a computer scientist and not a nuclear weapons expert on how a nuclear bomb works.

"A nuclear explosion is triggered by a material like plutonium or highly enriched uranium that is put under sudden and intense kinetic pressure from all sides, causing the atoms to squeeze together and trigger a thermonuclear explosion. There are two tricky components to this. One is creating material of such a pure state that it can explode. Second is placing your charges around the material in such a way that you get a complete compression effect. If there is an instability or a weakness, you can get a partial explosion or just eject a bunch of nuclear material at a high velocity without triggering an explosion, which, I should point out, is a terrible outcome too, because this creates a radioactive cloud of a disastrous proportion. An incomplete bomb explosion that's not completely belowground is still a dirty bomb.

"The Department of Energy, working in conjunction with the Pentagon, was tasked with figuring out if it was possible to use an explosion to trigger the explosion that set off the nuclear material. They realized that with well-placed shaped charges in the concrete cylinder around the warhead you could have a high probability of setting off the interior charges, triggering an explosion inside the missile silo.

"There were two goals of this research. One was in case the United States ever found itself in a situation where they could compromise people working in the nuclear program of an adversary that had access even to the exterior of a ballistic missile silo. The other purpose of this research was to explore the possibility of using specialized bunker busters to trigger detonation of these bombs on the ground via an aerial strike."

Theo tapped his keyboard and paged through different schematics in the document.

"This, of course, was just a theoretical exercise and, as far as we know, never implemented against an adversary. But the physics worked out and with a higher degree of certainty that it would cause an ignition event on ballistic missiles manufactured by the United States because the research study had access to precise details, including certain vulnerabilities."

Theo tapped his laptop again, and a logo of a schematic overlaid on the planet Earth came up next to a company name, Target Dynamic Systems.

"Target Dynamic Systems doesn't even have a web page," said Theo, "but you can see their name is one of the contributors to this research report. If you try to find out anything about them online, the most you'll find is that they are a government contractor that has put in place certain complex electrical systems at military installations.

"They're a subcontractor to several primary defense contractors that support our ballistic missile defense program," he explained.

"Trying to connect Seth Bakker to any of this has been made difficult because his military record has been whitewashed, as is any connection he might have had to government contractors. However," said Theo, "it only took me a minute to find out that during the first Gulf War, when Bakker was deployed to Iraq to assist with the search for WMDs, Target Dynamic Systems was working on a government contract operating out of the same military base and unit as Bakker. While I can't prove what he did for work after leaving the army, I wouldn't be surprised to find out that he remained in contact with, at the very least, the technicians that he met there. And likely became a contractor for them."

"Is this true?" Lumley asked Osterman.

"Our facilities are the most secure installations on the planet. We do continuous background checks on any individuals that may come in proximity to them, and we have no reason to think anything could be compromised," Osterman responded.

Jessica wasn't the only one who could pick up the faltering sound in his voice. He had told them the party line, but it was obvious he didn't believe it.

"Are you aware of the Matryoshka scenario?" Theo asked.

"I'm aware of a lot of scenarios, Dr. Cray. I assure you, we're confident that we've taken every precaution. That report likely indicates an extreme degree of technical proficiency and access to specialized explosive charges."

"Like the ability to make precision shaped charges?" asked Theo. He pressed a button, and a slide appeared showing the crater in Cleveland where Bakker's car had been located. "Allow me to present the résumé for someone extremely proficient in shaped charges and fixated on nuclear weapons systems."

"You're sweating a lot for somebody who says they're confident," Lumley told Osterman. "I suggest we make some phone calls."

EXHAUST PORTS

It only took twelve minutes for Colonel Osterman's attitude to change dramatically. Between Lumley's explanation of the situation and whoever else was at the other end of the line, orders came down from above to cooperate completely with the FBI and Theo Cray.

Where Theo had clawed for attention before, he now was the uncontested center of the emergency operation. With Jessica and Sloan's assistance, the command center had been reorganized, with several tables pushed into the center and Theo at the far end, standing before his laptop like a preacher at a pulpit.

Osterman stood next to him, speaking to somebody on his phone, then lowered it. "I can get my inspectors into the silos within the next thirty-five minutes."

"No," Jessica blurted out.

Osterman turned toward her. "What do you mean?"

Theo explained, "He'll have booby-trapped them. We don't know how many silos he got access to, but given what happened in Cleveland, I don't think he's going to let us simply disarm whatever he put in place."

"But we inspect those silos all the time," Osterman replied. "Nothing's gone off so far. I know that because we're still standing here."

"But how often do you inspect them? What's the schedule?" Theo inquired.

"Every nine days we have a team from Minot Air Force Base dressed in US Fish and Wildlife uniforms driving an official vehicle go inspect each of the silos. It's a three-day inspection routine," Osterman explained.

"When was the last inspection?" Theo asked.

"Six days ago," Osterman answered.

"If it was thorough enough to uncover what Bakker did, we have to assume that he knew to set the trigger after the inspection, based upon that pattern," Theo said.

"How would he know that?" Osterman asked.

"You tell me. We're still trying to figure out how long he worked with the contractors and what information he had access to."

"He was never on the service staff for this facility," Osterman replied.

"That may be correct, but that doesn't mean he doesn't know the inner workings here. We already know that a lot of these records have been available to foreign adversaries for a long time. We have to assume that he knew everything about what went on here," Theo replied.

"We can't just do nothing," Osterman declared.

"I know," Theo replied. "We need more than these maps. How quickly can you get me satellite data, real satellite data?"

"Maybe twenty minutes."

"Brad is inbound," Sloan told the group as she lowered her phone. "He's also got a team from Wind Aerospace coming in with drones. We can probably get this area pretty well canvassed within three hours."

"Which leaves three hours until the countdown ends," Jessica pointed out.

"I can't leave it to that," Osterman responded.

"That would have been a really great insight twelve hours ago," Jessica snapped. "We could be having this conversation with a lot more time on our hands, but here we are."

"Okay, but I'm going to need to have my teams in place by the silos, ready to disarm the warheads at a moment's notice," Osterman said.

"Fine," Theo agreed, "but I'm pretty sure that'll trigger whatever Bakker put in place. But I understand. Just make sure that they don't go into the silo or do anything that would trigger something."

"Define 'anything,'" Osterman demanded.

"Anything out of the usual," said Jessica. "I'm sure that there are other vehicles and inspectors and whatever else you do to contain the charade of the wildlife preserve. But if you have camera systems inside or anything internally, don't open any doors or hatches." She added, "Tell us how these things are disguised. What do they look like? They can't just be launch silos with concrete doors on top."

"No. I'm going to get you the images of that shortly, but they look like cisterns, sheds—equipment that might belong in a wildlife preserve."

"All right," Theo said. "I need you to explain to all of us here the construction of the silos. I've seen diagrams, but there's some variability there. Can you tell us what all sixteen of these have in common?"

"There's the launch port—that's the part where the missile exits. Like I said, that can be disguised as something else, even a shed that falls away. And then there's an access portal. This could be something as simple as a manhole cover or something else near there. To prevent them from being flagged by adversarial satellite images, they'll look like a trash can or something else to that effect, usually on a concrete pad.

"But as I pointed out before, those access points have twenty-four-hour surveillance, both below and above. We've got cameras everywhere. We would see him if he came near there. There're motion sensors. I get forty mule deer sightings a week," Osterman noted.

"That's assuming your camera footage is accurate," Jessica challenged.

"I'm not making any assumptions that they're not compromised, but that would be a really difficult thing to pull off. We have secure signals coming through the cameras back to the base, and trying to do a man-in-the-middle attack would be extremely complicated. I'm not saying it's impossible, but it would be something that you don't get a lot of experiments to try, and we've not detected *any* penetration."

"I see your point," Theo acknowledged. "I think you're probably right. That wouldn't be his point of attack because of the amount of surveillance, and he would have no way of knowing without precise insider information about the location of cameras. At least, I think so." He scratched his chin. "But I'm confused. You mentioned two points: the missile launch port and the access portal. What about the exhaust from the rockets? That's not ported directly upward, is it?"

"Correct. Each one of these systems is designed with an exhaust port. There's a flame tunnel that goes from the base of the silo to an exit approximately forty meters away. But those have cameras on them as well. There's a plug to keep wildlife from crawling in there. But as a precaution, those are heavily monitored."

"That's a lot of effort for some missiles I'm sure the Russians know you have," Sloan pointed out.

"They might suspect we have missiles there, but they don't know. We've got a number of locations like this, and part of an early defense system is to confuse the enemy with more targets than they're capable of attacking," Osterman explained.

"But there are bombs here, right?" Sloan asked.

"Yes," Osterman confirmed, "there are."

"Tell us more about the exhaust ports," Jessica told him.

"There's going to be variability for each of these silos based upon the geography, but they're pretty standardized. As I said, they're monitored just as securely as the other points of entry and exit."

"How often are they inspected?" Theo asked.

"Every nine days on foot, same as the rest of the facility."

"Tell me about the sensors you use," Jessica requested.

"Seismic sensors, infrared, even sound pickups," Osterman said.

"I'd like to see one of them," Jessica said.

"Any one in particular?" Osterman asked. "I can have a helicopter take us there."

Theo pointed to a spot on the map.

"That'll be tricky," Osterman responded. "Harder to get a helicopter there. We'll have to land it a couple miles up road."

Theo and Jessica exchanged glances.

"That might be a really good place to start, after all," Sloan remarked, picking up on their interest.

BURIED ALIVE

The exhaust port for the missile silo was indeed well disguised, Jessica observed, as Theo and she stared at the side of the hill.

"I'd walk right past that," said Jessica. "It looks like just a wall of dried clay."

"It makes you wonder what else is hidden in plain sight on public land," said Theo.

Jessica lifted a satellite phone to her ear. "How's it going over there?" she asked Sloan, who was inspecting another silo.

A moment later, she replied, "Yeah, it doesn't look like anything to us. I don't know what we were expecting." She ended the call. "Sloan is in a similar spot."

Jessica walked around the ridge, glancing at the trees, then pointed at one in particular.

"There's a camera there," she noted.

Theo glanced up at the limb she was indicating and could see a small black cylinder aimed in the direction of the exhaust port.

"I looked at the schematics. They all have power and signal cables running underground to a junction inside the silo. And they're all connected to the power grid."

Jessica added, "And the cameras have an encryption key attached to their data." She walked closer to get a better look at the camera. "You could put a high-definition display directly in front of there. It wouldn't be too hard to," she observed, "and then you could control whatever the camera saw."

"Until the next manual inspection. I agree," said Theo. "But Bakker seems more focused on systems. I'm still thinking a remote exploit is his style."

"I think you're right," Jessica acknowledged.

Theo stepped to the exhaust port, then knelt and stared at the plug, which was shaded like the brown rock of the ridge. "Explain the trick to me," he asked.

"What do you mean?" Jessica replied.

"It's an illusion, isn't it? We have sixteen silos, one or more of which Bakker might have visited without anybody noticing. Yet the audience"—Theo turned around and pointed at the camera—"has had the access points in view the full time. How?"

"I don't know. A deer costume," Jessica said sarcastically.

"Maybe he could fool the cameras," Theo suggested, "but there's still the motion sensors."

"Maybe with a distraction . . ." Jessica thought for a moment. "You know, I wonder if he could have disguised himself as a wildlife officer and run a parallel inspection before they did. If he had the ability to observe when they showed up and were here. If this was being monitored by the team back at the air force base on the surveillance system, would they notice an extra person disguised like they were?" she thought aloud.

"Send a message to Osterman and tell them to go back over the surveillance data," Theo instructed. "I could try to make an algorithm to look for an extra man, but we don't have time. They're going to have to put eyeballs on that. It's a great suggestion."

"I can tell by your voice you're not convinced," Jessica said.

"This guy is socially awkward. I don't know if he's going to put on a uniform and go through a whole charade of pretending he's somebody he isn't. I think he likes to work in isolation in the dead of night, when he knows nobody's paying attention. He went to great effort to hide himself in his trailer and remain unseen. It's probably something else. But definitely worth looking into," Theo encouraged her.

"I can't think of a specific magic trick that this fits. There are a few where you try to get into an impossible situation like a locked box, but it's not very dramatic. You want to be out in front of the curtain at the end so the audience applauds you, not hidden away," Jessica mused.

"Well, not being seen by anybody is exactly Bakker's MO," Theo said. "Maybe not literally like a magic trick, but more like pulling off an impossible closed-room mystery. How would you pull it off?"

"How would I gain access to the most secure facility on the planet?" Jessica responded. "Or make it look like I did? Because I could fake it with my own dummy silo."

"Interesting," Theo said, "but I don't think that's what happened here, and I know you don't either. Assume he has to get inside the real silo without being observed. How does he do that?"

"Buried alive," Jessica said.

"The illusion?" Theo asked.

"Yes," she answered. "Harry Houdini had planned to do the Buried Alive illusion in front of the Great Pyramid, but he died before it happened. What's kind of crazy is he wrote a story. Well, actually, he didn't write it. It was probably ghostwritten by H. P. Lovecraft. It described performing an escape from a subterranean passage below a pyramid. Really crazy, very weird. Clearly Lovecraftian. But the point is, this is basically Buried Alive in reverse—instead of trying to figure out how somebody got out of an underground chamber, we have to figure out how he got in."

"And how would you do that?" Theo asked.

"A secret tunnel," Jessica said.

They both scanned the area around them, looking for some other entry point.

"That's forty meters that he would have to dig through, not to mention drilling through the concrete," Jessica replied. "I don't think he did an escape into Alcatraz here. Not with all the cameras."

"You're probably right," Theo agreed. "That's not the way he would operate either. He looks for existing vulnerabilities."

The satellite phone rang and Jessica answered. She hung up a moment later.

"It turns out they led Sloan to the wrong spot. She'd been staring at a tree stump. The on-the-ground inspection team is at the other end of the reserve. There was some confusion about where the ports are camouflaged."

"Wait," Theo said. "Why is there confusion? Get Osterman on the line."

Jessica dialed the colonel and put him on speakerphone.

"What's the update?" he asked.

"We're still here. We're going to go check out the next facility," Theo replied. "But I have a question for you. Were there any changes to these installations?"

"No. They've been the same for eighteen years since they were constructed. There were no modifications made after. We've replaced some of the electrical cabling and the security systems, but nothing structural. Why?"

"When McPherson inspected the battery plant in Florida, it turned out that the facility's design specs were different from what was actually built. Bakker didn't cause the vulnerability, but he learned of it and took advantage of it," Jessica explained.

"We build these to very specific standards, I assure you," Osterman said.

"We don't doubt you," said Theo. "The question is, Were there changes made? The terrain is wildly different for each silo. I assume that was part of the camouflage. But in every construction site, they will have run into unforeseen challenges that they had to contend with." He stopped and stared up into space. "Hold on, we'll call you back."

"What is it?" Jessica asked after clicking off.

"We're making the same mistake again. I don't believe it. Damn it," Theo said quietly.

"I'm not sure I understand. What do you mean?"

"We're walking around here looking for things the way you and I would. It's not how he would do it. He could spot the vulnerability a mile away. Especially if he understood something about the construction of these silos, and let's assume that he knows more than even Osterman and his people."

"Okay, but how does that help us? We don't have that level of information. We've only got a couple hours left," Jessica said.

"I know, I know," he said. "Hold on." He reached into his backpack and pulled out a tablet loaded with the images of all the silos' exhaust port locations. "Let's take a look again but try it from his point of view."

Theo thumbed through the images. They came in pairs. The first image showed an aerial view of the missile silo location. The second was a diagram indicating where the exhaust ports were. He moved through them quickly and then back through again.

"I don't see anything," Jessica said.

"Me either," Theo replied. "Maybe we have too much information. Hold on." He selected some images, then opened up a new album. "Now look again." He flipped through the images.

"I can't see the diagrams here. I don't remember where the flame tunnels that lead to the exhaust ports were," Jessica replied.

"That's the point," said Theo. "I do, but I want you to tell me where you *think* the exhaust ports were for each silo."

"Well, that's easy," Jessica said. "They're usually at a lower elevation. The silos tend to be built up aboveground, and they put the ports in some natural declivity or whatever where they could vent the exhaust away."

"Okay," Theo said, "but I want you to point them out." He moved through each image.

"Here," said Jessica, "and here," she said on another image. "Here," she said on the third one, and they continued through the other thirteen.

"How did I do?" she asked Theo.

"Fifteen out of sixteen," he said.

"Not bad. I only missed one."

"Yes, and the reason you missed is interesting. That location is less than a quarter mile from here. I think we need to take a look there."

"Why that one?" Jessica asked.

"Because you looked at all the others and saw a pattern for the exhaust ports." He pointed at the image. "This location matched that pattern, but it's not where they put it." He looked at her. "Why is that?"

EXPANSE

Jessica glanced up at the helicopter flying by overhead. "They're still looking for a place to land," she said.

"And how far out is the inspection team?" Theo asked as they made their way through a shallow gully, then up and over into a steeper ravine.

"Probably another twenty or thirty minutes," she replied.

"Is this the spot you recall from the map?" Theo asked.

Jessica could tell he was testing her and assumed it must be for an important reason. "I was looking at aerial photos," she began, then looked around. "I think this is close to it."

They were standing on a rock bed that carried snow runoff in season. Similar to the last site they'd inspected, the ridge was made of brown and beige stone.

Theo checked the tablet, then glanced up. "The silo is about fifty meters from here," he said, pointing to the east over the ridge.

"And where's the exhaust port?"

Theo looked to the left, where a pile of boulders had formed at the bottom of the ridge. "It should be on the other side of there," he said, "around the bend."

Jessica inspected the surrounding trees. "I don't see any cameras here," she observed.

"According to the inventory, there aren't any. They have a couple on paths to and from the other side, but none over here," Theo explained.

"Too many cameras would cause too many false positives, particularly if they're not concerned about an empty rock wall," Jessica noted.

"Assuming that's what we're looking at," Theo replied.

"Why not put the exhaust port here? It seems like a perfect spot. It looks almost exactly like the other location."

Theo studied the wall alongside her. "There could have been some kind of geological issue in there, some rock that was harder to cut through."

She inspected the wall with Theo, then snapped her fingers. "Damn it, we're doing it again. We're seeing things like we do, not how he saw them."

"Exactly," Theo agreed.

She turned around and stared the other way, away from the wall.

The other side of the ravine was much lower and gently transitioned into a wide, weedy expanse.

"This seems like a perfect location for venting missile exhaust," Jessica said.

Theo pinched and zoomed a map that pointed out something. "Except for this."

Jessica could see that they stood at the outer edge of the reserve. On the other side of the scrubby expanse ran a road.

"Does that have public access?" Jessica asked.

"Yes," Theo replied. "There seem to be two perimeter fences, but they're chain link."

"Which means you could see this spot from the road with binoculars," Jessica said.

"I imagine so."

"And if you were suspicious about this area," Jessica thought out loud, "spotting a team of people staring at a rock wall every nine days like clockwork might attract attention."

"Precisely," Theo said. "But that might not be the kind of thing you realize until after you finish construction."

"So you think they actually built the tunnel?" Jessica asked.

"We'll know if we can find it."

"But wouldn't they fill it in?"

"Probably," Theo said, "but how completely? It seems unlikely that he could dig through forty meters of earth, but moving a couple tons of rocks from a concrete tunnel could be done in a couple nights."

They walked back up to the ridge wall for a closer inspection.

"What are we looking for? How does he access his tunnel? Use your magic brain," Theo challenged.

"The cover wouldn't look like a plug," she said. "It would look like dirt or rocks." She pointed to a bush and moved over to it. She started to grab the end of the weed, then hesitated.

"Wait, could this be booby-trapped?" She felt her pulse quicken. She gently released the stem, imagining that she might have been one tug away from thermonuclear annihilation.

"We've got less than two hours left." He reached down and plucked the large weed before Jessica could protest.

"What the hell?" She stared at him.

"Everyone here is pot committed," Theo said. "If it's going to blow, it's going to blow, and we've got to move fast."

"You can't just make that kind of decision for hundreds of thousands of people," Jessica protested.

"All right," Theo conceded. "I won't do it again. Now, that . . ."

He directed her attention to a square piece of plywood partially buried in dirt. Written on the cover in cursive was:

Abandon all hope, ye who enter here.

FAIL-SAFE

"Jesus Christ," said Sloan as she stared at the morbid sign. She had just come running from the helicopter, followed by Lumley and Osterman and two air force technicians.

"Who knew this guy had a sense of humor?" Jessica remarked.

"Who's the joke for?" Sloan responded.

"I'm sure he put a lot of thought into this," Theo said. He glanced over as Nicholas Zhao and his young FBI colleagues entered the ravine, followed by Brad.

"Perfect timing," said Sloan. "Now we all get to die together."

"What do we do?" Lumley asked as he stared down at the plywood lid.

"You guys can make a run for it," Theo offered. "That helicopter should get you pretty far away. I'll wait, but I'm going in."

"How do you know that won't trigger the booby trap?" Osterman questioned.

"I don't, but at this point we're pretty sure that missile is set to explode. So option A is we all get the hell out of here and hope it's a misfire and just creates a radioactive cloud like he tried to create in the first place. Option B: You get the hell out of here and I see if I can stop it before it goes off."

"You're not a bomb-disposal technician," Osterman observed.

"No, but I'm pretty good at puzzles, and that's what this is."

"Jesus Christ, your arrogance," Osterman muttered.

"He's also right a lot," Brad added.

"Let me check it for trip wires," said one of the air force technicians. He directed the request to Theo, not Osterman.

"I think you should take him up on the offer," Brad said, "considering Cleveland."

"Okay," Theo agreed. "Why don't we all step back and let Airman Lewis be the first person since Nagasaki to get killed by a nuclear bomb. We at least owe him that."

Lewis, who was kneeling down by the plywood, looked up at Theo. "I'm not sure I can do this," he admitted.

Then he shrugged and returned to probing the corners with his fingers.

After two minutes, he stood back up. "I couldn't feel any wires or sensors. But I don't make any guarantees. I'd really like to get my gear in here with a probe and have a closer look."

"We've got fifty minutes until the end of the sequence," Jessica said. "That's not going to help us now."

"Agreed," Theo said as he reached down and yanked the plywood out of the way.

Everybody froze, afraid of an explosion. But the only sound was the wood making a thud as it hit the ground.

"For fuck's sake," Lumley snapped. "Warn us."

"I'm sorry, it won't happen again," Theo said as he bent down and aimed a flashlight into a concrete tunnel barely wide enough for a person to squeeze through. "McPherson, any suggestions for how I back myself out of this?" he asked.

"We've got some rope with us. We'll tie it around your leg. It won't be comfortable, but we can just pull you out if you can't turn yourself around. Of course, it'd be a lot easier if you let me go instead."

He looked at her. "For the record, I'm okay not being the one that goes in here," Theo admitted.

"But you're the guy to figure this kind of thing out," Brad reminded him.

Theo squatted down and crawled into the tunnel. It was a long shaft that disappeared in darkness. His flashlight didn't reach any endpoint or turn.

"Hold on," a voice called out behind him.

"What?" Theo shot back.

"That floor looks pretty smooth. We've got a mechanic's dolly and a radio we use for inspections. We're flying it in now."

"Make it quick," Theo urged, staring into the void ahead.

"I assure you it'll help you move through there faster than crawling," Airman Lewis called into the tunnel.

Theo remained stationary two meters into the chamber and waited. A few minutes later, he could hear the sounds of footsteps and moving rocks, then casters rolling across concrete.

"Coming at you."

The dolly hit his boots, and Theo raised his body to pull it underneath his torso, then settled down on the wheeled platform.

"Thank you," Theo said, and he began to kick off against the ground and push himself farther into the tunnel.

The rest of the group watched as the rope being fed by Airman Lewis disappeared into the tunnel as Theo moved deeper.

"Airmen, do you have this?" Osterman asked Lewis and the other technician kneeling by the mouth of the exhaust port.

"Yes, Colonel," said Lewis.

"Okay," he replied. "I'm going to go back to the command center in Minot and supervise from there."

"Are you fucking kidding?" Sloan asked him.

"I'm being pragmatic," Osterman explained. "If we screw this up, there's an entirely different crisis we'll have to deal with. Any of you are welcome to come with me."

"I think we're good here," Brad remarked. "Right?" he asked Nicholas and his team.

Nicholas let out a nervous laugh. "I guess so, sure." He glanced over at Lumley.

The senior FBI agent shook his head. "I would never live it down."

"We either die here like heroes or drink ourselves to death as losers," Brad said.

"You have a very peculiar way of putting things," Lumley commented.

"How are you doing down there?" Jessica called into the shaft.

"Great," Theo's voice echoed back. "You all should try this. It's a lot of fun."

"You should go with Osterman," Brad advised Sloan. "You've got a kid and a husband."

Sloan wore a pained look. "I know. But I have a kid I have to look in the face every day. And I can't leave you all here."

"There's nothing for us to do right now but just wait," Jessica said. "You should go. I would rather you did."

Brad turned to Nicholas and the other FBI agents after thinking things over. "You guys should go too, now that I think about it. Our show of force isn't going to help Theo."

"I'm fine staying," Nicholas responded.

"What's the status on the command center?" Brad asked Lumley.

"We cleared everybody out. We're the only ones in the blast radius right now."

"How big of an explosion is 1.2 megatons again?" Brad inquired.

"These are designed to explode midair," Airman Lewis explained, "flattening everything. A missile inside a silo, it's going to leave a crater a few hundred feet across."

Brad started pacing. Jessica had never seen him even close to anxious. She could tell he was thinking something over. "What is it?" she asked.

Brad squatted down and stared into the tunnel. Theo's flashlight was a dim flicker.

"What do you see?" he asked over a radio handed to him by Lewis.

"There's some wiring here. It's nicely organized, but not part of the original schematics," Theo said.

"What does the wiring do?" Brad questioned.

"I'm trying to figure that out. I think there's some kind of pattern to it. I assume they're connected to the detonators."

"1.2 megatons?" Brad repeated to the man beside him.

"Yes," Airman Lewis confirmed.

"And we don't know for sure that he didn't booby-trap any other silos," Brad said.

"We don't," Jessica acknowledged.

Brad glanced back at the helicopter that Osterman was about to board. He looked over at Jessica, then to Sloan and shook his head.

"What?" asked Sloan.

"For smart people, we're pretty stupid," he said, then spoke into the radio. "Theo, we're going to pull out. I don't like this. I don't like this at all."

"I understand," Theo replied. "You guys go ahead. I think I can figure out this pattern."

"No, Theo," Brad insisted. "I mean, we're all pulling out."

"We can't let this explode," Theo argued. "You guys go ahead. I understand."

"Theo, we can't let you die."

"This is a nuclear warhead about to explode on American soil," Theo said firmly.

"We've detonated bigger nuclear bombs in three different states," Brad said. "This is North Dakota. Nobody's going to get hurt but you. It's not worth it."

"I think I can solve it," Theo said.

Brad grabbed the rope and began to pull. "I'm sure you can, buddy. I'm sure you can. But not today."

He gave it another yank and it went loose.

"Goddamn it," said Brad, turning to the others. "He untied it."

TRINITY

Theo stared at the intricate wiring and considered Brad's words. *Was* he trying to be too clever? Letting his arrogance put himself and everyone else into danger?

All his life, he had seen problems and tried to find solutions.

Part of this was motivated by his curiosity, but also by pain. When he lost his father as a child, the world didn't make sense to him anymore. It seemed unfair and unbalanced, and Theo looked for ways to try to understand things and fix them.

Theo knew it wasn't arrogance driving him, but he understood how it looked to everybody else. He didn't care if Bakker intellectually bested him. Theo cared about the problem at hand. Though Brad wanted to downplay the impact of a 1.2-megaton nuclear warhead exploding in a missile silo, it would irradiate a large portion of North Dakota and create fallout affecting people for hundreds of miles. A nuclear weapon had not been detonated this close to the surface since Nagasaki. Even the Soviet tests, which ran deeper, left craters the size of cities.

Letting this explode wasn't an option.

Theo heard a shuffling sound as someone began to crawl into the tunnel behind him. He ignored it and focused on the wiring in front of him. Bakker was trying to tell a story. Or at least there was a story in front of Theo, whether it was intentional or not. He had to figure it out. There had been no taunting message to the police, no clues, no manifesto, nothing—just chaos. Theo realized that expecting any deliberate clue or hint was futile. The joke on the plywood was the closest he had observed to Bakker having a sense of humor. Initially, Theo thought it was directed at whoever found the hatch, but now it began to dawn on him: It was probably an inside joke solely for Bakker's benefit.

"Hey, buddy, maybe we back the hell out of here and watch the boom boom from a distance," Brad said, inching his way closer to Theo.

"You have no idea how much I'd like to see a nuclear bomb go off with my own two eyes," Theo answered over his shoulder. "But not today, and not this close."

"That's what the helicopter's for," Brad informed him.

"I'd tell you to go ahead, but I know you won't do that. And also, given how quickly you decided to come after me, I'm guessing you forgot to tie a rope around your ankle. That'll mean getting out of here will take a while if we're both trying to shuffle in reverse," Theo said.

"Goddamn it," Brad muttered. "Maybe I'll just ride on your back." He aimed a flashlight at the complex wiring in front of Theo. "For crying out loud . . . How are you supposed to make sense of that rat's nest?"

"I don't know that I'm supposed to," Theo admitted. "I was hoping for some multiple choice test that I could whiz through and solve this thing. I'm now realizing that's not the case."

"Now you're realizing?" Brad asked, raising his voice.

"Better late than never," Theo said hesitantly.

"If I could punch you from here, I would," Brad growled.

"The helicopter left," said Sloan over the radio.

"Goddamn it," Brad swore again. "We've got, what, eighteen minutes left?"

"That's when the sequence ends. We don't know how long until the trigger goes. It could be hours," said Theo.

"It could be seconds. Screw that," said Brad. "We're gonna have to just keep running and running and hide behind rocks."

"That's not going to help," Theo replied. "Unless it's a partial explosion."

"What happens in a partial explosion?" Brad asked.

"The charges go off around the missile. There's a chance that the inner charges fire and damage the casing. We'll still have a contamination issue, but it won't be spread with the force of a thermonuclear blast."

"How bad is it on a scale of one to ten?" Brad inquired.

"About thirty, with a nuclear bomb being one hundred."

"Fuck," Brad muttered again.

"The warhead is just a few meters away from here," Theo said. "All this wiring around this section doesn't make any sense to me."

"Is it a game? You tell me."

"This guy doesn't play games," Theo responded sharply.

"No, he was willing to blow himself up," Brad said. "We found that out the hard way. I don't think there's a right wire to cut."

"You mean they're gonna all cause an explosion?" Theo asked.

"That's the point, isn't it? It's not a test for you. He doesn't want to give anybody else the chance to stop what he's trying to set out to do."

"He was willing to kill himself to prevent this from being stopped," Theo said.

"What's our alternative?"

"This is a precise arrangement, right? Everything has to work right to pull off the full ignition," Theo explained. "The research paper gave this less than even odds of succeeding even in the perfect scenario."

"And a perfect scenario being what?" Brad asked.

"Basically, complete encirclement along one axis of the warhead. Creating a ringlike explosion that blows inward."

"That sounds very precise," Brad observed.

"Yes, Bakker thought in extreme detail."

"Not at all chaotic, really, if you think about it," Brad commented.

"Oh, damn it," Theo groaned.

"What is it?" Brad asked.

"Well, I think you just made me see something that I wasn't seeing all along," Theo admitted. "He *hates* chaos. He sees it every day, in every face. That's what this is. All this cable cutting doesn't matter. It all leads to destruction."

"So what is this telling you?" Brad questioned.

"I was hoping for some clean, logical, simple solution," Theo explained. "An elegant way to defuse this. But there isn't."

"Are you saying there's no way we can stop it?" Brad asked.

"I don't think we can stop the explosion, but we might be able to stop the nuclear detonation, or at least prevent a full fission event," Theo told him. "*We* need to be the agents of chaos."

"And how do we do that?" Brad asked.

"Do you want the higher-chance-of-success way, where we both probably die, or the slightly less chance of success where we walk away from this?" Theo questioned.

"Just between you and me, I'll take the second one," Brad admitted. "But tell everyone I insisted on the braver option."

"I'm going to tell everybody on the radio to get the hell away from the exhaust port. And then I need you to slide up here next to me," Theo instructed. "And then give me your gun."

"You know a bullet won't set off C-4. It's designed to resist that. You would have to hit a detonator head on," Brad replied.

"I know," Theo said. "We just need to screw up his perfectly ordered system. We need to add chaos."

TRICK SHOT

Brad Trasker aimed his pistol straight down the tunnel at the center of the cabling.

Theo had left his flashlight at the opposite end to illuminate the tiny target. Sloan, Theo, and the remaining staffers were lying flat on the berm behind Brad, at his insistence. Their plan, which stretched the definition of the word, was for him to just start shooting at the cabling, in hopes that he would either cut something vital or otherwise affect the shaped charges Bakker had placed inside the silo.

Brad counted out loud, warning everybody within earshot. "Five, four, three, two, one."

There were seventeen rounds in Brad's gun. His goal was to place each one of them in a different spot.

Initially, he thought he would squeeze the trigger as fast as he could and empty the magazine but realized that was stupid. Precision was more important.

He had seventeen chances to create some kind of puncture or ricochet damage that would destroy the trigger or dislodge the shaped charges. Privately, he suspected the chances of the detonation going off the way Bakker had intended were low regardless of whether he interfered with the explosives. But not low enough.

He fired the first bullet, and despite the fact he was shooting from a bench rest far enough from the tunnel to avoid permanent hearing damage, the sound of the shot was still loud. Even for Brad, who had heard that *pop* more often than most people have heard their telephone ring.

Bang! He fired again: *Bang! Bang! Bang!* He continued in a steady rhythm, adjusting the placement of each bullet.

"This is the stupidest thing I've ever done," he muttered under his breath.

Bomb-disposal teams frequently used explosives or other kinetic methods to try to reduce the destructive power of bombs. But to Brad's knowledge, he had never heard of anyone trying to do *this*, let alone with a nuclear warhead attached to the target.

Once he had emptied the magazine, they were all going to make a run for it and hide behind a rock outcropping overlooking a ditch close to the access road.

But the ninth bullet had other plans.

The chances of him hitting a detonator were astronomical, but the moment after he squeezed the trigger and saw an orange jet flare from inside the tunnel, his heart barely had the chance to skip a beat.

The last thing he recalled was an acrid smell in his nostrils and feeling what seemed like a thousand pellets hitting him in the face and arms.

CHAOS AGENTS

The first solid thing Brad could recall was a pair of feet resting on the edge of the bed. They were attached to Theo Cray, who was sitting in a chair with his back to the window and a laptop in front of him.

"Why is everything so blurry?" Brad asked.

"You've only got one good eye right now," Theo said.

Brad slurred, "I like how you say that so matter-of-factly."

"You'll have an eye patch for a little while. All things considered, there were worse outcomes."

"What was the outcome?" Brad felt both tired and giddy and suspected that the IV drip next to him had something to do with that.

"Either you hit a detonator or we actually triggered the thing we weren't supposed to trigger," Theo explained. "The result was surprising but, after doing some computer modeling, very predictable."

"I'm guessing since you have all your hair, the shaped charges didn't go off," said Brad.

"Correct. Zero for two for Bakker trying to create a radiological event," Theo remarked.

"Well, I'll call that a win."

"You wouldn't think so from the media coverage, to be honest. Our little countermeasure managed to sever the ballistic missile in half, send it through the launch door, and into the wildlife preserve."

Theo paused. "It's not a comforting sight to see an unexploded nuclear weapon on the ground."

"As long as the word 'unexploded' is in that sentence, it's pretty comforting to me," Brad said.

"I concur," Theo agreed. "The media, of course, is having a full-on meltdown, which may be justifiable, given that this never should have happened in the first place."

"We did our best," Brad said. "Didn't we?"

"I think we did okay, but I don't have a lot of confidence that there won't be copycats," Theo replied.

"How much of the blame has fallen on us?" Brad asked. "And by the way, how long have I been here?"

"Five days. You and I actually had a great conversation yesterday, but I doubt you remember it." Theo closed his laptop. "Officially? We weren't involved. The air force is insisting that this was an accidental firing of an unarmed ballistic missile in a test that went wrong."

"You gotta be kidding me. Even after the evacuation order?" Brad exclaimed.

"You mean the preemptive evacuation order because they had a computer system flag a potential problem that they were then trying to . . . de-escalate?" Theo explained. "At least that's the story they're selling."

"So did we accidentally trigger the explosion or did he have a misfire?" Brad wondered.

"We'll never know."

"Where are Sloan and Jessica?" Brad managed slowly, aware that whatever drip he was on had just served him another dose.

"Sloan's back in Florida with her family. Jessica is assisting with the investigation," Theo answered.

"And you got stuck babysitting me," Brad muttered.

"Kylie's here too. She's in the cafeteria getting something to eat," Theo added.

"I am the worst employee ever," Brad admitted.

"I would have to agree," Theo said dryly. "But she considers you family, just so you know."

"She's a good kid," Brad sighed. "So have you and Jessica arrived at any deeper insight into Seth Bakker?"

"We were able to fill in some of the gaps that our friends at the Defense Intelligence Agency were trying to cover up. Nothing that would surprise you," Theo said.

"Was everybody else okay? Nicholas and his team?" Brad asked, suddenly recalling more about what had happened shortly before he blacked out.

"You took the full brunt of it," Theo explained. "They're good. They're back at Quantico. Jessica and I are going to fly out there once you're back on your feet."

"Aha," Brad slurred. "Have you two decided to become mentors to a new generation?"

"Something like that. They're pretty sharp. Hopefully we can have them learn from our bad examples and not put themselves into stupid situations like this one."

"We certainly have a lot of bad examples for them to learn from." Brad smiled at the disordered memories flowing through his mind.

"That's an understatement. I'm not as reflective as I should be, and I don't like to second-guess myself," Theo confessed. "Analyze, yes," he continued as he stared at the ceiling. "But not blame myself for decisions that weren't apparent. But if I was to go look back and point out one decision I made I should have done differently, it would be that I think I never should have left the classroom—maybe changed what I taught, but maybe not try to take everything on by myself, have a little faith that a younger, cleverer generation could learn from my experiences and build on top of them."

Brad let out a long snore as the pain medication took effect.

Theo shook his head and reopened his laptop. "And Jessica wonders why I talk to chatbots."

ABOUT THE AUTHOR

Andrew Mayne is the Amazon Charts and *Wall Street Journal* bestselling author of *The Girl Beneath the Sea*, *Black Coral*, *Sea Storm*, *Sea Castle*, and *Dark Dive* in his Underwater Investigation Unit series; *The Final Equinox* and *Mastermind* in the Theo Cray and Jessica Blackwood series; *The Naturalist*, *Looking Glass*, *Murder Theory*, and *Dark Pattern* in the Theo Cray series; *Angel Killer*, *Name of the Devil*, and the Edgar Award–nominated *Black Fall* in his Jessica Blackwood series; and *Impostor Syndrome* and *Mr. Whisper* in the Specialists series. He was the star of A&E's *Don't Trust Andrew Mayne* and swam with great white sharks using an underwater stealth suit he designed for the Shark Week special *Andrew Mayne: Ghost Diver*. He worked on creative applications for artificial intelligence and served as the science communicator for OpenAI, the creators of ChatGPT, and is the cofounder of Interdimensional.ai. For more information, visit www.andrewmayne.com.